ALBI

by

Hilary Shepherd

H NNO MODERN FICTION

First published in 2018 by Honno Press, 'Ailsa Craig', Heol y Cawl, Dinas
Powys, Vale of Glamorgan, Wales, CF64 4AH
1 2 3 4 5 6 7 8 9 10
Copyright: Hilary Shepherd © 2018

The Author would like to stress that this is a work of fiction and no resemblance
to any actual individual or institution is intended or implied.

A catalogue record for this book is available from the British Library.

Published with the financial support of the Welsh Books Council.

ISBN 978-1-909983-74-8 (paperback)
ISBN 978-1-909983-75-5 (ebook)

Cover design: Graham Preston
Cover images: © Shutterstock, Inc
Text design: Elaine Sharples

For Nick,

for naming things which then I see

ACKNOWLEDGEMENTS

Thank you to all those who have given me feedback during the writing of this book – particularly to Crispin Keith, Rebecca Trick-Walker, Chris Stewart and Christine Evans for commenting on the manuscript. Thanks to Brenda Squires, Lenka Janiurek, David Lloyd Owen, Richard Kipling, Alison Hayes and Thorne Moore for astute and stimulating critiquing sessions at Rhosygilwen, and David Llewellyn for getting us together and giving such encouragement. Thank you Rebbecca Ray and the Wyeside Writing Group for your support, and to Steve Evans for telling me how a plane of the period would sound in the ears of a small boy – I hope I've done justice to your wonderful description. This book would never have happened without the generosity of the people of Pitarque, Spain, who have welcomed us in and made us feel so very at home – special thanks to Pakita and Pedro and their family, and Juan Ramón Tena; also to Pierre and Marijke for sharing the workings of their mill. As for Casimiro and Guadalupe, Robustiano and Romualdo – you probably had no idea how big a part you played in our lives, and you always will. Finally, endless gratitude to all the team at Honno but especially to my editor, Caroline Oakley. And last but never least, thank you Nick Myhill for your endless patience, even through the last-minute upheavals of disappearing texts. It's been a long haul.

September 1938

The silence was all wrong. It wasn't the silence of harvest time when everyone was out in the threshing yards. It wasn't the silence of *fiesta* when everybody had gone to the Plaza. This silence was full of listening, of every man, woman and child in the village waiting inside their shuttered houses, behind their barred front doors.

Albi sat on his low stool. With the shutters closed it was dark as night in the kitchen. Just a ghost of light coming down the chimney, where the fire lay asleep under a blanket of ash, the afternoon burning at the finger-hole of the shutter like a single eye looking in at them. He stared back at it. There were six people in this kitchen, seven in the house if you included the grandmother sleeping in the other room. You would never guess they were so many, in the listening dark.

Beneath his feet, in the stable, a horse-shoe clanked on the cobbles as the mule shifted her weight. The sound was so ordinary. The animals didn't know the soldiers had come and everyone was waiting. That was the most difficult bit, the waiting. Not knowing what they were waiting for. Albi shuddered, but he was nine-years old, too big to let it show he was afraid. Not that anyone could see him, in the dark. He could be as scared as he liked and nobody need know.

Then he heard it. He lifted his head. He could feel the others listening too. From the far side of the village, the tramp-tramp-tramp of marching feet. Closer, then further away, as they came through the winding streets. So many feet, and they kept coming.

PART ONE

1

The writing on the wall, September 2016

The old man sits on a rickety chair, his walking stick between his knees, and keeps his eyes down. The hot sun made him dizzy – that and the stiff unfamiliarity of his best clothes – and it's pleasantly cool in this dusty store-room, but he should have stayed outside. The writing is still there, on the wall above his head, the faint pencil scrawl apparently forgotten even in this year of anniversaries. Forgotten by everyone, except him.

He stares at the red dust spoiling the shine on his shoes and listens to the distant voices as the priest intones, the small crowd gives the responses.

He might have explained his sudden faintness. *He was my best friend, that one*, he could have said. But it's a long time since he and Carlos were particular friends. Besides, how much of Carlos can be left in that shiny casket of ashes? That's the way they send you back from the city these days. Better to stay here in the village and go into the cemetery wall in a coffin. Or over the cliff without one and let the vultures pick your bones clean.

He pokes at the dirt floor with his stick.

It's no good. He has to look up at the scribble of pencil, fading away for nearly eighty years until it is barely legible:

On the 20th day of September 1938
Comandante Vicente Muñoz Barrosa
took control of El Rincón and surrounding territory
on behalf of the Nationalist Army

Is he the only one left whose skin is burned by those little words, like battery acid eating away the flesh? He turns his face away.

Outside, the priest's solemn voice drifts on the warm air, the words indistinct.

Through the doorway Alberto can see a human thigh bone, old and yellow, casually propped against the cemetery wall. It must have become separated from its owner when they moved bodies to the ossuary, and now nobody knows which family it belongs to. He looks away. Old ghosts rustle at his back. Bones. It always comes back to bones.

The priest raises his voice in blessing.

A pause. Then the voices start up, ordinary and cheerful, moving down the slope towards the gate. Somebody laughs. That's how they deal with you when, as Carlos was, you are eighty-nine: a bit of solemnity while they shove you into the chamber in the cemetery wall, a bow and a nod to God, then chatter chatter chatter all the way back down to the village.

Mari-Jé bustles in. Her hair is burnished brass this morning, and bouncy, so that she is unfamiliar, for all that she's his wife. Her voice is brassy too.

'Not like you to feel faint, Alberto.'

'Not faint,' he says, getting to his feet. 'A touch dizzy, that's all. Too much standing around in the sun. Let's go home. Those sheep will take themselves out if I'm not back soon.'

'You and your sheep,' she says. But not crossly. There'll be coffee and *magdelenas* in the bar this morning, that's what she'll be thinking. And all the city relatives here for the interment. You have to make the most of such moments at this end of the year. After *Todos Santos*, apart from the odd funeral, the village will be dead until Easter.

'I don't know what's got into you this morning!' Mari-Jé bangs the broom briskly round the legs of the kitchen table. 'Carlos wasn't a friend of yours. I don't remember you and him so much as passing the time of day.'

He shrugs. She doesn't appear to notice – she's too busy whisking her broom along the bottom of the kitchen cupboards.

'So what are you moping for?'

Her hair-style is subsiding and she hasn't got her teeth in, but even with a lisp she's as sharp as ever. She's a good wife, he reminds himself.

'We were best friends once.'

'You and Carlos? When?'

'In school.'

'School!' She comes round under the window and past the sink with her broom. 'You stopped going when you were seven.'

'Eight,' he says. 'But we were friends afterwards too.'

She stops sweeping and gives him the eye. Seems about to say something, then closes her mouth and starts sweeping again. 'Well *I* never heard you talking about him.' As if that is the subject closed.

A jealous woman, Mari-Jé. Especially of the past she wasn't there to share. She wasn't born till he was fifteen.

'I'm going out,' he says.

She thumps the broom around his vacated chair.

He walks down towards the river with the old dog at his heels. The streets are empty. The weekend's visitors will be back in the city by now. He passes the house with the leaning balconies, the deserted forge. Down the white concrete road he goes, out of the village. Raul's rabbit shed is all shut up. Raul will be sleeping off his Sunday lunch. So will Raul's son Santi, no doubt, after carousing in the bar late into the night with the city boys. It's always like that after funerals.

Across the valley, the great wall of the dam is flushed orange in the last rays of the setting sun. As Alberto crosses the meadow the light casts a ghostly glow across the surface of the river.

It's true, what Mari-Jé said. Carlos was a teenager when he left with his family to work in Valencia. But he came back every August and every Easter for the rest of his life. It wasn't the leaving that stopped them being friends.

There's no point thinking about this. Carlos is dead and there's nothing to be done about the past. He sits on the low wall, his stick between his knees, and stares across at the sun-flushed face of La Guadaña. Every cleft and crevice in the cliffs casts a sharp shadow. There are still marks where the water poured down the rockface in the big storm last April. Don't think.

Don't think.

But the names keep coming into his head. Carlos, Pepito, Rafa. Juanito Torrecillas. All dead. Carlos was the last one left, and now he's gone.

Alberto suddenly sees Carlos, not as the man he became but as the boy he once was – angular, pale-skinned, grubby, his thatch of blonde hair always uncombed, running across this meadow to hide in the bushes along the river-bank. *Let's go and spy on the soldiers*, he'd say. And whatever Carlos said, they did it, him and Pepito. However crazy.

The past has got its foot in the door. That night the nightmare comes visiting, the same dream he's been dreaming, on and off, for nearly eighty years. There are guns in the room, there is hay on the floor, and the *abuela* is screaming in the chimney corner, but he's too small and the soldiers are enormous: he can't do anything for her, though he knows she is going to die. Or maybe she's dead already. He looks across the room but she has disappeared and the dead fire on the hearth is a nest of bones. A crowd of soldiers looms suddenly between him and the chimney corner, the floor shudders under their boots, he can hear their caps knocking against the ceiling beams. Now his mama is there too, and his papa and his three sisters, cowering so close around him he can scarcely breathe.

8

In the jostle of dark figures that fills the room he glimpses the hem of a dress, covered in tiny flowers. He reaches out to touch it but the fabric whisks away.

And then the shooting starts.

2

The Soldiers

Alberto wakes with a jolt. He hears the rasping of his own dry sobs as he lies trembling in the dark.

The dream.

He places his hand on his chest and waits for his heart to slow down. A nightmare, he reminds himself. Not reality. Beside him, Mari-Jé stirs, and mumbles.

'It's nothing,' he says.

Nothing?

The dream is not what happened. But it's no good, he has to go back there to separate the dream from reality. In the real world, the soldiers arrived and there was no shooting. No faces, no uniforms visible, nothing but the tramping of boots as the troops marched through the streets while the villagers hid, blind in their houses with the shutters closed. He drags the jagged shards of memory back to the surface: the noises in the street, the sharp and mysterious clinking and clattering of steel toe-caps on cobbles and the un-nerving silences.

In their house, nobody slept. But nothing happened. Not until morning.

*

Perhaps he'd dozed off, perched on the stiff, upright chair, his head against the wall, because suddenly there was shouting in the next street and a din like the gates of hell being broken open.

'Rifle butts,' Papa whispered. 'On the doors.'

'Open up!'

Bolts rasped, doors crashed open, heavy boots ran up other people's stairs. The noises were muffled, then. When you are listening, you fill that space with terrible thoughts. Maybe the *abuela* was listening too because she started screaming, 'The devil's on his way, you sinners! Make way for the devil!' Loud enough for the soldiers to hear.

'Quick!' Papa hissed. 'Get her into the back room!'

Pilar and Inma pulled their grandmother out of her bed in the front bedroom and dragged her, screeching, through the kitchen into the back of the house, shutting the door behind them.

'That woman will be the death of me,' Papa said, his voice sounding strange in the silence left behind.

'Ramón!' said Mama. 'Don't speak of your mother that way.'

Outside, the soldiers were working their way closer, house by house. The floor trembled under Albi's bare feet as blows thundered down on their front door. Mama put her hand on Papa's arm, her face pale in the light of the single candle.

'Not you, Ramón.'

She ran downstairs.

Albi, squeezed between his sisters and his mama and papa, tried not to look into the muzzles of the guns but his eyes kept going there. In the corner of the kitchen the *abuela* was slumped on a chair, rocking backwards and forwards and whimpering. The soldiers ignored her.

'You! Name?'

The gun jerked at Papa.

Albi closed his eyes, but then he heard his papa say, 'Ramón

Álvarez Blanco,' so he opened his eyes again and saw another soldier writing the answer down in a black book.

'Age?'

'Sixty-three.'

'Occupation?'

'Farmer.'

'This woman is your wife?'

'Yes.'

'Name?'

'María Zapatero Irún,' Papa said.

'Age?'

Papa glanced helplessly at Mama, and shrugged.

'I am fifty-one, señor.'

So many questions, and all of the answers had to be written down. After Albi's mama, his three sisters. Then it was his turn, but the soldiers didn't seem interested any more. They were more interested in how many draft animals they owned. Three. How many breeding animals? Nine ewes, one ram, two goats, one cow. And the poultry and the rabbits. How much land, and where? Questions, questions, and all the while the guns waving about, and the fierce voices. Boots loud on the tiled floors, caps brushing the low ceilings.

When the answers had all been written, the soldier in charge made Mama fetch every knife in the house, along with the billhooks and the axes and Papa's gun, and even the old musket which didn't work any more, until they were all laid out in a row on the kitchen floor. The soldier who'd been doing the writing started tying labels round handles and bundling them into a sack.

Papa said, 'But señor! How can I kill a sheep without a knife? How can we cut sausage, even?'

The officer in charge stared down at Papa's leg. Then he raised his eyes to Papa's face as if to be sure to remember him. But all he said was, 'Stay out of trouble and you'll get them back.' He went to the door. The small knives were still lying on the floor, and the smallest axe.

11

'Anyone found carrying a weapon will be shot,' the soldier said, and then he went away.

Albi's legs were hurting from sitting all the long day in the shuttered house. His head hurt from the endless whispered arguments and from listening, listening, hour after hour. But all they heard was the soldiers marching about the streets, and once, fierce shouting.

Papa opened the kitchen shutter a crack to spy down on the street.

'What's going on?' Mama whispered.

Papa didn't reply. He closed the shutter.

In the end they had to lie down and sleep. They couldn't sit waiting for ever. But they all slept in one room, squashed up together in the three beds, the night heaving with bad dreams.

*

Alberto lies on his back beside Mari-Jé, who is snoring gently. The ache of his limbs and the heaviness of his feet tell him he's old. The street light shines upwards on the varnished beams and for a moment he is distracted that the beams are no longer whitewashed the way they used to be when his *abuela* slept in this room. No, that was long ago. The soldiers didn't shoot anyone in their kitchen. They didn't shoot anyone anywhere. They took over the village and nobody stopped them. Did a good job at scaring them all shitless, but nobody got killed.

I don't want to think about this.

But he must. The nightmare is so much worse than the reality was, in the beginning. We were confined to the houses. The soldiers searched for weapons. The next day (or was it the day after?) they made us all go down to the Plaza. That's all.

*

They woke to the stale darkness of another dawn. The street was already full of noise.

'Down to the Plaza!' a voice bellowed right outside their house. 'Every one of you! Now!'

'What? The *abuela* too?' whispered Mama, over the clatter of people coming out of their houses.

'You heard them,' Papa said.

Inma and Mama pulled the *abuela* out of the bed. In all the noise you could hardly hear her wailing. Albi followed them down the shadowy stairs, his knees weak as water. Outside, he blinked in the grey light. Young Jaime and his little wife Belén were coming out of the house opposite, supporting Old Jaime awkwardly between them because he should be in bed, like the *abuela*. Belén's face was white but Young Jaime's was dark and angry. The crowd swallowed them up.

'Move!'

Soldiers jabbed with their rifle butts. Albi stumbled, somebody grabbed his hand and squeezed it. Ramona. He was surprised into squeezing back, not caring who might see, until his sister's hand slipped away in the crush.

In the Plaza there were more soldiers. How many? He couldn't see to count, there were too many people pushed into the middle of the square, the soldiers crowding them close with their guns like dogs with a flock of sheep. There were nearly seven hundred people living in this village. That was a big number to all be in the same place at the same time.

A shot rang out. The crowd pushed back and suddenly a woman started screaming. A man's voice hissed, 'Shut up! Shut up! He was firing into the air!' and the screaming stopped.

A man was speaking, somewhere at the front. The crowd went very still, listening. It wasn't a powerful voice but the words were scary. They mustn't do this and they mustn't do that. The punishment for this and this will be death, the punishment for that will be imprisonment. And there will be all these other rules

13

besides: *curfews, permits, penalties*. New words Albi hadn't heard before. He stared at his bare feet and let the danger-words go straight through his head and out the other side to a place where they didn't matter.

'As from tomorrow, the factory and the school will open again,' the strange voice said. 'You will return to normal.'

He did hear that. And the bit afterwards, about going to church on Sunday.

3

The Comandante

'Who were you talking to?,' asks Mari-Jé, pausing to frown at him over the bundle of sheets on her way to the washing machine.

'Nobody. I wasn't talking.'

'Yes you were. Sounded like *Carlos*.' Her voice is suspicious.

He gives her his vague look, the one that stops her probing, usually.

'I was talking to Perrito,' he says, when she doesn't look away. The old dog hears his name and wags his heavy tail on Alberto's foot without lifting his grizzled snout from his paws. Alberto goes back to paring the curved handle of the new walking stick and his wife disappears into the front basement. It's obvious she thinks he's going gaga – he can hear her muttering about it as she slams soap into the dispenser and twists the dial.

Talk about talking to yourself.

It's quite cold in the back stable but he likes to sit here where he can see up the passage to the street at the front of the house, and at the back, through the door of the corral, down to the neat *huerto* where the last of the tomatoes gleam in the sunshine. The sheep in the pen keep him company, and so does old Perrito. All his dogs have been called Perrito or Perrita but this one it's a joke. Perrito has got wolf-hound in him, he's not small at all.

One of the ewes sighs. Nobody passes in the street. The village is empty.

Mari-Jé steps out into the passageway and stares at him as if he's surely up to something. He pretends he's too busy finishing off his new walking stick to notice she's watching. She sighs, and goes upstairs.

A few minutes later she's back with another armful of sheets. His guard is down. The funeral, the nightmare last night, and now Mari-Jé with the washing: the nagging memory flips upright suddenly and grabs at his heart. Not Mari-Jé but his mama, standing at the corner of the stairs with a basket of washing at her feet. He is nine-years old, the soldiers have come, and nothing will ever be the same again.

*

'Albi!'

'What?' Reluctantly, he put the rabbit back in her cage and went to see what his mama wanted.

She was standing on the stairs, balancing a basket of washing on the broad step at the corner. 'Take this.'

Women's work. He glared, but the girls had gone back to work in the factory this morning and there was nobody else, if you didn't count Papa, or the *abuela*. He picked up the basket.

'Wait.' She went back up the stairs to the kitchen and came down with another basket, filled to overflowing.

Outside in the street there was nobody – no old people sunning themselves by their front doors, no children playing in the dust, but no soldiers either. His mama locked the door and put the key in the usual place behind the pot of geraniums. Albi hurried after her up the street, hoping the soldiers didn't find it. He wished he was still in the kitchen with the front door safely bolted from the inside. He knew she was scared too, that was why she didn't want him to go out with the sheep today. He would have to take them out soon, though. They couldn't stay indoors for ever, eating precious hay.

Mama stopped so suddenly he nearly bumped into her.

'Read it to me,' she whispered, nodding at the piece of paper pinned on the stable door. He put his basket down and glanced over his shoulder. The street was still empty. He stumbled over the words, leaving the long ones out, but it was only what the soldier had said yesterday, about the factory and the school re-opening, and being normal. Mama walked off. He picked up his basket and followed her. As they went past the church he glanced up at the old *castillo*, perched on its rocky outcrop above the village. That's where the soldiers will be, he thought. They'll be watching Mama and me right now. We'll look like ants walking along a stick.

Down in the deserted Plaza, the slap-slapping of laundry from the wash house was the only sound. There were no voices, as if it was ghosts doing the washing. The hairs on the back of his neck prickled, but when they came round the front of the building it was full of women. He wanted to laugh. All those women and not one of them talking? Papa would be amazed.

He followed his mama through the crowd to a space at the back of the wash tank. The familiar faces looked pinched and scared as they bent to their scrubbing, not a child in sight.

His mama nodded to him to put the basket down behind her. He turned to go.

'You stay,' she said.

He pulled a face, but he didn't mind really. It felt safer here than out in the empty streets. He sat cross-legged on the stone bench which ran along the back wall and stared up at the dappled light on the underside of the tiled roof. Nothing had changed but everything was different, the women so silent, the sunlight in the Plaza so empty. Only the swallows were the same, chattering noisily as they dived in and out between the roof beams. A ripple of whispering began, too low for him to hear more than a word here, a word there: *Fascists… Nationalists… Rebels…* all those words for the bad soldiers who were the Enemy. Whisper whisper, all round the tank. *My Pedro says they're making the old Dormitory into a garrison…* Albi pricked up his ears.

'That's where the bloody soldiers are today,' Cristina added, not so quietly.

It felt better, knowing the soldiers were busy outside the village walls. The women slapped and rubbed and dunked their laundry in the tank. Somebody made a curt comment and her neighbours chuckled. The water gurgled and lapped and glugged the same as usual, the whispering became a murmur, the murmuring became a hum. Albi watched the swallows chattering over their heads. The soldiers shouldn't have come here, not to this village. Not when they had a castle, and old walls round the village to keep the bad soldiers out. But the *castillo* was a ruin and the village walls were broken in places, and castles and walls only keep you safe if you use them to fire guns at the soldiers to stop them coming in. No gun had been fired against the soldiers here in El Rincón, not a single one. The soldiers had marched in and taken charge while everybody hid in their houses. How could that be? Papa said they were saving their bullets for later, but what use was that when the soldiers had taken all the guns away? 'The ones they found they did,' Papa had said, looking at Albi sideways.

Two more women arrived, looking for a space. That would be *La Valenciana* with old Teresa. Last winter Teresa's son, Andrés, went to Valencia to join the Republican Army, but two months ago he'd come back to El Rincón with a new wife. Hardly anybody had seen her yet because Andrés's farm was out of the village, up on the *Meseta*. Albi stared at this new wife as she followed her mother-in-law round the tank. She was very pretty. Her dress had little buttons all down the front, not like anything the girls in the village wore. She wasn't wearing the usual canvas espadrilles either, but leather sandals unlike anything he had ever seen, with little heels, and criss-crossing straps over her neat toes.

The *Valenciana* squeezed into the narrow space between Teresa and Albi's mama, looking like a chicken that can't move its wings.

'We've had to leave the Torre and come down to the house in the Placeta,' Teresa whispered to Mama. 'The soldiers made us.'

That made Albi's insides go funny again.

He leaned back against the wall, staring at the backs of the *Valenciana's* bare legs. They were smooth and hairless and they weren't burned brown after a summer working in the sun.

'*Hostia!*' somebody exclaimed on the far side of the tank as the soap shot out of her hands and landed in the water with a splash.

Teresa turned to Albi. 'Alberto,' she said, not whispering. 'This is a job for you.' The others shushed her but they were laughing.

His mama said quietly, 'Albi, get the soap for Pepito's mama.'

He clambered over the parapet into the tank. The water was cold, even though the air outside the wash house was hot. The bottom of the tank was slimy and he had to be careful; he knew they were all waiting for him to fall in. He felt for the soap and handed it to Pepito's mama, climbing out quickly before anyone could trip him up to make the others laugh. He pushed his way out into the sun to dry off, ducking away from the wet hands that reached out to ruffle his hair.

Angelina cackled. 'Such sleek black hair that boy has, like a little dog! Always makes me want to stroke him.'

He hurried past her, into the blinding sun, and nearly ran into the man standing outside the wash house.

The hubbub behind him subsided like bubbles bursting. Albi stared down at the brown boots, which had a tiny sun blazing on each toe. Tall leather boots, such as a rich man might wear for riding. He lifted his eyes a little. Above the boots, green-brown cloth, pressed sharp and fierce. He looked a little higher. He got as far as the leather holster with the gun in it, then he stopped looking. He dived back into the wash house, anxious hands reaching out to pull him to safety.

From out in the Plaza the high-pitched voice from yesterday said, 'Carry on with your work.'

The women did as they were told. Albi leaned against the back wall, his heart pounding. He sank slowly down out of sight. Everything about the soldier was clipped and polished but his voice was pale like a small man's voice trapped in a big man's body. Albi stared at the sun-browned legs of the women in front of him, at their faded summer dresses, and the *Valenciana's* elegant pale legs and her dress all bright with tiny flowers. The soldier's boots rang out on the cobbles as he walked first one way, then the other, in front of the wash house. Thwack, thwack, went the soldier's cane against his thigh. He reminded them they were to return-to-normal-and-that-was-an-order.

'The Generalissimo intends the new Spain to be a place of hard work and honest citizens,' the soldier said to nobody in particular. 'Schooling is the root of good citizenship.'

Albi studied his dirty toenails. *Ciudadana.* That was a funny word.

'So why is that boy not in school?'

He froze. The man must mean him. Nobody moved, nobody said a word.

'Boy!'

Was there another boy? He looked around, hoping. He tried to stand up but his insides had knotted as hard as dried sausage and his knees wouldn't work. His mama stepped back until she was standing in front of him. She reached out behind her and put her hand on his knee.

'Señor Comandante,' Mama called out (her hand patting Albi quickly, secretly). 'My son is not in school because he has to look after our sheep and goats.'

19

In the silence, Albi's heart fluttered like Mama's hand on his knee. Not any old soldier, then. A Comandante. How did Mama know that?

The Comandante's voice said, as if he was making a joke, 'Sheep? I see no sheep.'

The women stared down at their hands. The water lapped quietly against the stone parapets. Albi shrank a little lower against the wall.

'Get him a permit from the *Ayuntamiento* then, not to be in school. All of you, observe the curfew. Remind your husbands: anyone found breaking the curfew will be shot.'

Nobody moved. They listened to the sound of the Comandante's boots walking away.

Angelina, who was very old, sat down on the edge of the wash tank and started fanning herself with her kerchief. The women who'd finished washing seemed in no hurry to leave. They too sat down on the parapet and fanned themselves, everybody whispering at once.

It was a very strange day. Not normal at all.

*

Alberto gets up stiffly in answer to Mari-Jé's call. He can smell it still, the homemade soap scumming the cold water in the wash house tanks, the smell of fear and then of relief on the women. He closes his penknife and puts it away in his pocket. Such a strange time that was, after the soldiers came, everybody watching their backs and trying to carry on with their lives while they waited to see what would happen next.

He goes upstairs, the warm smell of ham and chickpeas wafting down to meet him.

Presumably Mama got him a permit. He can't remember the details now.

4

Normal

Mari-Jé's mobile rings. She wipes her hands on her apron as she hurries to pick it up.

'Yes?' She frowns at the wall, then her face lights up. 'Rosa!' And away she goes, settling herself onto a chair for a long chat, talking loudly to be heard over the television. Rosa. Inma's girl. 'Yes, yes we're both well. Apart from your *tío* having a dizzy spell on Saturday, in the cemetery. The cemetery. Did you not hear? Carlos Perez? No, no. Just the ashes.'

Alberto picks up the TV remote while Mari-Jé is too busy talking to notice. Yet another anniversary programme about the start of the Civil War – Mari-Jé is fascinated by them, but then she wasn't born until years after the war ended. He flicks through channels. A studio audience, a man telling why he beat up his wife, the audience roars. He clicks again. A tiger stalks through shadows. He lets it stalk.

'Yes, yes,' Mari-Jé says, nodding earnestly to Rosa in Seville.

A powerful voice, Mari-Jé has. A country voice. This village was always full of them, from generations of shouting from hillside to hillside. His sisters Pilar and Ramona were the same, but not Mama, and certainly not Inma. Rosa is as soft-spoken now as her mother once was. He can't hear her half of the conversation. His eyes wander to the old photo on the wall. Inma, with her melodious voice and her kind ways. The strip-light glares in the glass, but he knows exactly what is there in the picture without needing to see it. It was taken the year before the war began. He's on the far right, not much more than five-years old, big eyes gazing at the camera. Inma is standing behind him with one hand resting on his shoulder. She's a soft pillowy girl of

21

eighteen in the photograph. Like her sisters standing next to her, her black hair is shoulder length, curled in the style that was fashionable then. Pilar frowns at the camera as if she is about to reprimand the photographer and beautiful Ramona smiles co-quettishly, but Inma is plain and comfortable. A homely girl with smiling eyes.

Inma the quiet one.

*

Papa said, 'Let the boy go, María. He'll be safe with the permit.' He reached out and put his hand on Mama's tightly folded arms. 'You know I'd go with him if I could.'

Mama looked up then, with a sad little nod.

'The soldiers won't touch him. It's not the small boys they're interested in, María.'

She gave another little nod of her head, so slight Albi wasn't sure he'd really seen it. He stared up at them anxiously. His papa must be worried: he didn't usually talk quietly, or call Mama by her name.

'Off you go, Albi,' Papa said. 'Go out past Ovidio's garden, they haven't got sentries there. But stay close to the village. And come back at once if anyone gives you trouble.'

Anyone? It was obvious who Papa meant.

Albi picked up his satchel. Carlos would be brave, or if he wasn't he would make it look as if he was. Albi could too, if he concentrated. That was what the old schoolmaster always used to say, when Carlos made his chalk screech across the slate. *Concentrate.*

The sheep and goats pushed at the gate of the pen. Including the lambs there were twenty-one altogether, and he couldn't hold them. As soon as the gate came open they ran past him into the passage and out onto the street. He had to shout at his dog to bring them back and even when he got in front it was tricky, because La Perrita couldn't stop them rushing him, and how could he keep an eye out for the soldiers if he was running? But the streets were empty, except for one *abuelo* hobbling down to his front door. At the corner, by the house with the leaning balconies, Albi glimpsed a woman's back as she slipped into an alleyway, but nobody else, and after a while the sheep slowed to a trot, and then to a walk, and so did he.

There were two flocks out already, walking up the track towards the cliffs of La Guadaña. He guessed from the numbers of sheep that one of the shepherds was probably Miguel, and the tiny figure higher up the slope might be Ovidio. He could hear sheep bells on this side of the valley too, somewhere above the trees. He certainly wasn't the only one out.

He had such a funny feeling as soon as he left the narrow twisting streets behind. It was as if the sky had been heavy and now it had lifted up again. He felt safe, that's what it was. Out here on the terraces he could see, and he could hide if he needed to. He wasn't trapped in the house like a fox in its earth.

He found a place where he could sit with his back against a rock. If anybody came, he would see them before they saw him. Away to his left the *castillo* shone bright in the sun, an empty shell. He looked the other way to where the great wall of the dam hung like a white curtain across the Tajubo valley. His heart jumped. There were soldiers there all right. A line of black figures, strung out along the top of the wall, too many to count. What were they doing?

Nothing much. Just moving about.

After a while he got tired of watching. He got out his penknife and began to whittle a stick. The soldiers hadn't wanted his penknife, even though it could cut a string with a flick of the wrist. They'd looked at it and put it down. Hadn't they seen how sharp it was? Anyway, he'd let Papa borrow it, next time he wanted to kill a sheep.

He whittled two sticks and sharpened points on them: you could use these to spear a sheep dead. Or a soldier, if you crept up behind him. If the soldier was asleep and didn't see you coming and you aimed for his throat. Or would it be better to aim for his heart? Where is your heart, anyway? He put his hand on his chest but couldn't feel his heart beating. Perhaps it had stopped. He whittled another stick.

Later, when the sun began to drop, he put all the sharp sticks in his satchel and whistled to Perrita to bring the sheep to him. If a soldier looked in his bag he'd tell him the penknife was allowed, the other soldiers had let him keep it. And the sticks were for his mama to use in the garden, he would say.

The black figures were still on the dam, moving about on the top of the wall.

Albi, in his corner by the kitchen fire, leaned his head against the wall and felt the voices go fuzzy in his ears. Then they went quiet.

Mama chuckled suddenly. 'He's worn out, the poor little thing.'

El pobrecito, she'd called him. He tried to wake up enough to protest, but the voices were murmuring again and if they thought he couldn't hear because he was asleep he had better listen. He woke his ears up and kept his eyes closed.

Ramona said, 'But Papa, the factory makes paper, not guns.'

'Paper for banknotes,' Papa said. 'That'll be Fascist money now.'

Silence.

'We can't be sure the war is over,' Inma said, in her low voice which everybody always listened to, even their papa. 'It might be Republican money yet.'

'But Ramon!' That was Mama speaking. 'How would we manage if the girls stopped bringing their wages home?'

'I will not have any child of mine conniving with the enemy!'

Albi opened his eyes. Nobody noticed.

'Papa, they've got a list,' Pili said. 'It's got our names on it. All of us who work in the factory.'

Inma said, 'She's right, Papa. They're saying they'll march us to the factory if we don't go of our own free will. And if they do that they won't pay us.'

A long pause. Then Papa said, his voice tired, 'It's not as simple as you make it sound, Inma. The road up to the *Meseta* isn't the only reason the Fascists are here. The factory is important too. They want to make sure that paper goes on being made but it'll be for Fascist banknotes now.'

Nobody said anything.

Was the same fight happening in every house? Albi closed one eye and squinted up at the photograph on the wall above Pili's head. He was only six the day that picture was taken but he remembered the photograph man as if it was yesterday, going round the village with his camera on its stand, persuading people to pay him to take photographs of them, each family lined up outside their house. It was like magic, the picture in a wooden frame with glass in it and them all inside it. It was still magic, because there they were on the wall, three years later, still fixed in the frame: *Abuelo* in the middle and next to him the *abuela*. On either side of them, Mama and Papa upright on their chairs.

He turned his eyes away. That picture was the family they used to be, when *Abuelo* was still alive and the *abuela* was a sweet little grandmother with cheeks like apples. Papa still the old Papa. Albi's sisters in the back row, one two three. And his brother. They weren't the same family any more.

Papa's voice rose: Pili was arguing and Papa never liked that.

Albi went to bed.

Next morning the girls went to work as usual. Papa didn't try to stop them, but as soon as they were out of the house he started shouting at Mama. 'Don't you realise? This isn't just about collaborating! Do you not know what those bloody fascists do to young women?'

Mama's hand flew to her mouth. She saw Albi standing in the doorway and shook her hand at Papa as if to say *Not now!* She picked up the broom and started sweeping. Papa didn't say another word.

What did soldiers do to girls? Albi walked out of the village on the path past the cemetery where there wasn't a check-point. He couldn't think of anything they couldn't do just as badly to boys. Bullets weren't fussy. It was surely more dangerous going out alone with the sheep than it was going to the factory with a great crowd of other girls, and men too.

When Albi got back with the flock that afternoon, Papa was in Julio's bar. He came in drunk. So drunk that Mama put him straight to bed and nobody was there to argue when the girls came in from the factory, Papa's snores so loud they barely heard the soldiers marching up the street at the start of curfew.

The next day the girls went to the factory, and the day after that. And then it was Sunday and they all went to church, even Papa, because the soldiers came with their guns and made them. There wasn't a priest, there wasn't a Mass. Just everybody in the church. They stayed in the church a long time not doing anything. El Comandante knelt at the front, praying as if he could save the world, while the soldiers stood by with their guns and stared at the villagers, ready to shoot anyone who caused trouble.

Albi stood between Inma and Papa. He let himself lean just a little bit against Inma. Her arm sneaked round the small of his back. He bowed his head and screwed his eyes up tight to look as if he was praying, but while he was about it he might as well ask God to make sure Papa bowed his head too.

5

Mena

Albi lay on his back, watching the October sun spark among the branches of the evergreen oaks as he listened with half an ear to the soft, rhythmic clanking of the bells. The sound told him the flock was still resting in the shade, chewing the cud.

Mama had made him promise to stay close to the village, but that was stupid. He hadn't seen any soldiers moving about today, not even on the dam, but there were two sentries right here on the road-block below the *castillo*. He'd been watching them all afternoon.

He turned his head to see what the soldiers were doing now. Nothing. Just lolling against the barrier and smoking.

Carlos said they must watch the soldiers, even when the soldiers weren't doing anything. He said it importantly, as if he knew more than Albi. Maybe he did. Carlos was only a year older but he was much taller.

A sudden yelp, like a dog being trodden on, made Albi sit up. Down by the *chorreta* the sun glinted on the top of a woman's head. Red-brown hair, all shiny. He stood up – it was the *Valenciana*. He scrambled down the bank. She was wearing the dress with all the buttons. He jumped across the water channel. She was wearing the sandals, too.

Now he could see the problem. A water-snake lay coiled on the bottom of the *chorreta* with its head up like a stalk, its snout sticking out of the water. Albi laughed and picked up a long stick.

'Don't kill it!'

Don't kill it? He stared, but she seemed to mean it so he hooked the snake out of the water and carried it downstream. The *Valenciana* watched him suspiciously until he'd dropped the snake in the bushes. It slithered away, and she set her basket down.

He made himself comfortable on the end of the *chorreta* wall.

The *Valenciana* glanced sideways at him. 'What's your name?'

'Alberto. Mostly people call me Albi.'

'And I am Carmen, but at home I'm called Mena.'

'Why?' He'd never heard a Carmen being called Mena before.

She placed a bar of soap on the edge of the parapet. She had fine white hands, with a ring on her wedding finger. Was it gold, like Pili talked about having one day? Mama's wedding ring was only made of brass.

'Because my best friend is also called Carmen. She stayed Carmen and I became Mena.'

'Can I call you Mena?'

As soon as he said it he wished he hadn't. He poked at a waxy plant growing in a crevice of the wall where he was sitting and his ears went hot. But when he looked up her eyes were smiling. Big dark-brown eyes.

'If you want to. You know, you look just like my little brother.'

He kicked his heels against the parapet. He'd be ten next year. Then he noticed what she was taking out of the basket and he stopped being cross. His sisters had petticoats with lace on the hems but those were coarse, hand-made things, nothing like this filmy white cloth with lace so delicate you might put your finger through it by mistake. His face went hot now, as well as his ears, but she was too busy plunging the clothes into the water to notice.

'Aren't you going to clean the *chorreta* out first?'

She looked at him in surprise, as if she didn't know the first thing.

'My mama always cleans it before she washes,' he said. Maybe she was a bit simple. He jumped off the parapet and picked up the old broom lying by the sluice gate. 'Take them out again. This is what you have to do.'

He lifted the wooden gate and the water emptied out of the *chorreta* in a rush. He swept the silt out of the bottom of the rock channel and gave the sides a good brushing down, like he used to for his mama. Then he put the gate back and sat down on the parapet to wait for the *chorreta* to fill again.

The *Valenciana* started to get the clothes out of her basket and lay them on the stone. 'What is a *chorreta?*'

So she was a bit simple. He gestured at the channel cut in the rock. 'It's the name for this. A washing place that isn't a wash house.'

She laughed. 'It must be an Aragonese word.'

He didn't know what she was talking about so he busied himself checking the gate wasn't leaking too much water, and told her about his sheep and which one was his favourite which was La Gorda, and by then the water was up to the top again. She started wetting the clothes and patting the bar of soap on them.

'That's not how my mama does it.'

'How does she do it?' She held out the soap.

He looked at her sharply but she wasn't laughing now. He glanced back towards the village, and the other way, past Ovidio's *huerto*, but there was nobody about, so he took the soap and showed her how to rub it into the cloth, then work the cloth about until the dirt lifted.

She took the soap back and started doing it the same way. 'I came up here while it was quiet, to practise.'

Practise? Surely girls were born knowing how to do washing, or was it different in Valencia? And wasn't she scared to come up here on her own with the soldiers about? She really was peculiar.

'In Valencia we… We have someone take our washing away to do it.'

He perched on the parapet again. If she was from a rich family why was she living in El Rincón? There was nobody rich here, not since El Caballero ran away.

'It's different here from Valencia. There are so many new things to learn but it's hard with everyone watching. Nobody seems to understand you're not born knowing these things, they have to be learned.' She made it sound like school.

'Why did you come here then?'

'Andrés couldn't live in Valencia. Because of the farm.' She turned her head and stared up at the rosy cliffs where vultures sailed on broad wings. The sun had moved over the crest of the rock lighting up all the little trees along the top, bright as candles. 'And my parents thought it would be safer here.'

Andrés's farm was up there on the *Meseta* beyond the cliffs. The sprawl of buildings that was the Torre de las Estrellas had a tower like a castle but nobody was fighting the soldiers from it. Instead, the soldiers made Andrés come down to the village every afternoon for curfew, just like everyone else, though it took an hour on a mule (two hours on foot) at both ends of the working day. The soldiers said anybody who disobeyed the new law would be shot. That didn't sound safe at all.

'Andrés's mother thinks it's safer if I stay down in the village all the time.' She gave a little nervous laugh. 'But I'd much rather be up at the farm with him.'

He could feel the loneliness breathing out through her skin. 'You can come with me when I take the sheep out.'

She laughed as if he'd made a joke. Above them, the sheep bells were beginning to sound restless. He jumped down off the parapet. 'I'd better go.'

'Thank you for my laundry lesson.'

Please don't say that in front of anybody else. Please don't. He ran back to his flock and shouted at his dog.

Albi looked at their five feet around the hearth. He liked doing sums. Five feet round the fender, steaming gently, and Mama's and Inma's four feet hurrying about the kitchen making the supper: five add four made nine. Pili's two plump feet tucked under the little table where she was sitting sewing made it eleven all together. If you counted the *abuela's* feet in the bed in the front bedroom it would be thirteen, but the *abuela* was quiet so she was probably asleep and her feet didn't count anyway because they'd stopped working.

Inma came to sit by the fire with a basket of potatoes, so now there were nine feet round the fire and under the table, and only two running about. Albi watched her peel the potatoes with the small kitchen knife the soldiers didn't take. She peeled the potatoes into her apron the same way Mama did. Had Inma grown up knowing how to do that because she was a girl, or did she have to learn it? He hadn't had that thought before today.

'I saw the *Valenciana*,' he said. 'Her name is Mena.'

'Mena?' Pili's voice wasn't friendly. 'What sort of a name is Mena?'

'What sort of a name is Pili?' he retorted, and got a clip round the back of his head.

'Pilar to you.'

What was she doing, anyway? That sewing looked like some of the things she kept in her enamel chest.

Mama came to the hearth with the heavy cauldron of water. As she lifted it onto the hook over the fire the chain came off the bracket in the chimney.

'Fix it for me, Albi.'

He tried, but the fire was too hot, and anyway he couldn't reach high enough. Papa took the chain. Even for him it was a struggle, with his head up inside the canopy of the fireplace, coughing from the smoke.

Albi looked down where Papa stood half in the ashes. 'Your leg is on fire!'

Papa hooked the chain back up and hopped off the hearth. Inma quickly filled a basin from the water jar and put it on the floor so he could stand his wooden leg in it. A sizzle of steam rushed up out of the bowl.

Papa winked at Albi. 'That was a close shave.'

Ramona laughed. 'If you keep doing that, Papa, you'll end up lopsided.' She leaned over and put another log on the fire. 'Do you suppose the *Valenciana* will want to work in the factory?'

'We won't see her there,' Pili said in the hard voice she used for people she didn't like, even though she'd never met the *Valenciana*. 'A stuck-up hoity-toity like that wouldn't want to get her hands dirty.'

Albi thought of the *Valenciana*'s slender fingers, and the flimsy things she'd been washing in the *chorreta*. He didn't think she was stuck-up but perhaps it would be better not to mention her not knowing how to wash clothes.

'El Caballero's back.' Papa said to the ceiling. 'And bloody Jesús with him.'

Albi looked up quickly. He saw Ramona and Inma exchange glances.

'Papa!' Pili said indignantly. She must know already, that would be why she'd got her sewing things out again.

'Papa nothing!' Papa sat up, suddenly fierce. 'Forget it, girl. That bastard Caballero is hand-in-glove with the damned fascists and bloody Jesús is his henchman so as far as you're concerned that's an end of it.' He made a swiping action with his hand.

Albi stared. Even if El Caballero had run away at the beginning of the war and Jesús with him, wasn't it a good thing they'd come back? Seeing as Jesús was Pili's *novio*.

'I will not have you fraternising,' Papa said, to Pili's bowed head.

Fretnising. That was a good word for Pili. She'd fretted when Jesús left. Now he'd come back it looked as if she was fretting again, even though she'd got some of those new white towels and aprons out again, after they'd lain such a long time in the enamel chest. He looked at Pilar, hunched over the table as if to ward off blows. Tears rolled off her chin and fell on the cloth.

'Ramón!' said Mama. She pulled a little face at Pili as if to say *Don't mind him*.

Alberto shivers in the crisp evening wind. The water sings in the *chorreta* at his back. A creamy-white eagle with dark markings on its underwings glides out across the sky. His eyes follow it idly: *la culebrera* – the snake-eater. To the south, a cloud of vultures is wheeling above the gorge as if there's something dead up there. It was stupid of him to come up to the *chorreta* of all places. Even all these years later it tugs at his heart.

Mena.

How can he *not* remember?

6

Papa

'Albi!'

He went to see what his papa wanted and found him sitting on the bed in the *alcoba*, one leg of his long underpants rolled up to expose his stump.

'Get some warm water. That damned sore is weeping again.'

Albi went to the kitchen. He got a basin down from the cupboard and filled it with warm water from the cauldron over the fire. Papa used to have two legs but the war happened to him, one day when he was away felling trees in La Selva. He didn't come back for half a year, and when he did he had a wooden leg. At the beginning Albi hadn't liked seeing Papa's stump but he was used to it now. Papa never let Mama or the girls help him. Albi was proud to be the one who bound the stump with cloths to lessen the chafing from the leather straps.

He knelt down on the floor and bathed the scabs gently, trying not to catch the one which was lifting.

'The stump will harden up,' Papa said, as he always did. 'Give it time.'

The cloth came away yellow with pus. Albi took the bowl to the kitchen and threw the water out of the window into the street. He left the cloth in the basin for Mama to deal with when she came in and went to find a clean bandage from the shelf in her cupboard. Papa was very brave, walking about on the wooden leg even though it hurt, but he still couldn't walk far enough to look after the sheep, and he couldn't milk the cow or feed the oxen because cattle and wooden legs don't go together. All these were Albi's jobs now, or his Mama's. What they couldn't do between them, like cutting the corn, they'd had to pay Miguel to do for the last two summers. Though Papa was still saying he'd do the ploughing next spring, *the devil take me if I don't.*

'Run along now,' Papa said, when Albi had finished fixing the bandage. 'Take the ewes out but leave the lambs. The gypsy is coming today.'

Albi looked up in surprise. Papa knew he would mind about the lambs going, why hadn't he said it before? But Papa wouldn't look at him.

'Go down by the river,' Papa said, 'but don't stay out long. If you come back past the *huerto* you can graze off the top terrace.'

Albi led the sheep and goats along the narrow path. They seemed so few without the lambs. He could see his papa was bobbing about on the *huerto* and loudly telling Mama what to do, so the gypsy must have been. He hoped Mama had the money safe.

At the bend in the path he stopped and pulled the branches of thorn away from the opening in the wall so flock could go through. He could see Papa wasn't really doing much, though he was being very busy about it, hopping up and down the rows and arguing. Their voices drifted across the *huerto,* Mama saying crossly, 'We must pick the last tomatoes before we go,' and Papa snapping back 'Why bother? The damned fascists will only take them off us.'

The tomato vines had turned black after last night's sudden frost. The last few tomatoes shone like green and scarlet balls in the cold sunshine and Mama went on picking them. 'If you want to live on potatoes all winter, Ramón, you can. The rest of us would like to live a little better than that.'

'You can like away, woman. Liking doesn't get. They're taking far more than they need. Probably selling it on the black market.'

'Really?' said Mama in a sneery voice, and Albi stopped listening. He watched the sheep spread over the terrace, nibbling fast at the bean haulms and onion waste, even though the frost had shrivelled everything up. He looked up at the clear sky, at the late sunlight shimmering all along the edge of the cliff. Down here, the cold shadow of the cliff was stalking out across the valley floor towards the *huerto*. Papa whacked at the tomato vines with his crutch and toppled the supporting sticks. Then he trampled on them with his one good leg so Mama couldn't pick the tomatoes.

She turned her back on him. So did Albi.

Next time he looked, Mama was loading the panniers onto the mule while Papa stood by, indignant on his crutches and still arguing.

Albi went over and helped her pile the potatoes into the panniers, and then the marrows, and the tomatoes Mama had managed to pick on the top – at least Papa had let her keep those. They led the mule off the *huerto* and Albi followed after with the flock. He thought they'd stopped fighting, until Mama said, 'A lot of help you've been, Ramón. I should just have taken Albi.' But Papa ignored her.

On the outskirts of the village Miguel was watering his mule at the stone trough and Mama stopped to let their mule drink too. Albi held the sheep back and waited for them.

Miguel frowned at Papa. 'I hear you sold your lambs, Ramón.'

'Needs must.'

'Do you trust him? Where's he selling them?'

'He's a sly one but he's clean,' Papa said.

Albi stared at his bare feet in the damp lush grass below the trough. Clean? The gypsy was even dirtier than he was. He almost didn't hear Miguel say quietly, 'The priest is back.' He looked quickly at Mama. She'd heard, but she didn't say anything.

'Is it the same one?' Papa asked.

'*That* crafty devil won't show his face again after buggering off like that. Unlike his mate El Caballero. No, it's no one we've seen before. Looks as if he's been eating very well, behaves as if he's here to stay. You'll see what I mean.'

The big church doors were hanging open, flanked by two soldiers on guard. The door of the priest's house next to the church was open too, and clouds of dust drifted out through the windows like smoke. A plump, middle-aged woman, dressed in black, appeared on the doorstep with a broom.

Albi's mama crossed herself furtively as she hurried past but Papa didn't notice. He was going so fast down the slope, his two crutches and his wooden leg going *lippety lippety*, Albi was certain he would fall. But Papa didn't fall. He didn't look once at the church, or at the soldiers, or at the small fat woman with the broom.

In the Calle San Juan, the neighbours huddled by Jaime's wall. Mama and Papa joined them. Albi heard the word *Zaragoza* and all the heads leaned in to listen. He lingered by the front door and the sheep went past him into the house.

'That woman is the priest's sister. She's been cleaning the church house all afternoon.' Martín's voice, whispering.

'Good thing there was nothing left in it then,' Young Jaime said out loud. 'Made her job easier.'

The others laughed, a tense, nervous sound, glancing over

their shoulders. Albi leaned against the doorpost and pretended to squeeze a thorn out of his hand.

'The soldiers say we have to report for work tomorrow,' Francisco from next door said. 'Those of us who aren't working in the factory. They want the church repaired.'

Albi had to go indoors then, to stop the sheep coming back out. The last thing he heard was his papa saying, 'We'll see about that.'

Was it true Papa was a trouble-maker, like Pili said? He shut the gate of the pen and went to fetch an armful of hay. Last night she said Papa brought trouble down on everybody else by talking against the factory in Julio's bar. If the girls lost their jobs there would be no money coming into the house. It was just as well the gypsy had come today, whatever Miguel meant when he asked if Papa trusted him. Mama said last night there was no more money left under the mattress. Now there would be some. For a while.

Albi climbed the stairs to the kitchen. He scooped a cupful of water out of the big water pot and drank it, then another. Below him, hooves clinked on the cobbles as Mama brought the mule in. The sound of Papa's angry voice came muffled through the kitchen floor. He was still arguing as he clattered his way up the stairs and banged in through the door.

'They can drive us to church like cattle on a Sunday,' he said as he threw himself down on a chair, 'but they can't force us to do the repairs. We'll all refuse and there's an end of it.'

Mama stood with her arms crossed, watching him unstrap his wooden leg.

'That's all very well for a legless man to say. Do you really think they'd want you?' She turned away to stir the fire. 'But if they did, you'd better not draw attention to yourself by refusing.'

'Pah.'

Albi edged round Papa and sat down in the chimney corner. He'd been walking all day and his legs were so tired. If only the girls would come in from work perhaps the arguing would stop, but it was early yet.

'It's bad enough being forced into church on a Sunday,' Papa said. 'If that damned priest thinks he's going to have a congregation any other day of the week he's in for a disappointment. I will not have you crossing that threshold out of choice, woman, and there's an end to it. You hear me?'

It was bad enough having the soldiers here, without Papa saying dangerous things. Albi pretended he hadn't heard.

Anyway, Papa was wrong. When the soldiers lined up the men in the Plaza next morning, all the men who weren't working in the factory, Papa was one of them. But when they picked out *You – you – you* to work on the priest's house, Mama was right. They didn't pick a crippled man, and nobody they picked dared refuse.

7

Permits

Santi says, '*Tío*! Let's go fishing!'

They drive off down the road, out of the village and along the valley, high above the river. The drifts of poplars below the road glow bright yellow in the afternoon sun. It makes the heart sing, that sun in the poplar leaves. Santi's pick-up swoops down the long bends towards the river, but just before they enter the jaws of El Portal, where the road squeezes through the narrow gap above the river, Santi swerves off the tarmac onto the track that leads back towards the dam. Gravel spits under the tyres.

'Sorry, *Tío*! Sorry!' he says, putting out a hand to steady Alberto.

'*Gran tio*,' Alberto says, pulling rank. It is Santi's father, Raul, who is his nephew. 'Slow down, lad. There's no point dying before we even get there.'

Santi laughs and puts his foot down. A white plume of dust rises behind them. On this side of the valley they're still in full sun, but away to their right the village is already in shadow.

A snake slithers across the track in front of them. A big black snake, so long it has almost arrived in the bushes on the far side before its tail is fully on the track.

'Did you see that, *Tío*? Did you see that!'

Alberto hangs onto the dashboard. He's vowed over and over he'll never go off-road with Santi again, but then he never has the heart to say no.

'Snake on the road,' he says through gritted teeth. 'Means it's going to rain.'

Santi gives him a startled sideways look. 'Who says?'

'My papa used to say it. Your great-grandfather. Where are we going?'

'To fish in the dam, *Tío*!'

Alberto stares out at the glowing rosehips speeding past. Is it that time of year already? Of course it is. The trout fishing is over, their permits are no longer valid.

Santi says, 'I didn't know you could remember Great Grandfather. *Abuela* told me you were still very young when he died.'

Alberto is surprised that Pilar should have talked of such things to her grandson. She's been dead more than ten years. How old was Santi when this conversation took place? He tightens his grip on the dashboard as Santi rams his foot on the brake.

'Well I'll be damned,' Santi says, looking away to his right where the old pill-box still stands, a squat, pale shape among the rosemary, looking out over the dam wall and the dark fall into the valley below. Beyond the wall, the dam-water shimmers. Alberto can never decide what colour you'd call that bright blue-green. Perhaps it's jade.

It isn't the water Santi is looking at. He is staring at the pill-box. The setting sun casts sharp shadows: in this light the pock-holes look startling, ragged, as fresh and sharp as the day they were gouged out of the cement. Santi jumps down from the cab and bounds like an ibex over the clumps of rosemary. He places his hands, one in each of the higher pock marks, and leans his forehead against the sun-gilded cement between them, standing for a moment like a figure crucified on a wall.

When he walks back to the cab his face is sombre and unfamiliar. He climbs into the driver's seat and sits for a moment. 'We shouldn't ever forget them,' he says softly. 'Those boys, and what they tried to do for us.'

Alberto shoots a startled look at the young face glowing in the fall of the sun, but Santi is quite serious. Pilar must be turning in her grave, he thinks, as he looks away and stares into the light and shadow of the rosemary where a smoky haze of insects dances. He lifts his eyes to the bullet wounds in the wall for a moment, then turns his gaze back to the track.

'Better get going, Santi. Get those rods set up before we lose the light.'

*

Albi hurried back to the village with his sheep. Above him, the wall of the dam glowed orange in the light of the setting sun. Were there soldiers up there, watching him as he went by? It was his own fault for coming back this way, but there wasn't any grass left near the houses and his sheep had to eat, and now it was late. He started running.

At the mid-point of the humped bridge over the river he looked back. Ovidio was coming down the track behind him, his great flock kicking up a cloud of dust. It wasn't curfew yet, then. Albi pressed his hand against the stitch in his side to stop it hurting and walked up the steep lane towards the village.

Just below the first houses, where the walls of the gardens

crowded in on either side, a new checkpoint blocked the road. He stopped, his animals milling around him.

Two soldiers were standing in front of the barrier, their rifles held ready to fire the minute he started making trouble. He wanted to turn and run but that would be dangerous. Besides, Ovidio was already climbing the lane behind him, his flock loud and crowded between the high walls. Albi walked up to the barrier, his knees threatening to give way any minute. He felt in his pocket for the piece of paper.

The soldier took the permit, staring hard at Albi before he read the writing.

'Pass.' He tossed the permit so it fell on the ground. Albi bent to pick it up.

'You! Stop there.'

He froze, but the soldier wasn't looking at him, he was staring at Ovidio. The barrier was still across the road.

'What are you waiting for?' The other soldier jerked his gun at Albi. 'Go round it, imbecile.'

Albi dived for the gap at the end of the barrier, barely big enough for a boy and a handful of sheep to pass, but the soldiers ignored him, their eyes on Ovidio. He forced himself to walk up the lane, not run, though his legs felt as if they might crumple. He wasn't going to look back, but then at the last moment he did. Ovidio was at the barrier, his flock right behind him, looking from one soldier to the other and talking fast, and all the summer had drained out of his face.

One of the soldiers suddenly lunged forwards, cutting upwards with the butt of his rifle. Albi heard the crunch of wood on bone. He turned and ran, and didn't stop until he fell over the doorstep into his house.

'What's happened to him?' Carlos whispered as Ovidio walked away along the path, his face so swollen and discoloured he looked like somebody else pretending to be him.

'It was yesterday,' Albi said. 'The soldiers on the new checkpoint on the road down to the river. They wouldn't let him through and then they hit him.'

'What with?'

'Rifle butt.'

'Spect they tortured him after that,' Carlos said. 'To make him that colour. They're just looking for trouble.'

The soldiers might torture them too, then, seeing as Carlos was supposed to be in school, and when he wasn't in school he was supposed to stay in the village. But Carlos didn't seem to care.

He nudged Albi. 'Where is this famous permit then? Go on – show me!'

Albi pulled the paper from his pocket and handed it over, hoping Carlos wouldn't see his hands shaking. If Ovidio hadn't been there yesterday the soldiers might have hit him instead.

Carlos peered at the writing. 'What does it say?'

'It says *Alberto Álvarez Zapatero is per… mitted to… to graze his flock outside the village pro-something he… rems within four kilometres of the church and obs the hours of curfew.*'

'Four kilometres? How far is that?'

Albi shrugged. 'About… to the waterfall? Or El Portal.'

The words shut his mouth. El Portal where the river ran fierce and narrow below the village. The rock walls closing in, the sky a strip above and vultures standing, big as sheep, along the skyline, waiting. A natural gateway keeping the bad things out for hundreds of years, ever since their village began. But not now. When they made the dam, years ago before he and Carlos were even born, they blew out the rock with dynamite to squeeze a road through beside the river. Where roads go, soldiers go, and all the trouble with them.

He brushed his arm across his face and put the permit back in his trouser pocket.

'C'mon, Rabbit,' Carlos said, jumping to his feet.

'Don't call me that.' But Carlos was walking off. Albi whistled to La Perrita to bring the sheep and goats.

They climbed further up the bank and spied on the sentries manning the road-block below the *castillo*, until they got bored. Then they took the sheep higher up among the trees and found a rock where they could sit and watch the village without being seen. They could hear the banging and hammering in the priest's house, tucked out of sight beyond the church. Albi was glad his papa hadn't been chosen to do the repairs today. The soldiers beat Roberto the baker last week, even worse than Ovidio, and all Roberto had done was refuse to bake bread for them.

He leaned a little closer to Carlos. It felt safer being two, even if Carlos didn't have a permit. 'Do you reckon the soldiers are going to take the same people to do the priest's work every day?'

'Maybe. But my papa won't be one of them. Nor my brother either. The soldiers won't take anyone who works in the factory. And they won't want yours, not with his leg.' Carlos chucked a stone into a gorse bush. 'I never thought it would be like this, being in a war. It's so boring. Nothing's happening.'

'Yes it is! People are getting beaten! And the soldiers might shoot us any minute.'

'Huh. Shoot us for what? Nobody's doing anything, except what the soldiers tell them to do. *Go to church!* We go to church. *Mend the priest's house!* We mend the priest's house.'

No they didn't, other people did. But he knew what Carlos meant.

'It's same as it always was, only worse. We're prisoners now. And what are we doing about it? Nothing!' Carlos pulled up his knees and leaned his chin on them. He stared over the crowded roofs of the village towards the dam. 'That's what we should be doing. We should be spying on the dam. That's why the soldiers are here, to stop us blowing it up. So that's what we should be doing.'

'Blow it up?' Albi screwed his eyes against the sun and stared at the dam wall, all white and empty. No soldiers on it today. 'Why would we want to blow it up? People would get drowned!'

'The people who did the blowing up wouldn't drown, would they,' Carlos said, as if he'd be one of the blower-uppers and not helpless in his bed or in the Plaza or in school when the blowing-up happened.

'My papa says the soldiers are here 'cos of the factory and 'cos this is the only road up onto the *Meseta*,' Albi said, but his heart was sinking. He knew what Carlos would want to do next. It was always the dangerous things Carlos was most interested in.

In the kitchen, the talking stopped as they listened to the flinty sound of boots marching past at the start of curfew.

When the sound got fainter the talk began again, the way it always did: the girls told the gossip they'd learned at work, Papa told the news he'd heard in the street, and Mama told what they'd talked about over the laundry and in the bakehouse.

Ramona said, 'Did you—' but Papa shushed her.

Screaming. Faint but terrified, not stopping even for breath.

'Mother of God,' whispered Mama, her hands to her face. 'They're beating a woman now.'

Papa, his hand still raised, shook his head. He listened intently. 'That's not a woman. It's a man.'

How could a man scream like that? High-pitched and piercing as a rabbit in the jaws of a fox.

'What's happening?' Albi whispered.

'We'll find out soon enough,' Papa said, when the screaming stopped.

It seemed impossible that a man could scream like a rabbit and still be alive the next day, but in the morning there was Hernán Irún, outside his house at the bottom of the next street. He had a black eye and his right arm was in a sling, but he wasn't dead.

'Silly old fool,' Pili said that night in their kitchen, as if it had been Hernán Irún's fault. But all he'd done was be in the wrong place when curfew started.

8

Church

Alberto goes along the lines of rabbit hutches stacked back-to-back, three rows high, down the middle of the shed. Here and there white fur protrudes through the mesh where a big doe lies against the front of the cage. Too lazy, most of them, to shift when he opens the door to fill the water bottle from his plastic can.

'*Tío?*' Raul's voice.

'Here. Doing the water.'

Raul appears round the end of the cages. He's carrying a large rabbit, and he's limping. His hip must be playing up again. He's eleven years younger than Alberto; calling him uncle is a joke from long ago.

'What you got there,' Alberto says. Santi would say *a rabbit*, but Santi isn't here.

'José Moliner's. I said I'd put her in with the buck.'

The doe is brown. Unlike these great white lumps with their red eyes, this is a real rabbit with firm flesh and strong bones, same as they used to have when he was a boy. Alberto reaches out and strokes her ears. The doe regards him with a steady eye.

'She's quiet.'

'She's used to being handled. Between you and me, he's made a pet of her.'

Raul opens the door of the buck's cage and pushes in the doe, who promptly wakes up. In the small cage it isn't clear whether she's running away from the buck or chasing him.

Raul laughs. 'Look at us! Watching fucking rabbits as if that's all we have to do all day.' He grabs the wheelbarrow from the wall at the end of the shed, throws a shovel into it, and a broom.

45

Always a ball of energy, Raul.

Alberto follows more slowly along the row of hutches. They're cleaning out this morning, as they do every Wednesday, regular as clockwork. That's the other thing about Raul. He likes routine.

'We'll never make our fortunes, not like some. Hey, *Tío*? Not like Carlos did.' Raul shovels rabbit pellets into the barrow.

Alberto sweeps behind him. 'Not sure he did make a fortune. Gold chains and fat cigars aren't the same as money in the bank.'

Raul snorts. 'He had that too.'

Carlos is dead and buried, what's left of him, but he's hounding Alberto. Everywhere he goes, even the rabbit shed, Carlos bobs up. It isn't as if he was significant. Mari-Jé is right. He isn't now, and he wasn't then. Carlos was always more of a noise than a presence, even as a boy.

Alberto takes his six sheep out after dinner and lets them graze on the deserted terraces by the cemetery. When he was a boy, all this land was gardens, full of the sound of running water in summer, full of birds, full of people. Now it's all grey thyme scrub, and wild roses running rampant along the edges of the old *huertos,* the hips bright and the leaves yellowing. And today he is the only one out here.

No, not quite. There's a thin column of smoke from a bonfire, somewhere down towards the old mill. Alberto sits on a flat rock and watches the smoke, so calm and quiet in the sunshine. He looks back at the village, at the crooked line of houses through the trees, curving away unevenly towards the great buttress of the church. The present is empty, but the past is full.

*

Albi sat out in the street with his rope-making, listening to Old Jaime's thin voice drifting down from the upstairs window of the house opposite.

'*Ho, ho is that your tune?* I said, and then I ran at him with my pitchfork. We had no more nonsense from him after that.'

Silly old fart, Carlos called Old Jaime, but Mama said he couldn't help it. When you get old your brain can go soft, like the *abuela.* Only, what if a soldier heard him? Albi glanced nervously down the Calle San Juan but all the people in the street were neighbours, busy working in the autumn sunshine while there were no soldiers about.

He pulled another handful of straw and joined it into the end of his plait of rope. He'd promised Mama he'd stay close to the house and listen for the *abuela,* and it was good to be sitting out in the street with everyone else on a sunny autumn morning. But he was jumpy, because who knew where the soldiers were today and what they were doing.

'*Look lively lads,* I said. *Quick march!*'

Old Jaime's stories weren't real, not like Papa's. Papa was pinned to the ground by an armoured vehicle with his foot trapped under the wheel, the Fascist driver he'd shot lying half out of the vehicle, nobody left alive to get him free, not even an enemy. He lay trapped in the mud for hours before he managed to get his knife out of his back pocket. He tied his red kerchief as tight as he could round his thigh, and then – Albi always had to close his eyes when he got to this bit of Papa's story – he plunged the knife blade into his knee.

Albi made himself go through every detail because he must never forget.

Papa worked the knife backwards and forwards in the joint, even though he kept falling backwards in a faint. Every time he came to, he worked his knife a bit more, until he'd sawn the bottom half of his leg clean off. *Good thing I always kept that knife so sharp,* he liked to say. *Pity I'd just used it to cut my breakfast sausage.* The blood ran into the mud, the mud got into the cut. He had to drag himself nearly a kilometre to the road, and it was only luck a Republican truck came along and not a Fascist one. The truck took him to the hospital.

It worried Albi, what had happened to the foot Papa left behind and the bit of leg attached to it. Was it still out there somewhere, lying on the ground? Or did the vultures take it? Was there a rocky ledge on some cliff with his papa's bones on it, picked clean and white, and a vulture grown strong on his papa's flesh?

'Is that you?' shouted Old Jaime, making him jump. 'Bring me the chains.'

It took Papa a long time to tell his story, in the months after he came home. He didn't boast about it, Albi had to plead to be told the details. It took Papa nearly as long to tell the story as it had taken him to come home, which was a long time because he got a bad thing from the mud, while he was still in the hospital in Valencia, and he had to have more of his leg cut off in a proper operation, leaving only a short stump. He was sick for a long time after that.

They'd had a different story at home. In their story Papa went away to cut trees in the spring and didn't come back until it was nearly winter, even though he'd said he'd only be gone three days, and by then they thought he must be dead. Papa's story was better. But he never quite said which battle it was, or what sort of armoured vehicle. How many men had been inside it? What happened to them? Mama said, 'Don't bother your Papa. He prefers not to talk about it.' Why had Papa gone to the war when he'd said he was going to fell trees? Why didn't he say good-bye properly before he went? 'I got caught up in it,' Papa said. 'One minute we were felling pines, Manuel Gomez and me. The next we got picked up. I didn't mean to go.'

Manuel Gomez still hadn't come back. He didn't seem to be there in the bit of the story where Papa cut his leg off. Papa said they'd got separated, he didn't know what happened to Manuel.

It showed it was safer to stay in the village because the war had been all round them, not so far away as people might have thought. A day's walk, Papa said. No more than that.

Up in his room, now, Old Jaime seemed to be pulling a mule-team out of the mud.

Albi coiled the new rope neatly the way Papa had showed him. He wished his mama would come back. He pulled out another handful of straw and began plaiting more rope.

High up among the roofs the church bell hiccupped suddenly into life. He stopped plaiting, puzzled. It couldn't be curfew time, they hadn't long had dinner, but the bell clanged insistently as if it was. The *abuela* seemed to think so too, screeching suddenly from her bed upstairs as if she'd just woken. 'He's coming. He's coming! It's bloody Saint Peter again, raping all the young virgins.'

The sound of running feet made him look over his shoulder: his mama, and Pepito's mama with her. They ran straight past him into the house and up the stairs. The *abuela* shouted 'Get your hands off me! I'm waiting for Saint Peter!'

She was still yelling when they appeared at the front door and hoisted her awkwardly over the step. Albi watched them hurry up the street. The bell clamouring made everything feel wrong. He jumped up and ran after them.

A small group of women had gathered in the road. Above them, the new priest stood by the open doors of the church, watching Mama and Pepito's mama haul the *abuela* up the steps. The priest spoke to them as they went inside the building, Albi saw his mouth moving, but if they said anything back it was drowned by the bell. The women who'd been waiting in the road climbed the steps after them and disappeared into the church. The priest went on standing there, stern in all his finery, until the bell stopped. Then he turned and went inside.

Albi darted up two steps and down again. Ran three steps towards home, came back. He couldn't go into the church and make his mama come out again, not without attracting the attention of the priest. Besides, Mama wouldn't take any notice, even if he threatened to go and find his papa. Mama was more scared of God than she was of Papa.

49

9

Jesús

'I'm going to church,' says Mari-Jé as she comes out of the bedroom, all shiny in her new blouse.

Alberto nods. It's Wednesday, the amiable new priest will be in town. She never used to be so keen.

She lays her mobile phone down on the table. 'Gloria might ring.'

He nods obediently. Daughter-in-law Gloria. He'll ignore it, then. If it rings.

Alberto strokes the blade of his penknife backwards and forwards, backwards and forwards, across the whetstone. At the top of Calle San Juan, in the church tower, the cracked bell creaks into action. Dang dang. Dang... Dang. Not quite a rhythm – Mari-Jé's cousin José is getting too old for hanging on to that rope. A few voices pass outside. Alberto can tell they're dressed in their church clothes, just from the sound of their voices.

Funerals and marriages, that's all he goes to church for. Old habits don't change just because you're old and the end is coming. However jolly the new priest is, Church means trouble.

*

Albi turned his eyes back to Mama, willing her to stay quiet, because Papa looked as if he might fizz over without her saying a single word.

'Not all priests are bad, Ramón.'

'I'll go and shut the hens up,' Albi said, even though it was early. He went to the door.

The *abuela* yelled, 'Get you behind me Satan. That's just the

50

way I like it.' She'd been shouting all afternoon, since Mama took her to church. He thumped down the stairs as loudly as he could on his bare feet but it didn't stop him hearing.

'How could you bring such shame on me!' Papa might as well have stood outside and shouted it in the street. Albi stuck his head out of the front door and glanced up and down but everyone was indoors. Probably listening, all the same. 'Supporting the bloody fascists in full view of everyone!'

Mama's voice quiet, private, 'There wasn't anybody else there, Ramón. Only a handful of women. And the priest.'

Albi closed the front door and hurried back along the passage towards the corral, where he was far enough away not to have to hear.

He stroked his rabbit, and then the little speckledy hen, and put them to bed. He could go upstairs now. The girls had come in from work, their voices making the kitchen safe again.

The *abuela* was still shouting and Mama and Papa seemed to have stopped talking all together, but the girls chattered on as if they hadn't noticed. Suddenly Papa roared, 'Get that old bat into the back room like I told you to! Get her out of earshot before the fucking soldiers come by.'

Mama didn't move, so the girls did it, Albi helping. They had to change the beds round too, and all the bedding, because the *abuela's* bed was too small for two people to sleep in.

'Why do they want to sleep in the same bed if they're not even speaking?' Ramona said, lugging the heavy wool mattress from one room to the other with Pili's help. Albi followed with the bolster.

Back in the kitchen they sat round the fire, nobody talking. Albi could still hear the *abuela,* but muffled now.

Mama said, 'I didn't want your mother to fall out with God this late in her life, Ramón.'

Papa gave her the same withering look he sometimes gave Albi, the kind which made him want to be somewhere else. 'You know whose side that bloody priest is on. Not ours. He'll keep us firmly in our places and rob us blind while he's about it.' The bell started ringing for curfew. Papa thrust the old pack of cards at Albi. 'Go keep your *abuela* quiet.'

He went out to the back room and stood in the archway of the *alcoba* holding up the pack of cards. The *abuela* stopped shouting as soon as she saw it.

'Sit you down, Saint Christopher,' she said. 'We'll have a round or two before Peter comes.'

It was very quiet in the house then, with nobody talking. The candle on the shelf guttered gently. He was dealing a second round under the *abuela*'s watchful eye when Ramona came and sat down next to him.

'I can't take any more of *that*,' she said, jerking her head towards the kitchen door. 'It's like being at a funeral.'

Albi started dealing again, for three. The *abuela* watched his every move, making sure he didn't cheat. She might not know which year it was, or the names of her children, but she was still a dab hand at cards.

'What does Papa mean, the priest will rob us?' he whispered.

'The Church tax,' Ramona murmured back. She picked up her cards. 'Papa thinks it will start up again now this new priest has come.' She looked at the *abuela* sitting upright in her bed with the black shawl over her shoulders. Her white hair falling out of its pins made her look like a mad woman. '*Abuela*, you could do with your hair being brushed.'

'Eh?' But the *abuela* wasn't listening, she was too busy looking at her cards.

'You go first, *Abuela*,' Albi said loudly.

The tallow candle flickered in the draught; the *abuela* put a card down on the board balanced across her knees.

'Don't make it too exciting, Albi,' Ramona whispered. 'Better if she falls asleep. There are hardly any candles left.'

Albi put his card down slowly but he didn't know how you could play a quiet game with the *abuela*. She got excited if she won, she got angry if anyone else did.

'Do you think Mama will take her to church again?'

'Who knows.' Ramona placed her card and the *abuela* let out a little sigh of satisfaction as she quickly put down two. 'Good thing the priest hasn't moved in yet. When he does there'll be a Mass every day.'

Albi played another card. How would anyone have time to go to church every day, even if they wanted to? He caught Ramona's eye and didn't ask.

'Walls have ears,' she murmured.

When Sunday came the soldiers made everybody come out of their houses, same as all the other Sundays, and marched them into the church, but not *abuela*. She was asleep when the soldiers came up the street and Papa said it was safer to leave her behind, given the things she'd been shouting these last few days. He glared at Mama as if that was her fault.

The priest led the Mass. The Comandante stood in the front row, El Caballero and Jesús beside him, and the soldiers stood round the walls with their guns across their chests, speaking the responses loudly. Some of the villagers mumbled along with them. Most stayed silent. Papa stood next to Mama in the middle of the congregation, angry and bristling. Albi kept his chin tucked down, staring at the floor. So many things to worry about. Pili might be looking at Jesús when Papa had told her not to. Mama was murmuring the responses on his right, on his left Papa's angry silence might erupt any minute. If they were going to argue, please please let it not be here in the church with the soldiers watching.

They didn't say a word. Not even when they were safely back in their own kitchen. Pili kept quiet too. In the *alcoba,* at the back of the house, the *abuela* was still asleep. Albi stopped feeling sick. He was ready for his dinner now. Until he remembered there might be another Mass tomorrow. Or the day after.

Notices went up on all the stable doors with new laws on them. Nobody must work on a Sunday or they would pay a fine.

'As if sheep don't eat on a Sunday,' Papa said when Albi read the words to him.

There was a long list of other things they couldn't do on Sundays either. Playing *pelota* was one of them, but there was no law saying they couldn't hang about by the *pelota* wall on a Sunday, even if Jesús *had* parked his motorcycle there.

'It's a Gilera,' Carlos said. 'That's the gear change on the petrol tank.'

'Hey, Rabbit!' Rafa called across to Albi. 'How fast can this thing go?' And Juanito said, 'How much did it cost then?' As if Albi would know, Jesús being betrothed to his sister.

The only thing he knew about the motorcycle was that it wasn't Jesús who had bought it, it was El Caballero, and he didn't think he would mention that. 'It's faster than a horse galloping.'

Miguel came across the Plaza just then, pushing a wooden wheelbarrow piled high with potatoes. The wheel of the barrow wobbled and squealed, shouting to the whole world that Miguel was doing an Illegal Act. Wasn't he afraid of the priest or the soldiers catching him working on a Sunday?

Miguel cast a sideways look at the motorcycle and spat in the dirt. '*Hijo de puta.*'

Albi stared. Did he mean Jesús?

The gobbet of spit stayed there in the dust, until Andrés came into the Plaza leading his big black mule and the mule trod on it. Mena was with him. She wasn't wearing the pretty dress with all the buttons, nor the sandals either. Albi hadn't talked to her since that day by the *chorreta* but when she saw him she waved. He would have waved back only Carlos was watching, so he turned away and studied the motorcycle instead.

Rafa murmured, 'Did you hear about Andrés's brother? He's gone to France.'

'What's he gone there for?' whispered Carlos.

'Something to do with the Government. Not this lot.' Rafa jerked his head in the direction of the two sentries visible through the Gatehouse, guarding the check-point. 'Andrés will have to be extra careful, now El Caballero's back.'

Why? Albi bent closer, but before he could ask Pepito said, 'Where's France?'

'Across the sea, stupid,' Carlos said.

'Carlos!' Carlos's papa loomed, sudden and angry. 'Leave that bloody machine alone and get off home!'

Carlos scuttled off like a dog that had been hit. He liked to say his papa was scared of him, now he'd grown so tall, but it couldn't be true. Albi turned to see if the others had noticed but they were running off too, they'd seen Jesús coming along the street from El Caballero's house with his riding goggles in his hand.

Albi hesitated. After all, Jesús was nearly family now. He might give him a ride.

'Scram, Ear-Wax,' the big man said, swinging his leg over the motorcycle. 'It's curfew time.'

The motorcycle roared into life. Albi walked away, listening as Jesús cut back the engine and putt-putted out of the Plaza. He heard the echo as the motorcycle drove out through the archway under the gatehouse, and the pause that would be Jesús stopping at the check-point. Then the bike roared away down the road. The sun had already dropped behind the cliff.

If it was curfew time, why was it a different law for Jesús?

In Albi's house all was quiet. He ran up the stone stairs and opened the door into the kitchen. His mama sat alone by the sleeping fire, wiping her eyes with the hem of her apron. Crying again? It couldn't be about church because they'd all been to Mass this morning, so it must be Manolo. Why did she keep weeping for his brother when she'd still got *him*?

Mama smiled a watery smile and patted the stool beside her. He went over and sat the way he liked to when nobody was there to see, with his head on her lap and her hands stroking his hair. He said, as he always did, 'I'm your best, aren't I?' And she said, as she always did, 'You're my best baby.' But that was never quite what he wanted to hear. Anyway, the church bell had started tolling for curfew and the girls would come in any minute. He got up and went to sit in another chair. The front door opened and closed again: feet on the stairs, then the girls spilling into the room, all three of them together.

'Papa's in Julio's bar, Mama,' Pili said. 'On a Sunday! Do they think just because they've got the door locked nobody will know they're all in there, breaking the law?'

Mama shrugged and said nothing.

'He shouldn't do anything to get himself noticed,' Ramona said. 'He doesn't want the soldiers asking awkward questions. You know what they did to Benito.'

Albi shuddered. Of course Mama knew. 'Anyway,' he said quickly, changing the subject. 'When I—'

The front door banged and they all went quiet, listening to the heavy key being turned and the bolts shot home. The girls jumped up, Mama too, and started being busy. Papa banged his way into the room, much too cheerful.

'What's new then?' He dropped onto his chair.

There wasn't any news that anybody wanted to tell him. Pili sat down at the little table with the oil lamp and started sorting her sewing things.

Papa picked up his crutches, and dropped one again with a clatter. 'Think I'll go and have a little lie-down.'

The bell stopped tolling.

'What are you doing, you bloody whore?' The *abuela's* reedy voice, a double thud as something hit the wall and fell to the floor. The girls stopped talking to listen.

Through the wall, Mama's voice murmured gently.

Albi sat in the corner by the fire with his favourite hen on his knees. She lay quiet while he stroked her silky feathers, her gold-circled eye glinting as she stared at the flames. If he stayed quite still maybe nobody would notice he'd smuggled her into the kitchen. Pilar had the oil-lamp lit on her work-table but she was very short-sighted.

Ramona stirred the fire, making the flames and the shadows jump up.

'Albi!' Pilar's voice was sharp. 'Have you got that chicken up here again?'

He looked at Inma, but she only said, 'Take her back down now, Albi.'

He dawdled over lighting the stub of tallow candle, hoping Inma would change her mind, but she didn't. As he went out of the room he heard her say, 'He does so love his animals, that boy,' but Pili said, 'He should love them down in the stable then.' And then she shouted, 'Draught, Albi. Shut that door.'

The candle guttered as he went down the stairs with the speckledy hen tucked under his arm. In the passageway the flame bent so sideways he was afraid it would blow out. He didn't like the dark. He wondered if Carlos was as brave in the dark as he liked to make out. Carlos said he'd crept out of his house last night and sneaked all round the edge of the Plaza and back indoors again without any sentries seeing him. Even thinking about it made Albi feel sick, but it was possible Carlos was making it up.

He put the hen on the perch with the others in the old pig pen and went back upstairs. In the kitchen, Mama had moved her chair next to Pilar at the table. The *abuela* was quiet, so perhaps she'd gone to sleep.

Mama patted Pilar's pile of cloth, her brass wedding ring

glinting in the yellow light from the oil lamp. 'But you know how very expensive paraffin is, Pilar.'

'It's my money that pays for it, Mama. I spend enough hours in that factory working myself stupid to get the money.'

'I know you do, I know you do. But it isn't just the money, Pili. You know there isn't any paraffin in the shop to buy.'

The door to the front bedroom opened and they stopped talking. Mama got up to start making the supper.

Papa paused by the table and looked down at Pili. 'What's that?'

Albi picked up his penknife and started being busy so he didn't have to listen.

Pili said nervously, 'A placemat, Papa.'

'A *placemat*? And what do you want with a *placemat* when you don't own a table to put one on?'

Albi shrank down in his chair, whittling faster. *Please stay quiet, Pili – please.*

But Pili never did. 'I *will* have one. Jesús will buy me one.'

'Like hell he will! Have you not listened to a word I've been saying?'

'I heard,' Pilar flared. 'You can't stop me sewing, Papa. And it's none of your business what I sew in my own time.' She ducked as Papa let go of his crutch and lifted his hand. The crutch clattered to the floor as the hand came thumping down on Pili's shoulder.

'Ramón!'

But Pili was already up from the table. 'Jesús will provide for me – not like you did for Mama, only ever living off what was already here in this house, like peasants.' She pushed past Mama and ran to the back bedroom, slamming the door behind her.

From the far side of the door the *abuela* started up again, drowning out the sound of Pili weeping.

*

Alberto leans on the low wall in front of the church steps and stares down into the deserted Plaza. It's nearly thirty years since Jesús died. Behind him, the sounds of the Mass drift down from the church: the rise and fall of the priest's voice, the thin replies of the congregation. The rest of the village is deserted, only the dead leaves moving, skittering across the concrete by the old wash house.

He was always a big man, Jesús, even at the end when the wasted flesh hung loose on his bones, and his thick mop of black hair was reduced to a narrow grey semi-circle. Alberto remembers him full-fleshed and tight-skinned when he was young, his dark features topped by heavy eyebrows which met in a single line. *Jesús's pet caterpillar*, Carlos used to call it.

He snorts, remembering.

Jesús was big, but El Caballero was very short. Seeing them in the street you'd never have guessed what power that little man wielded. Alberto had no idea, when he was a kid. It took him years to understand Papa's anger.

He sees them now, clear as if it was yesterday: El Caballero walking down to the Plaza, impeccable in his dark trousers and white shirt, Jesús bending to hear what the smaller man is saying. Papa, watching them from where Alberto is standing now and trembling with rage.

10

Mama

It was late, only the two of them left sitting by the fire, Inma's needles flashing in and out, in and out, to finish the second sock. Paco at the factory said he would buy them off her if she had them ready by tomorrow.

He could ask it now, the question he'd been wanting to ask all evening.

'Why does Pili fight with Papa?'

Inma let go of her knitting long enough to put her hand on his knee. 'It's late, sweetheart. You should go to bed.'

'But *why* does she?'

She looked at him as if deciding what to say. He held her gaze and waited.

'Pili is very unhappy,' she said at last. 'She thought she was going to marry Jesús but then he went away. When he came back she thought they would be married after all.'

He waited, but Inma didn't say anything more and what she'd said he knew already. Everybody did. Or did she mean Jesús wasn't going to marry Pilar now? Even though she had opened her enamel chest again and was doing so much sewing? Pili would certainly be cross if that was true.

Inma said, 'Jesús is not so dishonourable that he wouldn't marry Pili, even now, if Papa would let him.'

Albi stared. He knew Papa didn't like Jesús but the whole village knew Jesús was Pili's fiancé, it would be shameful if they didn't marry now.

Inma put her knitting down. In the dying firelight he couldn't see the expression in her eyes. She said softly, so that he had to bend closer to hear, 'It would have been better if Jesús had never come back, Albi. Pili would have learned to live with her broken heart. And in a while her heart would have mended enough for her to accept somebody else.'

Somebody else? But nobody else from the village rode a motorcycle!

'Go to bed now, sweetheart,' she said. 'Don't worry about it.'

In the morning Albi cleaned out the chickens, and the rabbits. He chopped kindling like his mama had asked him to before she went to the bakehouse, and tidied the woodpile. It was late morning when he went to the pen. He was unlatching the gate to take the sheep out when the church bell started clanging.

He dropped the latch and listened. Was it for a Mass? It wasn't a Sunday.

Where was Mama?

He ran outside and up the empty street. A group of men had gathered by the wall in front of the church steps. Albi's papa was there, jaunty on his crutches. More men were coming up the lane from the Plaza. The priest stood by the church door, but there was no sign of any soldiers today. In the neighbouring streets whispering wives huddled, kerchiefs over their hair as if they meant to go to church. Albi looked to see if one of them was the *Valenciana* but he couldn't see her. He went to stand by his papa.

The men were watching the women, so was the priest.

The bell stopped. For a moment nothing happened, then the kerchiefed women started hurrying towards the church but the men surged forwards to block their way and the women stopped. Some of them shouted and shook their fists at their menfolk.

Above them, the priest frowned.

More women appeared from the *barrio* above the church. They stopped when they saw the crowd of men and they too started shouting. Albi glanced at his papa but Papa wasn't taking any notice, he was staring the other way, towards the Calle San Juan. Mama was walking quickly up the street, her grey kerchief on her head. She ignored Papa, she ignored the crowd of men. She ignored the other women. She walked straight up the steps and into the church.

As if it was a signal, a surge of women pushed up the steps after her.

Papa roared at Mama. All the men were shouting now, but the priest went into the church and the big doors swung shut behind him.

After a while the men drifted away. An hour is a long time when you have a lot of work to do. Papa went to the bar. Albi had to take the sheep out, he wasn't there to see what happened when the Mass ended.

It was late afternoon when he came back into the village from the river. Away behind him he could hear a lorry on the track to the dam. Whatever they were up to, the soldiers were still busy doing it, but only some of them: the two sentries stood in front of the checkpoint below the village as usual. They checked his permit and nodded at him to pass. He felt their stony eyes on him as he edged round the barrier and walked up the street towards the turning into the Calle de Mora. At the top of the empty street there were two sentries standing outside the church. That was new.

Their house was quiet. He penned the sheep and gave them some hay, he took the cattle and the mule down to the *fuente* to drink. Papa was still in Julio's bar, Albi heard his voice, loud and argumentative, as he hurried past. When he came back the kitchen was empty but his sisters' clogs were there so they were home from work. The door to the front bedroom was shut and all was silent. Albi went through the back bedroom, glancing into the *alcoba* as he passed. The *abuela* was asleep on her back with her mouth open.

Out on the *solenar* at the back of the house his sisters were sitting in the cold like fugitives. The *solenar* wasn't really a room though it was as big as one. It was open all along the back wall like a balcony, and tonight the wind had an edge to it. Albi perched on the little stool beside Inma and whispered, 'Where's Mama?'

She patted his hand. 'In the front bedroom.'

'Is she ill?' Mama was never ill.

Ramona said indignantly, 'Papa hit her in the face with one of his crutches.'

Inma patted Albi's hand again and gave him a small smile as though to say he shouldn't be frightened, it wasn't as bad as it sounded.

'He could have taken her eye out.' Pili said.

Inma said, 'We should have been with her. He wouldn't have hit her if we'd been there. But we were at work.'

Albi sat close to Inma and didn't say anything. Priests were thieves, everybody knew that. That was why they were called sodomites. But what if there really was a God? What if Mama was right and Papa wasn't? And even if it was Papa who was right and not Mama, the priest was on the same side as the soldiers and it was dangerous to make a noise against *them*.

When Papa came in at curfew, Mama had to open the bedroom door and let him in because there wasn't any other bed for him to sleep in.

'He's so drunk he could sleep in the stable and not notice,' Ramona said.

'He's so drunk he's only fit to sleep in the stable,' Pili said.

Inma said, 'Sleep in my bed with me, Mama. Ramona can sleep with Pili tonight.'

In the morning Papa didn't say anything. Perhaps he didn't dare, with the girls staring back at him whenever he tried to give them bad looks. Even Albi was unwilling to be on his side. Mama had two black eyes from where Papa had whacked her across the bridge of the nose. Perhaps he was ashamed really.

But after the girls had gone to the factory, when Mama was getting ready to go to the bakehouse to make the bread, Papa hissed at her, 'Don't you go telling tales to your cronies and cooking up another rebellion.'

So then Albi knew Papa wasn't sorry, and the fight wasn't over.

He was on his way out of the village when the church bell started. He turned and ran back with the sheep at his heels, down past the houses of the Barrio Alto and round the corner. A group of men had gathered below the church, Carlos's mop of pale hair bobbing about among them. Albi stopped the sheep and drove them back into the corner. He pretended not to see Carlos waving, but out of the corner of his eye he watched as more men came up the street from Julio's bar, noisy and belligerent, with Papa hopping along in their midst. Behind them, a drift of women appeared,wearing kerchiefs as if they were going to Mass. Albi straightened up. One of the kerchiefs was his mama's. His three sisters were with her, their heads covered too. What were *they* doing here? They should be in the factory.

The hubbub died away as heads turned to stare back down Calle San Juan. The sound of marching boots was like curfew beginning but it wasn't even dinner-time yet.

The women parted to let the soldiers through. The Comandante was marching along in the front. His riding boots were polished till they reflected the sun. He had gloves on, and his stick tucked under his arm. The soldiers marched straight up the steps and into the church but the Comandante stayed outside. The priest came and stood beside him and they both looked down at the villagers, the crowd so silent, the men watching, and beyond them the women watching too.

The Comandante beckoned to the women. 'Come. You may pass,' he said, in that funny high-pitched voice which was so much slighter than his body.

But the women didn't pass.

Mama stood near the front of the crowd watching with her bruised-black eyes. The Comandante beckoned again, impatiently, as if they were children who needed to be commanded. Mama stared up at him for a long moment. Then she turned on her heel and walked back down the hill, Pilar and Inma on either side of her and Ramona following behind.

The bell stopped. The distant slam of their front door sounded loud in the sudden silence.

The other women turned and slipped away like ghosts, down the hill to their various front doors. The men didn't make a sound. Albi sneaked a look at his papa. He couldn't tell anything from his expression.

The Comandante stared down at them. 'You!' he commanded in his strange voice. 'If you have work, go to it. If not, get inside the church.'

The crowd melted away like butter in the sun. The Comandante turned curtly on his heel and disappeared into the church. The priest followed.

In Julio's bar afterwards there was hardly room to move. Albi stood next to his papa at the counter. Papa leaned on Albi's shoulder and raised his beaker of wine. 'There are big wars, and there are small ones,' he said, his voice already slurred. 'And my wife is a Leader of Women.'

*

Mari-Jé comes into the kitchen, flushed with the glow of the righteous.

'You missed a good sermon,' she says. She's been working on Alberto for years but these days her tactic seems to be to talk as if his not coming to church is just a one-off and he'll be there next time for sure. She starts unbuttoning her blouse. 'Have you been out with the sheep?'

'I'll go after dinner.' He watches as she slips the blouse off and folds it carefully. How chaste her crumpled flesh is, so white and exposed in the pale autumn light. It's a long time since her flesh was anything but chaste. His too. The innocence of decay.

She pulls the everyday blouse off the back of the chair, talking all the while as she wriggles into it and does up the buttons: who was at church this morning, and what they said. Mostly the gossip seems to be a list of ailments.

She picks up the folded blouse and hurries away with it into their room. 'Is the stove still going?'

Obediently, he checks, and throws in another log.

Mari-Jé bustles a frying pan onto the cooker and pours oil into it. They have a wood-burning stove like a little silver dustbin, and a calor gas stove for cooking – such luxuries. A fridge, and a sink with hot and cold running water. For all that, it's still the same kitchen he grew up in. The window is glazed now, but through it he can see the same small square of view: the house wall opposite, with the bottom corner of the balcony window just visible. Alberto turns his head. He looks up at the varnished beams that used to be whitewashed. He looks down at the old red tiles that Mari-Jé curses because so many of them are cracked. He listens to the sound of her clattering plates and glasses from the wall cupboard and thinks, if you didn't look too carefully, you might think it was Mama still, moving around her kitchen.

11

The Mill of the Devil

Albi stared at his mama standing, unrelenting, on the corner stair. 'But—'

'No buts,' she said. 'Saddle the mule.'

But he could barely lift the wooden saddle onto the mule's back without Papa's help, and Papa was still in bed. 'His bad leg is playing him up,' Mama had said, but the truth was both Papa's legs were playing him up after a long afternoon in the bar yesterday. Lots of buts, Albi thought, as he struggled to lift the saddle onto the partition. He climbed up on the manger, the old mule watching him with interest, her ears pert. She hadn't been out for days, other than to the *fuente* to drink. It was true the mill was too far a walk for a man with only one leg, but that didn't stop Albi being annoyed he had to go instead.

He grunted as he lifted the saddle and swung it over the mule's back. He hopped down and fished for the girth under her sagging belly and climbed back up on the manger to put the bridle over her head – up down, up down. When he'd done all that, he led the mule out into the passageway towards the front door. The pale winter sun, slanting low over the rooftops, lit up the front of Young Jaime's house across the street.

Mama was waiting, two stairs up, with the sack of grain at her feet. As Albi stood on the step beside her to fasten the buckles of the bridle, she leaned forwards and blew gently into the mule's soft muzzle.

'Seen better days, haven't you, old girl. Like me.'

He frowned. He didn't like her talking that way. 'Why can't Miguel go to the Molino for us like he did last winter?'

She stopped crooning and said sharply, 'We can't pay him, Albi.'

But she must know! She must know about El Ciego. The blind man could take his eyes out and hang them down his cheeks. And sometimes he put them back in again the wrong way round, that was why they were so chalky. You couldn't go to the Molino without dealing with the blind man, not now that there was nobody else to grind the corn. There was Joaquín, but he was simple. Joaquín was good at grinding corn but he couldn't talk. Some people whispered that he was really El Ciego's son but everyone knew the blind man had never been married and anyway, Joaquín was Joaquina Zapatero's son, and he didn't have any of the blind man's names. The blind man did have names of his own, though mostly he was just called *el ciego*, the blind man.

When he was little, Albi used to go to the mill with his papa sometimes. Even with his papa he'd been scared, because of its strange name, *El Molino del Diablo*. The Mill of the Devil. Maybe El Ciego really did sup with the devil at night, like Carlos said he did.

Mama helped him tighten the girth. 'I rely on you, little one,' she said, putting her hand on the back of his neck, which stopped him minding the *little one* too much. 'You shouldn't be scared of poor old José-Luis. He can't help being blind.'

So she did know he was frightened. It made it worse.

'Come on,' she said. 'Let's get this sack loaded. The sooner you go, the sooner you'll be home again.'

It took them a long time, heaving and pulling and pushing, and the poor old mule staggering about, until the sack was balanced across the wooden saddle. Then they roped it down.

He went down towards the river. Maybe El Ciego wouldn't be there. The two soldiers on duty at the check-point stared at him briefly. Then they stared with rather more interest at the mule, but she was too old. Their eyes moved away to the middle distance as they nodded at him to pass. He was relieved. The soldiers took people's mules, if they liked them.

The mule plodded quietly behind him, down the sandy track. He glanced up at the looming wall of the dam. There were figures, dark and menacing, moving around on top of it. They were up to something. He shuddered, but it was nothing to do with him. He had enough to worry about without worrying about soldiers.

Maybe it would only be Joaquín today.

He crossed the old stone bridge, looking neither right nor left, his shoulders hunched against the edgy wind. He was too dispirited even to think about yesterday and his mama being a Leader of Women. The mule trudged behind him as if the excitement of being out of doors had already worn off. All the same, when they left the river behind she woke up enough to snatch mouthfuls of grass from the side of the track. They rounded the bend and there was the Molino del Diablo, crouched among the bare poplars, the low red roofs going every which way and the tower looming at the back where the water from the *acequia* fell down the shaft to drive the machinery. His papa showed him once. It was very dangerous – those great stones turning, turning. 'They'd grind you into flour if you got in the way,' Papa had said. And now Albi must go there on his own. I won't go inside, he thought. Whatever El Ciego says, I'll stay this side of the door. Please let him not be there today.

The blind man was sitting on a bench under the porch with Joaquín beside him. El Ciego was tall and thin but Joaquín was head and shoulders taller and he was all muscle, with big shoulders like a bull. But his head was too small. It made him look funny, like a boy in a man's body. Like the Comandante but different, because Joaquín didn't talk.

Albi could see by the angle of the blind man's head that he was listening to him coming. Joaquín stood up and went indoors.

'Ramón's boy?' El Ciego said.

It didn't really sound like a question so Albi didn't reply. He tried to shrink very small and invisible, keeping the mule's head between himself and El Ciego. How did the blind man know it was him? Could he see really, or had Joaquín told him, even though he was dumb? He sneaked a look round the mule's long nose. The blind man's eyes were safely in their sockets but they did look as if they were back to front, they didn't look like eyes that could see.

'What have you got for me today, Ramón's boy?'

'Please, señor, a bag of rye. For flour.'

El Ciego got up and came close. Albi shrank back as the calloused hands ran along the mule's neck to the saddle and then over the sack, feeling for the knots. The blind man didn't ask him to undo them, he ran his hands over them and suddenly they were all undone. Then he lifted the sack onto his shoulder as if it was a feather bolster and disappeared with it inside the mill. He might be old but he was strong.

As soon as El Ciego was safely out of sight Albi led the mule away from the mill towards the meadow. He heard the sudden rush of water falling in the tower behind him, and the rumble of the machinery beginning to turn. He looped the lead rope round the mule's neck and let her graze the winter grass. If El Ciego couldn't see, he couldn't object. All the same, Albi was scared. He sat watching the mule from the safety of the trees, keeping one eye on the doorway of the Molino in case Joaquín reappeared, because Joaquín might tell on him if he saw the mule grazing their pasture. Though how could he without talking?

Joaquín didn't reappear. After a long while the blind man came to the door of the mill and shouted 'Boy!'

Albi ran as quietly as he could and caught hold of the mule. He walked her to the mill. The sack was leaning against the door-frame, bigger now that it was flour instead of grain, but El Ciego picked it up and threw it over the saddle as if it was nothing. He felt for the ropes and re-tied them. Was he just proving that he could? He turned towards Albi and held out his hand. Albi scrabbled in his trouser pocket for the coins his mama had given him and threw them into the dusty palm so hastily he nearly missed. He grabbed the mule by the bridle and turned to go.

The blind man cocked his head as if he was listening for the words Albi should have said. '*Adios*, boy.'

'*Adios,* señor.' It came out in a whisper.

12

Carlos

Carla gets a notebook and pen out of her bag and puts them on the table. This is beginning to look serious. Alberto sips his thimble of wine and waits to see what it is that deserves a notebook.

'You knew my *abuelo,* right?'

'Which one?' he says, because both her grandfathers were born here, and both were called Carlos.

'Papa's papa,' she says. 'Carlos Perez.'

'We were nearly the same age.' He chooses his words carefully, still waiting. 'We were friends when we were kids. But I didn't see much of him by the time he left Rincón.'

That's a big notebook and there's nothing in it yet.

'I want to write a book,' Carla says. 'About my *abuelo*'s experiences during the Civil War. It's a long time ago now and most people who were alive then are dead. It needs to be told before it's too late.'

'What does?' He's playing for time.

'You know. The things that happened. In nowhere places like this. It'll be a book, definitely, but TVE has already expressed an interest. They're thinking it would make a good documentary for Channel 2.'

'What sort of things?'

She looks at him as if he's either stupid, or senile. 'The factory being blown up? The shootings? The murders?' She seems surprised he could forget.

Alberto goes very still inside.

'I tell you what,' he says at last, 'you tell me what you know, and then I'll tell you if there's anything I can add.'

She smiles at him. He's not sure whether she's being condescending, or kind.

'*Abuelo* had such a lot of stories,' she says. 'It would take quite a long time to tell you everything I know but let's start with that *maquis* who got caught after they blew the factory up – is it true he was your brother?'

Alberto gives the smallest of nods. He thinks he knows what's coming and he doesn't want to hear it.

'Shall I get you another?' she asks, gesturing at his glass.

He puts his hand over the empty glass and shakes his head. He wants to get out. The bar feels hot and loud, the voices are echoing off the tiled walls, the TV in the corner is shrill. Mari-Jé will be watching that at home, he thinks, glancing up at the chat-show that fills the large screen with distorted over-bright people, all grins and shiny lips.

'Well,' Carla says. 'I know my *abuelo*'s part in all that, of course, but I'd like to put it in context. Could you tell me what *you* remember?' She gives him that smile again, and definitely it is condescending. The echoes boom in his ears. He feels the sweat pricking on his forehead, his hands going clammy on the table-top. It's all right, she won't know. She'll just think he's old and stupid and losing his marbles. He stands up, a bit too abruptly, and reaches for his walking stick. 'I'm sorry. It's so hot in here, and I've not been feeling well lately. Would you mind if we left this till another time?'

'Of course.' But she looks disappointed as she jumps up and places a caring hand on his elbow. 'Trouble is, I'm going back to Madrid tomorrow and I don't know when I'll be back. It would be helpful if you could give me some idea how much you'll be able to tell me?'

He gives her the blandest of smiles. 'The truth is I was only nine or ten years old. It's all very hazy now. I'm not sure there's much I could tell you that you don't know already from your *abuelo*.'

Is that relief in her face? He walks out of the bar, returning Raul's greeting as he goes, careful to keep his back straight and his head up until he's well out of sight. I shouldn't have done that, he thinks when he reaches the *fuente*. He sits down on the wall of the trough. I shouldn't have done that. Now she'll think it's all true, what Carlos said.

It starts to rain.

'You'll catch your death!' says Mari-Jé, coming downstairs and finding him sitting in the passage on the bench against the wall. He shrugs, and waits for her to go away. It's raining hard now.

72

Water pours off the roofs and runs down the middle of the concrete street, a temporary river. He doesn't want to go upstairs to the warm kitchen. Carlos is waiting for him. Somewhere in the past he leans on the wall of Old Jaime's house opposite, the same way he always did when they were boys.

*

'Scaredy rabbit.'

Albi looked up in time to see Carlos waggle his hands over the top of his head like rabbit's ears. 'I'm not scared,' he said crossly. 'But I've got *them* in tow.' He jerked his head towards the sheep.

'So? We'll take them with us. You need some cover when you're spying.'

He couldn't think of an answer to that, apart from the same old one that Carlos hadn't got a permit, which Carlos thought was a scaredy sort of objection. So he whistled to Perrita to bring up the flock.

All he could see in front of him was Carlos's bottom as they scrabbled up the hill through the prickly leaves of the evergreen oaks. Every now and then Carlos dislodged a stone, forcing Albi to duck to one side as it crashed down past him. They weren't exactly being quiet and there was an easier way up, but you don't go on paths if you're having an *aventura*. Only, it was worrying how far behind them the sheep were lagging. He paused to make sure they were still following, Perrita weaving about at their heels. He turned back to the climb.

Carlos was a long way ahead, now, his bony rump wiggling quickly from side to side as he went up the steep slope on all fours. Then he disappeared into the trees and everything went quiet, the silence closing like a door shutting.

Albi stopped again and listened. The silence was full of the sound of the wind sighing in the pine trees higher up the hillside, and the grunt and scrabble of the sheep coming. He could just go home, but it was Saturday afternoon. No school for Carlos, so perhaps it didn't matter quite so much him not having a permit. No Pepito, because he was helping his mama clear up the *huerto,* as Albi was supposed to be helping his. There would be trouble when he got home. He might as well follow Carlos, now, and spy on the dam. He waited for the sheep, then turned back to the climb. They wouldn't go very close, it should be safe. Carlos's idea was that they would climb up onto the plateau below La Guadaña and creep round under cover of the trees until they were above the dam. He wanted to see what the soldiers were up to.

At the edge of the trees a wall of rock stopped Albi going any further. It wasn't so high – about the height of three men standing on each other's shoulders – but there was no way of knowing which way Carlos had gone. Could he have gone straight up? Albi squinted up against the brightness of the sky, but the wisps of cloud racing along the limestone edge made him feel giddy and he had to look away. When he looked again, two feet were dangling over the edge. Two dirty bare feet. And like a moon hanging over the top of them, Carlos's face loomed forwards with a lopsided grin. 'Where've you been, snail?'

He'd rather be a rabbit than a snail. 'How did you get up there? Did you climb?'

Carlos looked as if he was going to say he had, but then he said, 'Path's along there,' pointing with his chin. Albi was relieved. Sometimes it was hard to keep it a secret that he didn't like heights, even climbing trees. Anyway, sheep can't climb cliffs. He waited for the flock to catch up, then he led them the long way round. Far away in the distance Miguel was calling to his sheep with the high *hee-wit, hee-wit* that meant he wanted them to keep moving. The clonking bells told Albi the sheep weren't hurrying, they were walking steadily, so Miguel was probably moving from one bit of grazing to another – he must have been out for a while already. It felt safer, knowing Miguel was there, even if he was out of sight and didn't know the two of them were there too.

By the time Albi got to the top of the path, Carlos was running off again, along the rocky ledge towards the Tajubo valley. He followed reluctantly. The sheep were happy enough grazing and Perrita would keep them from wandering. There was no hurry, they didn't need to run, but Carlos always wanted to have what he called *aventuras*. In the old days, before the soldiers came, *aventuras* had sounded exciting, but not now. The closer they got to the dam and the soldiers the less exciting it felt.

When they got near the edge of the escarpment Carlos dropped down, so Albi did the same. Side by side they crept forwards on their hands and knees. Low down in the scrub like this only the top of the hill opposite was visible, and the big water-pipe drawing a line straight up it and making a little bump against the sky as it went over the top. They crept forwards. Now the lower part of the hill was cliffs, dropping straight down, the pipe was still just a pipe, and he couldn't see any soldiers. Forward a little more, the stones cutting into his bare knees, the gorse scratching his shoulders through his shirt, until they could lie on their bellies among the rosemary bushes and peer down over the edge at the bright water that wasn't blue and wasn't green but was no colour they'd ever learned in school. To their left, at the bottom end of the pipe, the dam wall looked like a line drawn with chalk across the valley from one side to the other. Beyond the white line everything looked hazy and much further away. The inside of the dam wall was dark. The water was always low at this time of the year, before the winter rains came and the melting snow filled it up again. Suddenly, Albi's eyes woke up: at the far end of the wall there was a funny building that never used to be there. He looked back at this end and there was one there too.

'So *that's* what they've been doing,' Carlos said.

The buildings were small. Grey-white, all shiny new in the

sun, they had six sides and flat roofs, slits like sideways windows at the tops of the walls.

'Pill boxes,' Carlos whispered, but how did he know? 'They're made that shape so you can see out all round and shoot in any direction. If we were closer we'd probably be able to see the guns.'

Albi stared down. 'Why have they made them there? And why do they need two?'

'Like I said. Somebody might try to attack the dam.'

'But who would do that?'

Carlos shrugged. 'Somebody might. Somebody *de fuera*.'

Albi shuddered. *De fuera* – from outside. A stranger. But they didn't have strangers in El Rincón, except for the soldiers. He stared down at the bright water. And Jesús. Jesús was *de fuera*, he came from Zaragoza. Papa said El Caballero was *de fuera* too. Really.

Carlos said, 'Anyway, my brother says you wouldn't have to blow up the dam. If you blew up the pipeline you'd stop the water getting to the reservoir and then there wouldn't be any electricity in Valbono and they wouldn't have water for their *huertos* either.'

Albi leaned his chin on his arms and thought about it. It wasn't fair that Valbono had a whole dam on the Rincón side of the mountain to make electricity in their houses as well as in the streets. In El Rincón all they got was the little bit of electricity left over from pumping the water over the hill, so they only had lights in the streets and none in the houses. They had lots of water of their own, from the waterfall valley, but it didn't make electricity. That was why the Rincón people didn't like the people from Valbono. That, and them supporting the rebels instead of the Republicans.

'Anyway, when the water's this low it wouldn't make *too* much trouble to the village if you blew the dam up,' Carlos said.

'Wouldn't it?' Albi peered at the glittering surface, so quiet in the sun. How big a space would that water take up if it was all let out at once? Some of the village would surely be swallowed up, even at this time of the year. The Molino certainly. And the garrison.

The red roof of the new garrison was just visible, beyond the dam wall. It used to be a dormitory for the workers brought in from other places when they built the dam. It had stood empty ever since Albi could remember: a dead-eyed, lonely building, looking out over the junction pool where the Tajubo river and the El Rincón river met, right in the path of the water if the dam broke.

The thought made his blood stop moving. To some people that might be a reason to blow the dam up. If they had any dynamite.

Carlos elbowed him. A movement by the nearer pill-box: there were two soldiers lying on their backs on the grass. For one heart-stopping moment Albi thought they might be dead, but then he saw they were only enjoying the November sunshine. He and Carlos peered along their imaginary rifles and blasted the soldiers into bits. They couldn't hear them screaming in agony but that was because they were too far away.

'Now we'll run across the dam and attack the other pill-box. And then we'll bomb the pump house,' Carlos whispered.

'If we did that we wouldn't have any streetlights!'

'What use are streetlights when we're not allowed out of our houses after dark? Why should the soldiers have the electric light but not us? That's what my papa says. We built the pump house, they didn't.'

Albi's papa said the same. It was a scary sort of thing to say.

'Anyway,' Carlos said, 'if there weren't any street lamps they wouldn't be able to see to stop us doing things, would they?'

'What things?' asked Albi.

Carlos looked at him as if he didn't need to know, and started shuffling backwards away from the edge. 'I'm hungry. Let's go home.'

*

It's *Todos Santos*. The village is full of people for the holiday weekend and Mari-Jé is in her element because the kids are here too, and all the grandchildren.

From the sheep pen, where he's putting hay in the rack, Alberto hears adult voices just over his head. His sons and their wives are out on the *solenar* enjoying the late autumn sunshine and the last of the view before they set out on the long drive back to Barcelona. He suspects Mari-Jé has told them he's been behaving oddly, that they should all come this *Todos Santos* in case it's the beginning of dementia. They've been looking at him too tenderly, a little suspiciously. And now, as he closes the gate of the pen, he's listening to them talking about him, Ana's voice affectionate, his sons more matter-of-fact, his other daughter-in-law, Gloria, not saying much.

It's the book Carla is writing that's set them off. If her *abuelo* was old enough to have memories of the civil war, their papa must have them too.

'But he was just a kid,' Bernardo says, his voice sounding surprisingly close through the floor over Alberto's head. 'He was younger than Carlos, wasn't he?'

Marco says, 'Not by much. But there was that funny thing about Papa not talking.'

'What thing?'

'José Molino told me his mother used to say Papa didn't talk when he was a kid. They all thought he was dumb. Surprised everyone when he came back from Zaragoza talking. He'd have been in his twenties by then.'

'I never heard that before,' Ana says. 'I always thought he was just quiet. By nature.'

'I never heard that either.' Bernardo sounds as if he feels he should have been told.

'But it would explain why he's never talked about the war,' Marco says.

'Why? Not talking doesn't mean you don't hear. It doesn't make you not remember.'

That's Gloria's voice. Alberto nudges Perrito with his foot to stop the old dog scratching.

'Papa would have been six or seven when the war began. That's old enough to remember quite a lot, I'd have thought,' Bernardo says.

'What do *you* remember from when you were seven?' Ana asks, and Marco says something that makes the others laugh.

Alberto slips along the passage in his canvas shoes, out into the street. He feels as if he's just stepped out of his skin and a stranger has taken his place.

He climbs down below the old bridge at the bottom end of the Plaza, where he can sit on a rock undisturbed and think. It's such a long time ago and he's never told anyone. Not telling has made him safer, but it's been like carrying a stone in his stomach. He can feel the weight of it, sometimes icy, sometimes hot, but always smooth and heavy. If he tells, what will happen to that familiar weight? It might be all that keeps him balanced. And what is there to tell? It's a story of nothings, perhaps. But if it is, why has he always felt so guilty?

Above him, in the Plaza, there are busy sounds of leaving. The kids will be packing up their cars and wondering where he's got to. They'll be waiting to say goodbye, thinking his disappearance is another worrying sign. If they don't have that thought for themselves, Mari-Jé will have it for them. But he can't do it, he can't go through the motions, pretending there's no turmoil inside him. He couldn't look into Ana's eyes, even if he could manage Bernardo and the others.

He strikes the end of his stick against a boulder. The stream is running slow and torpid, waiting for the winter rains. He'll have to go and say goodbye. He can surely manage that, whatever is going on inside his head.

*

79

Late that autumn the lorry came to the factory and took away the paper from the store. The girls were working for the enemy now, like Papa said would happen. And so was Carlos's papa, because he worked in the factory too.

'You got to keep alive somehow,' Carlos said, his voice echoing. 'If he didn't work, how would we eat?'

Albi sighed. He lobbed another rock into the shadowy water. Papa hadn't prevented the girls from going to work in the factory, but that hadn't stopped him shouting about it. Their house was full of arguments these days. Perhaps Papa should talk to Carlos's papa. Albi balanced precariously on his bare feet and picked up a bigger rock. This was their private place, under the bridge at the bottom end of the Plaza. Nobody else came here, not since last winter when the aeroplane circled over the village and they thought they were going to be bombed. He dropped the rock into a pool with a hollow splosh and shivered, remembering the sour smell of fear, his own and everyone else's, as they crowded under the stone arch of the bridge.

'Tell us again about the soldier kissing the girl,' Pepito said, lobbing in two small rocks one after the other.

Carlos told the story again. He was always seeing things from his bedroom window in the middle of the night. Last time it had been a soldier aiming his gun and threatening to shoot a man, but the man ran away up the street before Carlos could see who it was. He didn't see who this girl was, either. Very convenient, Albi thought, chucking in three pebbles: *clink clink… clink*. And anyway, what was a girl doing out in the streets after curfew? Was Carlos making it up?

'*We* should be going out at night too,' Carlos said, picking up a small boulder. 'Creeping round and stuff. There's lots of men doing it now.'

Albi's skin went cold. 'Who is?'

'Dangerous to mention names, Rabbit.' Carlos chucked the boulder into the water and made such a splash they all got wet.

Pepito said nervously, 'But *why* are people doing that? The soldiers would shoot them dead if they caught them.'

'It's called Resistance. It's our duty to resist. My papa says so.'

Important sounding word, *resistencia*. Albi liked the word but it was better sometimes, when Carlos said things, to pretend he hadn't heard.

Whatever Carlos's papa said about Resistance, nothing happened. People went about their business as best they could. They complained a lot, but they were getting used to the soldiers being here.

'Don't get used to it,' Papa said quietly when Mama wasn't there to hear. 'This is the quiet time, Albi. Things will start happening, you wait and see. Keep your eyes peeled but be careful. And stay away from the dam.'

Albi nodded. They hadn't been *that* close, him and Carlos. Not really.

He kept his eyes peeled, like Papa told him to, but there was nothing to see. No more new buildings went up. The soldiers marched round the village and to their sentry posts, they marched out to their new pill-boxes. They roared up and down the road in their trucks and on their motorcycles, and made everyone go to church on Sundays. When they weren't doing any of those things they stayed in their garrison and did drill. The leaves fell off the poplar trees, the same as usual. The river ran cold and blue and the brown trout quivered, hanging quietly in the sunlit water, but the sun had less power now, and some days it rained.

13

Los Regresados

Albi led the sheep out of the village by the upper mule path. He walked past the stone water-trough, past the almond tree, its trunk black in the rain and all its leaves fallen, counting off each of these things as he passed to keep track of where he was. He was wearing a sack over his head against the rain and he couldn't see much, only the stones on the path, and his bare feet walking. He crossed the *acequia,* which was no more than an empty ditch now the sluice gates were closed for the winter. His feet were cold and it made the stones prick harder. Soon he would have to force his feet into last winter's boots and they would pinch, because he *had* grown, even if Carlos laughed at him for saying so.

Halfway to the waterfall he stopped to let the sheep graze. The rain came down, patter patter in the evergreen oaks. Tap tap in the bare willow twigs. Splat splat on the fallen poplar leaves. If you look at the yellow leaves on the ground the day feels bright as if the sun is shining. He looked up at the sky and the day went grey again. He pulled the sack closer around his neck but the wind was bitter so he called La Perrita and started along the path again. La Gorda, his bell-sheep, followed close behind him and the others followed La Gorda, and behind them his little black dog trotted along, her bright red tongue hanging out. He turned his eyes back to the path. He could see by the marks in the mud that nobody else had been out this way. On either side, the box bushes were pungent in the rain. The trees dripped, and small animals rustled unseen in the wet undergrowth.

When he was nearly at the gorge he turned onto one of the paved mule paths and climbed away from the main track, up onto the wild bit of land that ran along the base of the cliffs. It was like a skirt, this slope, dotted with bushes and trees. He let the flock spread out while he looked for a place in the rocks where he could sit out of the rain. The cliffs rose sheer as a wall, with high ledges where the vultures roosted, but there were clefts in the base and it didn't take him long to find a good place. He made himself comfortable and pulled the damp sack close. Nobody could come up on him here and take him by surprise.

What did Papa mean when he said something was going to happen, and how did he know?

The mist came down like an old cloth being drawn slowly, slowly over the top of a great bowl, the rain made dark streaks down the cliffs. Albi looked behind him into the narrow cleft. This would be a good place to hide food from the soldiers. But if you did, the rats would take your provisions instead, and the foxes would take what the rats left.

The sound of stones slithering made him jump round. On the far side of the river a man ran across the steep hillside in the direction of the waterfall – one moment he was in Albi's line of vision, the next he was out of sight.

Silence. Had he imagined it?

A shot rang out, echoes rolling like thunder round the cliffs. He looked round wildly – he was trapped like a rat up a drainpipe. Dropping to all fours he scrabbled up the cleft, over a fallen rock lodged at the top end, slipping and sliding, to crouch behind it. Where was Perrita? There she was, looking at him from the entrance, wagging her tail as if she thought it was a game. She bounded towards him, sending little stones clattering. He grabbed her and pulled her down.

Silence.

The narrow vertical strip of outside world was an empty sliver of grey scree, impassive rock, mist blowing. He stared until his eyes and ears ached but he heard nothing more. He couldn't even hear the sheep bells. Had they scattered? He crouched in his hiding place, wondering what it was he'd seen.

A man running. A big man, moving clumsily. Ordinary clothes, so it wasn't a soldier. Did the man have a gun? He didn't think so. The shot had come from this side of the valley, so it wasn't the man shooting, and whoever fired that gun was between Albi and home.

He waited some more. Nothing. Just the wind moaning.

He shuffled carefully back down the cleft, stopping to listen every few feet. The view widened but the hillside opposite was empty. No soldiers, no sign of a body. At the cliff edge he peered out to his left. Then to his right. There were the sheep, not far away, grazing as if nothing had happened. But it had. He strained his eyes against the mist, examining this side of the valley, and then the other. He listened. The sheep grazed steadily. He couldn't hear anything except the squeaking of their gums on the tired grass.

All along the path back to the village his eyes flicked nervously from side to side but there was nothing unusual. In the distance the village nestled in its armpit of hillside. It looked empty. In the falling mist he couldn't even see smoke from the chimneys. Perhaps he was the only person left alive, only he didn't know it yet.

A blackbird clattered out of a bush.

He ran, his animals running close on his heels. He didn't see anyone until he was almost back among the houses, and then it was ordinary people, doing ordinary things. When he got to his house he pushed the sheep quickly into their pen and ran back up the street to Julio's bar. The door stood open, the bar noisy, crowded with men snatching a last cup of wine before curfew, but all they were talking about was the weather. And they were laughing at Emilio because he was drunk and getting angry over his game of cards. Papa wasn't there. Albi slid away again, back to his house to feed the sheep.

That night, in the kitchen, his teeth wouldn't stop chattering. Was it from being cold all day, or from being scared? Had something happened, or hadn't it? He watched Papa's face but he couldn't see any sign of him knowing anything special. Papa wasn't angry, he wasn't excited – he was nothing much at all.

Nobody said anything the next day either, or the day after. Had he imagined it: the tense dark figure, feet sliding on the stones as he tried to run? The gunshot? Or had he seen something nobody else knew about?

He didn't even tell Carlos and Pepito. If they were disbelieving it would make it hard to believe he hadn't dreamed it. That running man.

In the sleepy warmth of their kitchen Mama was telling the girls the bakehouse gossip while she cut Albi's hair with Pilar's sewing scissors. He hoped she was concentrating, she was very close to his ears.

The gossip was all small things. He hoped she might have seen Mena in the bakehouse, but if she had she didn't mention it.

'You know those cardoons,' Mama said. 'Belén puts them in the house as decorations!'

Pilar tutted and Ramona laughed, but Albi thought decorating your house was a nice idea. He didn't say anything. He looked down at the black shiny locks of his hair on the floor and stirred them idly with his foot.

'Sit still, Albi!' Mama cut sharply round the back of his head with the snaggy scissors – all the little hairs on his neck, making them short. The trouble with having his hair cut was the old women would want to stroke him again.

'She's young,' Mama said. 'She'll get over it. When she starts having children.'

Later, when the thin supper of cabbage and potato and only a tiny bit of ham had all been eaten, and Pili had gone to the back bedroom to organise things in her enamel chest, and Papa had gone to bed, Albi sat dozing on his stool in the chimney corner, leaning back against the wall. It felt hard and cold through his new haircut but he didn't want to go to bed yet. It was warmer by the fire than up in the attic.

Mama was sitting next to Inma by the fire, their chairs drawn up close, their knitting needles busily clicking. Mama said softly, as if only Inma was meant to hear, 'I saw Josefina's Esteban today,' and Albi woke up, keeping his eyes shut so they wouldn't stop talking. Inma didn't say anything but he could feel she was listening. 'I'd never have known it was him,' Mama murmured. 'Thin as a rake, his hair all matted. And such a beard on him. Like an old man's beard, except it was black. I was walking back from the bakehouse with Josefina and he stepped out of the alleyway by Pedro Iranzo's house. He gave us both such a fright. I didn't recognise him but she did. She knew her own son straight away.'

Cold sweat ran down Albi's back. Was the running man Esteban, trying to get back to the village? Somebody he knew.

'How long ago was it that Esteban went away?' asked Inma.

'It was before potato planting last year, because Josefina had to plant all the potatoes on her own.' A long pause, then Mama said. 'He didn't seem to have been wounded but I couldn't really see. I expect Josefina will tell me tomorrow.'

Pilar came back in then, all huffy and puffy in Albi's ears as she brought her sewing things to the fireside, and the talking stopped. He heard Ramona sit down too, the scrape of her chair on the floor-tiles. He opened his eyes and looked at his sisters and his mama sitting there, the fire rosy on their faces. You could see they were the same family, even though they were different heights and different shapes and only Mama still had her hair long. Would Consuelo have looked like them? It would be five women by the fire if his other sister was still here. He couldn't remember what she looked like because she wasn't in the photograph, she'd already died by then.

He looked up at the two rows of figures in the picture. Manolo was there because he hadn't gone away to fight when it was made. If the two boy babies before Manolo hadn't died when they were born they'd have been in the picture too. And then there was *Abuelo*, who died when he was old. Mama's parents hadn't died but they weren't in the picture because they lived up on the *Meseta*. They were still living there now, even though the soldiers said nobody must live up on the *Meseta* any more and Mama worried about them every day.

He looked at her, frowning over her knitting in the firelight. When she looked at the four of them who were sitting round the hearth did she see only them, or was her kitchen full of ghosts of all the missing people? He didn't like that thought, it made the new-cut hairs prick on the back of his neck. Anyway, he preferred it the way it was. Four of them and Papa and the *abuela* was quite enough.

In his cold attic room, shivering under the thin blankets, he couldn't sleep. What if Manolo came home again, like Esteban? If he did he would be a *regresado*. That was what they called them in the village, the boys who came back: the returned.

If Manolo came home he would take back this room. Albi would mind that now. There was nobody here to tell him to send the cat out. She was lying stretched out along his thigh right now, her silky warmth better than any scratchy old blanket. Nobody to tell him not to watch the soldiers through the window. If Manolo came home, even if he let Albi share his room, it wouldn't be the same.

He turned on his side and stroked La Gatica. Her purring made the bed vibrate. Manolo went away so long ago, right at the beginning of the war. All he'd left behind was a big shadow and the echo of a deep voice, and Papa so proudly telling everyone, 'My son has gone to the Front.'

Albi sighed. La Gatica stopped purring and half-opened one eye. She stretched out her paws, flexing her claws sleepily, and started purring again.

They hadn't seen Manolo since. Sometimes little scraps of news had filtered through – a message sent with another boy from the village who was in the army too, or someone had met somebody who knew him – but not for a long while now.

If Manolo came back he would take charge of the sheep and goats instead of Albi, and all the other jobs. He'd do the ploughing too, even though Papa said he was going to plough next spring and the devil take him if he didn't. Manolo would laugh and do it himself. Which was what Albi would do, if he were bigger, because Papa only said it to be brave.

If Manolo came back, Albi wouldn't be so important any more.

If Manolo came back, he could go to school again.

The thought surprised him so much he stopped stroking. The cat stirred and stretched out longer against his leg. He'd so liked school, when the old schoolmaster was in it. The quiet of them all being busy in one room. The smell of the chalk, the smell of the slate. The way you could draw on your slate, or write a sum, then rub it all out and start again. The way the old schoolmaster used to say, 'Look around you. Look what a special place this valley is!'

They looked, but they saw only the same old terraces, the same old *acequias* bringing the water to the *huertos* and the same old mule-paths criss-crossing the valley, surrounded by the same old cliffs.

'No no no,' he said. 'You're looking but you're not seeing. Look again. Those cliffs were carved by water.' And they laughed, because the river was in the bottom of the valley and nowhere near the cliffs. 'And before that, this was all once a sea,' the schoolmaster said, but anybody could see it hadn't been. Where would the water have come from? And it would have run out of all the holes, like it did now when it rained hard. So the old schoolmaster told them all about the Moors coming and how they'd made the *acequias*. A Feat of Engineering, he called it.

'Feat of engineering, my arse,' Papa said when Albi told him what he'd learned in school that day. 'It might be clever but it was us Spaniards that did it, the old Conquistadors. It was never the Blacks. Cousin Javier was in Morocco. He'll tell you.'

Albi turned over and lay on his other side with his back to the cat. The new teacher was a lay priest. Nobody liked him. Besides, Carlos would laugh at him if he went back to school now.

*

'I don't understand why you won't even talk to her,' Mari-Jé says. She won't let it drop: Carla this, Carla that. It's not the book that is firing Mari-Jé up, it's the possibility of being on television. 'It would put Rincón on the map,' she says. 'And you surely remember enough to be useful to her. What the village was like, back then. What her *abuelo* got up to when he was a boy.'

'There's nothing I can tell her she doesn't know already.'

Mari-Jé gives him a look but Alberto can't tell what it signifies. She says in a resigned voice, 'Well, maybe it's for the best.'

He doesn't know the significance of that, either. He glances up at the clock on the shelf.

'Where are you going?' Her voice is sharp, suspicious.

'To the rabbit shed.'

'It's Monday.'

He doesn't bother to reply. It's Monday, yes, but Raul is in Montesanto this morning, getting his truck repaired, and Santi is feeding the rabbits. Santi never says no to some company.

In the passageway Alberto kicks off his slippers and shuffles into his old canvas shoes. He'd never admit it to his wife but he's been thinking of nothing else since that day he met Carlos's granddaughter in the bar and she told him what she was planning. It's like a cold wind at his back, blowing him all over the place. He knows he must sort out his past, before she re-writes it. He's been raking through his memories but his thoughts are tangled; there are things he remembers as if they happened yesterday but the meaning of them has disappeared. Like the man running on the scree, the day he heard the gunshot in the valley but never saw who fired it. Did he never find out who the running man was?

He opens the front door onto a bright morning, the sky a strip of blue between the tall roofs, the sharp winter shadows cast long in the street. Perhaps it was a *regresado*. Alberto walks down the silent street, remembering those bearded, ragged men who slid through the streets like shadows until someone somewhere let them in. And then there were the others. The ones everybody knew about but didn't tell. Not local men with homes to go to. The *maquis*.

*

Men started coming to the village who were not village boys, so they were not *regresados*. In the privacy of the back stable Papa sat with Albi, carving wooden spoons to replace the broken ones, and told him to be careful if he saw one. The *maquis*, Papa called these men.

'How will I know it's one of them?'

'They'll look like *regresados*,' Papa said. 'But you won't know their faces.'

'What do they do? They don't have homes to go to.'

'Someone always takes them in,' Papa said softly as he sharpened his chisel. 'But like the *regresados*, it's a dangerous business. The soldiers have been here long enough to notice an unfamiliar face. The priest too.' He leaned towards Albi, his voice so quiet Albi had to stop what he was doing to hear. 'You know the way the priest stares at the faces as he passes down the street? He's twice as dangerous as the soldiers. You never know where he'll turn up next, creeping about in those soft-soled shoes of his. Twice as dangerous. You remember that.'

'Yes, Papa.' He shivered so hard it made his chisel skid across the wood. If the soldiers caught you hiding a *maquis* they would shoot you, same as if they found a *regresado* in your house.

'Don't you worry about it,' Papa said. 'But if you meet one, pretend you don't notice he's a stranger. And tell no-one. No-one except me.'

Albi nodded. But he didn't mention the running man on the scree.

'The *Meseta*, that's where they're headed. Trouble is, strangers don't know the proper paths. It's only a matter of time before one of them falls.'

What did they want to climb up onto the *Meseta* for, where the winter winds scraped the distances white like old bones laid bare? And what about Manolo? If the war was over, would he come home like the other *regresados*? But he didn't want to hear the answer so he didn't ask. Besides, Papa was still talking.

'A man can hide for ever on the *Meseta*, Albi. That's why the *maquis* are coming here. It's why the soldiers have stayed.' He peered at Albi's carving. 'Good. You can start shaping the back now.'

Andrés's farm was up on the *Meseta*. Did he see these *maquis* men hanging about? Maybe he let them come in his house out of the cold. Albi turned the block of wood over and slowly, carefully, pared away slivers of wood. It was a good thing Mena was safely down in the village, not up at the farm.

That was a strange thought, the village being safe. And then it was sad. The soldiers being here when nobody wanted them, the *regresados* and the *maquis* having to hide. Was it going to be like this always, now?

'Is the war over, Papa?'

'No, Albi. The war is over but the war goes on.' Papa leaned closer, his tobacco breath hissing in Albi's ear. 'They're afraid, the soldiers are. They know they'll never catch those boys, not once they make it onto the *Meseta*. No matter how fast the soldiers drive their trucks up and down that road and all the way over to Las Hoyas.'

The rabbit shed is locked. No sign of Santi. Alberto clicks his tongue, and walks on down towards the river. He remembers the sorrow of those bearded *regresados*, each one of them like another nail in the coffin as they came back from a war that had been lost, to a village which was not safe, but where nothing was happening. And the *maquis* too, who should have been their hope.

14

Telling

They listened, spoons suspended over the bowl of steaming cabbage and potatoes, as steel-shod boots pounded down the next street. A stranger's voice shouted 'Halt or we'll shoot!'

'They want us to be scared,' Ramona said.

A woman started screaming. Inma put her arm round Albi's shoulders. After a while the screaming stopped and it was just the soldiers shouting, but nobody could eat after that, not even Albi who was always hungry. Mama took the pot away. Would she serve it again tomorrow, or would the chickens get it?

That night he slept in Inma's bed and Ramona had to sleep with Pili.

In the morning the story went round as fast as fire in dry summer grass. Before Albi had even got out of the village he'd heard the news: it was old Felipe Moliner, forgetting there was a curfew and trying to go to Mario's bar in the Plaza but the soldiers caught him. His daughter ran out into the street as soon as she realised what was happening, she was the one doing the screaming. But in the end the soldiers didn't shoot, they shouted instead. Told Laura to take the key out of the door in future and hide it.

'You see,' Pilar said that night, when they were sitting by the fire in the dark, saving candles. 'You see! The soldiers are here to restore order. They won't hurt us.'

Papa did the shouting then.

In December a wind from the south brought a spell of bright, mild weather, but the nights were cold and the grass was tired. Albi came back early and let the sheep and goats eat hay in the stable. It was like old times, to sit out in the street with his papa and his mama, and all the neighbours outside their houses too, doing useful jobs. Better than being on his own all the time.

Above them, Old Jaime's voice, thin and ancient, drifted out of the window. 'I looks at his toes and I says, *That's frostbite, my boy. We must get you to the medico*, I says. So I puts him on my back and off we go. But he lost all his toes after. Every single one of them.'

Papa stopped what he was doing and listened for a moment, then he picked up his adze and went back to work on the clog he was making for Mama.

'That's Young Jaime's story he's telling,' he said quietly. 'Jaime needs to move his *abuelo* into the back room before anyone starts paying attention.'

Mama clucked her tongue, maybe agreeing, maybe not, and went on with her sewing.

Anyone? Albi slid the blade of his penknife under the bark of the forked stick and pared it away. The new catapult looked white and naked under the bark. Why did Papa say *anyone* when everybody knew the story already? How Young Jaime (who wasn't young really) had escaped from the battle with nothing worse than a string of bad stories that had happened to other people. Did *anyone* mean the soldiers?

The bark looked like long strings of apple peel.

He glanced at his papa, frowning at the half-finished clog in his hands. *Anyone* probably meant El Caballero too, he was friendly with the soldiers. But El Caballero must already know Young Jaime had been in the army, and about him being at the Battle of Teruel. Jesús would have told him, if he didn't know by himself. Jesús would certainly know, because of Pili.

He stopped whittling his stick and looked from his papa to his mama. Mama went on quietly sewing up his torn trousers, Papa went on making Mama's clog. The sparrows went on cheeping on the roof-top and the neighbours, sitting outside their houses all down the street, went on chattering like birds. A movement in the sky – he looked up as a big vulture sailed lazily overhead with barely a flap of its wings and disappeared out of sight behind the rooftops. Pili. She surely told Jesús things. Jesús would tell El Caballero. El Caballero would tell the soldiers. After all, he was hand-in-glove with them, Papa was always saying so. Especially now that El Caballero had re-opened his shop but the soldiers were the only ones who went to it.

At the bottom of the Calle San Juan the neighbours stood up suddenly and went inside their houses, leaving their chairs in the street. They closed their front doors loudly. Papa paused, watching them, Mama looked up from her sewing. Old Jaime's voice drifted down, 'It was bloody good wine, too. Pity to waste it.' Three soldiers appeared round the corner at the bottom of the street, not marching but strolling. All the rest of the neighbours got up hurriedly and slipped into their houses. Mama stood up so suddenly her chair fell over. Papa grabbed his crutches and hopped quickly indoors, Mama pushing Albi after him. She slammed the door shut and shot the bolt. They stepped into the front stable, the three of them, and stood in the shadows waiting for the soldiers to go by. This was their silent rebellion. Everyone's silent rebellion, whenever any soldiers came by.

Up in his room, Old Jaime was carrying on his own private

rebellion at the top of his reedy voice. '*You fascist curs,* I shouted. And then I gave them what for.'

The old mule turned her head and looked at the three of them standing there, then she closed her eyes and sagged back into sleep. Through the little window Albi could see the disembodied heads of the soldiers as they stopped to listen. He saw the way the soldiers looked at one another and up at the window where Old Jaime was still ranting. Then they laughed and walked on.

In the half-light he saw the tremor that passed over his papa and the way he squeezed his eyes tight shut. With a shock he realised his brave Papa was frightened.

Mama put her hand on Papa's arm. 'We'll go and eat,' she said.

The *abuela* woke up when she smelled the omelette cooking.

'Huh,' said Papa. 'Forgets who she is but never forgets to eat, does she.'

Later, when Papa was lifting the *abuela* for Mama to pull the soiled sheet from under her, the *abuela* shouted in his face. '*Hijo de Puta! Hijo de Puta!*'

Papa began to laugh. Then suddenly he roared, 'Son of a whore, am I? Whose son am I then? Whose son, you stupid old goat!'

'Ramón!' Mama said. 'She's old. She can't help it.'

'All these crazy old people!' Papa said. 'Eating food we can't spare and selling us to the devil all the while.' He went out to drown his sorrows at Julio's.

Mama was crying, but whether she was crying for Papa or for the old people, Albi couldn't tell.

José Cedrillas was standing at the front door. 'I've come to collect the church tax.'

Papa looked up and down the street to check which ears were listening. 'We're not paying,' he hissed. 'Turncoat!'

Albi hovering in the passageway in case there was an argument.

95

José spread his hands. 'Come on, Ramón. Be reasonable. A man has to bring home something if he's to keep his family alive.'

Papa folded his arms and stood firm.

'Ramón, if you refuse to pay you will end up behind bars. Better a few pesetas than the lock up, surely?'

But Papa stood with his arms folded, saying nothing, until José went away.

Mama waited until Papa went out of the house, then she took the money to José Cedrillas. She told Albi not to tell Papa.

Wouldn't the priest say that was a bad thing, one person in a family hiding things from another? It wasn't right. It wasn't Papa's fault he didn't want to pay the tax. All the priest did was walk about the village telling everybody whose side God was on: the soldiers' side. They shouldn't have to pay money just to keep him here, and his housekeeper-sister too – the fat little woman, dressed all in black but her hair cut short and curled in the modern fashion.

'You can be standing in the queue in Valentín's shop,' Mama said as they sat by the evening fire. 'You'll be minding your own business, waiting with your ration-book to buy your bit of cooking oil and sugar, and suddenly she's there in the shop with you. That stops the chat sharpish.'

'Same as when the soldiers come in the bar,' Papa said.

Albi looked up from his whittling. He didn't know the soldiers went to the bar. 'Why does Julio let them in?'

Papa looked at him as if he was stupid. 'If we see them in time we lock the door and pretend nobody's in there but Julio can hardly tell them to go away if they come in at the door. Besides,' he added, sourly, 'Julio quite likes their money.'

Next evening, when Papa came back at curfew, he was buzzing with bar-talk.

In Las Hoyas, twenty kilometres away across the *Meseta*, they'd always hated priests because it was an Anarchist town. At the start of the war the townspeople took the priest and threw him into the gorge and that was the end of him. But now the soldiers were in Las Hoyas, just like they were in El Rincón. Two days ago, Papa said, soldiers seized ten men from the town and made them stand in a line in the place where the priest had been pushed over the cliff.

'Shot them dead,' Papa said. 'The poor buggers went over the edge the same way the priest did before them.'

'Ramón.' Mama jerked her head in Albi's direction and Papa stopped talking.

Albi sat very quiet in his corner. What had it felt like, standing along the edge of rock, staring into those guns, with the dizzy drop behind them and the up-draught cold on their backs, knowing they were going to die? He wished he hadn't eaten so fast, he could taste the garlic in the back of his mouth. He licked his lips. All those bad things the soldiers do to you – it was supposed to be secret but everybody knew, whispering it in doorways, in stables, in chimney corners: *They cut your tongue out if they catch you spying so you can't tell anyone what you saw… They stick red-hot pokers up your bum… They hang you up by your finger-nails… They hammer nails into your eyes…*

In their kitchen, nobody spoke.

Then Pili said, 'Maybe it's just a story. You know what they're like in Las Hoyas. The soldiers haven't actually shot anybody here, have they. Not even Geronimo Gonzalez that night they caught him trying to creep back into the village after curfew. They took his sheep and goats away but they didn't hurt him.'

'Oh yes they did,' Papa retorted. 'How do you suppose he'll keep himself and his family now he hasn't got the sheep?'

Pili said, 'He could work in the factory.'

He wouldn't, though, even if there were any jobs to be had: Geronimo Gonzalez said the factory was owned by a Capitalist Pig, which was a funny thing to say. Don Fernando owned it and he was a gentle old man who lived in Zaragoza and hardly ever came to El Rincón.

The river runs quietly in the sun, the old bridge as tranquil as it appears on the postcards Josefina sells in the bar. Alberto sits on the wall, keeping his ears open for Raul's boy, but the river wind is blowing cold and Santi was always a late riser. He gets to his feet.

On the summit of the bridge he almost turns back. He has walked these paths all his life, he should be at ease with them, even this one that goes past the Molino del Diablo – but from the corner of his eye he can see that the hand holding his walking stick is trembling. He grips the stick more tightly and keeps walking, an undercurrent tugging at him, buried deep in his guts. Just go and look at the Molino. Look, and remember. Not, as he's done all these years, choosing to forget.

*

Albi pulled La Perrita up beside him, onto the top of the giant rock, and sprawled in the winter sunshine to eat his bread and the piece of sausage that used to be one of the ewes, Perrita watching him all the while.

She took her eyes off the sausage and stared down at the path, growling deep in her throat. He stopped chewing to listen but there was nothing. Nothing, then the distinctive tap-tap that was El Ciego's stick, coming round the bend in the path. Albi grabbed Perrita by the snout before she could bark. Her eyebrows shot up and down and strangled sounds came out of her throat as the tap-tapping came closer. He held her tight against his chest and leaned across until he could peer over the edge of the rock at the path below. He was looking straight down at the top of the miller's head, there was a small bald patch right in the middle of the dusty grey hair.

El Ciego stopped. He turned his blank-eyed face up to the sky as if he was listening.

'Boy! Come down here.'

Albi lay very still, his hand round Perrita's muzzle, and gave his dog a little warning shake. If they kept very quiet El Ciego would surely go away, he couldn't be certain there was someone up here.

'Come down at once, Ramón's boy. Or I will tell your papa how disrespectful you are towards your elders.'

He didn't dare pretend he hadn't heard that. He scrambled down the rock. 'How did you know?' The words tumbled out all scratchy. 'How did you know it was me?'

El Ciego inclined his head and pursed his lips. 'The sheep bells. Your *abuelo* had that big bell before it was your papa's.' His eyes were in their sockets but the pupils were as pale as if they'd been scrubbed out. 'What's your name, boy?'

'Albi.'

'Ah. Alberto.' The blind man didn't say anything more.

'I thought you couldn't see.' Albi looked down at their feet on the path – his feet in the too-small boots, the blind man's in his espadrilles. The skin of the blind man's feet and ankles was all red and cracked. It was late in the year to be wearing espadrilles and surely the blind man could afford boots, when he had the mill? 'Don't your feet get very cold in espadrilles?' But it wasn't the question he really wanted to ask.

'So, you want to know how I can see when I have no eyes, same as everyone else wants to know. Eh?' The blind man sounded disappointed, his unseeing face turned away towards the sky. His eyes might look dead but his face looked alive, only not in the way that other people's faces did. His face looked like ears listening. 'You think you can see but people with eyes see nothing much.'

He didn't say anything more for so long Albi thought the conversation had finished.

'I knew I was coming near the big rock where you were lying by the echo of my footsteps. The sound the sheep bells made told me the sheep were lying down and cudding so I knew the shepherd would be nearby. I could smell goats as well as sheep so it wasn't Miguel. Not many animals, so it wasn't Ovidio.'

'But how did you know I was up on the rock?'

'By the shape of the stillness where you were sitting.' El Ciego stopped, his face pointing up at the sky as if he was reading the wind. '*Adios,* boy.'

'*Adios,* señor.'

He watched the blind man walk away along the path and it seemed to him he made a particular show of tapping with his stick as he went towards the village.

'Ah,' said Papa later, when Albi got to the end of his story. 'He wants people to think he's helpless because he's blind. Keep it to yourself, lad, what he said to you about what he sees. It's a kind of message he's entrusted to you, to see if you can keep it secret.'

*

The roof of the Molino has fallen in. The distinctive tower stands at the back where the water from the *acequia* used to drop, driving the machinery. Alberto leans on his stick and gazes at the broken edges of the roof where beams have collapsed, dislodging tiles. The shutters are all closed as if there is still something within to protect, even though the walls are no more than a hollow shell enclosing a piece of broken sky. The porch has long gone but the door is padlocked. Alberto goes to it and leans his ear against the rough wood, listening. Nothing. No ghosts, only the wind moaning gently through the tumbled roof beams inside the mill.

There is nothing here, as if what he remembers is another place entirely, the roof whole, the porch intact, the machinery well-oiled and rumbling as water rushes down inside the tower shaft. Was that this place, or somewhere else? He knows the answer, but that is how he feels it. Was he the same person then that he is now?

He slashes with his stick at the brambles growing thickly beside the door. It must be here still, hidden beneath their tangle: the low arch like a black mouth in the base of the wall. Inside the arch, deep in the dark underbelly of the mill, the great cog-wheels that once turned water into power. He can hear them in his head, the lumbering wheels, louder even than the rush of water driving them. The smell of blood should hit him, now. The iron smell, so thick in his throat it seems to have travelled with him all his life. But the only smell is the fragrance of crushed leaf: it's just an empty ditch. Alberto stares, listening to the silence.

'Are you all right, *Tío*?' Santi says, staring into his face. 'You look as if you've seen a ghost!'

Alberto pats his hand. 'Shall we get going, lad?'

Santi keeps glancing at him as they go down the rows of hutches, as if he thinks his great uncle might keel over any minute. Alberto focuses on the task in hand, shutting the questions out. Rabbit feed comes out of a sack these days. None of that carrying great bundles of greenstuff on his back, which is just as well given the number of rabbits in this building.

'That's better,' Santi says, cutting open a new sack. 'You've got your colour back now. You worried me for a bit, *Tío*.' He fills Alberto's bucket, and then his own.

For a moment Alberto wants to say something, but what would he say that Santi could hear? He's only a boy. The world he lives in is so far away, with its cars and its computers and even, in Raul's house, its oil-fired central heating.

He picks up his bucket and walks away from Santi, filling the feeders one by one.

*

'If they must take firewood why the devil can't they chop it themselves?' Papa shouted, staring at the empty space in the

101

corral which he and Mama had spent days stacking with split logs.

The church bell started ringing for the daily Mass which nobody went to. Mama passed her hands over her face. Albi could see she was thinking it was a good thing Papa hadn't been here when the soldiers came for the firewood. He might have got them in bad trouble.

'I'll just have to start again,' she said, picking up the axe as if she was going to do it that very minute. But her voice was so tired.

'No, Mama.' Albi took the axe off her.

'Bah,' said Papa, turning away and hopping up the passage on his crutches . He'd be going to the bar and Mama didn't like it, but she couldn't stop him.

The truth was, Papa couldn't chop wood without falling over. There was a piece missing on his wooden leg where he'd lost his balance and the axe had glanced off the chopping block and sliced into his wooden leg instead. Mama had taken the axe off him then. She said she'd rather have a man with one leg than a man with no legs at all.

Papa had cried afterwards. Albi heard the sound from the byre and ran out to the corral, thinking he must be ill. Papa was standing with his unshaven face lifted to the cold, empty sky. Tears were running down his cheeks and a funny noise came out of him. Albi crept away and pretended he hadn't seen.

'Papa's really letting go of himself,' Pilar said that night when Mama was busy with the *abuela* and Papa was helping her. 'He forgets to shave, even. He can hardly blame *that* on his leg.' Her voice was thin and angry as if everything was Papa's fault, but it wasn't.

Albi looked at her sitting at her table with her sewing. She wasn't like she used to be. In the old days she liked to tell stories about how strong Papa was, and how brave. How he could cut down a pine tree and peel off all the branches with his axe quicker than any other man in El Rincón. She used to tell how, once a year, Papa would walk all the way to Escucha, which took him a whole day, just to have his axe blade set and sharpened by the blacksmith there, because that blacksmith was the best in the Maestrazgo. And then Papa walked all of another day to come home again.

Pili especially told those stories after Papa disappeared, when he didn't come home from the new moon before Easter until nearly the new moon at grape-picking time and they thought he was dead. Which made the stories all the more hurting of the heart.

15

Christmas

Mari-Jé is hatching plans for Christmas. She's persuaded the kids to come, and all the grandchildren. 'We'll make it special,' she says, regarding Alberto with an appraising eye as if something is his fault. What's she up to? Usually the children prefer to stay in Barcelona, afraid they might get stuck in the village if the weather turns bad. They may not get snow like they used to in the old days but they did have a heavy fall last New Year. The village streets were perilous with ice for weeks afterwards.

Alberto feels unsettled, like an old dog. The trouble is, if the kids come, they will try to persuade him and Mari-Jé to go back with them to Barcelona for the rest of the winter. They always try, Mari-Jé is always tempted. His answer won't have changed: *I can't. I've got the sheep to think of.*

It's worth hanging on to those sheep.

She comes off the phone at last and he waits for her to tell him what's been decided, but all she says is '*Jamón* for supper? Or cheese?'

In the morning he wakes in the dark and leaves Mari-Jé sleeping. He lights the stove and puts on his trousers. It's hard to manage his socks these days so he doesn't bother, even in winter. Just slips his feet into his canvas shoes. His feet are as cracked as the blind man's used to be.

His knees creak as he goes down the stairs. Old age is a bugger. Opening the front door he greets the morning, the half-light of winter very still in the deserted street. He looks up the road, looks down, takes a deep breath of cold air and blows out a cloud of steam. The sky above the shadowed roofs is a delicate blue, streaked with rosy clouds, the cliffs are bright with the unrisen sun. He goes back inside to feed the sheep.

Christmas.

Buried memories rise like fish, breaking the surface.

Christmas 1938 – the first winter after the soldiers arrived. The war not yet finished but in El Rincón it was already over. He can't remember why there was no curfew that one night, or where the soldiers were. If they were in the church, why hadn't the villagers been driven in there too?

Something else. Something to do with Carlos. Fire-crackers! That was it.

Alberto pours the bucket of concentrates into the trough. Is that a memory? Or is it a tangle of dream?

*

There were five fire-crackers left in the old box. Carlos had been given them by his brother.

'We'll have some fun with these,' Carlos said, huddled in the

104

corner of the Plaza with Albi and Pepito. They hadn't had fire-crackers since before the War.

'Shall we let them off now?' Pepito asked.

'Later.' Carlos led the way into the basement of his house.

'Is that you, Carlos?' a quavery voice called down the stairs.

'Yes, *Abuela.*'

Albi looked up in surprise. When Carlos spoke to his *abuela* he sounded like a different boy. A good sort of boy. But that wasn't what he was being. He'd climbed on the manger and was feeling all along the top of the ceiling beam.

'Aha!' He jumped down with a box of matches in his hand. 'Thought there'd be one of these up there somewhere.'

They ran down the street, past the suspicious gaze of *abuelos* who had brought chairs outside to make the most of there being no curfew. It was a cold night, very still, and the stars and the frost were already glittering. A sickle moon slid along the top of La Guadaña, hunting its own shadow. People had brought braziers out and sat round them, shawled in old blankets.

In the Placeta de la Perdiz, Andrés and Mena were sitting with their neighbours outside Andrés's mother's house. The flames from the brazier lit up Mena's face and she was laughing.

'What are you up to, Albi?' she called as he went by, but he was too busy looking at the man sitting in the shadows next to Josefina to reply. The man didn't have a beard any more, or long matted hair, but it was Josefina's son, Esteban. The one who had been away and then came back. And he wasn't the running man, he was too small and narrow.

Andrés was cracking walnuts. 'You boys want some?'

They took a handful between them and ran off down the Calle Pelegrín.

'Did you see him!' Albi asked when they stopped in the Plaza to share out the nuts. 'Did you see Esteban?'

'They're all out tonight, the *regresados,*' Carlos said, as if you could see them any old time. 'Didn't you see Javier sitting with

105

his papa and Tomás and Miguel? They don't think the soldiers will notice them tonight with so many people about.'

But Albi wasn't listening. He was thinking how, even cleaned up, the *regresados* didn't look like the men and boys who'd never been away. Esteban's hair was too newly cut, his face still pale where the beard had been, his clothes looking unaccustomed like clothes that had lain too long in a chest.

'Anyway, you shouldn't have stared like that,' Carlos said. 'These *regresados* don't want you to notice them.'

Down by the bridge a group of boys was hanging about looking bored. Carlos showed them the firecrackers.

'What do you mean, wait for the soldiers to go to Midnight Mass?' Rafa said. 'It's only firecrackers. And they're probably duff anyway.'

'They might be duff but they're mine,' Carlos said. 'I'll decide when and where we let them off.'

Around ten, Carlos went off to get something to eat and Albi hurried home to grab a piece of bread. In the kitchen Mama was sitting all alone by the fire. She dried her eyes on her apron when she saw him and he sat beside her on his stool and leaned his head on her knee. She stroked his hair.

'Am I your best, Mama?'

'You're my best baby.'

It made a bad taste, knowing she was sad. Was it about Papa? Or money? Or was she weeping because she couldn't go to the church, this night of all nights? But probably it wasn't any of those things. There were so many coming back, but not the one she wanted.

He sat with her for a while, but the excitement outside was pulling at him. He kissed the back of her hand and promised he'd be back soon.

Anyway, Manolo might be dead.

The streets were humming. Men spilled out of the bars with their beakers of wine and cider, women pulled their chairs closer, the better to gossip. There were children everywhere, running wild. Small shadows jumped out of doorways, bigger shadows turned on them and punished them with a good tickling. Even bigger shadows slipped away in pairs. Once Albi thought he heard Pili's laugh, but he didn't see her. He looked over the low wall by the church and saw Pepito down in the Plaza with a group of older boys near the wash house. He turned to run down and join them and bumped into Miguel.

'Hey – steady, lad.' Miguel looked over the wall at the bustling Plaza and shook his head. 'They're going to regret this. They'll think they've unleashed more than they can deal with.'

Albi had no idea what he was talking about. He ran away laughing.

The church bell started to toll and he stopped running. Everybody stopped. They were listening for the sound of marching feet, but when the soldiers appeared they weren't marching. They strolled up to the church and in through the big doors, and they left everybody else alone.

The silence in the streets began to bubble. When the cracked bell finally stopped, the talking and the larking about began again.

Albi ran down into the Plaza.

There were far too many boys wanting to let off the firecrackers now. They argued about where best to do it.

'At the sentries. Throw them at the sentries,' one of the older boys shouted, but Carlos ignored him.

'Through front doors,' Carlos said. 'Go for the *abuelos*, they can't run so fast.'

They lit the crackers and threw them into doorways, then ran away laughing before angry *abuelos* could catch them.

'I'll give you such a thrashing, when I get my hands on you,' Felipe Moliner shouted, shaking his fist. But he was an old man, he couldn't run. The cracker had only made a bit of noise, and besides, in a minute or two he would have forgotten all about it.

They whooped and giggled down the street and up the other side and chose another house. They might have got in real trouble if the fire-crackers had gone off properly. The sentries might have thought it was shooting and come after them with their guns. But Rafa was right: none of the crackers made much of a show, except for the one they threw last, into José Iranzo's mother's doorway. That one went off with a satisfying bang. They ran away, screaming with laughter.

Before they'd even got to the corner José was after them.

'Come here, you little buggers!'

José Iranzo wasn't so old. José Iranzo could run. The boys scattered, diving down different turnings. Albi followed Carlos back down into the Plaza, Pepito close on their heels. José was still behind them. They fled across the Plaza and up the lane towards the church. The lane was steep but the slope would slow down a fully-grown man more than it did half-grown boys. At the top they glanced back over the wall but José wasn't there – he was already nearing the top of the lane behind them. They turned and bolted down the Calle San Juan and into Albi's house.

'Quick.' He pushed the door shut but there wasn't time to lock it. 'Out the back.' In the dark, the other two stumbled on the uneven floor making such a noise.

'Albi?'

'Yes, Mama?' He didn't stop. He slammed back the bolt on the door to the corral and they spilled outside, but the outer door was locked and the key wasn't on its nail. He scrambled up on top of the rabbit hutches and from there onto the high wall of the corral. Pepito jumped up after him. They knelt on the narrow wall and pulled Carlos up between them. They weren't laughing any more. Somebody was banging on the front door.

The moon gleamed on the top of the wall as Albi led the way to the place where they could jump down into the *huerto*. They fled across the terrace and down the steep steps into the gully and the shadows of the trees. There was a bit of a cave here which José had probably forgotten. They stood squashed up together in the narrow dark. It smelled of damp earth, and of fox.

'He's a bit sore, isn't he?' Pepito whispered.

'Shh,' Albi said, 'I'm listening.'

His mama was shouting his name. José Iranzo was shouting it with her. There was going to be trouble now.

José bellowed, 'Come back here or I'll have your guts for sausage skins, you little vermin.'

Whose side would the soldiers be on if they heard him now?

On Christmas morning, Albi was beaten by his papa and Carlos was beaten by his. Pepito had no papa to beat him, so all his uncles beat him instead.

José Iranzo came to Albi's house and took him roughly by the arm. 'You must never do that again. You could frighten an old person to death with such silly tricks.'

Albi looked at Papa. Wasn't he going to tell José Iranzo that he'd already been beaten for it? Papa looked down at the floor.

Upstairs, the *abuela* was raging.

When José had gone Papa jerked his head towards the ceiling. 'You should have saved one of those fire-crackers for that one up there.'

Why had Papa beaten him then? It hadn't been a hard beating but it had hurt his feelings. Papa saying that made it worse. Albi looked at him and wanted to say so, but Papa always said real men don't talk about feeling things.

Papa said gruffly, 'José expected me to beat you.'

Albi watched his papa make his awkward way up the stairs on his crutches. If ever he had sons he wouldn't beat them just because somebody else wanted him to do it.

Before Papa had got to the top of the stairs the shouting started. Soldiers came hammering up the street.

'Everybody out! Get in that church!'

The Mass went on for ever, the priest and the soldiers grim as devils.

When at last the priest let them go, the whispering began. Neighbours flitted from doorway to doorway, furtive, excited, passing on the news. *Somebody stole their horses!*

Who did?

Three men with flour sacks over their heads. Holes cut in them for eyes.

But who was it inside the sacks?

'Jesús says it wasn't men from El Rincón,' Pili said that night in the kitchen. Her eyes were sparkling with so much knowing.

Afterwards, her eyes were red.

'Anyway, he can't thrash me like he could when he still had two legs,' she said, when Papa was safely in bed and Mama too. But Pili was limping when she went out of the kitchen to fetch her sewing.

'Very cocky, our Pilar,' Ramona said. 'Now that Jesús has said they can be married next year.'

Albi's head shot up. When did that happen? Had Papa changed his mind? He opened his mouth to ask, but Inma gave him a little warning shake of the head.

So nothing had really changed.

For days the excitement bubbled nervously in the streets as if there had been some kind of victory, though nobody knew who it was who'd taken the horses. Gypsies, probably, people said. Nobody from round here.

Perhaps it was true. The soldiers scowled, and jerked their guns, and waited. But there were no *denuncias*.

They were all punished, just the same. The new curfew lasted from three in the afternoon until eight in the morning, and every morning for a week the villagers were rounded up in the Plaza and made to stand in the cold. Rounded up like sheep, while the soldiers went round the houses, seizing hay and oats and barley wherever they could find it, for the new horses which had arrived to replace the stolen ones. They took other things too, and none of it was written down in any book. Chickens from the coops, a rabbit, a mattock off the wall.

Afterwards, the soldiers rode around the village in pairs, and six abreast across the Plaza. High-stepping horses, their necks curved, their ears pricked. The soldiers staring down at the villagers with haughty eyes. Albi was shocked to recognise the fair-haired soldier who sometimes said hello to him. Up on the horse the soldier didn't look so friendly.

He watched the soldier pass along the street. When I am a man I will have a horse like that. And some of those long leather boots to go with it.

16

Snow

Mari-Jé gets her way: they are eleven round the table for Christmas Eve, twelve when Santi comes to join them after the meal. It's hot and cramped in the kitchen, and afterwards Marco and Santi retreat to the *solenar* for a cigarette. Ana goes too, though she doesn't smoke. Mari-Jé is in the church with Bernardo and Gloria. The grandchildren are off with their mates, hanging about the streets, under-dressed as usual. They're good kids. Modern as they are, they love El Rincón. Rincón has been good to all the grandchildren: summers and holidays, the village still buzzes.

Alberto whistles tunelessly as he sits by the stove carving the handle on a new walking stick.

Two days later, he and Mari-Jé are alone again and the house feels hollow. He understands the little tear he sees in the corner of her eye as they go down together for the bread, though she says it's just the cold wind. They wait for the van to come from the bakery in Valbono, sitting on the unforgiving stone bench and swapping gossip with four or five of the few neighbours who live in the village all year round, people they've known all their lives. The youngest is sixty-something.

'Help me with the beds,' Mari-Jé says, when they get back home. She takes the key to next door from its hook on the wall. The house belongs to her cousin now. It's rarely used, except at Easter and in August. One or other of the cousins usually has family here then.

Alberto follows Mari-Jé up the narrow stairs. She was born in this house, her mother Margarita was Ramona and Inma's best friend. He shivers in the frigid air. He's not surprised she wanted company this morning, though he isn't much help at stripping beds, she's much too authoritative for him, pulls the sheets right out of his hands. After a while he leaves her to it and wanders into the old kitchen. It's barely changed since he was a boy and used to bring buckets of embers for Margarita when she'd let the fire go out. She'd had thirteen brothers and sisters to look after, their mother dead with the youngest. He looks at the hearth. Like theirs, it has a stove sitting on it now, but otherwise the kitchen is almost the same as it was when he was a boy. The view through the small window, over the long red roofs, is unchanged too. He hears the echoes of the missing voices: the children squabbling around Margarita's feet in this kitchen, the *abuela* faintly screeching through the thick wall, next door in their house; Papa's voice suddenly, very close as if he's in the same room, on a grey day like this and a heavy sky lowering.

*

Snow. Fine, dry snow at first, blowing like grains of white sand and collecting between the cobbles. Everything white except for the cliffs, which didn't look white any more but dirty grey.

'Go down and bolt the front door, Albi,' Papa said when the girls came in from work early because of the blizzard. 'I doubt we'll be going out again before curfew.'

They sat by the fire, Papa carving a new bell-collar, the girls telling the bits of gossip they'd heard in the factory, but it was all things they knew already. When curfew came they fell silent, listening to the church bell tolling and then the muffled crunch of the boots marching up the street. Inma's knitting needles resumed their clicking, and Pili bent again to her sewing. The wind came in through every crack, through the cat-holes, under the doors and between the shutters. It whistled round their feet, scattering the wood shavings on the floor. Albi watched snowflakes come down the chimney and hiss in the flames. Every now and then a puff of smoke billowed out into the room.

Papa cocked his head on one side, listening. 'Wind's from the north,' he said. 'You can't hear the river.'

'Morning wood?' Mama said uncertainly, but Albi could see by her face that he was in with a chance. She was always short of sticks to start the fire.

'I'll get a really big bundle.'

'Very well. But keep close to the village.'

He ran down the stairs. She shouted after him, 'And stay away from that Carlos. I don't want him getting you in trouble again.'

He pulled open the heavy front door. Carlos detached himself from Jaime's wall mouthing, '*Stay away from that Carlos.*' Albi

113

grinned and put a finger to his lips. They ran laughing down the street, their boots echoing in spite of the snow. The shutters of his house banged open and his mama's voice shouted, 'Alberto?' but they were already round the corner and into Calle de Mora.

'Where shall we go?' Carlos asked when they found the others. Rafa, Pepito, Juanito Torrecillas, all the usual crowd.

'Let's go to the waterfall, it'll be frozen,' Juanito said, but only he and Albi had permits and most of the others didn't want to get caught out of the village without one. Not now, with the soldiers still being angry.

'Let's do some spying, then,' Carlos said.

Rafa said there wasn't much point in the snow. Anywhere you went, everybody would see you'd been there. So they made a den in the woods above the *chorreta,* pulling poles out of a log-pile somebody had made and covering them with thin branches that had been stacked nearby. At the end, when it was getting towards curfew time, they knocked the den down so the soldiers couldn't use it. They put the poles back where they'd found them, and Albi ran around quickly picking up dead sticks to take home to his mama.

She was waiting at the front door when he got back. The church bell was already ringing.

'You call that a big bundle?' she said, her voice not friendly.

The next afternoon she was very unfriendly indeed. Somebody had been messing about with Luis Irún's woodpile and the blacksmith seemed to think Carlos was involved. Albi hadn't been there too, had he?

'No, Mama.'

You have to learn to lie.

The cold made everything difficult. The ice in the *fuente* heaped itself up over the side of the tank and flowed in a motionless stream of glass over the cobbles. The livestock had to be taken down to the river to drink and buckets of water carried back up the hill, under the eyes of the sentries, for the rabbits and poultry and for the kitchen too. Even in the kitchen, with its thick walls and the fire burning all day, the water jars had a skin of ice on them by morning until they got the fire hot again. Mama said the bakehouse was the warmest place in the village in the early morning, but by dinnertime it was deserted and the oven was cold.

Albi took the sheep out, but they had to scratch holes in the snow to find anything to eat. Papa said it was taking more condition off their backs keeping warm than they would put back from the grazing, so after that he stayed at home. Just him and his mama and papa, now the factory was open again: the girls walked to work, snow or no snow, but the days were short.

He sat in the byre with Papa mending potato sacks. The two heavy oxen blew their warm breath and the cow grunted and sighed and went back to chewing her cud. And the new pig grumbled in the pig pen under the stairs. It was a very small pig. Papa had taken it off Benito's widow because she couldn't keep it any more, but Mama said the wool he'd given in exchange was worth more to them than the pig was, and how could they spare scraps for a pig when they didn't have enough to eat themselves? 'Besides, the soldiers don't bother taking wool but they do take pigs.'

'Not this one, they won't,' Papa said. 'And the pig will make lard if it doesn't make much else.'

The cow stirred and scratched her neck on the side of the manger. Papa paused in his work and watched her. Amapola was old, like the mule. She was thin and shrivelled but her belly was swollen.

'She's too old to get away with being fed so little,' Papa said. 'We should have eaten her before now.'

She was barely giving any milk. The goats had long stopped giving any. There would be no milk now until the new calf came and the goats kidded in the spring.

'It's not her fault,' Albi said.

'One more calf. Then she will have to go.' Papa passed his hand over his eyes. 'Please God this winter doesn't go on like this too long or the oxen will have to go too.'

Albi went very still inside. How would they plough if there weren't any oxen? What about milk and butter if there wasn't a cow? And the mule? Was Papa going to say the mule must go too? There would be such shame in having no big animals. They'd be no better than Pepito's mama.

Papa cleared his throat suddenly as if something had got stuck in it. 'We'll hire the oxen out this spring. Even if I can't plough we'll get something from other people for using them.' He didn't say it, but Albi knew he was hoping he'd be grown enough to plough the year after. He might be. He was bursting out of his clothes before they wore out now, and Mama had to keep going to the chest where she'd put Manolo's clothes. If Papa would only wait until he was bigger he would do the ploughing.

But then he looked up and saw Papa frowning at his needle as it went in and out of the sacking. Manolo might be home by next spring, that was what Papa was thinking.

Albi bent again to his mending and forced himself to think about something else. What had Mena been wearing on Christmas Eve? A coat? Probably not the sandals. Or the dress with all the buttons – not in the cold, even under the coat. It would be very cold now, up on the *Meseta* in the snow with the north wind whistling close to the ground. Perhaps she was staying all day in her mother-in-law's house down in the village and not going up to the *Meseta* at all. He thought of her sitting in Teresa's kitchen in the house in the Placeta de la Perdiz. Mena, all bright and strange and unknown. It was hard to imagine her in a smoky old kitchen.

The front door opened and the wind whistled along the passageway and into the byre. The door slammed shut again: Mama had been down to the wash house, though nothing would dry in this weather, not on the lines over the street. It wouldn't dry on the *solenar* without any sun. They would have to sit all evening under the dripping washing, hung on the strings across the kitchen.

'Oh, there you are.' Her old coat was pulled across her chest and fastened with a big safety pin. She had a shawl over her head and her cheeks were red from the cold. She came in and leaned against the cow to warm up. Amapola sighed, and leaned against Mama.

'We've been ordered to collect new ration books tomorrow. From the *Ayuntamiento*.'

Papa nodded. The silence filled up again. The cow farted.

Mama said, 'And Luis's Santiago is back.'

'That's a dangerous thing to know, María.'

Albi felt her looking at him so he pretended he hadn't heard. *Regresados* were dangerous even when the soldiers weren't being as jumpy as they were now.

'They're coming back too soon, the cowards,' Papa said suddenly. 'The war isn't over yet.'

'Hush, Ramón,' Mama said. Her eyes were wet.

When she looked at Albi, did she see him or did she see Manolo's clothes and Manolo not in them?

Old Jaime had pneumonia. Young Jaime had moved his bed so his *abuelo* could lie by the stove at the back of the house.

The soldiers came with their black book to take provisions from all the houses in their street. When they'd gone, Belén told Mama Old Jaime had been coughing too much to say anything at all the whole time the soldiers were in their house. So that was one good thing.

In Albi's house, after the soldiers had been, there were only twenty-three jars of tomatoes left, and all the biggest jars had gone. There were only five cheeses and six strings of garlic. A third of the corn in the bins had been taken, and the sack of walnuts was a quarter empty. One of the mutton hams had gone. He could do his sums. That wasn't one tenth, just as it hadn't been a tenth the first time the soldiers came. Papa could only do numbers if the numbers were sheep, but even he knew that one tenth of a full sack of rye was not half a sack. He was angry enough about what he saw. Albi didn't tell him the things he hadn't seen – that the soldiers should only have taken four jars of tomatoes at the most, and two strings of dried figs.

Mama was almost more upset by the things the soldiers didn't take. 'What's wrong with my sausage?' she kept saying. 'So it's gone a bit dry – it's still good enough for us. Who do they think they are, turning up their noses at it?'

The soldiers didn't take the skinny little pig either. They laughed at it. But they did take the young cockerel Mama had been going to kill when it got bigger. And they took two laying hens. Not the little speckledy hen, but how long would it be before they did take her?

When the soldiers left they placed a little column of coins on the bottom stair. It was far less than the chickens and rabbits and everything else was worth, Mama said, but at least it would buy them a few things in Valentín's shop.

'Don't tell Papa I said that,' she added.

Inma put her hand on Mama's shoulder. How small and thin Mama looked, next to Inma.

'How long can we go on like this, Mama?' Inma said in a low voice, but not so low that Albi didn't hear. 'We haven't enough left for ourselves.'

Pilar said, 'When the *Guardia Civil* take over it will be different. There will be a proper system then.'

The *Guardia Civil*? Even Inma looked scared at those words. How did Pili know they were coming?

'Mother of God,' Mama said, sitting down suddenly on the nearest chair. 'It won't be better, Pilar.'

Pili shut her lips up tight and threaded another needle.

17

The *Guardia Civil*

It is the Hunting Fraternity lunch. There's one every year, and this time it's Valbono's turn. Alberto sits in the bar which once belonged to Jesús and Pilar and now belongs to their daughter, Concepción. Raul's sister. Two long tables have been set out along opposite walls. In the space in the middle the little children tumble and squabble while the bigger ones try to keep them out of mischief, and they all of them trip up Concepción and her daughter as they rush about with great plates of food.

There are nearly thirty people here today, sitting down to eat. Alberto looks at all the different ages, sad that neither of his sons is here to share it. He has to make do with Santi instead. Santi is sitting with his cousin at the far end of the table and whatever it is the lads are saying, their elders are amused. The television is on in the corner and the noise level is deafening. Everybody is telling stories. When they run out of stories from today's hunting they'll tell the ones from last month, from last year, from ten years ago. Nobody minds how old the stories are. They improve with telling.

Alberto turns away from the table for a moment. The noise is hurting his ears. Outside the window the afternoon is cold and grey, a thin snow beginning to fall. Through the hatch to the kitchen he can see Concepción, stout and red-faced, busy about the pots. She looks just like her mama.

'You all right, *Tío?*' Raul shouts from three feet away across the table.

Alberto laughs. How could he not be, in such company?

'You just say when you've had enough. Santi will run you back whenever you want.' Raul goes back to picking his teeth. Further

119

down the table Mari-Jé is deep in discussion with Raul's wife, Josefina, their faces deadly serious.

Santi appears at Raul's shoulder and asks his papa for the keys to the truck. He wants to go off with his cousin to... To do something, but Alberto doesn't hear what. He watches, amused, while Raul argues: Santi has been drinking and what if the *polizia* are out?

Santi raises his eyebrows. '*La polizia*, Papa? On a Sunday? Here?'

Santi doesn't take after his paternal grandparents. Pilar was always plump, and Jesús was a big, broad man, as Raul is, but Santi is small and wiry, bright-eyed. He moves quickly, is reckless, impulsive, and has the most engaging grin. When Santi smiles, you cannot say no to him. Just as Raul is failing to say no to him now.

'Such a smile, that boy has,' Alberto says, when Santi has taken the keys and bounded out of the room.

Raul says, 'We always think he takes after you.'

'Do you?' He is startled. 'I was never so giddy.'

'Mama always said he was the spitting image of you when you were young.'

Alberto is silenced. Pilar speaking out of the grave sets the nerves pricking all up and down his spine. It's more than ten years since she died. He remembers his surprise when she confessed once, as if it was a shameful secret, that of all her grandchildren Santi was her favourite.

It casts a strange light on the past, this sudden new piece of information dropped by Raul so casually at his feet. Santi was Pilar's favourite, but she thought Santi was like him?

He looks through the window where Santi is striding past, down the alleyway. All those opportunities the boy has had, the late last-born of ageing parents, and what is he doing now but hanging about back home in the middle of nowhere.

Santi grins as he starts the engine. 'Did you think I'd forget to come back for you?'

Alberto shakes his head, but of course that's just what he did think. He does up his seat belt in the front passenger seat, wondering if Santi is sober yet, and Mari-Jé climbs into the back. It's still trying to snow as they drive out of Valbono and over the switchback mountain road to El Rincón. As they crest the summit the view opens up to the west: wave after wave of grey rock and dark valleys, all the way to the distant horizon where a gleam of setting sun cuts between pillars of cloud. To their right, the cloud is like a black curtain dropping. It could be rain but it looks like snow.

Santi drives fast down the long sweeping curves of tarmac, into the shadowed valley. Just before El Portal a black and tan dog runs across the road, the truck spits gravel as Santi brakes and swerves into the side of the narrow road.

'That was my damned dog! Did you see her, *Tío*?' He jumps out, leaving the door hanging open, and runs down the track towards the old factory.

Alberto turns in his seat. Mari-Jé raises her eyebrows but she's smiling. *That boy!* her eyes say. The wind whines in the rocks that tower above them, a scatter of gritty snow blows into the cab. He gets out and goes round to close Santi's door. The boy has disappeared into the factory. Alberto pulls his scarf tighter: he might as well go and see what he's up to.

The building, long deserted but still whole, sprawls along the bank of the river: the clay tiles and cement walls of El Caballero's replacement factory. Brambles climb up the walls, the big doors hang broken. Inside, the machinery has long gone.

Santi's voice echoes in the emptiness. 'Preetty! Preetty!'

Funny name for a dog, sounds foreign, Alberto thinks as he picks his way over the cracked concrete. There are old bricks lying about, and lumps of fallen render, and it's dark in here, a thicket of bramble and briar growing up and over the gaping window holes.

A dog whines.

'Oh Preetty! Clever girl. You clever, clever little dog!'

Alberto makes his way towards Santi's voice.

In a corner of a side-room, on an old sleeping bag, the bitch lies watching Santi with wary eyes. The unmistakable smell of pups and dog-milk tells Alberto what he can barely make out in the shadows. She's whelped, that's what she's doing here, though why here God only knows.

Santi approaches her cautiously. This is one nervy little bitch, but she lets him put his hand close and even wags her tail a little. He straightens up.

'I knew there had to be a good reason for her running off. We drowned her last litter, that's her problem.' He looks down at her, cooing, 'You got round us, didn't you! You little devil, you.' The dog watches with careful eyes as Santi turns away. 'I'll come back in the morning. No point trying to do anything now.'

Alberto clicks his tongue in agreement.

'Well look at that!' Santi is staring at the wall. 'Fancy that still being here after all this time.'

He peers where Santi is looking. He can just make out the scribbled words:

> *I was here*
> *masturbating*
> *to keep up the old tradition.*

Alberto coughs. It occurs to him, if Santi's seen it before, he may be the one who wrote it. He starts walking away towards the big square of light and the broken doors.

Santi follows him out. 'I saw that the first time I ever came in here. I didn't know what it meant then, of course.'

The river is loud, rushing out of sight beyond the brambles.

It used to power the machinery inside the factory; this one, and the ruined one beyond. Alberto looks at the rickety pinnacles of the two remaining corners of the older building, sticking up among the trees. It's years since he last came down here. He glances at Santi. In this light Santi's face looks older. It's like glimpsing into the future, watching the boy stare at the old factory.

'I know *Abuela* worked in there, but she never talked about it.'

Ah. For all her surprising confessions, Pilar did have her silences, then. Alberto waits for Santi to ask him questions, but he doesn't. They walk back to the truck.

'It's full of history, this place.' Santi says, his voice reverent.

Alberto looks down at the red roof sprawling below them along the river bank. To him, this is modern, this is the new factory. This isn't where his sisters worked, though Carlos did. There is history, and then there is history.

*

At *Semana Santa*, the same as every other Easter, the *acequias* were re-opened for the growing season. It sounded cheerful, the water singing in the streets again, but it didn't feel cheerful. Not even when the soldiers issued new permits so that people could go to their outlying lands, up to a distance of seven kilometres from the village. *For the purpose of cultivating only*, the new permit said. Albi read the words on the piece of paper to Papa. He had the old permit still in his pocket. It was worn and dirty and going soft along the creases, and the ink was smudged on the front, but on the back the paper was blank. He could write on that, and try making sums. If he had a pencil.

'For the purpose of cultivating only?' said Papa. 'As if we'd go all that way to sit in the sun!'

Papa was sore because Miguel was doing their ploughing again this year, not him, and then the harrowing too. They paid him with the last of the cheeses, the shoulder of cured mutton, and a promise of a share of the harvest if he did the reaping for them when the time came.

The *tierras* were too far for Papa on his crutches. It was Albi who did the sowing, walking up and down the prepared ground in the cold spring sunshine.

When he'd emptied the satchel of seed corn he fetched the sheep from the lower terraces where Perrita was watching over them and they set off the long way home. From their *tierras* it was a very long way, if you didn't want to go past the dam and the guns listening in the slits of the pill-boxes, and a harsh voice shouting, 'Halt! State your name and business and show your permit,' like happened this morning. So he went home the long way, dropping down the valley at the back of the ridge which was called La Espalda.

Even the long way was bad. As he came down near the road he held the flock back and listened, but all he could hear was the noise from the factory. No trucks, no motorcycles, no metal-shod horses trotting along – he whistled to Perrita and ran onto the road.

He hurried towards the factory, glancing down over the wall to see if his sisters were in the corral below or sitting on the benches under the trees by the river, but everyone was inside working. The roar of machinery echoed off the walls of the gorge even louder than the rushing water, making it impossible to hear. He ran faster; past the factory and through El Portal, past the track to the garrison and over the river bridge to where the old mule path led back to the village.

As soon as he dropped down off the road onto the narrow path he felt safer: away from the noise of the factory and the roar of water through El Portal he could hear the world again. He passed the junction pool at a distance. On the further bank the blank face of the garrison, shuttered and silent, was visible through the trees. Faded uniforms were spread out on the walls to dry in the

124

sun. Jesús might know things other people didn't, and he might even tell some of them to Pili, but the soldiers were still there. He'd been wrong about that.

Two evenings later, the sound of the soldiers marching at the start of curfew was brisker, harder. Albi saw his papa raise his head to listen, and his mama too. He saw the look that passed between them.

That was how the *Guardia Civil* arrived. On an ordinary afternoon when they were busy doing their usual things (Albi out with his sheep, the girls at the factory, Mama washing the *abuela*'s sheets) the *Guardia* had come and the soldiers had left.

'Without a backward glance,' Mama said, though how did she know?

'Without even saying good-bye,' Ramona added.

'Not that that matters to *you*, Ramona,' Papa said, but Albi knew what she meant. He had got to know their faces, especially the one with fair hair who had asked him about the sheep, until Papa said he would beat Albi if he caught him fraternising again. After that whenever the soldier looked as if he might talk to him Albi pretended he hadn't noticed.

Fraternising. It wasn't anything to do with *fretting* after all.

He'd seen Ramona talking to that same soldier, once or twice. Did that mean she'd been fraternising? He stole a look at her as she sat in the kitchen with her head bent over her darning but she looked like the same old Ramona. He couldn't tell if she was happy or sad that the soldiers had gone.

The *Guardia* weren't like the soldiers. They didn't lounge on the church steps when they were on sentry-duty, looking like ordinary men who wanted to go home. 'The *Guardia* are professionals,' Pili said. Whatever that meant.

They were certainly different. They stood smartly on guard, they marched sharply in time, and there were more of them. Their Commandante never smiled. It felt as if the soldiers' time had been

125

quite a good time; it didn't feel like a good time any more. The *Guardia* stopped men and searched them roughly in the street. And women too – Alicia, Ramona's friend, was stopped and searched while her mama wailed and wept and wrung her hands, like a duck trying to draw the hunter off her brood.

It would be even more dangerous now if you had a *regresado* in your house. When the *Guardia* came to seize provisions, the hidden men would have to slide through back-doors or dive under beds, or wherever else they could find a place to hide. 'But never in the grain bins,' Mama said: 'The *Guardia* always thump their rifle butts down into the grain bins in case there's someone hiding there.' She didn't say anything about them noticing Papa. Papa in full view with his stump of a leg so obvious, so impossible to overlook. The *Guardia* would know Papa was a *regresado* too, because he was, even if he was old. And he wasn't paying the church tax either. If the *Guardia* hadn't noticed him, the priest would surely point him out. They might throw him in the lock up.

Every day, when Albi passed with his sheep, his eyes were drawn to the tiny window of the prison. Imagine spending the night in there, the thick mud walls as hard as rock, the door so small and narrow a fat man wouldn't go through it, but the key to the door was enormous.

When they were little they used to say to one another, *We're going to lock you in the prison and leave you for a week and nobody will hear you crying and at the end you will be only bones and the rats will have eaten all the rest of you, even the gristle.* He was older now. Julio's bar was just across the street and somebody would hear you screaming. Besides, there was only one key and the *Guardia* had it. And before them the soldiers had had it, and before the soldiers – long ago, before he ran away to Bilbao and then came back again – El Caballero had the key and was in charge of putting people in the prison if they did something bad. But in the old days the prison wasn't used very often. It was different now.

Albi came down the Calle San Juan late one afternoon and there was his mama in the street, passing a cloth-covered bowl through the window of the prison to somebody inside, even though a *Guardia* man was standing on guard right outside the door. Albi couldn't stop, the flock was running past him and he didn't know if the door of their house was open to let them in, but as soon as he'd shut the sheep and goats in their pen he turned back to see what his mama was doing.

She was there in the passage already, her face white. She pulled him to her and held him very tight. 'They've taken Papa.'

'Is it the tax? Is it because he wouldn't pay the tax?'

'I've been paying the tax,' Mama said, distracted. Her voice suddenly woke up. 'Don't you tell Papa that! Mind you never breathe a word.'

That evening it rained very hard and Mama went up to the attic to put basins under all the drips, the same as she always did. It was too wet to sit out on the *solenar* with the rain blowing in so they sat in the kitchen. The *abuela* was shouting because she'd got used to lying out on the *solenar* on the folding bed, now the weather was getting warmer, but today she'd been in her bed in the *alcoba* all day and the back door was shut.

Albi watched Inma sitting by the fire, stirring the pot of potatoes and cabbage and saying nothing. What she was thinking? That the *Guardia* would send Papa away to the big prison in Las Hoyas, like they did to Antonio Gonzalez when they caught him hiding a stranger who might have been a *maquis*? Nobody had seen Antonio since.

Pili said, 'Do you suppose Papa said something stupid? He might have insulted them.'

Inma knocked the spoon against the side of the pot and laid it down on the hearth. 'The *Guardia* punish anyone they think might have been fighting for the Republicans. Papa didn't need to say a thing.'

'We should have hidden him. Like the other *regresados*,' Albi said. His sisters looked at him as if they'd forgotten he was there in the corner by the fire.

Pilar tilted her head warningly in his direction. 'Walls have ears,' she said to Inma. 'Wait till the rabbit's in its burrow.'

In the morning he fed the oxen and the cow. He felt the calf's foot, sticking out like a knob in the smooth wall of Amapola's belly. He put his face close and whispered, 'Are you ready to come out yet?' But Papa had said the calf would be born around the time of the next new moon. That was half a moon away still. He put hay in the big manger, spreading it across in front of the cow and the two oxen, careful to keep out of the way of their wide sweeping horns. He spread it thin to make it look more than it was. Then he went through to the stable and did the same with the mule, hurrying now. When he'd finished, and before his mama could get back from the bakehouse with the new bread, he slipped out of the house and up the street to the prison.

Papa got up off the stone bench where he'd been lying. His face loomed winter-white in the shadows as he hopped to the window, one hand on each wall to keep himself from falling.

'Go home,' he hissed. 'Don't let them see you here.'

But he couldn't go home. If they took his papa away he might never see him again. He put his hands through the bars and the tears ran down his face.

Papa's eyes stopped being cross. He took hold of Albi's hands and rubbed the backs with his rough thumbs. 'I'll be home before you know it. Run along to Mama now, there's a good lad.' His voice was gruff and his moustache was trembling. Albi nodded and did as he was told.

A little while later, after Mama got back from the bakehouse, there was Papa, swinging down the Calle San Juan on his crutches as jaunty as if he had just won a game in the *fiesta*.

'Let off with a warning,' he said to Mama, making it sound like some kind of prize.

But later, when Albi was dawdling outside in the corral, loving his rabbit, he heard voices above him on the *solenar*. Papa said, 'Somebody must have told them.' Albi's head jerked up in surprise but Papa couldn't know he was down in the corral listening. 'And we know who,' Papa added.

He worried about it all the rest of the day as he walked through the flowering thyme and the rosemary, the birds singing in every bush, and little blue butterflies flying up from under his feet. Papa had stopped talking as soon as he looked over the rail of the *solenar* and saw Albi in the corral below. 'Get those sheep out, lad, before they starve,' he'd said, as if he was cross.

Albi went inside to let the flock out of the pen. Papa's voice came muffled through the ceiling. 'That boy's got ears as long as his bloody rabbit's.'

It wasn't fair. They were always saying walls had ears but nobody told him the things that really mattered.

'You should be grateful,' Pili said.

Albi looked up in alarm as Papa lifted his hand. 'You tell him to mind his own business.' But he put his hand down again without hitting her.

Him? Jesús?

Later, Albi tried to ask Inma but all she said was, 'Perhaps we shouldn't blame Pili.' That didn't tell him anything.

The next night Papa and Pili started arguing again but Mama said, 'Not in front of Albi.'

Nobody said anything at all after that, Pilar snipping angrily with her scissors, Inma and Ramona studying their sewing as if nothing more was happening than their needles going in and out of the cloth.

Suddenly Papa shouted, 'I am beset by women.' Even though Albi was in the room.

*

129

Alberto speaks with Bernardo on Mari-Jé's mobile. It's mostly about the grandchildren – Mateo has just done an exam, Leon has a new girlfriend – but Bernardo seems touchy and distant as if something has upset him, so Alberto hands the phone back to Mari-Jé.

Afterwards she says, 'You shouldn't make him jealous.'

'Bernardo? Jealous?'

She shrugs, with just a suggestion that it's Bernardo at fault, really, even though she seems to be saying otherwise. 'You told him about the dog and the pups. In the old factory. He thinks you're much fonder of Santi than you ever were of him. Or Marco,' she adds, but they both know Marco isn't touchy the way Bernardo is. Bernardo has always felt he's missing out.

'Santi is just a harum scarum without an ounce of common sense in his pretty skull,' Alberto says. 'What's there to be jealous of?'

Mari-Jé chuckles. She's rather fond of Santi too. 'No he isn't. He's taking a while to grow up, that's all.' She pulls a length of crochet yarn from the ball on the table. 'It's not like when we were young.'

'What would his grandmother think if she'd lived to see him now?'

'If Pilar was here now she'd be a hundred and two.'

It's a shock, Mari-Jé saying that. In his mind, Pili is still about twenty-four, which would make him nine.

'Anyway,' Mari-Jé says, 'You can do something about Bernardo being jealous. If you tell Santi things you don't tell the boys, it's bound to hurt.'

What things? He isn't conscious he's said anything to Santi or to anyone else. He looks at his wife, wondering what she's talking about. She frowns at her crochet. Was she really talking about herself?

*

130

Albi put some of the soup in a bowl and walked through the back bedroom, past the *abuela* asleep in the *alcoba,* out onto the *solenar* where Ramona, Inma and Pilar were sitting in a huddle. They were crying. All three of them. He looked at Inma questioningly but Pili gave Inma a little shake of the head not to say anything. It must be *women's business*, so it was probably Jesús again.

He sat down on a stool by the balcony rail and dipped his spoon in the bowl. The soup was thin and watery but it had been near a ham-bone so it was better than it might have been. When he'd finished he wiped the bowl out carefully with a piece of bread. The coarse, heavy bread, more rye flour than wheat, which made everybody sad for the past.

The girls blew their noses and wiped their eyes and tried to look as if they hadn't really been crying. The last thing he'd heard before he stepped out onto the *solenar* was Inma asking, 'Does Mama know?'

A cold dread seized him. Was something wrong with Mama? It could be that. Some sickness which Mama didn't know she had, like happened to Carlos's mama. That would explain the three of them talking in secret. If they knew, then Papa must know.

But when Papa came out on the *solenar* it didn't look as if it was anything he knew about it.

Later, Albi heard Papa in the front bedroom saying 'What's the matter with the girls?' and Mama replying, 'Jesús told Pili.'

'What did he tell her?'

'That it wasn't how you said.' Mama looked through the doorway then and saw Albi. 'Walls, Ramón.'

Papa didn't say anything more.

Why did everybody keep saying that about walls having ears? What was all this talking that he wasn't supposed to hear? What Mama said meant it couldn't be about her; that meant he was the only one who didn't know. He lay in his room trying to go to sleep but the questions kept bounding about like rabbits, keeping him awake. He couldn't make sense of any of it.

'Catch me if you can, Rabbit!'

Carlos jumped off the wall and was off down the alleyway before Albi had even scrambled to his feet. He glanced back at his sheep. They were dozing in the shade, Perrita lying with her nose on her paws guarding them. He charged down the slope and round the corner into the Calle del Horno, just in time to see Carlos's *abuela* coming out of the bakehouse and Carlos ducking round her and disappearing down the steps to the Plaza. Albi went to do the same, but the *abuela* reached out and grabbed his upper arm. Her grip was like iron.

'Not so fast, young Alberto.' She glared short-sightedly into his face. 'Getting my grandson in trouble again, are you?' She was no taller than him, but she was strong.

'*Non*, señora!'

She shook him, as if she might shake a different answer out of him.

'Ow!' He tried to pull away, but she held on.

'Seems to me wherever you are, trouble follows after. You leave him alone.'

'*Si*, señora.'

She let go. He walked away, not daring to run, and she whacked him on the behind with her stick.

'You leave him be, now! Leave him be.'

By the time Albi got to the Plaza, Carlos was sitting at the base of the *pelota* wall, deep in a game of jacks. The white pebble glinted as he tossed it, scooping up the knuckle bones with his other hand.

'Ha!' said Albi, as Carlos left two behind in the dust. 'My turn.'

He dropped down, settled his back against the wall and picked up the jacks – bones out of a rabbit's back, worn smooth and dark with handling. *Your cousins*, Carlos called them, when he was being mean. Albi picked up the pebble in his left hand. He was good at this, but Carlos was even better. If Carlos had been cleverer at numbers he'd have known he was winning, game for game, but numbers went out of Carlos's head like cuckoos in the middle of summer.

Albi tossed the pebble and scooped up the jacks. Carlos tried to put him off with jokes and rude comments, but he closed his ears and kept going. Then it was Carlos's turn again. Neither of them noticed the big *Guardia* come into the Plaza, or Miguel, but when Albi looked up, the *Guardia* was sitting at a table outside Mario's bar and Miguel was standing facing him across the table, looking crabbed and crooked like a tick that's fallen off a sheep and wishes it were somewhere else.

Albi nudged Carlos.

'Sit down!' The *Guardia*'s high-coloured face made him look like a country boy but he didn't talk like one: he'd used the familiar command, even though Miguel was so much older.

Miguel scowled but he did as he was told. He didn't look scared, only annoyed, as he sat there staring down at the table. The *Guardia* glanced across at the doorway of the *Ayuntamiento* where two sentries stood, one on either side of the great arched door, their chins up as if they weren't listening, their silly hats pulled down over their noses. Their uniforms were as neat and close-fitting as skins they'd grown into, like lizards. The soldiers had been raggedy compared with this. Was that what Pili meant when she said *these Guardia look professional?*

The man stared at Miguel from under his pointed hat as he reached down and pulled the gun from his holster. He laid it on the table. Miguel watched, his face not moving.

Carlos's breath blew hot in Albi's ear. 'That's an Astra! It's a Modelo 400.'

Albi glanced sideways, distracted. How did Carlos know that?

The *Guardia* said something and Miguel's expression changed, the muscle in his jaw twitching, the way it did when he was angry. 'I didn't ask you to.'

'I'll do the talking,' the *Guardia* said. He reached out one hand and spun the pistol on the table top. The sun glinted on spinning metal as if it was a game. The man put his hand out suddenly and clamped it down on the gun.

Miguel didn't even jump. He kept his eyes on the *Guardia*'s face, and the muscle in his jaw twitched again. Once. Twice.

'Next time you cross me, *comrade*,' the *Guardia* said, making the word *comrade* sound like a joke, 'you'll be target practice. And I never miss. Now scarper.'

Miguel's chair scraped loudly as he stood up. He walked away. His bow legs gave him a jaunty swagger but the fear showed in the way he walked, so stiff and proud, as if he was waiting for the bullets to hit him in the back. Albi held his breath, his eyes fixed on the grubby white of Miguel's shirt where the burst of blood might come at any moment.

The *Guardia* got to his feet. He turned towards them as he picked up the gun. 'It's a Luger, not an Astra. German.' He lifted the gun above his head and fired into the air.

Albi jumped as if he'd been shot.

When he looked again, Miguel was still walking down the Calle San Jorge, all proud and aloof. Albi looked down at his hands shaking. He looked sideways at Carlos's white face and startled eyes. He looked at the *Guardia*, calmly putting the pistol back in his holster before he walked away.

A figure moved out shadowed doorway of the *Ayuntamiento*, the same green uniform, the same three-pronged hat. How long had he been standing there? The *Guardia* stopped in front of him and stood to attention. The other man looked him up and down with a grim face, as if it had been some kind of test. Then he nodded once, as if the answer was yes, and led the way back inside.

As soon as they'd gone, Carlos scurried over to the place where the *Guardia* had been sitting. He searched the ground and

134

pounced. When he stood up he had the spent cartridge in his hand. How could he grin like that when Miguel had nearly been shot right in front of their very eyes? Albi scrambled to his feet and walked away.

'Where are you going?' Carlos shouted after him.

'Back to my sheep,' he said.

He hovered behind Mama as she opened the front door with trembling hands. Only the *Guardia* knocked like that.

There were five of them.

'Provisions. Your turn to cough up.'

It was the man from the Plaza with the gun. He looked different up close, his rosy face not boyish after all. He had mean blue eyes and a weak chin, and he seemed to be in charge.

The *Guardia* prodded the pig in its pen under the stairs and made it squeal. They laughed and left the pig behind, the same as the soldiers had. In the corral, they stood with the poultry around their feet, looking them over. Albi felt his mama's hand grip his shoulder to stop him crying out if they picked his special hen, but they didn't choose her. They took two of the biggest birds instead. Then they stood in front of the rabbit hutches so that he couldn't see what they were doing. The *Guardia* with the red face pulled out a rabbit and turned to make sure they saw he was holding the buck. Mama let out a little cry. If they took the buck there would be no more babies, Albi knew that. The man held the rabbit by the ears, watching Mama and grinning slyly as if he might be teasing but might not. The other men were pulling two of the young rabbits that were ready for killing out of the next hutch. Albi felt his mama relax her grip on his shoulder as the buck went back in his cage. She turned away so nobody would see her face.

The men went through the whole house taking things, and all the time they were poking with their rifle butts in the grain bins and prodding in the cupboards they watched Albi and his mama as if to read things from the expressions on their faces. They went away with a sack of corn and half a sack of flour, with the rabbits and the eggs, the pots of preserves and the strings of dried figs. Albi's stomach hurt, seeing all the things they were taking. The men made Mama put her thumb-print on the sheet of paper before they left, but what difference was that supposed to make, if she couldn't read what was written on the paper?

Papa fell over the threshold when he came in at curfew and lay helpless on the kitchen floor. Mama didn't mention the *Guardia* had been.

'People with wooden legs shouldn't get drunk,' Pili said, but not to Papa's face, only afterwards to Albi and Ramona as they sorted dried beans out on the *solenar* in the pale light of evening.

She shouldn't talk about Papa like that.

'You said the *Guardia* would have a proper system,' he said, giving her the eye, 'but they haven't. Just more paper and more writing.'

Pilar pretended not to hear.

18

Hunger

'What did you eat when you were a kid?' Santi asks.

'Not fish,' Alberto says.

Santi laughs and settles back against his rock. The lines stretch out in front of them, into the quiet water. They've been here several hours without a single bite.

'We won't be eating fish either, at this rate.' Santi pulls a giant *bocadillo* out of his bag and bites noisily into the crust.

He doesn't know he's born, Alberto thinks, turning back to

the jade-green water of the dam, so bright in the sunshine he has to screw up his eyes.

'So what *did* you eat?'

'Potatoes and cabbage mostly,' he says. 'One bowl and many spoons.' Would Mari-Jé class this as telling things? 'Did you ever hear about the giant fish?'

'What giant fish?'

'There was one in this dam when I was a kid. Lots of people saw it. Carlos Perez and I did, once.'

'How big?'

Alberto stretches out his arms as far as they will go until Santi's eyes widen in amazement, then he brings his hands closer together and grins. 'About… twice the length that *bocadillo* was before you started chomping. Hey – looks like you've got a bite.'

Santi thinks he's joking but he isn't. One of the lines has tightened and it's starting to twitch.

*

'Keep it quiet it was me did the killing,' Miguel said, slicing the pig apart with a stroke of his long knife. The carcass opened up like a cupboard, all the gleaming bits hanging neatly inside. 'The *Guardia* think the soldiers took all my knives.'

Papa grinned and pulled his old hunting knife out from his one boot. 'They thought they'd had all mine too.'

Albi stared. Where had that been hidden all this time? Not in Papa's boot, surely, because he had to take his boot off to go to bed and Mama would have seen it.

Papa looked across at him and winked. 'Don't even ask. Least known safest.'

The pig turned out to be mostly fat and only little bits of meat sandwiched in-between.

'Huh,' said Mama when she came down to the byre to fetch the blood to make *morcilla* sausages. She didn't need to say, *I told you so.*

137

Papa winked at Miguel.

'She'll be glad of the lard,' he said, when Mama had gone back to the kitchen.

'Well there'll be plenty of that.' Miguel wiped the sweat from his forehead with one elbow. 'Tie that dog up, Albi.'

Perrita was licking the gobbets of blood on the cobbles where the little pig was hanging from the beam. He grabbed her and took her out. When he came back, Miguel was wiping his sharp knives on a piece of old sacking. 'Another visit last night,' Miguel said, looking at Papa. 'Checking the house again.'

Albi froze, staring at the gleaming blades of Miguel's two knives, the long one and the short one. Was it the same *Guardia* as that day in the Plaza, or different ones? If they'd found those knives they really would shoot him.

But Papa said, 'If anyone asks, we killed the pig with Albi's penknife.' He was grinning as if it was a joke. 'He'll run over with your share of the *morcilla*, Miguel. When María's finished making it.'

All the things that penknife could do... Papa shouldn't laugh.

It was late in the season for killing a pig, but they ate well for nearly a week. After that, the rest of the meat had to be cured and kept for next winter.

All round the edge of the muddy pond frogs were lying low in the shallow water, only their snouts visible. Whenever Carlos or Albi moved, the banks of the pond woke up and mud-coloured shapes plopped hastily into the water, so they were being very careful. No creeping up as close as they could and then jumping up to make the frogs leap. They weren't here for fun, they were here for an experiment.

Carlos was organising the experiment because it was his idea.

Albi watched him make the grass string into a loop and carefully anchor it in the notch at the end of the stick.

'That won't work,' he whispered.

No frogs jumped but Carlos frowned as if they had. He had the same pale blue eyes as his sister, like his mama used to have, under his thatch of untidy blonde hair. The dirt showed up more on his pale skin than it did on Albi's, and the sun made him flush red.

'It *will* work,' Carlos turned his back slightly so Albi couldn't watch.

'The frog will fall out.'

Carlos ignored him. He held the stick gingerly and eyed the bank below them for the nearest frog, then he lowered himself onto his belly and worked his way forward like a snake. This could take all day.

The nearest frog threw itself into the water and all the others followed. Plop plop plop, like a watery fuse, all the way round the pond. Plop plop. And then lots of froggy eyes watching from the water, dark heads skulking.

'You need a longer stick,' Albi said out loud. He went off to find one. But a longer stick meant a longer piece of grass string, too, and he was the one who had to make it.

An hour later they still hadn't caught anything, though once Carlos was close enough to claim he'd had the loop over the damned frog's head.

'One frog wouldn't be enough anyway,' Albi said, looking on the bright side. 'Not for two of us.'

Carlos didn't reply.

Albi watched the water, the beady eyes of the frogs, the sun mellow on the brown surface, the air very still. A dragon-fly buzzed over, and Carlos re-positioned his stick. They waited for the frogs to lollop slowly out of the water again. According to Carlos, French people liked to eat frogs' legs, but even if it was true, you'd need an awful lot of frogs. Albi rested his chin on his arms. Cutting the legs off would be like cutting up a rubber ball. He'd had a rubber ball once, a small one. It was hard and round at the beginning and then it went soft and not round. And then it wasn't there any more. Things come and go like that. He didn't remember who'd given it to him, he didn't know where it had gone in the end. Two boys in the village had proper footballs – not the usual sheep's stomach sewed up with string – but the footballs were getting old and saggy. Nothing like that had come to Rincón since the war started, and even if a pedlar came with one for sale now, nobody would have the money to buy it.

The air vibrated again with the sound of frogs as one by one they clambered out onto the mud.

He looked over his shoulder to check the sheep were still grazing quietly. Would he rather have a football or a good dinner? That was a difficult question. He was hungry all the time. It made it harder to want to play football, even when he was there to join in.

Carlos slid a little to the left and manoeuvred his stick carefully. Albi watched. It would be easier to shoot a bird with his catapult. Snares would be good too, if it was birds. Perhaps Papa could show him how to do it. Anything, to catch some meat. His stomach gurgled loudly at the thought.

Concentrating on the end of his stick, Carlos hovered just behind a very large frog which was squatting a little way up from the water's edge. Big legs on him – even one of those legs would be something. Albi watched the trembling noose inch forwards. He could see the bright stain of the frog's bulbous eye as if it was watching them, wary but not afraid. The frog shifted on his haunches and the stick stopped. How was he so fat when they were both so thin? It wasn't fair. He was only a frog, but they were boys, with nothing to eat but old cabbage and floury potatoes, and that was all there would be now until the new things grew on the *huertos*. Potatoes and cabbage and black bread, while this frog looked as if it lived off the fat of the land.

Carlos's stick hovered, Albi held his breath, the noose dropped down. For just a moment the string was over the frog's head but he leaped sideways, into the water, and all round the pond the water plopped and gurgled as frogs hurled themselves in.

'Nearly,' Albi said.

Carlos got to his feet. 'Anyway, the schoolmaster says it's a filthy French habit, eating frogs.' He threw the stick down and walked off.

Albi unknotted the string and put it in his pocket. Carlos walked away, the sunshine pale in his hair. To their right La Guadaña reared up all bright and cheerful in the afternoon light. In front of them, the hillside on the far bank of the dam loomed nearly as high. All round them the Prados stretched out wide and shallow under the cliffs, like a flat bowl tilted up towards the pure sky. Carlos looked small in the middle of it, as if he was shrinking in the sun. Albi ran after him. If they didn't eat they wouldn't grow. Behind them, the frogs in the pond barked like dogs. *Ha ha ha.*

'We could look for snails instead,' he panted when he caught up. But he knew as well as Carlos did that everybody else had been doing that all through the winter, and snaring wild rabbits and little birds too. There was hardly a snail or a rabbit left within walking distance of the village, and all the pigeons from the pigeon lofts were gone. The village was quiet without them.

'Even a fool knows it's only worth looking for snails at night. Once the weather gets warm,' Carlos said. He sounded tired and grown-up.

Albi stopped to cut grass for the rabbits at home. At least there was lots of grass, now the spring had come. The sheep trotted up behind him and pulled at the grass in his bundle. He smacked their noses crossly. They'd been eating all day, the greedy things. It was different for boys.

They came to the rim of the Prados where you could look over the edge at the dam below. Was that colour green or was it blue? He crinkled up his eyes, considering.

'That's where we should be,' Carlos said, staring at the shimmering surface. 'Lots of fish in there.'

'Mmm.' Albi had been thinking the same thing, but even

Carlos wouldn't want to fish in the dam right now. Not since the *Guardia* caught those men with their lines out and fired at them. The men had run away, up the secret paths the long way round La Guadaña until they could climb over the top and come down to the village past the waterfall, as if they'd been no further than their *tierras*.

Carlos said, 'Remember that fish?'

He nodded. A fish seen once and never to be forgotten. Him and Carlos out together, three summers ago, climbing trees near the dam when their mamas thought they were safely somewhere else. A big black fish, lazily gliding about so close to the surface they saw the fin on his back break clear of the water. It scared them so much they stayed away from the dam for a long time afterwards. Now they were bigger and braver, but they'd never seen the fish again. You might think you'd dreamed it except that other people talked of it too. When people described it, the fish was sometimes so big it was nearly a monster, sometimes it was just a large fish.

People were talking about it again now, that mythical fish. It would feast a whole family. It would feed a family for a week. It would feed a whole street and there would be meat left over for the following day. Anything was possible. 'Remember the loaves and the fishes?' Tomás said to Papa. 'We deserve a miracle in this village. It's about bloody time.'

Instead of a miracle, a new sign went up on the stable doors in the village, and another by the bridge over the river to remind people as they went out.

IT IS FORBIDDEN TO FISH IN THE DAM
ANYONE CAUGHT FISHING WILL BE PUNISHED

Sunday, and they were all in the church. Albi stood between his sisters, hot and itchy in the tight press of people. He was too short to see anything. Up by the altar, out of sight, the priest droned and El Caballero rang the altar bell because he was altar server now. 'Of course he is!' Papa said. 'He's one of them.' But he didn't say it in the church, only in the stable at home.

The droning and the long murmuring silences went on and on. Albi stared up at the flaking pink and gold paint and did sums in his head to pass the time. Three cherubs on the left, three on the right, and two over the top. That made eight, but if two flew away it would be six. It was very hot. There weren't any chairs to sit on, because what the villagers hadn't taken when the last priest ran away they had burned in a big bonfire down in the Plaza. 'Paying for it now,' Papa said, but he didn't sound sorry.

The congregation dropped raggedly to its knees, heads obediently bent, and Albi dropped with them. He looked from under his eyebrows to check that Papa was doing the same. Beyond Papa, a splash of colour caught his eye: something blue, like a piece of the sky come inside the church. He kept his eyes on it as they stood again for the Blessing. Blue of the sky, and a glimpse of coppery hair – the *Valenciana*.

At last they were all released, flooding out into the cool fresh shade of the plane trees. Albi wormed his way quickly through the crowd and down the steps. In the street he stopped as if he was waiting for his family to catch up. Yes, there was Mena in a sky-blue dress, coming down the steps on Andrés's arm. For a moment her eyes held his, and then she smiled.

She smiled, and his heart sprang up like a bird flying out of a bush.

*

Deep in the black depths of sleep the room is choked with people. Alberto can't breathe. In the press of bodies he can't see. Friends, or enemies? He doesn't know, but it feels bad. Somebody starts wailing – that will be the *abuela*. He fights his way through the crowd to find her but the house is all wrong and the room goes on for ever.

143

Suddenly Mena is there, pushing her way towards him, and they're not indoors at all but at the bottom of the dam. It feels like black trees crowding a room as thick as soldiers, but he knows he's in the water because he can't breathe. Everything is dark except for Mena in a blue dress, her bright hair tumbling about her shoulders and her eyes fixed on him. She's got a book in her hands and she is saying something but he can't hear it, only the sound of it, as if she's mocking him. Suddenly her eyes are like lasers, boring into him, and he knows for certain he's about to die.

He surfaces like a desperate fish, gulping for air.

'Alberto!' Mari-Jé's voice is urgent in his ear. 'Wake up! You're dreaming.'

He lies on his back, heart pounding, and stares at the ceiling. He feels her hand rest on his chest. Slowly, he puts his hand on top of hers. The pillow is wet. He's been crying again.

'What is it?'

He can hear she doesn't expect an answer so he doesn't say anything, just squeezes her hand.

'These dreams, Alberto. You need to see somebody.'

He shakes his head impatiently on the damp pillow. The very idea of therapists and counsellors makes him want to say nothing to nobody.

Her voice comes out of the darkness. Her practical getting-things-done voice, but he can hear the fear in it. 'Nightmares can be an early sign, you know. Of Alzheimer's.'

The dreaded word. Out in the open at last.

PART TWO

19

Las Cabreras

Albi waited in the kitchen for his mama to come in from the bakehouse with the new bread before he took yesterday's bread down to feed to the hens.

'Oh, there you are,' she said when she came in. Where else did she expect him to be?

The door to her bedroom was closed as if Papa was still sleeping but he came out just then, shutting the door behind him.

'Ah, Albi,' Papa said, as if he hadn't expected him either.

What were they up to? Had the war just ended and the Reds had won after all but nobody had remembered to tell him? It couldn't be that, the *Guardia* had marched past for curfew ending this morning, same as usual. He went down to feed the chickens.

He was collecting the eggs in the old pig pen when Mama came out to the corral with a small parcel in one hand and his satchel in the other.

'I want you to go to Las Cabreras,' she said. She stared anxiously into his face. Of course he was surprised. It was a long way to Las Cabreras. He hadn't been there for nearly a year, and never on his own. 'Can you do that, little one? The *Guardia* won't take any notice of you, they'll just think you're shepherding as usual.'

He did mind. Especially her calling him *little one*. What if they stopped him while he was out? Las Cabreras was much further than seven kilometres, and in the opposite direction from their *tierras*. They would look at his permit and be very angry. They might be angry enough to put him in the lock up. Or worse.

He stared down at the three eggs in his hands, so warm, so perfect. One of them had little freckles on one end. Didn't she love him better than to ask him that?

'Must I make the *abuelos* come back with me?'

She laughed and patted his head. 'No, big eyes. I want you to take them some bread and sausage, and some soap. I want you to tell me how they are. That's the important bit – I need to know they're all right.' She touched his cheek. 'They won't come back with you, *cariño*. You should go now before it gets hot. I'll finish doing the feeding here. Oh, and stay the night.'

He was astonished. He started to argue but she said 'Nobody will notice. Come back tomorrow afternoon as if you've been out for the day the same as usual. Here – I've put the sausage in your satchel, and some nice fresh bread for you to leave with them. And this packet is the soap.'

On the path by Ovidio's *huerto* he passed four *Guardia* coming into the village. They looked at him and away again. Just a boy and his scrawny sheep, their expressions seemed to say. They didn't even demand to see his permit.

Just a boy. He'd show them. He'd show them, one day, when he'd grown.

The sheep dawdled, snatching at the fresh young growth on either side of the path. At the turn-off up to the *Meseta* he waited, whistling to Perrita to hurry the flock. La Gorda was already there, right behind him as always. He rubbed her ears for a moment and she turned her head this way and that, enjoying it. Her mouth turned up at the corners as if she was smiling. He'd never noticed that before. The rest of the flock came up. He turned onto the *Meseta* path.

It was a steep climb. Below him the gorge was still in shadow, the cold morning wind blowing out of it, but he was climbing into the sun. The air sizzled with the smell of thyme, the rosemary was a haze of blue. A lizard ran out on the path,

148

stopped, and ran back again – no time to try to catch it, he had a long way to go. He hurried up the narrow alleyway between the rocks, climbing now like steps on a staircase. The sheep skittered after him, his little dog with her tongue all red and her black coat all shiny-hot in the sun as she followed close on their heels.

Too close.

'Get back,' he shouted.

Nobody up here to hear him. Nothing but the warm wind moaning. Up, up. The vultures wheeling above him against the fierce blue of the sky. The black crows throwing themselves off the ledges of the cliffs and flying upside down for fun. Once, an ibex jumped onto the path ahead of him and paused to look back, the sun shining into her eyes as if they were made of glass. She leaped away into the bushes. Up, up, up he climbed, till his chest hurt and his legs were tired as dry sticks.

And then suddenly he was at the top, standing on the very edge of the *Meseta* and looking down into the shadowed slit of the gorge. Only he wasn't looking too hard, in case it made him feel dizzy. Across from where he stood, the line of trees along the rim of La Guadaña seemed so close he might lean out and touch it, but the dam was tucked out of sight in the cleft of the Tajubo valley. Up here, everything was white rock and shimmering green trees stretching as far as he could see until the distances looked blue. Empty distances. Not a man or a sheep visible anywhere. Not even a house.

He stood waiting for his lungs and his legs to catch up. The sheep began to graze, La Perrita flopped down in the shade of a rock. A vulture soared out from the cliffs below him. He sat on a boulder so as to feel more solid and looked down over the edge at the great brown and black wings. If he were to lie across those wings he wouldn't reach from one wing-tip to the other. What would it be like to ride on a vulture's back? The thought made him queasy but he couldn't leave it alone. It would be like being

149

on an aeroplane. How much bigger than a vulture is an aeroplane, to fit a grown man inside it? How does an aeroplane stay up in the air when it can't flap its wings? How does a vulture, when it can?

From far away across the *Meseta* came the sound of a vehicle and Albi turned, shading his eyes with his hand. A long way away to his right, where the dirt road crossed the *Meseta* going from El Rincón to Las Hoyas, he could see a tiny plume of white dust. It was nothing to worry about, it was going in the opposite direction to Las Cabreras. The sound travelling on the wind made it seem closer than it really was but, just to be safe, he called Perrita to bring the sheep and started walking quickly across the flat ground towards the pine wood.

It was cooler among the trees, and he was less visible if a *Guardia* truck came along the track, but he had to keep the track in sight. He could get lost up here, nearly as easily as the *Guardia* could. When you're older you know where all the places are, and the paths to get there, but when you are a boy, or a stranger, you have to learn them.

His eyes darted from side to side, his ears listening: nothing but the sweet sighing of the breeze in the pines. If the *Guardia* came on mules or horses he wouldn't hear them, not if they weren't talking. And they didn't have to stick to the tracks, either. That thought wasn't nice.

The sheep were happy to walk fast, there wasn't much to eat under the trees. At the far side of the wood he turned away from the track and walked back towards the gorge, to find a place to rest where the sheep and goats could graze. He sat on a rock in the spring sunshine and ate the bread and the bit of black sausage. Then the apple, but last year's apples were shrivelled and tasteless now. He drank a little water from his leather bottle. He was still hungry. He looked in his satchel but there was only the loaf of bread and the special piece of sausage his mama had put there for his *abuelos,* and the bar of soap wrapped in a piece of sacking.

Fat pig: fat for soap. You can make a lot of things with a pig, and not all of them can be eaten. Unless you're a rat. Mama said the rats ate all the soap once, when she was a girl and still lived at Las Cabreras.

If he ate the sausage and took the *abuelos* only the soap they would never know there should have been sausage too. How could Mama expect him to grow big enough to do all Papa's jobs if he didn't have enough to eat? He stretched out his arm and looked at it. It was very skinny. He studied his shins. But it wasn't only him that was thin. Mama was too. And she might find out about the sausage. Next time she went to Las Cabreras she might ask, *Did you enjoy the sausage?* And his *abuelos* would say, *What sausage?*

He closed his satchel and stared at the horizon where Las Cabreras lay unseen in its hollow. He probably had about five kilometres still to walk. From here on it was level, but very open. The only places for hiding were the sudden little valleys like this one in front of him – not wide or deep, but it had rocks like walls on either side and it was big enough for a shepherd to walk up it, and graze his sheep too, and be invisible to anybody out on the *Meseta*.

Did water make these hidden valleys? He wished the old schoolmaster hadn't had to go away during the war. He would have known the answer.

If he couldn't get down into a little valley to hide, and if he wasn't in a wood, he'd stand out in all this emptiness like a flag-pole. If the *Guardia* came, even if he had time to jump behind a rock, the sheep would still be visible. The *Guardia* would guess there was a shepherd somewhere and probably they would want to ask the shepherd what he was doing so far away from the village. It was very dangerous, this long next bit. Even though he thought Las Cabreras might be visible when he got to the top of the next shallow rise, it would still be a long walk. He stood up and whistled. La Gorda raised her head and her bell clonked, which made the others look up and their bells sounded too.

Sheep music. He picked up his stick. If he hurried them now he could take longer coming back. If he didn't stay the night.

Why had Mama told him to do that? Why did she want him to do something that was against the law? It wasn't like her. It didn't feel right and he didn't want to do it.

Las Cabreras looked as if nobody was living there any more, the houses tightly shuttered and padlocks on the gates to the corrals. But his *abuelo*'s small flock was grazing the bright green grass by the spring, where the water trickled noisily from the stone trough. Albi left his sheep to mingle with his *abuelo*'s and walked up the short lane between the locked buildings to his grandparents' house at the end. There were no voices anywhere. No cattle lowing. Just some chickens, squabbling out of sight.

The door to his grandparents' corral wasn't barred like the others. He lifted the wooden latch and pushed the door inwards.

His *abuela*, dressed in black as usual, was standing in the middle of the corral.

'Who is it?' Her voice was tight and scared.

'It's me, *Abuela*. Albi.'

'Albi!' She opened her arms for him to come and be hugged. When he got up close he saw her eyes were as milky as an old dog's.

'Fetch your *abuelo*,' she said. 'He's chopping wood in the byre. You'll have to shout – he's gone very deaf. I can't see and he can't hear.'

He went to the door of the byre.

His *abuelo* jumped. Then he shouted 'Hombre!' and threw down the axe. He hugged Albi tight, his old arms trembling. 'All this way,' he kept saying. 'You've come all this way all on your own?'

On the old bench against the front wall of the house, under the gnarled grapevine which was breaking into bright new leaf over

152

their heads, Albi's *abuelo* sat on one side of him, his *abuela* on the other, patting his knees and both talking at once. He gave them Mama's packages, glad now about the sausage because they looked so tiny, the two of them, as if they hadn't been eating. If *Abuela* couldn't see any more, how could she do any cooking?

She felt inside the parcel. 'Soap!'

Abuelo opened the other. 'Sausage!'

'How long can you stay?' they both kept asking, but he didn't quite answer because he didn't quite know. Mama thought he couldn't do the long walk twice in one day, but he could, and surely it was safer to do what the *Guardia* said.

'I have to be home by curfew,' he said. 'Did you know there is a curfew now?' His *abuela* patted his knee as if she did but *Abuelo* went on talking as if he hadn't heard.

'We will eat out here,' *Abuelo* said, 'under the grapevine. Bring the olive oil, *Abuela*, to eat with María's bread. And some of that new cheese you made.'

Albi pricked up his ears. Cheese! They hadn't had any at home for ages. Maybe he'd stay after all. Food was special at Las Cabreras. All those feasts they used to have, eating in the shade of the grapevine in the paved corral at the front of the house, with a red and white check cloth to make the table mind its manners and forget that this morning it had been used as a work-bench for mending an old boot, or disembowelling a rabbit. Big meals with lots of people, when they came up from Rincón to help with the harvest, or at Easter to plant the potatoes. Rich cheeses made of ewes' milk. Mutton stews full of herbs. Great legs of ham, and glazed apple tarts. But today there was no table-cloth, no ham, no stew. *Abuela* brought out the oil and the new white cheese, feeling her way with her hands but not like El Ciego did, she was timid, and she made mistakes.

Albi poured some oil on Mama's sweet-smelling bread. The oil was musty and tasted rancid as if it had been kept too long in a bad place. He bit into the cheese to take the mustiness away but the cheese tasted worse. He chewed and swallowed, trying not to retch, but their old faces were so full of pleasure at him being there, they seemed not to notice anything was wrong. *Abuela* chattered on about the old days, *Abuelo* lit his pipe. Albi watched his *abuela* feeling with her hands for the things she couldn't see. It never used to be like this. *Abuelo*, who used to hear the sheep bells from the house when the flock left off grazing and started to wander, hardly heard a thing that was said, though he pretended he had.

When they'd eaten, and Albi had managed to refuse more cheese without it sounding rude, *Abuela* said he should go inside and lie down and have a little nap because it was such a long walk home, but *Abuelo* went on talking, so he couldn't.

At last *Abuelo* went off to relieve himself in the lane. *Abuela* giggled like a naughty girl. 'Come on,' she said, 'I need a nap even if he doesn't.'

He didn't see what was wrong at first. The kitchen was so dark with the shutters closed. The only glimmer was the pale square at the back of the hearth from the light coming down the chimney. But he could smell what he couldn't see. He could smell dogs, and musty food, and badly preserved meat going rotten, and clothes not washed. He could smell urine, too, and not from a dog or a cat.

After a while his eyes got used to the gloom. He lay on the little bed against the wall, which his *abuela* kept for visitors. They had brought their bed down to the kitchen too, she didn't explain why. In the dim light he could see unwashed clothes and sheets everywhere, piled up on the table and on all the chairs. There were flitches of salt mutton hanging from the hooks in the ceiling. That was where the worst smell was coming from. He was sure he could see maggots wriggling, even in the dark.

He forced himself to stay on the narrow bed, pinching his nose and breathing though his mouth, until he was sure his *abuela* was properly asleep. As soon as she was snoring soundly he staggered outside, gulping fresh air.

From the byre came the sound of the axe. He went to help his *abuelo*.

Abuelo stopped chopping to wipe the sweat off his forehead and let Albi take a turn with the axe.

'She doesn't know. It isn't only that she can't see. She can't smell either. She won't let me clean the house. She says that's a woman's work.'

Albi nodded and raised the axe. He split the log. He split a second, wondering who had sawn the logs to length. The knotty pine was difficult to split.

After the fifth log *Abuelo* took the axe back. 'Save your strength, lad. It's a long walk home.' He put out a thin hand to touch Albi's arm. 'Don't tell your mother about *Abuela*. No point her fretting.'

'But *Abuelo*!' he blurted out, seizing hold of his *abuelo*'s hand. 'You can't stay here like this! You should both come back with me and live in our house.'

His *abuelo* stared at the mud floor and waited until Albi took his hand away. 'We were born here. Both of us. Did you know that? Me in this house, your *abuela* in the house on the end. We've lived all our lives here.' He looked up from under his shaggy white eyebrows and his big moustache twitched. '*All* our lives, lad. And that's the way we want it. Understand?'

He would have stayed, if only the kitchen didn't stink so. He hated to leave them almost more than he hated the stink. But it wasn't only the kitchen that scared him: his grandparents smelled old and musty. It felt all wrong, this place that was once so full of life deserted, and that sour smell in it.

He lingered, sitting on the bench under the grapevine in the afternoon sun with his grandparents, one on each side of him, stroking his arms and patting his knees as they told stories about Mama when she was a girl, and her sister and her brothers who went away. He didn't like to leave them, but in any case he confused the time. The light was different up here on the *Meseta* where there were no tall cliffs for the sun to drop behind. It was still quite high when *Abuelo* came with him to the water trough to help part out his sheep.

20

The Secret Valley

Albi walked a long way, his nerves strained with watching and listening for distant vehicles, before the realisation dawned that it was much later than he'd thought. He stopped and stared about him. The sun hung low over the horizon. At his feet, in the shadowed crevices of the limestone, the violets looked black. La Guadaña lay below him now, he was standing so high up on the top of the world. The cliffs shone with the afterglow of the sun that came after curfew, if you looked out from the *solenar*. Their safe, shady *solenar*, where they could sit out of sight of the whole world and look at the cliffs which had once protected them, but now the *Guardia* marched about in the spaces between the cliffs and rode their mules and horses along the paths and none of it was safe any more.

He thought of his grandparents' house, and the hollowness of the empty houses on either side, and whether he should tell his mama, even though his *abuelo* had told him so sternly he mustn't. It wasn't just the smell; it didn't feel safe there any more. He started to run, wishing he was home with his mama and his papa, with his sisters, even. The sheep ran obediently behind him.

After a while he stopped. He was already too late. He turned and began to run back the way he'd come, towards Las Cabreras. If he could get there quickly enough his *abuelo* wouldn't have bolted the door. *Abuelo* said he always bolted it when the sun went down and after the sun had gone down he wouldn't open it to anyone – *not to anyone*, he'd repeated sternly – but the sun hadn't quite dropped to the horizon yet. Albi ran, and then he walked for a while holding his side because it hurt. He ran again. Even that stinking kitchen would be better than being outside all night on his own.

He was halfway back across the open ground when he heard an engine. He jumped behind the nearest juniper bush and crouched down, calling Perrita. The sheep drifted away and started grazing. He held Perrita tight and peered through the top of the bush: the track stretched, as naked and empty as before, all the way to Las Cabreras on his left, and on his right to where it dropped out of sight over a long limestone bank.

The sound of the truck faded. He stood up, thinking he would whistle to the sheep and go on, but the sound came again, very close suddenly, climbing the slope towards him. He ducked down and grabbed Perrita to stop her barking. The vehicle came closer, closer. He waited, expecting it to brake and the doors to bang open as the *Guardia* jumped out to see who was out here with sheep, so far from the village, at this forbidden hour. But the vehicle didn't stop. It went right past.

He crept out from behind his bush. It was a *Guardia* truck, bumping in the direction of Las Cabreras. He had so hoped it would be somebody who didn't matter, even though he knew that wasn't possible. It *could* only be the *Guardia,* or El Caballero, because they were the only people who had petrol now.

He thought of the truck going to Las Cabreras and felt sick. *Abuelo* said that he and *Abuela* always hid in the house with the door bolted if the *Guardia* came. If they poked about in the outhouses and corrals or if they didn't, his *abuelo* said, he had no idea. 'Whatever they get up to they never bother us.' But he was deaf and *Abuela* couldn't see. How could they know when the *Guardia* were coming, or when they had gone away again?

Albi sat down suddenly on the ground. He couldn't go back to Las Cabreras, not until the truck came back this way again, and even then, how would he know they hadn't left a guard behind? Or the truck might be going beyond Las Cabreras – the *Guardia* might not come back at all. He wasn't going to wait to find out. He jumped up, whispered to Perrita to bring the sheep, and started running back towards Rincón. If he could get to the pine trees he would surely be able to find somewhere to hide until morning.

As he ran across the wide open *Meseta*, the light failing fast now, he remembered the secret valley near the place where he'd stopped to eat his breakfast this morning. There was grazing in the bottom of that valley. He could stay out of sight there, no matter how many trucks rushed backwards and forwards along the track.

Rushing trucks. His grandparents all alone at Las Cabreras. Wouldn't his mama want him to go back and make sure they were all right? He shut the thought out. Perrita brought the flock after him as he ran towards the edge of the gorge, looking for the opening into the secret valley. It was getting dark. Night birds churred close to the ground. A moon like a three-parts cheese had risen above La Guadaña but it wasn't lighting anything much, yet, just making shadows.

The secret valley wasn't where he'd thought it was. It opened up so suddenly in front of him he nearly fell into it. He turned his back on La Guadaña and walked back along the edge of the little valley looking for a safe way down, but the white rock dropped away below him about thirty feet, sheer as a wall.

At the top end of the valley the cliffs shallowed until natural ledges made wide steps going down. He jumped from ledge to ledge in the deepening dusk, with the sheep and goats behind him, until the rock gave way to grass and stone walls. A long time ago this valley had been terraced. The grass was lush, it was a good place for a shepherd to hide his sheep and he stopped hurrying. At his elbow, La Gorda's breath came hot and moist. He called Perrita close and let the sheep spread out to eat their fill.

Suddenly Perrita froze. She was staring off to one side, growling deep in her throat. He peered into the shadows. There was nothing, just an old wall built up under an overhang in the cliff, one of the field shelters made by the ancients to keep out of the sun. The white rock loomed in the nearly-dark. He, too, had heard something – a murmur, a movement, a faint clink of metal – all of these things, or nothing, he couldn't tell. Perrita went on growling. He reached out and took hold of her by the scruff of the neck in case it was a wild boar, keeping his eyes fixed on the confusion of shadows. He saw the paleness of the rock and the dark of the shadow. He saw the outlines of the stones in the wall under the ledge, placed one on top of another by unknown hands, maybe hundreds of years ago. Resting on the top of the wall there was a small, perfect circle of metal. A gun. Pointing straight at him.

21

The *maquis*

'It's just a kid,' the voice said. 'Just a kid and his sheep.'

Other voices came spilling out of the rock shelter and the valley filled with moving shadows. Albi hung on to Perrita to stop her running at them. She struggled in his arms, growling fiercely.

A man shouted to someone further down the valley, 'It's all right! It's only a kid. He's brought us dinner.'

Who were they? Not voices from round here.

A match flared. Faces leaned in to light cigarettes. He saw the gleam of an eye, a fall of black hair, the dark puff of a beard. Smelled the sweat and the unwashed clothes, and the strange, pungent smell of their tobacco. This wasn't the *Guardia*. And they weren't soldiers, though they had at least one gun between them and they had matches. They must be the *maquis*.

He'd told them over and over how he came to be here, but they didn't seem to believe him.

He'd tried hard not to mention his *abuelos*. There were stories of the *maquis* stealing things from farms on the *Meseta*, it was better for them to think nobody lived at Las Cabreras. But it made it hard to explain why he was so far from El Rincón. For the summer grazing, he'd said, over and over, but then they'd found the sheep's cheese in his satchel. They were hungry men. They tore the cheese apart. There were seven of them and it was a small cheese. He watched them in the rosy the light of the campfire. (Another match, he'd noticed, shocked at the wastefulness of it.) The men chewed on the cheese and he waited for them to spit it out. If they weren't so hungry, they said, they would.

'Doesn't your mother make better cheese than this?' the big man said. The one with arms and hands like a blacksmith's and a red kerchief knotted round his brawny neck.

'My mama didn't make it,' he said indignantly. He felt better now he could see their faces. He counted again: yes, seven. And they were only men, however dirty and unshaven. Men like the *regresados* in the village: they were on the right side.

'I saw a *Guardia* truck,' he said, wanting to be helpful. 'On the track.'

'I know where you've been,' the blacksmith man said suddenly.

'Those old *abuelos* in that place by the spring. They your grand-parents, by any chance?'

'Yes,' Albi croaked, but the big man was laughing too loudly to hear.

'I knew it!' he said. 'Once tasted, never forgotten.'

The others laughed too. The man with his arm in a sling said something and they all roared again. Had these men been to Las Cabreras and his grandparents had given them food? His *abuelos* said they didn't see anybody. They'd lied to him.

Or had they only said they didn't see the *Guardia* and he didn't think about the *maquis*?

The big man stood up saying he had business to attend to. 'Throw on the wood, lads. Throw on the wood.'

They left Albi alone then and threw wood on the fire until it was blazing. He watched the sparks rising into the dark sky and wondered that they were not afraid of being seen. The man with the glasses had a guitar on his knee and was quietly strumming. Soon they were all singing. One of the men told Albi to sing too, but he didn't want to. He wanted to go home. He wanted to be safely in the kitchen with his mama and his papa and his sisters. The guitar man kept looking at him over the top of his guitar. The glinting lenses of his little round spectacles made him look wise, like the old schoolmaster. Except this man wasn't so old.

The singing was loud enough for the *Guardia* to hear, even if they hadn't noticed the fire.

The men kept looking at him as if there was some kind of joke that they all knew about and he didn't. He stood up and said he thought, if they didn't mind, he'd be getting home now.

'You sit down,' a sharp voice said. The man with brown hair and a scraggy little beard which looked as if it wasn't used to being on his chin. '*You* won't be going anywhere tonight.'

There was a rifle lying on the ground next to scraggy-beard. Was it the same one? Did they only have one gun between the seven of them? He sat down, his legs suddenly too wobbly to

161

hold him up. He'd had a bad thought. If the *Guardia* came they would think he was one of the *maquis* and they would shoot him too. The men went on singing, the fire blazed. Albi sat hunched up on the ground, trying to decide what to do but not managing to think of anything.

After a while, when nothing happened, the crippling fear in his chest eased a little and settled in his guts instead. Being hungry didn't help. The bread and cheese *Abuela* had put in his bag for his supper on the way home had all been eaten by the men, even while they mocked.

The big blacksmith man loomed over him and flung something on the ground. 'You'll want this back. I've borrowed the rest.'

Albi looked down. One glassy eye, filming over with dust, stared out over the proud arch of La Gorda's nose. Her severed neck still had the bell collar on it, but all of the rest of her was missing.

He screamed and leapt up, threw himself at the big man. Hands reached out to grab him but he darted away. The firelight blurred as he whirled back at the man, kicking and dodging, flailing punches, Perrita at his side snarling and snapping in a fury of black fur.

The blacksmith man laughed. He picked Albi up under one arm, and Perrita by the scruff of the neck with his free hand, and thrust the two of them on the ground by the fire. 'Keep them quiet, you lot, while I get on with the business.'

Many hands pulled Albi roughly down. Somebody kicked Perrita. She would have bitten him if another man hadn't grabbed her by the snout and held on to her. Somebody shouted, 'Control your dog or I'll shoot it. And you as well if you don't shut up and sit down.'

It was the older man shouting, the man with one arm in a sling. He had a pistol in his good hand and he meant it, he wasn't just saying it. Albi grabbed Perrita and sat down quickly. Kept very still, then. Perrita shaking in his arms, whether from fear or from anger he couldn't tell. He sank his chin down until it rested on Perrita's warm doggy-smelling head, so it wouldn't show he was trembling just as much as she was, and stared furiously at the men. One by one they sat back down. The glasses man picked up his guitar and pulled a face at him as if to say, *Don't fret, lad.*

How could he not fret when they'd murdered his best sheep! Why had they done that? His bell-sheep. La Gorda who'd been his ever since he'd kept her alive on a bottle when she was a tiny scrap. Who nuzzled him with her lips the same way she did her newborn lambs, now that she was big and had lambs of her own every spring. La Gorda who stood over him as he lay on his back in the sun, flicking her ears if she thought it was time to move on and he didn't. Who he loved more than his sisters (except Inma), and who loved him more than they did because she was his friend and she was with him every day, more than anybody else in the whole world apart from La Perrita.

And now, behind him, the big blacksmith man was skinning his lovely Gorda as if he was undressing her. Though she wasn't the same without her head on. And he was talking all the time. 'Cutlets tonight, lads. We'll take our fill of them. And make a big fire tomorrow and the next night and spit-roast the shoulders and legs. Sausages with the rest. I'll use the guts for skins. Not as good as pig skins but we'll have to make do. I'll be needing saltpetre, though, if I'm to make sausages. Any chance of you getting some for me, Toni?'

The man with the glasses and the guitar winked at Albi. 'Vicente used to be a butcher.'

A butcher, not a blacksmith.

'Used to be? Still am, lad. Butcher of Fascist Pigs, that's me.'

They talked over his head, then, about Fascists, and pigs, and how long it was since they'd eaten as well as they were going to eat tonight. The butcher man squatted on the ground at the edge of the firelight, cutting and slicing. The smell of raw meat was strong in the cool air. Albi tried not to let it come inside his nose.

The man with the spectacles kept saying things to cheer him up. He didn't want to be cheered. Tears kept filling his eyes so that he couldn't see. What happens to your thoughts when your head isn't on your body any more? Where was the real La Gorda now? Not in the ragged pile of guts on the ground beside the butcher. Not the red bits that were beginning to sizzle over the flames. None of that could be his Gorda.

A terrible fragrance pushed the innards-smell away, assaulting all his senses with pangs of hunger. 'She was two weeks off lambing,' he shouted. 'You *never* kill a sheep just before she lambs!'

The butcher scowled into the fire as he juggled chops on spears of juniper wood. 'Course not, kid. But a skinny old ewe who's put all she's got into her lambs is a damn sight better than the nothing *we* were about to have for supper, so shut your trap and stop trying to teach me my business. Come on, cook yourself one of these.' The butcher thrust a bloody cutlet in his direction but Albi turned his back. The others were busy spiking chops on sticks and holding them over the flames but he pretended they were all in another place he didn't know about. He pretended he was all on his own here, just as he'd thought he was going to be. He sent them all to hell in his mind, pretending the fire was hell and they were burning in it. It wasn't only that it was his favourite sheep, it was the shameful waste of the lamb not-born that might-have-been. Two lambs, even: the butcher had said *lambs*. Wasted, after all that precious fodder through the long winter. And the meat, would be tough and stringy, mostly bone and gristle. La Gorda had been putting all her condition into the lambs, the way a good ewe does.

But the scent of the sizzling cutlets clawed its way into his nostrils, no matter how he tried to squeeze them shut. Through his nostrils and down into his stomach. All his juices sat up and crowed to be fed but he would never ever accept anything off that butcher. He wasn't a cannibal.

The glasses man put his guitar down and took two chops off the fire. He peered sideways at Albi and quietly passed him a smoking cutlet on the end of a stick. Albi looked away but the man leaned over and nudged him with him one elbow. Albi wouldn't look at him but he took the greasy chop and took a bite. Then another.

'Eat up, comrades,' shouted the butcher, piling more branches on the embers. 'Hey, Student! You look after yourself, the kid can cook his own.'

The glasses man grinned and took no notice. He had two more chops cooking on his sticks now. He winked at Albi. Was he really a student? He was much too old to be in school. The meat sizzled and the flames crackled and sparked. The fire lit up the white rocks until it looked as if they were running with blood. Seven men round the flames. Only seven, though they had seemed such a crowd at the beginning. He sneaked a look at each of them in turn but he'd never seen any of them before.

'Hey,' said a voice out of the darkness above them, making him jump. 'Don't forget us! Don't pig the lot before we get a look-in!'

So there were more of them out there in the dark. Good thing he hadn't tried to run away.

Everybody was joking and laughing now, the voices growing garbled.

'The meat is making them drunk,' the glasses man said in a low voice. 'We've eaten nothing at all for two and a half days.'

Meat was making them drunk? He'd supposed it was the wineskin they were passing round. The butcher man took it and poured a stream of ruddy liquid into his open mouth before passing the skin to the glasses man. The glasses man drank. Then he thrust the skin at Albi. Albi hesitated. His mama didn't like him to drink wine, but he was very thirsty and he would feel silly drinking water from his own little wineskin. He took the proffered skin and poured a thin stream into his mouth. The wine had a bitter, earthy taste. He took another mouthful and it tasted better. The man was playing his guitar again. One by one, the others joined in the singing.

When at last they stopped singing, the glasses man was still strumming quietly on his guitar. 'You all right, lad?' he murmured.

Albi refused to answer. Of course he wasn't, he'd just eaten his best friend. Well, next best after Perrita.

After a while the man said, 'What's your name?'

He wanted to pretend not to hear, but the man had been kind to him. So he told him.

'Albi.' The glasses man strummed gently. 'Is there a girl called Carmen in your village who came from Valencia last year to marry someone? I don't know his name.'

He couldn't mean Mena, surely? Nobody else had come from Valencia to marry a man from El Rincón.

The man said, 'We were at the same Medical School in Valencia, Carmen and me, studying to be doctors. Before the war started. It must be somewhere round here, the place her husband farms. This side of Las Hoyas, anyway. Such a waste,' he added. 'She'd have made a bloody good doctor.'

Albi peered at the glasses man's face and saw he wasn't laughing. It couldn't be *his* Mena the man was talking about. Anyway, how could a woman be a doctor, especially a pretty one who didn't even know how to wash laundry. So he just shrugged.

'Hey, Student!' shouted a voice. 'Let's have another song.'

The glasses man struck four loud chords and the singing began again.

The Student shook him awake. 'You'd better go now.'

A thin streak of light showed along the eastern horizon, lifting the night-clouds on its back. When had it gone cloudy?

When had he stopped hearing the singing?

In the tired light he could see the shapes of men lying wrapped

166

in blankets all round where the fire had been. Someone had put a blanket over him too. He crawled out of it, confused.

The Student said, 'It was my turn to watch. I didn't need the blanket.'

He was a kind man, then. The nights on the *Meseta* are very cold in April, even if you're awake and watching.

The nights are cold even if you have just stuffed yourself silly. With a horrible jolt, Albi remembered. He stood up in a panic. Where was the rest of the flock? Had the Butcher killed them all? But then he saw them lying cudding in the half-light as if they didn't care that a friend of theirs was lying all in bones chewed bare and discarded on the grass. He counted the sheep and goats quickly. Eleven. Only eleven now, without La Gorda. He looked at the bones on the greasy, trampled grass. Does a battlefield feel like this, your heart all hurting at the bits left behind? He bent down over La Gorda's head, lying on the ground, the eyes gone dull. A big black slug was crawling over her proud nose. He carefully took hold of the bell, his hand on the clapper so as not to wake anyone, and drew the collar off the severed neck. He wrapped the bell in the sack he used to keep the rain off, to stop it making any noise, and put the bundle and the wooden collar into his satchel.

The Student peered down at him. 'Ready now?'

He nodded.

The man put his hand on Albi's shoulder, but gently. 'Say nothing to anyone. You didn't see us, you slept out here on your own. The ewe fell over the cliff, that's why you're going back one short. If you say anything,' he whispered, bending forwards and jerking his head towards the others, 'they'll know it was you who told. Understand?'

Albi nodded again.

'Good,' said the man, and he ruffled Albi's hair briefly. 'Off you trot now.'

All round where the fire had been the grass was trampled. If any *Guardia* looked over into the valley they'd see the *maquis* had been here, even if they didn't see them still. Albi wondered why the men weren't more careful. But then, who would know that the valley was here, if they hadn't ever been here before?

Unless somebody told them.

He was scared, suddenly. He wanted to be somewhere else, but the sheep were looking at him as if something was missing and they didn't follow when he walked off. It was La Gorda, of course. They wanted La Gorda. He didn't dare call or whistle in case he woke the Butcher from his snoring, but Perrita understood. She ran round the flock. The goats came hurrying after Albi and the ewes followed the goats. He glanced back at the glasses man and hesitated. It wasn't safe here, but it was safer than where he was going. Ahead of him the night was still sleeping blackly in the gorge. The *Guardia* wouldn't be sleeping, they would be prowling about. The darkness was still theirs.

22

The Molino

The stream by the Molino was wide and shallow but the sheep jostled, drinking noisily, and wouldn't cross. All Albi could do was wait, even though they were right next to the mill and somebody might see them.

He was almost too tired to care. He'd gone the long way round for fear of any *Guardia* seeing him so early in the morning. It had been rough going, crossing the river above the gorge and scrambling up through the thick scrub to skirt along the base of La Guadaña, coming down off the Prados at a safe distance from the dam. He'd taken the bells off the remaining bell-sheep and the two goats and put them in his satchel with La Gorda's bell, muffling them with with the sack so they didn't clank.

The church bell had already rung for curfew ending but it felt all wrong to be out at this time and trying to get into the village when he should have been safely in the house thinking about coming out. He waited for the sheep to finish drinking, his head as thick as an old blanket so his thoughts didn't come straight.

'Boy!'

The blind man was standing in the doorway at the back of the mill, his face turned up towards the sky.

'Boy! What are you doing?'

Did the blind man know which boy he was? His thoughts fell over themselves, all in a tangle, but he couldn't refuse to speak so he said the truth. 'I'm letting the sheep drink, señor.'

The blind man tilted his head as if he was listening. 'Why have you taken the bells off?'

Albi looked at the listening face. He looked at the drinking sheep. He looked at Perrita trying to hassle them across. 'I have the bells in my bag, señor.'

'That isn't what I asked.' The blind man seemed to consider for a minute. 'Turn them onto my meadow but put the bells back on them first. And then come inside. Quickly now.'

El Ciego went inside the back of the Molino where Albi had never been.

He could pretend he'd misunderstood and go straight home, but the blind man had ordered him and it would be disrespectful if he disobeyed, his papa would be angry. So he put the bells back on and told Perrita to guard the sheep, then he went to the door by which El Ciego had disappeared into the mill.

'Señor?'

A delicious smell was wafting down the stairs.

El Ciego, in his kitchen, looked more ordinary, a tired man getting old. His thin hair was greying and his features were rugged.

Albi sat at the table, good bread in front of him and a ration of ham that was neither too fat nor too dry but tender as if it had been freshly cut, and kept his eyes down. The blind man was busy at the fire. He brought a pan with an omelette in it and slid half of the omelette onto Albi's plate, and the other half onto a plate for himself.

'Eat, boy. Eat.'

So he ate. And when he had eaten, El Ciego gave him more. More bread, and even more ham. And a cup of mint tea to wash it all down.

'Where have you been, boy?' El Ciego said at last. 'You were coming from the wrong direction, with no bells on the sheep as if you did not wish to be heard. They would notice you for that. Where have you been?'

Albi had his story ready. He'd been thinking about it all through the omelette and all through the ham. He could tell this half of his story and it not be such a bad thing to do. He'd gone to see his *abuelos*, that was the safer secret to tell – that they were still living at Las Cabreras even though the *Guardia* said they mustn't. El Ciego might be able to make them come home, if he knew.

'So why were you creeping back so early in the morning? Did your *abuelos* throw you out before dawn?'

Albi kept his eyes down, glad the blind man couldn't see his face.

'Or did you spend time with someone else on the way?'

He stopped breathing, staring at his empty plate on the table, which had bread-crumbs all over it, and a bit of fluff.

'Or with several someones, perhaps? Half a dozen or more. And one of them a big man who was once a butcher? The men who smoke the bad tobacco which is mostly asphodel root that I can smell on you now. As the *Guardia* would smell it too.'

Albi's chin sank onto his chest. The secret wanted to jump out, he had to hold it down with his chin and with both of his hands gripping the table edge.

'Because,' said the blind man, 'it seems to me you had twelve animals in the flock when you passed above my garden yesterday morning on the path to the waterfall. But today, coming back by another path entirely, you have only eleven.'

Albi looked at the eyes which could not see. He looked at the ears which seemed to hear more than seeing people hear. El Ciego knew. He knew about there being perhaps eight or nine men, and one of them the Butcher. He knew about La Gorda. He wouldn't be telling anything the blind man didn't know already.

El Ciego said as if he'd answered (though he'd said nothing), 'And did you see anything else?'

'I saw *Guardia* up on the *Meseta*, passing in a truck.'

'In which direction?'

'First, in the morning, going towards Las Hoyas. Then again in the evening, going towards Las Cabreras.'

'How many in the truck?'

'I didn't see.'

The blind man rubbed his chin and seemed to be thinking. His eyes didn't change but his listening face went inside itself, as though he was looking at the inside of his own head.

'Good,' he said at last. 'You didn't tell me the things you must not say. And you didn't tell me the things you do not know. Good. Well done.'

The sun was quite high when Albi called Perrita to gather up the flock. He crossed the river and toiled up the steep lane to the village. The blind man had made him rub his clothes all over with an onion cut in half, to hide the smell of the tobacco on him, and told him to roll in the patch of mint at the back of the Molino as well. He felt stupid doing these things but it was worth it when he passed the sentries on the edge of the village and they

171

barely looked up. Only a boy, their bored expressions seemed to say.

In the village, the streets were busy with late morning: women coming back from the wash house, old people sitting out in the streets in the spring sunshine. In their house, the *abuela* was being querulous upstairs in the back room and Papa was being cross downstairs in the byre, but he was surprised out of his crossness when Albi came in with the sheep and goats.

'Back so soon, son?' Papa said, following him out to the corral. He sounded disappointed, as if he meant *too soon*.

Albi said what the blind man had told him to say: that he'd been caught out yesterday on his way home (like he really had), and he'd had to hide all night and come back only when it was late enough to be safe.

'But why didn't you stay at Las Cabreras? Your mama wanted you to stay with the *abuelos*.'

All the secrets filling him to overflowing and he must not tell, so he told this smallest one. How the *abuelos* lived in a dirty house and the one couldn't see any more and the other could not hear.

'*Madre mia*,' said Papa. 'Don't tell your Mama. She worries about them enough as it is.'

So then he knew he'd done the right thing because the small secret made him safe. He could keep the big secret deep inside, only the blind man knowing it. The blind man wouldn't tell anyone else. And then Albi told his papa La Gorda had fallen over the cliff, as the blind man had ordered him to say, and the glasses man too, and after that his papa was so angry with him for being careless that he wouldn't have noticed a secret even if it had jumped up and bitten him on the nose.

23

Amapola

Albi took the cattle down to the Plaza to drink at the *fuente,* then brought them back, tied them up again, and gave them their hay and some oats. All he wanted to do was lie down and go to sleep. But then he saw the wall.

The far end of the byre was solid rock, with the rest of their house built up on it. The rock had a hollow in it, like a small cave scooped out. In the old days a stone wall had partitioned the cave off to make a bit of a cellar for storing wine, but then the wall fell down and nobody got round to building it again, though the stones still lay where they had fallen long before Albi was born. Now the wall had been built up, and not leaving a doorway this time. All the jobs to be done at this time of the year and Papa had built a wall they didn't even need.

'Why?'

Papa hovered as if he hadn't finished building the wall and was waiting for Albi to get out of his way. 'Why what?'

'Why have you blocked off the little cellar?'

Papa glanced behind him as if he'd forgotten the new wall was there, and shrugged. 'Just tidying the place up. If you've finished with those beasts your rabbits want feeding.'

Albi was in the corral with the rabbits, filling their water pots from the big jar in the corner, when Papa came out with a secret look on his face.

'Tell you what,' Papa whispered, glancing up at the *solenar* where Ramona and Pili had come home from work and were squabbling, 'Let's not say anything about the cellar and see how long it takes them to notice, shall we?'

Albi sighed. So many secrets, it hardly hurt him to keep another if it amused Papa, but the girls rarely came down to the byre. Their hours in the factory were long and they were always very tired when they came home. It would take them ages to notice.

After supper Mama took a candle and went downstairs with a pot of leftover food. Albi was offended. Feeding the hens was his job, even if he was very tired. And that was good food too – April food, chard and borage and new little white onions. He'd have eaten it if he'd known it was going to the hens. Mama came back with the empty pot. She might not have shut the chickens up properly against the polecats and the genets. He went down to check, but the gate to the poultry pen was as he'd left it and the birds were all sleeping quietly on their perches. There was no sign of the food anywhere, not on the floor and not in the wooden trough.

When he went down in the morning, Mama was sitting on her rush-seated chair in the corner of the byre. Such a strange place to be, between the beasts and the wall, saying her prayers. The next evening she was there again, murmuring. For a moment, spookily, God's voice seemed to murmur back and Albi went cold all over. But then she said '*Madre mia* but you scared me, creeping about like that!' as if it was his fault, when he hadn't done anything worse than having the speckledy hen up in his room.

Maybe she was going crazy. It might be what Pili and Ramona and Inma were talking about, that time they were crying on the *solenar*. He looked into her face.

She didn't look mad, only sort of glinty-eyed, as if she was excited.

The next day she made some little cakes, the first for a long time, even though there was hardly any sugar left and they needed what there was for their mint tea. That was quite a mad thing to do.

*

'But why won't you come?' Carlos demanded.

'Because I'm watering the cow.'

Not that Amapola seemed bothered about going to drink. Albi slapped his hand down on her bony back, exasperated. It should be obvious he couldn't come down to the bridge, he wasn't free like Carlos was. Even Carlos was supposed to be chopping kindling for his *abuela* right now, but he was going to pretend he'd forgotten. Wasn't he scared of being beaten by his papa? Albi thumped the cow again and shouted at her until she began to plod slowly up the street on her quiet feet.

'When you've watered the cow, then,' Carlos said.

'Then I'll be watering the oxen. And after that the mule.'

Secretly, he was glad. So long as they were in a public place like this it wasn't too bad, but if they went off by themselves he might find himself saying something he shouldn't. The big secret he'd been carrying round inside him for five nights and five days wanted to jump out into the daylight: *I was with the maquis. I had a real true aventura.* The words rattled round and round inside his head, and sometimes in his mouth.

'You're no fun any more,' Carlos said, and stalked away up the street, hands thrust deep in pockets, shoulders hunched.

Albi watched him go. The cow was dallying again, scratching her chin on the corner of the wall. He took hold of her tail and twisted it round his hand to make her walk on.

When they got to the fountain Miguel was there, watering his mule. He glanced across at Amapola and laughed. 'Look at the way she's loosening up. You'll have a calf by sunset tomorrow.'

Albi looked but he couldn't see anything, except that Amapola's udder was tight and pink-skinned with the milk inside it, but it had been like that for several days. He tried to look as if he knew what Miguel was talking about.

There was nobody in the house when he got back after watering the oxen and the mule, only the *abuela* fussing loudly in her bed. Everything was tidy, the water jars in the kitchen were full and the hearth was swept. He went to the back bedroom and looked into the *alcoba*. The *abuela* lay regally in her bed, her hair like a white bird's nest. She cackled with laughter when she saw him. 'Who are you?' she said. 'Bugger off.' So he went away again. He peeked in the bread crock and wondered if Mama would notice if he broke off a piece of bread, but then he heard her downstairs so he put the lid back down.

Mama came in with herbs in her basket. Her face was shining from the sun and her eyes were shining too. He knew what they'd be eating tonight: omelette with fresh oregano in it. And soon, when the cow calved, there would be new cheese.

He was dreaming of cheese. Deep deep deep in the white curds he was swimming like a fish, though he couldn't swim, when Mama shook him awake.

By the tricksy light of the candle he saw her warning finger on her lips. 'The cow's calving,' she whispered.

He followed her down the dark narrow stair to the kitchen, then down to the basement. Papa was in the byre with a lantern. Even before Papa said anything, Albi knew: two waxy feet were sticking out of the cow's back end but the feet were upside down. That meant the calf was coming backwards.

Mama and Papa were arguing in whispers – the girls were sleeping overhead and they didn't want to wake them. Mama wanted to move Amapola to the stable, Papa said there wasn't enough room in there. He said they must stay here to have room for pulling. But how could Papa pull a calf?

Papa propped his crutches against the manger and steadied himself along Amapola's back, the rope in his hands, until he got to her tail. He tied the rope around the calf's feet and Amapola bellowed sadly. Why are we whispering, Albi wondered, when she is making so much noise? The cow shifted suddenly and Papa nearly fell. Amapola's eyes bulged, the whites glaring, as she twisted her head against the rope tether.

'She's too old,' Papa whispered. 'She's too old for this.'

The spasm in the cow's belly passed and she stood quiet again, her legs splayed and her back arched.

'We're going to have to pull,' Papa hissed.

But what good was a one-legged man pulling? Albi took the ropes off him. Papa gave a sad little shrug and hopped out of the way.

'Wait,' whispered Mama, picking up the other rope. 'Wait, Albi. There's no point pulling except when she strains.'

When the next spasm came they pulled as hard as they could. The gleaming feet came out a little bit, and when the spasm stopped they sucked straight back in again to where they'd been before.

'This is no good,' Papa muttered. 'We'll have to take the ropes round the beam.'

Amapola moved to one side suddenly and the rope jerked out of Albi's hand. She moaned as if she was telling them how bad it was.

Mama went forwards and peered into her face and stroked her ears. 'She won't take much more of this. Her ears have gone cold.'

They had the rope round the beam now. The cow began to strain again. Mama took up her rope, Albi took up his. They pulled and pulled, their feet sliding about in the wet straw, and Papa grunted and struggled behind them on the ends of both ropes, trying to keep them taut so that when the cow stopped straining the calf's feet would stay out the little bit they'd gained. But even with the ropes braced round the beam the feet still slipped back.

'At this rate,' Papa said, not whispering any more, 'we'll be all night getting the damned thing out. We'll have to call the girls.'

Mama said hastily, 'But we can't. Not Pili, Ramón!'

Albi wondered why Pili should be let off when he'd had to get out of his bed. Amapola groaned. They grabbed hold of the ropes again and pulled. Why didn't Mama want them to call the girls?

Amapola barked suddenly like a great dog and then he was pulling too hard to think any more.

When the straining stopped, and Papa had secured the ropes round the beam, they stood in the slippery straw and looked at Amapola's back end by the weak light of the lantern and they thought that yes, maybe they *had* gained a little more that time. Mama wiped the sweat off her face with her apron. They waited. And then they waited some more. But there were no more contractions. Papa told Albi to take the lantern up by Amapola's head so he could see her face. The old cow stood humped up with the calf's feet still sticking out, eyes half-closed and her ears drooping.

'She's given up,' Papa said. 'We couldn't do much with her help, we certainly won't do anything without it.'

'Shh, Ramón,' Mama whispered. 'Keep your voice down.'

They stood waiting. The two oxen went on cudding rhythmically as if nothing was happening.

If it wasn't curfew they would have fetched somebody. They needed a strong man or, better still, two.

'Albi could go to Miguel's house,' Papa suggested.

'The *Guardia* will shoot him, Ramón!'

'If he went out through the corral and round the back of the houses they wouldn't see him. Or he could knock on Martín's back-door.'

Martín lived two houses down. Like theirs, his house had a door onto a terrace at the back, but Martín would never hear knocking from his bedroom on the first floor at the front. Backwards and forwards they argued, and Albi listening in a fright because this was about him. He would be the one who did the running across the dark terraces, who did the quiet knocking on shuttered windows and locked doors.

A stone fell out of the new wall behind him and thudded onto the straw. He saw the scared look on his mama's face and whipped round. There was a hand hanging out of the wall. A disembodied hand. As thin and as white as any ghost's.

24

Manolo

The cow stared. Albi stared. Another stone fell out of the wall.

'Stop,' whispered Papa. 'Stop a minute and I'll help you.'

And there was his papa, and his mama too, taking down the wall Papa had built only a week ago.

They worked quickly, piling the stones to one side. As soon as the hole was big enough, a man climbed out of it. He climbed out and then he straightened up. He was small, no taller than Papa, and very thin. He had black hair sticking up all over his head and a black beard, and his white wrists were hairy too, where they hung out of the sleeves of his jersey. A jersey Albi recognised because he'd seen it not very long ago in his mama's chest where she kept Manolo's clothes. What was she doing giving Manolo's clothes to this stranger?

And then the stranger said, 'Hello, Albi,' and it was his brother's voice.

They didn't talk, they pulled the calf. Manolo might not be big like Albi remembered but he was strong. He pulled, and they pulled, and poor old Amapola didn't push any more but was tossed about on the end of the tether tying her to the manger, and it was a wonder that the whole street didn't wake (let alone the girls and the *abuela* in the room over their heads), with all their grunting and all the cow's groaning. And in the end, there was the calf in the straw at their feet, covered with yellow ointment and the silvery skin of the caul he should have been born out of the other way round. It was a bull calf and a big one, and he would have been valuable but now he was worth nothing because he was dead. Had been dead for hours, Manolo said, as

179

if he knew about these things. Best not to eat him, not now, Manolo said. So Amapola had had her last chance because she was too old to have another calf, especially after all the tearing and bruising there would be inside her.

Albi sat on the three legged stool and leaned his head against Amapola's warm flank, which smelled sweetly of grass, and cried as he milked a bucket of the thick yellow first-milk. He wept for all the summers Amapola had had, the same number as himself plus one more. He wept for the shoes she would make, at the end when her milk dried up and she wasn't useful any more, and the leather apron, and the dog-meat and the glue, and her horns that would be made into buttons. Because all these things had their uses but they were nothing compared to a sweet cow living and breathing and speaking to him gently as he put cut grass in her manger. He cried for La Gorda too. And while he milked, his face pushed up against her flank to hide his tears (the rhythm of the milking inside the hurt but soothing the hurt too), his mama and papa built up the wall again with Manolo inside it. Now they too had a *regresado* in their house, and if the *Guardia* came they might find him.

'You saw nothing,' Papa said. 'Understand?' Albi nodded. Another secret to carry. One to balance another, perhaps. But he would have to stay right away from Carlos now. He couldn't hide all these secrets from Carlos, not now it was real life instead of *aventuras*.

Mama gripped him by the shoulder so hard it hurt. 'You know, don't you Albi, if you let slip a word, a single word, it could be the death of him. And of us too.'

He nodded obediently, but there were other *regresados* in the village – why was their Manolo so special? And he remembered the pots going full to the basement and coming back empty, and the little cakes, and his mama sitting praying by the byre wall. The same wall behind which his brother had been hiding all the while. She loves Manolo more than me, he thought. And she always did.

Nobody woke him next morning. The girls had already gone to work when he came down to the kitchen. His mama was back from the bakehouse. She'd done some of his jobs, she said, and the calf was already skinned, the hide rolled up ready for him to take to Ovidio to be cured. He could take it to Ovidio's house when he went out with the sheep.

She looked at him keenly. 'Your Papa thinks you should take the sheep to the far *tierras* today. Spend all day up there. There'll be a lot for them to eat now.'

She wanted him out of the way. There was no more grazing on their other piece of land today than there had been yesterday and the day before, and it was stupid to go so far when the ewes were about to start lambing. It would slow him down if any of them lambed while they were out because he would have to carry the lamb all the way home again with the ewe fussing round his legs and tripping him up.

His papa said the same as Mama, only he gave better reasons. 'I want the fallow terraces grazed off before the weeds get too long. You can check how the corn is coming up. Take your time. You need to be there long enough for the flock to rest up as well as eat. Don't come back until mid-afternoon.'

*

'Carla was here over the weekend,' Santi says, pushing the coffee across the bar.

Alberto sits himself carefully on the stool – he's always nervous of falling off, these days. This morning it's just him and the TV and he can hear what Santi is saying. He watches the lad as he wipes down the bar and rinses the cups from the early morning rush. There are three cups.

'Where's your mother this morning?' It is rare for Josefina not to be where Santi is standing now, and Santi on this side of the bar, perched usefully on a stool.

'She went to Las Hoyas. To the dentist. Or was it the physio? Anyway, she won't be back for another hour at least. Did you want her?'

Alberto shakes his head. It pains him to see Santi wasting himself in here. What were Raul and Josefina thinking of? She should have locked up for the morning.

'*Tío*, Carla wants to know, do you have any idea where the hole in the wall is, where they used to hide the *maquis*?'

Alberto goes very quiet inside. 'What hole?'

'The one her grandfather talked about. In the wall of the stable of the house in the Plaza, the one he lived in as a boy. We looked really hard but we couldn't see any sign of where it might have been. All the stonework seems old, and none of it looks as if it's been disturbed since it was built. She thought you might remember.'

Alberto raises his eyes from the counter and gazes out into the narrow street where nothing moves except the winter wind, ruffling up the dead geraniums in the window boxes. How would he know the secrets of other people's houses, any more than they knew the secrets of his? But Carlos's house – in the Plaza, near where Mario's bar used to be? Next-door-but-one to the old *Ayuntamiento*, and within sight of the gatehouse, and the checkpoint beyond? It seems unlikely.

He turns his eyes from the window to find Santi watching him. It's the romanticism of the *maquis* that is shining in Santi's face. A desire to claim a past he's made into a picture inside his head.

'In Carlos's stable? I don't remember anything like that. But why do you think you'd be able to see any sign of it? Don't you think the *Guardia* would have been looking even harder than you?'

Santi's eyes widen. His expression says, *So you do remember that time. I knew you did!*

*

182

Albi walked to their far *tierras* the long way round, as before. It was a very long way round, and he was so tired after last night.

He sat in the sun, and sometimes in the shade of the trees, while his sheep and goats ate their fill, rested, got up and grazed again. It wasn't the same without La Gorda. They all seemed lost, even the cheerful goats. He made a necklace of wild flowers for his mama but then crumpled it up again. He looked for pebbles for his catapult. He practised shooting flowers off the bushes, and once he nearly hit a bird – a brown bird, with a speckled chest. His mama could have cooked it, if he'd hit it. But then she might have given it to his brother to eat. His brother who made their house even more dangerous than it was already.

He slept in the grass. The ants walked over him. A shiny beetle walked past.

Manolo. But not the Manolo he'd been thinking of all this time. Not a tall Manolo, with a big voice. Manolo no bigger than Papa. Manolo's voice, but no deeper than his papa's voice was. When he thought about it, of course Manolo would be quite like Papa. Did that mean that he would be too, when he'd finished growing? He so wanted to be tall like Carlos's brother. Was he only going to be the same as Papa, then?

The sun crept up across the sky. Very faintly, from a long way away, he heard the church bell ring for Mass.

Had Manolo been hiding in their house all the time, even before Papa built the wall?

Thinking made him sleepy again. He slept some more, until a brown ant bit him. A bump swelled up on his arm, red and angry. Papa knew they would all be shot if the *Guardia* found Manolo hiding. His *padres* loved his brother more than they loved him and his sisters. They must do, to put them all in such danger. He never wanted to go home again. What was the point? His mama wouldn't miss him, not now she had Manolo. She'd be too busy talking to the wall and cooking little treats. And his papa bobbing about on his crutches like an excited polecat – it had all been for Manolo, all the time.

I'll go and join the *maquis*, he thought. I could.

But he knew he wouldn't. Who wanted to live like that, hungry and hiding, if they didn't have to?

I'll go and live with the *abuelos*.

But that smelly kitchen and the rancid food – he couldn't stomach even the thought of it. And what if their house was where the *Guardia* had been going that night?

Anyway, he would be sad to leave Inma behind.

He walked the long way back, past the factory and through El Portal, with a bundle of grass for the rabbits over his shoulder. He didn't see anyone until he was quite near the village, on the main mule path that crossed the river meadows. Two *Guardia* were riding towards him, one on a strawberry-roan mare and the other on a bay gelding with a white star on its forehead. He gathered the flock to one side of the path so they could pass, watching the horses pick their way towards him on hoofs as neat as polished boots. When they came close he kept his eyes on the ground, afraid the men might read things in his eyes he didn't want them to know.

'Where have you been, boy?' The nearer man reined in his horse.

'To graze off our far *tierras*, señor.' He started to pull the permit out of his pocket but the sheep were pushing forwards, La Perrita fussing at their heels and making the horses prance about. The *Guardia* cursed, Albi pressed back against the wall. His heart was beating so hard he couldn't even whistle to Perrita to stay back. The men swore. As they urged their horses past one of them leaned down and snatched the bundle of grass and rode off with it, shouting over his shoulder, 'Move your arse and get back to the village.'

Albi started to run but his legs had gone to jelly. If he'd met those *Guardia* six days ago they might have smelled the *maquis* on him.

He didn't say anything when he came in. It was nothing out of the ordinary, after all, being stopped by the *Guardia*. Even so, his mama and papa kept looking at him oddly as if there was something wrong with him. He was so tired that he fell asleep on his chair in the kitchen, and Mama had to wake him up to tell him to go to bed. It was early, but he didn't mind.

In the middle of the night he was shaken awake. Mama with the candle again.

Not another calf, he thought blearily. Then he remembered and jumped up hurriedly. 'Is one of the ewes lambing?'

She shook her head, laughing. The laugh didn't have a happy sound. 'We need you to do something,' she whispered. 'Get up quietly and put your trousers on. And your jersey – it will be cold.'

In the kitchen she put a finger on her lips not to make a sound and handed him his satchel. He glanced inside it, confused. Two pieces of sausage, bread, two new onions; a small package wrapped in a piece of cloth that smelled decidedly like mutton ham; four five *six* hard-boiled eggs, still warm! What was all this luxury for, in the middle of the night? But Mama shook her head and pushed him gently towards the door. She followed him down the kitchen stairs and pushed him again, towards the byre, where Papa was taking the wall down, stone by stone. Very carefully, so as not to make a noise.

Manolo climbed out. His hair was cut short now and his beard had gone. 'I never want to see the inside of that shit-hole again,' he said in a low voice, reaching back into the hole and pulling out a kit-bag. He stretched, and rubbed his back with both hands, staring all the while at Albi. Papa was looking at him too.

'Your Mama went to see El Ciego yesterday,' he said quietly. 'He told us something we didn't know.'

Albi went very still. He looked at the three of them looking at him. Then he looked at the floor. He didn't want to answer questions. He wouldn't know what he ought to say. He looked very hard at a piece of straw by his foot that was shining in the light of the candle.

A hand rested on the back of his neck. His mama's hand, all rough from the *huerto*. 'El Ciego said you must take Manolo to the place you know about,' she whispered. 'He says you should go tonight, just the two of you, no sheep. Don't come back to the village until the middle of the day tomorrow. When you come back you must go to the Molino and report to El Ciego. Bring a bundle of sticks but make sure nobody sees you until you're close enough to the village to look as if you were only out fetching firewood at a normal time. Do you understand?'

He was full of questions but he couldn't ask them. He was full of objections. He never wanted to see those murderers again! And what about the *Guardia*? What would Manolo do up on the *Meseta*? How would he live? But he was also thinking, good – he will be away from here.

Mama held Manolo very tight as if she thought she might never see him again. Albi watched her and felt sharp and sad inside. But then she hugged him close, too, and that made him frightened, even more frightened than he already was.

Papa said to him, 'Don't forget: nobody must ever know. Understand? Not your sisters, not Carlos or any of the other boys. Not our neighbours, especially not Martín. And never never *never* the *Guardia Civil*.'

They slipped out through the back door of the corral and Mama quietly shut and bolted it behind them. They couldn't go back now. You could jump out of the corral but you couldn't jump in.

Albi stepped across the *acequia* that ran along the corral wall. It was dark by the wall but the tiniest sliver of moon was rising, and the starlight was so bright it made faint shadows all by itself.

Manolo put a hand on his arm. He couldn't see Manolo's face but he felt him lean down to murmur in his ear, 'Don't go too fast.'

The shadows of the trees lay thick on the terrace but Albi had been all his life in these places and he could see them with his bones, he didn't need moonlight. He had to slow himself to Manolo's more cautious pace. Was it only that Manolo had been away too long? Or was it to do with being shut inside the wall? So many questions he wanted to ask. All the things he'd thought of yesterday, while he was banished to the far *tierras*. While Mama was finding that her little Albi wasn't so little after all, that he knew things, but he hadn't known she was finding that out. He'd been dizzy with all the knowing but still he hadn't told. He hadn't broken his promise.

Don't come back until the sun is at the top of the sky. That was what Mama had said. *And tell the maquis that this time El Ciego sent you. He said most particularly you must tell them that.*

That made him feel better, when he had time to think about it. But would the *maquis* still think he had told things he hadn't? *Tell it like it is,* Papa said, and shook him by the hand as if he was a man.

They walked in silence, Albi leading. His bare feet and his brother's espadrilles passed silently over the rocky ground. He walked along the edge of the *acequia* in the dark of the trees and waited for Manolo to catch up, trying not to hurry him.

Rustlings everywhere. Not human noises.

When they came to the edge of the trees Manolo put a hand on his shoulder to stop him going on. They stood a long time, waiting for their eyes to catch up with the darkness, to see the shapes in it. The stillnesses, or any tiny give-away movement. This is what the blind man sees, he thought, the shape of the dark. He felt the cold wind on his face. It was coming from the direction of the waterfall, from the place where the gorge spewed out its river, night-black and silvery. The sky was clear. Hundreds of stars winked. Some of them were red. The cliffs cut ragged black patches out of the stars. The blind man couldn't see that.

Manolo touched his shoulder, telling him to walk on.

The waterfall path was pale and clear, even in the dark. It would be easy enough to follow. But they must not. If any of the *Guardia* were out on patrol, this was where they were most likely to be – on the easy paths nearest the village. He already knew that, Manolo didn't have to tell him. But he did. 'Only a little way,' Albi whispered back. Manolo knew these paths equally well, he should know that the quickest way up to the path that ran along the *acequia principal*, higher up the slope, meant going along the main path as far as the big almond tree first.

It was like leading a blind man: all the things Manolo remembered but the instinct had gone out of them with lack of use. He wanted to turn too soon, or he walked past a turn without remembering it. Again and again Albi had to remind him.

They climbed until they could hear water. The big *acequia* made a silver ribbon to follow, reflecting the sky as it ran swift and deep between its banks. The rush of the water was noisy. It shadowed the sound of their footsteps, but now they were like deaf men because they could see but they couldn't hear.

'I don't like this,' Manolo whispered after a while. 'Let's climb higher.'

Albi filled with pride that his brother should talk to him like an equal.

They scrambled upwards, pushing through the scrub, tearing themselves on gorse and thorn trees, stepping lightly over stones and around rocks. Once Manolo unbalanced a small boulder with his foot and it rolled down the slope, crashing loudly as it went. They froze as the echo rebounded off the cliff face above them, trying not to breathe so they could listen properly. But the valley lay silent. The faint glow made by the streetlamps was already a long way behind them.

Not until they were on the path up to the *Meseta* and climbing the staircase of rock leading to the top of the cliffs, did they stop long enough to catch their breath. It was strange to be out with no dog and no sheep, stranger even than being out in the middle of the night. The darkness was thinner up here, nearer to the sliver of moon and the multitude of stars. It felt as if they were standing with their heads in the open air and their feet still in the dark heaviness of the valley.

Manolo hissed, 'What's that?'

Albi couldn't hear anything. Then he saw in the starlight that Manolo was pointing. He peered into the distance. 'It's the lights of the pump house shining upwards on the poplars.'

'Bloody Fascists,' Manolo said. 'We built it. Our sweat and blood built it and now we should blow it up.'

He sounded like Carlos when he said that.

By the time they climbed out onto the *Meseta* the thin moon had set and it was very dark. So dark Albi wasn't sure where to go, he had to stop and think. 'We go along the edge of the cliffs. Keep the cliffs to our left but look out to our right.'

Manolo laughed softly. Left and right – he'd never seen the sense in them, he said, not until he was in the army and it was a matter of life and death. He tousled Albi's head and for a moment Albi was sorry he'd be leaving his brother behind tomorrow.

'When we get closer,' Manolo said as they walked, 'we must be very careful. We don't want to get ourselves shot.'

He'd felt safer, being with Manolo, until he said that. Maybe it was less dangerous stumbling across the *maquis* the way he had, just a shepherd boy with his sheep, than it was finding them on purpose.

At last, when he was beginning to think they must have walked right past it, the secret valley was there in front of them like a broad deep channel cut in the ground. They followed the channel towards the cliffs until they got to the hollow place where the little valley opened out above the gorge. He led the way down into the hollow.

It was even darker down here. The stone walls of the terraces were invisible. Only the density of shadow between the glimmer of rock on either side reassured him that they were in the right place.

Manolo stopped so Albi stopped too, waiting and listening. In the darkness he could feel Manolo looking from side to side, working out his bearings. It was dangerous, entering a narrow space like this. He wasn't surprised when Manolo's hand rested on his shoulder and the warmth of his face came up close to whisper in his ear, 'Not yet. We'll go back for a bit.'

Now Manolo was the leader and he was the led. His senses all awake – he's there, I'm here, there's a rock, mind that bush it might be gorse – as he followed him back to the edge of the gorge. The sky they stood up in was bright with stars, but the gorge in front of them was solid darkness. It reminded him of pictures in the priest's books when he was small: down was hell and up was heaven. It *felt* like that. Was that the way the people of the *Meseta* saw the people of El Rincón? Was that how Mama saw Papa, before she came down off the *Meseta* to marry him? And what was Manolo doing now, skirting off along the edge of the gorge away from the *maquis*?

Over to their right, an outcrop of limestone rose up, black against the sky. Manolo moved towards it, a shadow among shadows, but in his hurry to keep close Albi got caught up in some bushes. He pulled himself free, panicking a little, but Manolo was waiting, laughing softly. What now?

'We'll wait for daylight,' Manolo said, keeping his voice low. 'Don't want to scare them. Better if they can see us than if we stumble over them in the dark.'

Albi felt about for a place in the rocks where they could sit with their backs against a boulder. He wondered about snakes. He always was afraid of snakes in the dark, though Papa had said many times, *snakes don't like cold, lad*, and it was cold now. He shivered. Manolo rummaged in his kit-bag.

'Have some of that, little brother,' Manolo whispered, thrusting a blanket round his shoulders.

Who was this brother he'd never thought of as kind?

'Budge up, let me have a share,' Manolo said, sitting down beside him and pulling half of the blanket over his own shoulders. They sat staring into nothing. Just space, and space, and more space beyond that. The stars very bright, the outlines of the hills along the bottom of the sky very black, and nothing else visible, nothing at all.

This is what the blind man sees.

Far below them, in the gorge, Albi could hear the distant roar of the waterfall spewing over the rock wall. He shivered, but Manolo's warmth was seeping into him, inside the dark tent of their single blanket. This brother, who used to torment him or ignore him but nothing in-between. Now Manolo began to talk. About being holed up in the wall. 'Anything would be better than that,' he said. 'I'd rather be dead than be buried alive.' About Papa, asking how they managed now he couldn't work any more. He made it sound as if Papa had been careless, losing his leg and causing them so much difficulty.

'Papa does still work,' Albi objected, 'And he *was* very brave.'

But Manolo didn't seem to be listening. 'So Caballero's back, is he, and Jesús with him? Turned tail when things get hot but back they scuttle soon as their cronies seize power. I never trusted that Jesús, not once he started working for El bloody Caballero. The servant learns from his master.'

Albi said, 'Uhuh,' as if he knew what Manolo was talking about. He asked how many battles Manolo had been in, but he said that was all in the past and they had to make themselves a future now, in spite of these fascist scum taking over the way they had. And then he fell silent.

Albi thought about Carlos, tucked up in his bed in his father's house. Carlos would be amazed if he could see them now, but it was a story Albi would never be able to tell.

'Is the war over?'

'No, it's not over yet. We will resist!' The blanket moved as Manolo punched at the sky. 'Resistance is the name of the game now. Harass them and needle them and attack them where we can.'

Albi thought of the men in the secret valley and it was hard to see what they were resisting. They didn't even have tobacco, so how could they have bullets for their guns?

That was an interesting thought. He hadn't had it before this moment. Had they pointed a rifle at him without any bullets in it? But then he remembered they did have matches, and a sharp knife to kill La Gorda. And anyway David killed Goliath with a catapult and a pebble. You can do big things with not very much.

Manolo started asking questions about the pump house. Where was this pill-box thing then?

'There are two,' Albi said. 'One at each end of the dam wall.' How many sentries on guard? He didn't know, but the most he'd seen was six, three in each pill-box. How often did the sentries change? He didn't know that, either. Did they go to and from the pill-boxes using the old Tajubo road on this side, or the track on the far bank of the river that went past the garrison? He didn't know what their routine was, he'd seen them on both tracks. 'We'll need to know more,' Manolo said. 'Can you find out more?'

What? He'd thought the *aventura* they were having was terrifying enough. After all, they might be shot by the *maquis* or knifed in the back if they weren't careful. Why look for more trouble?

Carlos would do it. He'd spy on the pump house and the pill-boxes. He would count guards, memorise patterns. For all he knew Carlos had spied on the pump house often enough to know the answers to these questions already. But would he believe everything Carlos said, even if he could ask him?

'So how come you've been running messages for El Ciego? My little brother, eh!'

He could hear that Manolo was impressed, but it was a mistake because he hadn't taken any messages. Had he?

His brother started talking about the *abuela* in her bed in their house and how bad it sounded from his hiding place in the wall and his voice was sad. He used to be her favourite. It must be hard knowing she wouldn't recognise him now.

'Will you go to Las Cabreras?' Albi asked. Maybe that was what Manolo had been planning all along. After all, he could hide up there. The *abuelos* would feed him and look after him and give him a bed to sleep on. But what a bed. He felt the blanket move up and down as Manolo shrugged. Should he tell him about the *abuelos*? But before he'd decided, Manolo said, 'Don't suppose you've got any baccy on you?' He shook his head. 'Too bad.'

An edge of light had opened up along the horizon in front of them. Somewhere far away an ibex whistled. Albi felt Manolo turn his head to listen. The *maquis* might eat ibex, if they had enough bullets.

'Have you got a gun?'

Manolo scratched idly. 'I did have. Once.'

You could make a bow and some arrows, Albi thought, for hunting ibex with, and wild boar. But you wouldn't want a wild boar to come after you, if you only wounded it with your arrow and didn't kill it. Dogs – that was what the villagers hunted with as much as guns, before the soldiers came, when hunting was still allowed. Had the *maquis* had a single dog? He didn't think so or La Perrita would have had something to say about it. You can't feed a dog on asphodel roots.

His thoughts rambled quietly on and ended up back at Las Cabreras again. 'It's not the same any more.'

'What isn't?'

'Las Cabreras.' How strange to have a brother to say these things to when he hadn't had one in such a long time.

'What's different?'

'It's dirty now. It smells. It's not like it used to be.'

'I wouldn't be going there for fun.' Manolo's voice was hard like a man's, but then he said in a different voice, 'Do you remember how we used stay up there all summer long? I remember *Abuela* bathing you in the water-trough. You screamed like a little pig. Consuelo too. Two little pink pigs.'

Albi didn't like being told he'd cried like a baby, but Consuelo – that was something else. He'd forgotten her and then suddenly she was right there, sitting with them in the dark. It was confusing, because he was nine and a half years old but Consuelo, who had been older than him, was still only little. She would never be more than six. 'Tell me about Consuelo,' he said.

'I'd forgotten how small it all is.'

Not Consuelo. This place, he meant. Albi turned his head, looking from side to side of the wide horizon. It wasn't small at all, and that was only the half of the world that was in front of them. He could see the outlines now, the crags and the cliffs pale against the dawn sky, and the dark slashes of the clefts. The bold trees growing obstinately out of the white rock, but below them everything still in shadow. Far away to their left, the thin lights of El Rincón winking.

Then he realised Manolo was looking at the village.

He nudged him and poked his arm out of the blanket to point. On the skyline, behind them and to their left, a big male ibex stood outlined against the paling sky. His enormous horns swept upwards like long curving blades. You could see how weighty they were by the careful way he turned and stepped down off his rock and disappeared into the shadows.

'That was a good one,' Manolo said. He got up and stretched. 'Time we started moving.'

Albi scrambled up, his legs stiff with sitting. He could see Manolo quite clearly now in the half-light. Mama had tidied him up, because that is what you do with *regresados*, but soon he would look like the other wild, hairy men hiding up here among the rocks.

They began to walk quietly, back towards the secret valley, straining their eyes against the deceptive light. When they reached the valley Manolo whispered, 'Put your hands on your head. So they can see we haven't got guns. And walk. Whatever happens, don't run. Understand?'

He did as he was told, his teeth chattering with cold and with fright.

Manolo nodded grimly, his hands on the top of his head like a naughty boy in school, then he turned and led the way into the little valley.

They walked the whole length of it. They had to use their hands to scramble up over each of the terrace walls, Albi's heart jumping with fear that the *maquis* would catch sight of them at that very minute and not realise they didn't have guns because their hands weren't on their heads.

Nothing. From one end of the valley to the other in the gathering light, nothing. Not even the ashes of a fire and the old cigarette butts. He was relieved, and then he was even more scared: Manolo would think he'd been making it up.

They passed the wall under the ledge of rock where the *maquis* were hiding last time. He nudged Manolo with his elbow to tell him but Manolo whispered 'Don't look. Keep your eyes straight ahead. Walk if I walk, stop if I stop.' But he didn't stop. Albi kept pace beside him. At the top of the valley they took their hands off their heads and scrabbled on all fours up the rock ledges. He was nearly crying. Manolo would never believe him now.

But Manolo didn't sound disappointed. He just said, 'Now they've seen us and they can see we're not the *Guardia*. We'll go back and wait and let them come to us in their own good time.'

They walked back the way they'd come, jumping down the terraces, this time keeping their hands on their heads. The rim of the sun was sliding up into the sky like a coin rolling upwards behind Muela Mala. In a minute it would be shining full on them. They passed the wall under the rock and didn't look at it. They passed the place where he thought the fire might have been, because now he could see traces of it. And then, where the valley widened, Manolo stopped and whispered, 'Sit down with your back to me.' So he sat down on the ground, and Manolo sat too, and they leaned against one another with their hands still on their heads. Albi could feel the warm rise and fall of his brother's steady breathing, and the less certain rise and fall of his own, rubbing against Manolo's back. They waited.

If they'd been born at the same time they'd be twins. But there was a gap of sixteen years between them, and four sisters, one of them now dead. His brother was already working for Uncle Pedro when Albi was born.

Manolo went still. 'Don't turn your head. One downhill to my left, two up.'

Albi slid his eyes to the left and to the right of him. He could see nothing to his right, but uphill he saw the Butcher. As he stared he saw the rising sun glint on the lenses of the glasses of a slighter man standing behind him, the one they called *Student*. The Butcher had a pistol.

'Well, well, well,' said the Butcher, jumping down the rocks and coming up close. 'So you couldn't stay away. And what's this you've brought us this time? Nothing for dinner, just another mouth to feed? Get up!'

The command was so sudden that Albi ducked, but Manolo stood up so he did too. He'd brought these *maquis* a comrade but they were treating them as if they were enemies.

'Name?' snapped the Butcher.

'Manuel Álvarez Zapatero.'

'Company? Number? *If* you have one.' The Butcher had come very close and his voice was mocking. The Student stood behind him with another gun, and he didn't look friendly any more.

The Butcher eyed Manolo as if he was a beast in the market he was sizing up for slaughter. Manolo stood very straight. He stared over the Butcher's shoulder and snapped out a name and a number.

'Search him. And the boy.'

The tall blonde man Albi recognised from before stepped forward and ran his hands quickly over Manolo, and then over him too, patting him all over.

'Nothing.'

'Search the bags.'

The blonde man emptied both bags onto the dewy grass. The Butcher looked, and sneered. 'So, you've brought us no guns? No bullets? No knives or grenades? Just you and this boy here who we've seen enough of already.' He turned on Albi suddenly. 'And what were you doing telling, you little rat.'

Albi jumped. He looked at the big man's narrowed eyes, the fierce rough beard hiding everything except his eyes and the glint of teeth, one of them missing. 'El Ciego…' he tried to say, but the words had dried up and they came out shrivelled. He licked his lips. 'El Ciego said I should bring my brother to you.'

He felt the change at the word. The Butcher looked surprised, a little uncertain. He lowered the gun.

'El Ciego?'

Manolo went on standing very straight, like a soldier. He didn't move his head as he snapped out, 'I have no gun to bring you because I lost mine in the mud of the Ebro. I have no bullets because I fired every last one at the fascist bastards. What I bring you is the things I know. I was born here. I know this place like the inside of my own head.'

Albi thought, but he doesn't know it like I do.

'And if you've heard of the Battle of Gandesa,' Manolo went on, 'then you've heard of me. Because I was there.'

It seemed to Albi that they were like two dogs circling one another, Manolo and the Butcher. All the other dogs in the pack drawn up in a circle round them and watching. Manolo was pretending to be the new dog, but that wasn't the role he was going to accept. Not in the end.

25

The Blind Man

It was after dinner-time when Albi got down near the Molino. He came along the side of the *acequia* with a bundle of firewood on his back, as he'd been told to, and a message in his head. 'Send us soap,' the Butcher had said, 'and a razor. And some scissors. We're tired of living like foxes.'

Foxes were neater. And they smelled better.

He went to the back of the Molino and knocked on the door in the wall of the corral, because that was the way he'd gone in before, but when the door opened it was Joaquín looking down at him, his small head cocked sideways and his eyes vacant. Joaquín shouted something over his shoulder but the shout didn't seem to have any words in it.

El Ciego's voice came from inside the mill, 'Take him up to the kitchen.'

Joaquín jerked his head and Albi followed him along a passage full of the smell of baking bread. Through an open doorway he glimpsed a big chimney with a bread oven in the base of it. The blind man had an oven all to himself.

Upstairs in the kitchen, Joaquín gestured at the table and sat down. Albi perched on the chair opposite. Everyone said Joaquín was dumb but he'd made that funny shouting noise. Did that mean he could speak really? They sat in silence, the two of them looking at the table as if it had words written on it, as if they could both read.

The blind man came in and Joaquín went away. El Ciego closed the door. He stood by Albi's chair and laid his hand gently on his head. Then he took Albi's face and turned it towards him. He ran his thumbs lightly over his forehead, over his eyelids. Skimmed his cheeks, finished on his chin.

'Good. This time you have not been so afraid.'

But he had. He was sorry El Ciego didn't see everything after all. Though it was true, this time he had not cried, even when he'd thought they might both be shot, him and Manolo.

'The Butcher sends you a message,' he said.

The blind man put a finger to his lips. 'Never speak if Joaquín is near.'

Albi glanced round quickly but the door was still closed and the room was empty.

El Ciego felt along the table top. He picked up a tomato and rubbed it between his hands. 'Never tell anybody things they do not need to know.' He felt for the cutting board and putting the tomato down on it. 'A man is like a bucket with a hole in it. If you fill the bucket to the hole it will leak. Better to put nothing in it except what has to be there.'

Albi nodded. Then he remembered the blind man couldn't see. 'Yes. Señor.'

'Now you can tell me the message.'

Albi told him: soap, a razor, scissors, and the man with the glasses wanted some iodine to treat their blistered feet and the septic places where they'd had thorns. The Student. The one who said he knew Mena, but he was surely mistaken.

El Ciego said, 'How many men this time, not counting your brother?'

He couldn't remember. His mind searched wildly for the number but he couldn't see it. Albi stared at El Ciego's unseeing eyes. He could make it up, the blind man would never know.

199

But he didn't really believe he wouldn't know, not when he seemed to see so much. Carlos would know what to say, but something told him Carlos would exaggerate and the blind man wouldn't like it. Had Carlos been in this kitchen? Had he been asked, and told lies, and El Ciego had sent him away?

'How many, boy?'

He looked inside his head again and counted up the faces he thought he definitely remembered. 'I don't know,' he said at last, and had to repeat it because he didn't say it loud enough. 'Nine? Or it might have been more.'

El Ciego's face twitched as though he was angry. Albi shrank down in his chair wishing he was somewhere else, ham or no ham.

'Good,' the blind man said. 'But next time, count. And remember.'

His face twitched again. It was a smile. Carlos couldn't *ever* have been in this kitchen. He would never have kept quiet about it if he had.

El Ciego got up and ran his hand along the stone shelf until his hands touched a pile of plates. He lifted three down. 'You'll eat with us, and then you will go home and take your sheep out as usual. But the day after tomorrow call by here as you go out with the flock. This will be your employment now. I need a boy to graze my animals and fetch firewood and rabbit food. Say nothing to your parents. I will come to your house tomorrow and have a word with your father. The day after, when you call by here in the morning I'll tell you what jobs I have for you. Firing will only be one of them.'

He was as tired as if he'd walked to the moon and back. He took his sheep and goats out in the afternoon and slept under a tree near the *chorreta*. Nobody disturbed him. The first lamb was born, that was all that happened.

He came home, carrying the lamb in his arms while its mother crowded at his heels and the other ewes followed after. He watered the cattle at the *fuente* in the plaza, and took them back to the byre. He milked the cow, and fetched water for the kitchen, and did all his other jobs. Then he fell asleep again on the floor of the *solenar* while his sisters, newly come in from work, told Mama the latest gossip and Papa said nothing much but smoked his pipe. The girls assumed Albi had still been in his bed when they'd gone out to work that morning. They teased him for being such a sleepyhead, sleeping so late in the morning, and sleeping again on the floor in the evening and it wasn't even dark yet.

Next morning, Mama was back from the bakehouse with the fresh bread, and Albi was down in the sheep pen busy with his jobs, when there was a knock on the open front door. From the passageway he could see the blind man standing in the street. He heard his mama call down a greeting from the kitchen window, and the blind man calling back that he wanted to speak to her husband.

Albi went on feeding and watering the rabbits as if the blind man was nothing to do with him, but he was listening to the sound of Papa shuffling down the stairs, then the click of his crutches as he hopped over the front step, his voice all jaunty as he greeted El Ciego. Albi slid along the passage like a shadow and up the stairs to the kitchen. He pretended to be busy putting food in his bag for his dinner, but really he was listening to what they were saying outside in the street, his papa and the blind man. Mama was listening too, her hand at her throat. All the street would be listening, through every open window. They would hear El Ciego telling his papa he wanted a boy to collect firewood and rabbit food and look after the few sheep and goats belonging to the Molino.

'You know how it is,' El Ciego said. 'More often than not a family wants to pay me with a sheep or a goat but what use is that to me if I can't take a flock out to graze? Joaquín is no good at that sort of thing, even if I could spare him from the mill work.' The words rang out, clear and precise. 'A lad your boy's age is what I need.'

Papa said, 'What's in it for me?' and the blind man replied 'Your flock can have the grazing of my land – the boy would run my animals with yours. And I will give you bran and cleanings from the mill for your pig.'

Papa seemed to be thinking. Then he said, 'We don't have a pig,' and the blind man said 'Well then, I will give you a quarter-share of mine when the time comes to kill it next winter.' Papa said, quick as a flash, 'Forequarter or hindquarter?' and the blind man paused, then said firmly, 'Forequarter.' Which was what Albi expected him to say, but he was disappointed. A hindquarter would have been better, but best of all the blind man might have offered to pay real money, like his sisters earned. A pig might die before it got to being eaten.

'Tell him to come every morning after curfew ends. But Saturday afternoons and Sundays you can have him at home. Oh, and I'll feed him when he's with me.'

His papa didn't say yes. He said he would think about it until tomorrow. Tomorrow Albi would come to the Molino with the answer.

From the kitchen they heard the tap-tap-tap of the blind man's stick as he went away down the street and the clumsy tap-and-shuffle of Papa climbing back up the stairs. He was grinning when he hopped through the door into the kitchen. He propelled himself on his crutches straight through the house, Albi and his mama hurrying after him.

'Who's that?' screeched the *abuela* from her bed in the *alcoba* as they went past. 'Only us, *Abuela*,' Mama said soothingly. But she didn't stop, she went straight out onto the *solenar*. They could talk more safely out here, so long as they kept their voices low.

'This is good,' Papa whispered. 'This is very good. If you do well, Albi, there will be more work for you at the Molino when you get bigger. That Joaquín isn't good for much. And a mill always does well, in good times and in bad. He might pay you money later on.'

Albi stared at him. His papa was talking as if the other night hadn't happened, as if working for the blind man meant only running a few extra sheep with theirs and collecting a bit of firewood. As if the blind man would not send him back to the *maquis*.

'Ramón,' Mama said. 'I don't want him working for El Ciego.'

'Don't be a fool, woman. The Molino has lands all over the valley and up on the *Meseta* too. If the boy runs the Molino sheep with ours he'll have the right to go anywhere. El Ciego can get a permit for him to be up on the *Meseta*, even. Then he wouldn't get in trouble even if he did run into the *Guardia*. Don't you see? We'll be able to send food to Manolo any time you want.'

His papa was selling him like a mule. For Manolo.

He saw the look on his mama's face and a knife turned in his heart. But she said firmly, 'No. Not both my boys, Ramón.'

Albi surfaced and stared into the dark. His heart was clattering in his chest. Rocks had been crashing down one into another, breaking open his sleep. Where was he?

Not rocks – metal on wood. A man shouting. La Gatica stirred against him, the streetlamp poking a shaft of light through the finger-hole of the shutter above his head. He was in his attic room.

He leapt up, dislodging the cat, and knelt on the bed. Very slowly, he unlatched the shutter and pulled it open. A group of *Guardia* stood in the street in front of their house, banging on the door with the butts of their pistols. Albi jumped backwards as one of them tilted his head back and looked up.

In the kitchen below a door creaked open, feet ran down the stairs. Not his papa, then. He heard the bolts of the front door being drawn back, the rasp of the key in the old lock, and Mama's voice, very scared. Then the harsh clatter of boots. He rolled into a ball under the blankets and clamped his hands over his ears but he could still hear the voices in the kitchen, the scrape of a chair, the door to the attic opening.

Boots on the stairs. He heard them. He didn't hear them. He was in a wood. He was hiding in a cave. He wasn't here.

'Get out of that bed you lazy little bastard!' The blanket was ripped off him. Towering figures, hands grabbing at him, yanking him upright. 'Get your arse down to that kitchen!'

He hesitated. In the hectic light of the electric torches he couldn't see where he was going and he was scared of falling down the stairs. Something hard smashed across the back of his head. He stumbled down into the kitchen.

It was crowded. Even the *abuela* was there, Pili and Inma holding her up. It was the *abuela* who was screaming.

'Shut it!' The *Guardia* raised his fist – the same *Guardia* who had been in the Plaza with Miguel, that day of the gun.

Mama said, 'She can't help it, señor. Her mind has gone. Please don't hurt her!'

The *Guardia* narrowed his sly eyes at Mama, but he let his arm drop.

The *abuela* looked like a ghost in her white nightgown. Pili and Inma too, and Mama. Papa in his long underpants with his shirt hanging out and his hair sticking up all over his head. Their terrified faces jumping in the jostle of shadows.

'Get in line,' barked the *Guardia*, shining his torch on Albi. The muzzle of a pistol gleamed cold and steady in his other hand.

From the stables, below, the crashing of things being overturned and ripped off the walls, and the sharp clinking on the cobbles as the terrified mule jumped about, snorting in alarm. Were they knifing all the animals? He looked sideways at Papa. The left leg of Papa's underpants hung empty as he balanced on his crutches and stared at the floor. He looked naked without his wooden leg.

The two *Guardia* who'd pushed Albi down the stairs were searching the back bedroom. A metallic crash – that would be the enamel chest going over. He stole a sideways look at Pili, standing next to him in her curlers, her eyes fixed on the red floor tiles. She was shaking. A draught licked round his bare feet: the door to the *solenar* must be open. The *Guardia* shouted, voices answered from down in the corral. One of them laughed. Albi was trembling so badly he was afraid he would fall down. He leaned against Pili. She put her arm round him. The man with the gun jumped and pointed his pistol straight at them.

Flashlights crowded back into the kitchen. 'Nothing, Sarge.'

The sergeant jerked his head at the men to go downstairs. He moved his torch-beam across Papa's face, then each of them in turn, taking his time as if he was learning what they looked like, even the *abuela*.

'This is a warning. Watch your step. All of you.'

As he went out he kicked Papa's crutch out from under him so that Papa toppled over and sprawled on the floor like a beetle turned on its back. The sergeant laughed all the way down the stairs, leaving them in the dark and the house full of night wind.

Silence. Then the door to the back bedroom slammed in the wind like a pistol shot and they all jumped. Pili whimpered, the *abuela* started screaming again. When had she stopped? Albi wished he could make her stop now. A match flared as Inma lit two candles; she thrust one at Mama and ran downstairs with the other.

'Come on,' Ramona ordered. 'We'd better get the *abuela* back into bed. That might shut her up.'

She took the candle off Mama. Albi followed her into the back bedroom, the shadows trembling on the walls. He closed the door to the *solenar* and the candle flame steadied, revealing the chaos, everything turned upside down.

They lifted the *abuela*'s bed the right way up and put the mattress back, and all the bedclothes. Pilar didn't do a thing to help. She had lit a third candle but all she was doing with it was staring at the contents of her enamel chest, tipped out on the floor.

'They shouldn't have done that,' she said in a shocked voice. 'They shouldn't have done that.'

Well they were all pretty shocked. Albi went to the kitchen with Ramona to fetch his *abuela* back to her bed. Mama was sitting in a heap on one chair and Papa was on another, too dazed the pair of them to do anything useful. Inma had quietened the animals and locked the doors downstairs and the house was still again. The *Guardia* would have been looking for hidden men, that was why they'd turned the beds over and pulled the wall cupboards open. He helped Ramona and Inma right the other beds and heave the heavy mattresses back. The whole street would have heard, as they did last night when Hernán Irún's house in the next street was searched. Papa had been brave and all-knowing when it was happening to somebody else. 'They're trying to scare us,' he'd said yesterday. But now it had happened to them and he didn't say a word.

Albi climbed into Inma's bed and tried to sleep, but the thoughts wouldn't let him alone. If the *Guardia* had come two nights earlier they might have found Manolo.

'In the old days,' Papa said, 'a squirrel could cross from one side of Spain to the other without touching the ground.'

In the old days, the inside of your house was safe, even if nowhere else was. Papa was talking as if last night hadn't happened. Perhaps that was what you had to do, otherwise how could you go on living?

Albi looked up from plaiting his rope and did his best. 'What? Squirrels could fly?'

Papa gave him a pitying look. 'No, Albi. They could hop from tree to tree.'

206

'It would have to be very long hops.' *Crashing on the front door. The harsh clatter of boots running up the stairs.*

Papa said impatiently, 'There were more trees, lad. Before they cut them all down. That's the point.' He looked at Albi, waiting to see if he'd caught up. 'That was how they had the money to build such fine houses – they sold all the trees.'

Albi looked at the street. *Trying not to see the black jumping shadows and the gun.*

Fine houses? They were just the ordinary ones, though it was true some of them did have fine stone arches around massive doors, and the planks of the doors were all heartwood and hard as nails.

But not hard enough to keep the Guardia *out, not if they wanted to come in.*

No worm in those doors, even though they had stood there in the wind and rain and sun for ever. And no worm in the big old beams inside the houses either. But it was still just the ordinary people living in them, and nobody was rich, and they were all afraid.

Papa said, 'Our ancestors were wealthy, Albi. Never forget that. You don't believe me? Look at the timbers in our house. Every one of them two hand-spans deep and two hand-spans wide and six paces long. Squared timber too, all the sap-wood cut away. Think of the size of tree it took to make beams as big as that. And the rings in the wood so tight you can't see to count them.'

Couldn't count them if he could see them. And why was Papa taking it on himself to talk like the old schoolmaster when he couldn't even read or write? Last night the *Guardia* had come and Papa said nothing about it.

He nodded.

'In the old days, long before your *abuelos* were born,' Papa said, waving his arms to indicate the hills all round them, 'this was all forest. But then merchants came and bought the timber. In three generations it was all cut down.' He jerked his chin over his shoulder and said in that special voice he had whenever he talked about Valbono, '*They* made even more money out of it. That's why they've got all those carved balconies.'

'Oh,' said Albi, his head full of the noise of boots on midnight floors. They plaited more rope. And some more.

Papa leaned forward and gripped him by the wrist. 'You have to go on, lad,' he said quietly. 'Don't let them get to you. That's what they're trying to do – wear us all down.'

Was that what they were talking about really? Papa hadn't said anything brave last night. Which was the real Papa? This one, or the silent shaken one after the *Guardia* left?

Albi lay sleepless in his attic bed. The night was full of threatening shadows, the silence suspect. Perhaps he did fall asleep in the end, because the shouting of the *Guardia* in the street seemed to come out of nowhere. He lay very still, terrified and disbelieving, waiting for the blows to crash down on their front door again. But when they came, it wasn't their door. This time it was Young Jaime's turn.

Mama was taut-faced in the morning, waiting for curfew to end so she could hurry across the street and find out what had happened. Albi followed her down the stairs, but there was Belén on the doorstep, pale but unhurt, and Jaime standing tall in the doorway behind her.

Albi had another story now. How the *Guardia* had come in the night and he'd thought they were all going to be killed. And it was all right to tell it, which made it safe to be with Carlos and Pepito again. So he went to find them, under the bridge at the bottom of the Plaza, and when Pepito had told about his mother beating him for one of the rabbits getting out, Albi told about the *Guardia*.

It made a space for the secrets to hide behind, and the fear of being with Carlos melted away. He was glad. It had been lonely, steering clear of his friends. He pinged two pebbles into the stream, one after the other, making hiccupy echoes as they hit the water.

'Were you scared?' Pepito asked.

'A bit.' He lobbed a bigger stone. It made a deep, satisfying *plop.*

'That's why they do it,' Carlos said. 'To scare people. You were lucky they didn't torture you.'

Albi shuddered. 'What do they do when they torture you?'

'Torture?' said Carlos. 'They've got all sorts but the main one is pulling your finger nails out.'

Albi looked at his hands and so did Pepito. That must hurt badly.

Carlos started rolling rocks over and looking underneath. 'I saw two men on the roof of one of the houses in Calle de las Monjas yesterday. In broad daylight.'

Pepito's mouth hung open as he stared at Carlos. 'On the roof? Oh – you mean mending it.'

'Not mending it, stupid. Creeping about. I 'spect they were snipers.'

Albi hadn't heard that word before but neither had Pepito, so he could pretend he knew what it meant.

'It would have been Republicans,' Carlos said. 'Hoping to shoot some of the *Guardia.*'

'What sort of guns did they have?' Albi asked, really alarmed now.

Carlos shrugged. 'They were too far away to see. Anyway the point is, once you get out on the roof you can creep from one house to another and nobody can see you from down in the street.'

'You did,' Pepito said.

'From up the hill you would,' Albi objected. From up the hill, if you were one of the *Guardia* and you saw men creeping about on the roofs, you'd be able to pick them off like pigeons on a roost with the pistol you kept in the shiny leather holster on your belt.

Carlos picked up a small boulder. 'You'll see.' He chucked the boulder in the stream with a loud splash.

They couldn't argue with that, and when Albi told them about his new job working for the blind man it didn't sound very special after all. Not after a sniper on the roof.

26

Secrets

The sound of the stream came furling through the open window, into the Molino kitchen where the blind man's fingers rustled among the dried bean-pods on the table. 'You see only with your eyes,' he said. Albi glanced up at the dead eyes staring at nothing as the blind man picked out the beans and put them in the bowl. 'But I see with everything except my eyes.'

Albi chewed on his new bread and salty ham and gazed out of the window. The blind man couldn't see the bright new leaves dancing in the sunshine.

'You think you can see and a blind man doesn't, but it isn't true.'

He watched the hands moving among the papery bean haulms. 'But *what* do you see?'

'What is this *seeing*?'

The haulms rustled. The birds sang outside in the brilliance of the afternoon, the air was soft as goose-down. Was that what he was talking about? But the blind man said, 'I see the dark things moving.'

Albi shivered, as if the dark things had moved right over his skin, but he said nothing. He wanted the blind man to go on talking.

'Especially at night, I see them. It's clearer at night, the sounds and the smells and the distances. I see the ibex bounding over the rocks from the loose stones skittering. The stillness when they stop running to stand and watch me. I hear them whistle to warn the others.'

Would the blind man know if it was a man sending the loose stones falling and not an ibex? Probably he would. How did he find the paths? How did he find his way back to the village again? So many questions Albi wanted to ask, but he didn't.

'You have to learn how to see. That day I met you on the path, remember? I knew I was coming near the big rock by the warmth touching the side of my face but I could hear it also, from the way my footsteps echoed. How do *you* know where you are when you walk about the village?' El Ciego's voice was mocking, as if he thought Albi didn't see anything much at all.

He couldn't make his thoughts into an answer. He watched the calloused fingers rustle among the bean pods, seeking out the full ones and shelling them into the enamel bowl. A scrap of dried pod fell in the bowl with the beans. He wondered if he should mention it.

El Ciego pushed the bowl away and stood up. 'I'll show you what I mean. We should go back to the village now. Curfew will be soon.'

They walked past the sentries and up the slope towards the houses. At the point where the gardens ended and the houses began the blind man stopped. He stood in the middle of the road with his finger pointing to the sky. 'Listen.'

Albi listened, but he didn't hear anything except the things you hear everywhere. Distant voices, a sheep bleating, water rushing.

'Can you feel the warmth on both sides of your face?' the blind man said, so quietly Albi had to lean close to hear. 'That is the tall walls enclosing the path – we're coming into the village. But there is more heat on your left cheek than your right and you can hear the echo of the river bouncing off that wall. That's because we are standing under Luis Irún's house, which faces the sun and the river.'

Albi looked up at the vulture face. It had no emotion in it, just the chalky eyes listening. If there was a man hiding up on the roof, would El Ciego be able to tell that too?

'I know every inch of this village,' the blind man said softly. 'I can taste the shape of it in the sounds my feet make. The walls talk to me.'

Albi was suddenly afraid. That was the way a mad person talked.

El Ciego grinned. 'And your house I know by the smell of your mother's bread dough.'

'Her bread dough?'

'It smells sweeter than in any other house.'

They'd reached the corner of Calle de Mora. The blind man stopped and turned to face Albi, but not quite where he was standing.

'From now on leave the lambs behind when you come out in the morning. You'll be walking fair distances to the Molino grazing and they won't keep up. They'll feed well enough when the ewes get back at the end of the day.'

Emilio Serrano passed them, turning his head to stare as he went by, but the blind man seemed unaware of him.

'Goodbye, boy.' He turned away and marched off up the Calle Agustín, his stick tapping sharply along the base of the wall as if he wouldn't know where he was without it.

Was he making a special show of his blindness as a kind of joke?

El Ciego got him another permit. It said Albi was working for El Ciego and could graze all the Molino lands, in the valley and up on the *Meseta*. He needn't be afraid of being more than seven kilometres from the village and nowhere near their far *tierras*.

It didn't stop his heart jumping into his throat and choking him every time the *Guardia* demanded to know where he'd been. Three times he showed the new permit at the check-point on the edge of the village. Three times they scowled at the writing, and let him pass. After that they stopped asking and the new permit stayed in his satchel.

He fetched the extra sheep and goats from the Molino corral every morning, and at the end of the day he parted them out again. El Ciego gave him breakfast before he went out, and fed him again in the afternoon, and every day he gave Albi something to take home in payment – a packet of ham, sliced off the bone and wrapped in a scrap of cloth, or a bag of flour, or oatmeal. A rabbit once, skinned and cleaned and ready to go in the pot. A jar of last year's blackberry jam, a brace of quail. This was the way the villagers paid El Ciego, if there wasn't enough milled grain for him to take a share and no money either. Sometimes, when the debt had grown big, the payment was a whole live sheep or a goat.

Albi was certain now that Carlos had never been inside the Molino kitchen. If he had he wouldn't ask the questions he did, whenever Albi could snatch a half hour with him and Pepito in their special place under the bridge. *How does he eat if he hasn't got a woman?* He could tell them the answer to that, but *Have you seen him take his eyes out?* He couldn't say he had, not without lying. *Have you seen the Molino ghost?* He couldn't answer that, either. What ghost, anyway?

'Have you seen the two long spoons then?' Carlos demanded

'What two long spoons?'

'The ones for supping with the devil.' Carlos gave him the eye, Albi stared back. He knew Carlos was trying to scare him because he was jealous, so he started listing all the things the blind man gave him to eat – the ham, the sausage, the omelettes made freshly just for him – until Carlos was nearly frothing at the mouth and Pepito clutched his belly and moaned out loud.

'And then there's the bread,' Albi said. 'Not black bread like we eat at home. There's no rye in the Molino bread, only wheat flour. Sieved so fine it's white.'

'That's the bread he makes for the *Guardia*,' Carlos said.

That made them go quiet, all three of them.

Pepito said, 'Is it true what they say, then? The blind man sells bread to the *Guardia*?'

'It's probably a double bluff.' Carlos went to sit down but stood up again, whimpering, as the seat of his trousers pulled tight across his buttocks. His papa had beaten him last night for playing truant from school. 'It's just not worth it!' He wiped his eyes on his ragged sleeve. 'But I'll show him! He might be able to beat me into going to school but he can't beat me into learning anything.'

'No he can't,' said Pepito. As if he knew about learning. Pepito had never learned a single thing in school. Or if he had, he'd forgotten it.

Sitting out on the *solenar* with his Papa, waiting for supper, Albi had stories too, now. Things the blind man had told him, or things he'd learned. How many rabbits the blind man had in the long row of hutches against the wall. Who he'd seen at the mill that day, what they'd brought to be milled and what they paid for it. Papa was very interested in everything about the Molino.

They never once talked about the other thing, not even when it was only him and Papa there and nobody else to hear. Papa never asked how he had known where to take Manolo, or what had happened when they got there. 'Words are dangerous, Albi,' Papa said once, looking him in the eye, man to man. 'Words are more dangerous than actions.'

Words.

Miguel came to the house and spent a long time talking quietly to Papa in the stable. Lots of words, first Miguel speaking, then Papa. When Miguel left, Papa said, 'No need for you to know, son. Least said safest.' He patted Albi on the shoulder. 'It's all about networks.' He lifted down the rope hay net from the hook on the wall and held it out. 'See those knots? A line of string between each one?' Albi nodded. 'Each knot on its own doesn't mean anything. But all linked together' – Papa shook out the net and thrust some hay into it – 'the knots make something useful.'

He could see what Papa meant, but it didn't answer the question gnawing at the inside of his chest: if El Ciego made bread for the *Guardia* every day he was working for the enemy. Where did networks come into that?

One worry bred another, like worms in a heap of manure. How could a blind man work with a dumb man? Was it that Joaquín could talk only he pretended he couldn't to hide things? Or could the blind man see really? Was he the one pretending? Perhaps everything was a trick. He watched carefully to see where the trick was, but the blind man's face was unreadable.

He tried coming at it sideways. 'Could you see when you were young?'

'See? What is this seeing?' the blind man said, like he'd said it before, as if *seeing* was something nobody in their right mind would miss for a minute.

'Can't Joaquín talk?'

'Talk? What is this talking?'

He thought about this for a long time, in different places; lying on a rock in the sun, walking his sheep, watering the oxen at the *fuente* at the end of the afternoon. But he still couldn't see how a blind man could see a dumb man talking with his hands.

'Today, you will go back to that place you know of,' El Ciego said, his voice careful so that Albi would hear it: *that place*.

215

It was a shock. He'd stopped expecting it. He glanced up at El Ciego's face but the blind man was staring at the wall.

'You will take these things.' The blind man pushed a loaf of bread and half a sausage towards him. 'Not for you, mind.' He held out an old shirt that might have been Papa's but wasn't. Finally, a lump of bacon fat. All things Albi might have in his satchel and it wouldn't be surprising to other eyes looking in at them.

There was nobody on the path, only Ovidio with his sheep in the scrub down by the river, the young lambs crying like babies wailing and the flock moving slowly.

Albi turned away and started the long weary climb up onto the *Meseta*. He found the secret valley and walked up it with his sheep. The *maquis* came out of their hiding places when they saw it was him. Manolo punched him gently on the shoulder as if he was pleased to see him and the others crowded round to see what was in his bag. He handed over the bread and sausage, the shirt, the lump of bacon fat.

They ignored the bread and sausage and the shirt but they fell on the fat, pulling it apart as if they were truly starving.

Then he saw it wasn't that – they were looking for something hidden. One by one a dozen or more bullets spilled out onto the flat rock. The bile rose swiftly in his throat. The *Guardia* might so easily have taken that fat off him.

Next day there was no special food, and the blind man told him to take the flock to graze up on the Prados under La Guadaña.

The day after, a piece of ham, half a loaf of bread, a wedge of cold *tortilla,* and the secret valley again. His throat tight all the way up the path in case he ran into any *Guardia* and they looked in his bag and wondered at him eating so well.

But there was nothing hidden in the bread, nothing inside the *tortilla* except potato and onion, and the *maquis* seemed pleased to see him. Manolo too.

A week later, El Ciego gave him four hard-boiled eggs and a loaf of bread to put in his bag, and a packet of ham sliced off the bone, and he guessed where he would be sent. From the shelf, the blind man took a ball of twine, a tube of ointment, a small pair of scissors. Albi put them in his satchel.

The blind man said, 'You tell them, the weather is changing. Tomorrow the wind will be from the west.'

'*Si,* señor.'

'Say it back to me.'

'There'll be a west wind tomorrow.'

'No no! *The weather is changing. Tomorrow the wind will be from the west.* Say it exactly as I say it.'

Confused, Albi repeated the words.

El Ciego put out his hand out and rested it on his head. 'Don't forget. Exactly as I said it. And ask them for their reply.'

Nobody looked surprised at the message.

The Butcher said, 'Tell him, *the eagles have rebuilt their nest but there are no eggs in it.*'

Albi nodded.

The butcher raised his eyes to heaven. 'Say it back to me, boy.'

Whether he was sent to find the *maquis* or whether he wasn't, he never said at home where he'd been and Papa didn't ask, neither did Mama. Perhaps they didn't want to know how dangerous it was. Perhaps they didn't realise what was going on. But once, when he was with his mama in the kitchen and there was nobody there to hear, she murmured, 'Is he well, Albi? Is he all right?'

He looked at her and considered pretending he didn't know who she meant, the same way she was pretending not to understand it was so dangerous. But he didn't have the heart. 'He's very well, Mama.'

'You would tell me, wouldn't you? If ever he wasn't?'

He nodded his head quickly, wondering if he would.

'Next time you climb the hill,' she said, 'take that pot of honey with you. Don't say anything, just take it from the cupboard.'

He never knew when he was going to the secret valley, not until he got to the Molino in the morning and El Ciego told him where to go. Besides, he was taking them food as well as messages and that was surely enough. So the honey stayed where it was.

Carlos and Pepito would have been more difficult to deal with than Mama, had Carlos's papa not resorted to the horse-whip. But Carlos was in school every day now, since the whip, and Pepito on his own was easy to shake off. No need to worry about him.

He knew the names of all ten *maquis* now. The Student, who sometimes they called *el medico*, was Sergio really. The blonde man they called the quartermaster, as if it was a joke, was called Toni. There was a José and a Paco. And the butcher of course, but it was hard to think of the butcher by his name – *Vicente* sounded like a gentle sort of man. A Vicente would not kill your friend.

They were all his brothers now, the men said. They told him a warning signal to make so they would know who was coming. 'Whistle like this. As if you're whistling up your dog,' Toni said.

They were always glad to see him because he brought them food and other useful things, and sometimes there was a message as well. Apart from the bullets that one time, the *maquis* seemed more interested in what they could eat than in anything else. They were lean, hungry men, except for the Butcher, who was built like a wrestler. The Butcher alone never seemed pleased to see Albi. 'Don't mind Vicente,' Sergio the student said. 'It's just his way.'

Manolo always milked the two goats before Albi set off for home. He milked into a jug he'd got from somewhere. Where? Jugs don't grow on trees. The Butcher watched him milking and sneered.

'Who wants to drink that muck when wine is so much better?'

Manolo took no notice.

Albi wouldn't let him take any milk from the ewes. That would be stealing from their lambs. As it was, when he got home and Mama went to milk the goats and found hardly anything there, she looked at him hard. She didn't say a word, but she didn't look cross either, even though the pot of honey was still in the cupboard.

27

The Torre

Alberto hobbles along the passageway. His foot is hurting this morning and he has to use his stick, even in the house. In the sheep pen, five ewes stand by the trough. Five?

On the far side of the pen, beyond the hay rack, the sixth sheep lies stretched out on the dirt floor, one glassy eye staring up at the roof beams. The ewe he calls Titi, nearly as old as Old Perrito, which is saying something. Even a sheep can die of old age, but Alberto's eyes fill as he stands looking down at her. It isn't just Titi, it's La Gorda he's thinking of, and himself as a child, lost in the past.

'Are you down there, Alberto?' Mari-Jé calls down the stairs.

He hurries out of the pen, not looking back as he shuts the gate behind him. Glad that the corpse is out of sight, should Mari-Jé come down. 'What is it?'

'Raul. On the phone. He wants to know if you'll give him a hand with the rabbits this morning.'

'So, *Tío,*' Raul says, putting the broom and shovel neatly against the shed wall. 'What's this little job needs doing? You're being very mysterious.'

Alberto leans the wheelbarrow against the wall, next to the broom. 'One of the ewes died last night. The old one. I need to get it out of the house.'

'Sure. It'll mean a trip to Las Hoyas, though. And paperwork. Bloody EU regulations!'

Alberto isn't thinking about rules. All he wants now is to get that dead sheep out of the house before Mari-Jé notices. Any excuse and she and the kids will gang up on him to get rid of his last few sheep. He starts to say this to Raul, but his throat goes tight and the words don't come out properly. His vision blurs. All he can see is glassy eyes staring, not at the ceiling but at the open sky, and himself as a child, terrified out of his wits as his best friend's head lands at his feet.

'*Tío?*' Raul's hand on his arm, his face coming close. Alberto wants to pat the hand reassuringly but he can't. He is here with Raul, but he is there too. 'Alberto! What is it?' Raul takes hold of his elbow, as if to support him.

It is strange to hear Raul call him by his name. He brushes his free hand across his eyes. 'Mari-Jé thinks… She thinks I'm going senile.'

'Why? Why does she think that?'

'She says I'm behaving oddly.'

'Really?' Raul stares at him for a moment, then shrugs. 'Well *I* haven't noticed. But then maybe I'm going senile too.' He kicks off his rubber boots and shoves his feet into his old trainers, glancing at his watch. 'Come on, *Tío*. If we're quick we can get this dead sheep of yours sorted while Mari-Jé is out collecting the bread. If she notices one's missing you can tell her I've taken it off you. You don't need to tell her it was dead.'

They go out to the truck. Raul opens the driver's door and pauses, looking at Alberto over the roof of the cab. 'There's nothing wrong with your mind, Alberto.'

Alberto shrugs, but he feels better for hearing it said out loud.

Bread comes three mornings a week from Valbono but you have to be waiting in the Plaza when the van comes, otherwise you might miss it all together.

Raul glances across at the gossiping women as he drives past the end of the Plaza. 'Such a lot of time they spend waiting for that van. It would be quicker to make the bread themselves.'

Behind them, in the back of the truck, the ewe lies stiff and unrelenting, covered with an old blanket against prying wifely eyes.

They drive in silence up the empty main road, which cuts great curves up the steep hill. Papa would have been amazed by this road, Alberto thinks, as he always does when he comes up here. So much road and nobody on it. You get used to things and then you forget how different it used to be. The road swings up over the crest of the valley and there is the *Meseta*, spread out before them to the great blue distances. It's unchanged, even if the new road has cut it in half. Away to their right the broken back of the ruined Ermita de las Estrellas still rocks against the sky, but the road doesn't go near it now.

Raul keeps turning his head, peering to their left and then to their right. 'Santi's up here somewhere. He's out with my brother-in-law's sheep today.'

Alberto nods. That's a big flock; it's good the lad has something to keep him busy, and sheep are as good a way as any to earn a living. He stares out across the sheets of bright white rock and patches of pine trees, dark against the sun, but there are no sheep anywhere. No humans either, and precious little grass. Just rocks, and trees.

'More than eight hundred sheep, Manuel has now,' Raul says.

That's more than Raul ever had, Alberto thinks, and more than four times what he himself possessed. He smiles, gazing across the rolling plain: he can always place the different stages of his life by the number of sheep he owned at the time. Seventeen ewes: that was the year after he came back from

Zaragoza. Twenty-five sheep was the year he married Mari-Jé. A hundred and eighty-four – he was in his fifties by then. A hundred and eighty-four sheep and a shed full of rabbits, and most years a pig or two. That was my prime, he thinks, as they hum over the top of the world, Raul and him. He'd been proud of those numbers – the *abuelos* would never have dreamed of owning so many – but now they seem so small. He has only five sheep left, and neither of his sons wanted the rabbit shed so it's gone to Raul. After Raul it will go to Santi, if he's still here. If he wants it.

*

'Come here.'

He was getting used to this. He went up close. El Ciego's hands passed over his face, gentle as butterflies, as if by feeling Albi's face he would be able to read his expression.

'Today you are going to La Torre de Las Estrellas,' El Ciego said. 'You will give this message to Andrés Prieto Ibañez.'

He was careful to keep his face very still under the blind man's fingers but that was Mena's Andrés. Was Andrés to have messages then, like the *maquis*? Even though he spent every night in the village?

'Listen and remember. The message is, *tomorrow evening three one six*. Repeat it.'

'Tomorrow evening three one six.' The numbers jumped about in his head. They meant nothing so they weren't memorable. Then he remembered El Ciego saying once that numbers had colours. He tried putting colours to these: *three* is blue like the sky, *one* is green like the summer oak trees, *six* the white moon. *Three one six* – the blue sky over the green oaks with the white moon rising. *Tomorrow evening*.

The blind man took his hands away. 'You do not tell him this if there is anybody else there to hear. Understand? Walls have ears and you don't want to put yourself in danger. Be careful to be back here well before curfew. It's a long walk to Estrellas. You should go now.'

Albi crossed back over the river bridge the way he had come that morning and skirted the village. He climbed quickly by the small paths, keeping a safe distance from the houses and the *castillo* until he could join the main track to Las Hoyas higher up the hill. The Molino had lands on the *Meseta* bordering Andrés's farm and he had his permit safe in his satchel giving him permission to go up there to graze his flock. All the same, he was scared, climbing the Las Hoyas road in full sight of anybody who cared to look. The *maquis* perhaps, watching from the cliff edge above, waiting with a gun. The *Guardia* perhaps, down in the village looking up, with many guns. Or Carlos, playing truant and sitting all on his own outside the *castillo*, risking the horse whip.

'Don't try to hide,' El Ciego had said. 'That will only look suspicious.' That was easier to say than to do. 'The Molinos lands lie beyond Estrellas on the southern side. You have every right to be there.'

It was a long, weary climb, the old track twisting backwards and forwards like a snake. This was the only road where a vehicle could get up onto the *Meseta* but it was a dirt track and very rough. Even so, Papa said the road was the real reason for the *Guardia* being in El Rincón. It made Albi jumpy. He kept looking over his shoulder, even though he knew he would hear a *Guardia* truck toiling up the steep escarpment long before it got close. This was the road Mena's Andrés had to climb every morning, and come back down again every afternoon in time for curfew. And in-between, do a hard day's work.

Why hadn't El Ciego given Andrés the message himself, before Andrés started out this morning?

He climbed, and the village shrank below him until it was only a cluster of orange roofs tucked into a fold of the valley. The track spiralled upwards from the village, a white thread like a kite string, with him as the kite. He stretched out his arms and swooped along the flat between one hairpin bend and the next. But then he remembered somebody might be watching so he stopped. La Perrita grinned, tongue hanging out, trotting backwards and forwards as she brought the flock up behind him. The sheep were panting, the sun was too hot for climbing such a steep road. He stopped to let them rest, pulling his shirt over his head like a tent to protect him from the sun as he stood on the side of the track and looked down over the edge. In the distant dam the water glinted like a mirror. It would be so cool in that water, if he could dive into it from here. If he could swim. The sheep jostled, pulling at the tired tufts of grass. The green was burning off everywhere, the ground smelled hot.

A grasshopper jumped, like an ungainly girl showing her sky-blue petticoats. He pounced. If he had a grasshopper, and a thread to tie on it, he could make a circus. A circus came to El Rincón once. He couldn't really remember it but they still talked about it in the village – the man who could turn somersaults, and the girl who walked on a wire and you could see her drawers.

The grasshopper got away.

He whistled up Perrita and trudged on, up and over the rim of the valley and onto the great rolling table-land of the *Meseta*. Now he was cut off, no valley visible below him any more, not a living being in sight. Just the small outbuildings where the shepherds used to store hay in the old days, where they would sleep for weeks on end in the summer while they grazed their flocks up here on the plains. But not now. Not since the soldiers came.

The road dipped and rose again, and swung to the north, and then the Ermita de La Virjén de Las Estrellas came in sight, standing up on the skyline like a broken bedstead. Even without its roof the chapel was the highest point on the *Meseta*.

It was a good name, Virgin of the Stars.

The last bit of the climb towards the Ermita, and all the world was spread out in a blaze of sun. White shoulders of rock pushed up through shaggy grey thyme; blue distances stretched, wave after rolling wave, blanketed with trees in places like dark stains, the valleys hidden. You could lose yourself in so much space.

He whistled to Perrita to hold the sheep while he scrambled up the bank to the great arched doorway of the ruined chapel. The ribs of the arches that once held up the roof framed only the deep blue of the sky now, the little dry plants growing along the ledges of the walls shivered in the hot breeze. Papa had told him the story once; how lightning struck, long ago, killing the people inside, and the Ermita had been ruined ever since, the sun and the wind rubbing out the carvings on the stone pillars until only shallow bumps and hollows were left.

He jumped back down onto the track, not wanting to think about bad things like lightning. The track was descending now. Soon the Torre de Las Estrellas came in sight, first the jutting tower, and then the farm buildings clustered round it. Mena was in the yard, shielding her eyes from the sun as she watched him come down the slope. It made him self-conscious, so he ran to get there quicker. He'd thought she would be in the village, in Teresa's dark house. Not up here in the sun, close to the sky.

When he arrived in the yard she was laughing.

'I thought it was you! Why all the hurry? What are you doing here anyway?'

Her voice was light and surprised. And pleased – she sounded pleased! He didn't know what to say. He was too shy to look at her face so he looked at her feet. She didn't have her sandals on, just espadrilles, but she was wearing the dress with little flowers on and lots of buttons only he hadn't recognised it at first, it was so faded, and the hem was torn.

'You look hot,' Mena said. 'Come in.' She led him inside the house, waving one hand airily when he asked what to do with the sheep, as if it didn't matter where they wandered.

And then he was in her kitchen.

It was cavernous, like a church. But not like a church, because the ceiling was smoke-stained, same as in any other house, and the great canopy of the fireplace was like theirs at home except ten times bigger. He sat at the table when Mena told him to and peered about him, but it was so dark with the shutters closed against the hot white light outside he could hardly see what he was looking at. A dull fire glowed in the hearth. A fireplace a whole family could sit inside and not get burned. If they wanted to, if it wasn't summer.

Mena put some sticks on the embers to wake them up. As the flames caught, it was easier to see the big stone flags under his feet, the wooden settles on either side of the fire, the great table squat in the middle of the floor.

A grey wolfhound watched him from the hearth, then laid its shaggy head back on its paws and sighed. Mena was busy doing something in a cupboard in the wall. On the table there was a big brown jug with five heavy cardoon heads in it, glowing bright purply-blue. He thought of Belén decorating her house, and Mama laughing at her. The flowers made Mena's kitchen look happy.

She brought him a plate of new bread and a beaker of milk. She cut him a slice of new cheese. How did she have these things? A girl who hadn't known how to wash clothes until he showed her. Did she know about setting milk with cardoon sap to make cheese? Did she make the bread her very self? He saw the flash of her teeth in the gloom as she smiled at his questions.

'Oh yes! I like to be here with Andrés. I made the bread, Andrés is teaching me to make cheese.'

He ate quickly, in case any of the food should disappear as easily as it had come, watching her all the while. How could she do these things and get all the way to and from the village every day? He didn't ask, he didn't want to be rude.

A shiny red tomato appeared on his plate, freshly polished on

Mena's apron. 'You are very honoured – that's one of the first tomatoes I've ever grown.'

'How did you know how to grow them?'

'Andrés showed me.'

He heard it in her voice – all that summer happiness, her pleasure in learning about the growing of things. Her and Andrés, here on their own in this place, doing these things together. Something hurt inside him, as if somebody had squeezed his heart. He wanted this, whatever *this* was. He wanted it for himself, a quiet house with somebody like Mena in it, so light on her feet, and so graceful and nice to look at, and a big table with cardoon flowers on it, just for decoration.

He looked round the room. Now his eyes were getting used to the shadowy light he could see the wooden rack on the wall with the spoons in it, like in their house – one for each person, but here there were six in the rack, not seven like at home. Six, when they used to be so many here, eating at the great table, but only her and Andrés to use them now.

Or were there other people too, hiding somewhere? The house was silent, only the murmur of the low fire, the sigh of the dog, a cat mewing as it rubbed round Mena's slender ankles. He tasted the feel of the room. No, it was only him and Mena here. He looked at the stone shelves with the old plates on them, and under the plates the same lace edging they had at home, yellowed with smoke. Mena moved among these things as if they were her own but they must have been new to her a year ago, just as they were new to him now. New but familiar, in this house not so far from his own but on a different scale entirely. And where in his house they were seven people in a small space, here the space was enormous and they were only two. And outside, the vast world stretching all the way to the horizon.

'Are you still hungry?' she said. 'My little brother was always hungry, back home in Valencia.'

He minded that, even while he nodded, but she didn't seem

to notice. She was too busy breaking eggs into a basin, talking all the while, as if she had spoken to nobody in weeks. *That* made the house feel empty.

'I'm making an omelette for Andrés when he comes in. If you wait you can have some.' She put a pan on the fire to heat. 'Could your mother use some eggs?'

She might. The *Guardia* had been to their house again yesterday while he'd been out with the flock and taken all their eggs. Did they never come here too?

'They come,' she said, her voice suddenly tight as if her throat had closed off and swallowed the words. 'But not so often. Not in a while now.'

The omelette smelled good. Too good for him to keep worrying, even when she told him that yes, she and Andrés were supposed to return to the village every night for curfew, like everybody else, but they didn't. It was too far. There was no petrol for the truck, it took so long in the cart, and besides it was too much to ask of the mule after a hard day working in the fields. 'And who is to know?' she said. But the *Guardia* went checking! Did Andrés not realise his mother might be questioned? That she might be knocked about if she couldn't give the right answers, even though she was old? *He* knew this, so how could Andrés not know it?

Or was it only Mena who didn't know? She seemed so untouched in her happiness, as if a light was shining inside her as she moved round the shadowy kitchen. He watched her while he ate the thick wedge of hot omelette and drank another beaker of milk. The potato in the omelette melted in his mouth, the eggs were creamy. Still Andrés didn't come and the message sat heavy on his stomach, weighing down the omelette, curdling the milk.

'Why are you here?' she'd asked, and he'd said (as he really was) that he was taking the sheep to graze the Molino lands that lay beyond La Torre de Las Estrellas.

'The Molino has lands up here? I didn't know that,' she said, as if she was the same age he was, after all, and every day still learning new things she didn't know before.

At last he couldn't dawdle any longer. Andrés hadn't come. When Albi asked if he'd be here soon, Mena waved her hand vaguely and said 'I never know when to expect him, when he's out in the fields.'

What would he do if he didn't see Andrés now? It would seem strange if he called in a second time today.

'Will you be coming back this way?' Mena said. 'Come to the kitchen as you go by. I'll give you eggs for your mother then. You don't want to carry them all day in the sun.' She looked away, out through the door towards the brilliant light. 'Your mother has been kind to me.' Her voice was suddenly sad, as if her life wasn't all bright sunshine and the happy growing of tomatoes after all.

He got up to go. 'Don't you like it in the village?' he asked, not knowing how else to touch her where she was hurting.

'I prefer it up here. The people in the village make me uncomfortable. Especially in the beginning they did.'

'They don't mean to. They're afraid of strangers. Strangers bring bad things.'

She laughed, and ruffled his hair. 'Wise boy,' she said. 'Old head on young shoulders.'

They looked up at the sound of boots on the stones outside and there was Andrés. 'Albi! I wondered whose sheep it was in my corn.'

Andrés went with him to get the sheep out of the wheat. He wasn't cross really. The sheep were too busy eating round the edges to have done much damage, which was lucky because the wheat was ripening and they could have spoiled it. Who would thresh it when the time came? That was a big job for two people on their own.

When they were safely away from the house, and nobody visible anywhere in the whole wide world, he murmured to Andrés, 'El Ciego says, *tomorrow evening three one six.*' He saw the surprise, eyes widening, as if Andrés was looking at him properly for the first time.

'Well well well. I never thought he would send a child.'

The pride in Albi's chest went down like a punctured bladder at that word.

Andrés looked at him kindly. 'Next time you come, pen your sheep in the corral by the house. I won't want them in my crops again.'

'I'm very sorry. I told my dog to keep them on the grass by the house but then I was a long time because you didn't come and I didn't know what to do. I didn't want to leave the message with *la señora.*' He said *la señora* carefully. He didn't know if Andrés might mind him calling her Carmen. Even worse, Mena.

Andrés tousled his head. 'You did quite right.'

All through the middle of the day, the sheep grazed and rested on the lush Molinos meadows. When the sun began its slow descent, Albi set off for home.

Mena gave him bread with honey on it when he called by for the eggs. 'Our land of plenty,' she'd said. 'Tell your mama she can give the basket to my mother-in-law tomorrow.'

Down down down the winding track he went, the sheep hurrying him because they wanted to get back to their lambs. El Rincón lay in a huddle below him, so close it looked as if he could reach down and touch it, so far away that everything looked tiny. The church was no bigger than a thimble, nestling in a tumble of red roofs.

The slope made his knees hurt and the basket of eggs was heavy on his arm.He stopped and put the basket down for a moment, the flock standing in the road and panting a little. They were impatient to get back and relieve the tension in their

230

straining udders but it didn't do to let them rush and get overheated.

There were two black trucks on the road out of the village, one going out, one further away coming in. The *Guardia*, or maybe one of them was El Caballero's truck: those were the only people it could be. Andrés had a truck still – he'd seen it standing, dusty and sad, in the lean-to at Estrellas – but there'd been no petrol for a long time, if you were an ordinary person, because the *Guardia* and El Caballero kept all the petrol for themselves.

The two trucks down by the village looked like two tiny black beetles meeting on a thread of white grass, one backing up to let the other pass, then beetling on. The sound of the engines was small and thin like an insect whining. He glanced back at his flock, swelled to twenty-five now with the Molino animals, and whistled to La Perrita.

On they went again, down the steep track, the clanking sheep bells loud in his ears. Nobody would ever *not* hear him coming, but he wouldn't hear them.

*

It doesn't take them long to dispose of the dead sheep in Las Hoyas. Afterwards, Raul suggests a coffee and a small glass of brandy to go with it, so they go into the bar opposite the *Guardia Civil* building. The streets are busy. Las Hoyas is a bustling little place these days, but Alberto isn't sorry when they're back in the truck, weaving their way out through narrow streets. The sun is dancing in the naked poplars as they cross the bridge over the sluggish slip of a river. In a corner, behind the Municipal dustbins, the mountain road looks like an afterthought.

They climb the steep slope, the cloudless sky peeping bright and keen between the pale looming crags. Up onto the *Meseta* they drive, the dead grasses blowing in the winter wind. Still no sheep anywhere in sight, though there are some black cattle in the distance and a white truck, speeding away from them along a track, throws up a plume of dust. Raul turns his head from side to side as he drives and Alberto does the same, scanning the glistening view, so bright and alive in the windy sunshine, for any sign of Santi and the sheep.

Coming from this direction it is harder to ignore the ruined Ermita dominating the skyline, and the Torre nestling beneath it. As they come closer, Alberto averts his gaze. He knows what's there: the buildings neglected, the old roofs beginning to fall in. The old guilt nags at his belly.

Raul says, 'The Torre's been sold again, did you hear?' Alberto gives a non-committal grunt, his eyes fixed on the opposite horizon. 'It's changed a bit since your day, *Tío*.'

Startled, he turns his head, but Raul is busy looking for Santi, not really watching the road, or the Torre either.

'An English man this time, apparently. So *he* won't be troubled by any old ghosts.'

Alberto goes very still inside. What does Raul know? He wasn't yet born when all that happened. Is this something else that Pilar used to talk about?

28

Plans

'It's too fucking hot to kill a sheep in the day-time,' the Butcher said. 'And too fucking noisy to leave one behind for killing later. You'll have to stay here and go back in the morning. Nobody will miss you.'

Mama will, Albi thought, hoping it was true. 'I have to go back. The lambs will shout all night if they don't get any milk.'

'They'll just have to shout then.'

He looked at the Butcher's closed-in face and stopped arguing. At least the Butcher had agreed which sheep to kill this time. One of El Ciego's.

That night, the *maquis* stuffed themselves with tough meat that had done too much walking, and Albi sat with them by the fire and ate until he was full. The night-birds were noisy in the dark, the frogs were singing, and he was no longer scared. Though something was going on between Manolo and the Butcher, sitting on the far side of the fire. What was there to argue about? The Butcher was only a butcher, but Manolo could snare partridges and rabbits and hares. He could tickle trout in the river. Or he could if he cared to climb down so far and hide up all day on the river bank, climbing back up the hill after dark with his catch gleaming in the moonlight. He talked about making a spear to kill game without wasting precious bullets. The Butcher could do none of those things. He couldn't even milk a goat. Until the war started, the Butcher had lived all his life in a town. So had the others.

There were more *others* tonight, four new faces since last time he was here. New faces who watched him with suspicion because they didn't know he carried their secret deep inside him where nobody could see it. For a moment he was proud, but then the same old question shrivelled up his heart and made it shake like a withered plum hanging in a tree: if the *Guardia* questioned him, would he tell things he shouldn't? Thoughts like that made it feel safer up here where the great black arc of the sky was so full of stars and the rock enclosed them like walls, the faces glowing in the firelight.

A safer fire tonight, now Manolo had told these city men how easily they might have set the whole *Meseta* alight, flames running through the summer grass and up into the trees, all the juniper bushes burning like bonfires. Animals can run in front of the flames but it's different for men. Especially the hidden men.

He stared into the fire. Voices rose. Manolo and the Butcher again.

'Well what do *you* suggest then, comrade?' the Butcher said, not too friendly, and Manolo said, 'Blow it up.'

Albi stopped breathing. Were they talking about the dam?

'What with?'

'Dynamite of course.'

'Oh yeah. Dynamite. I forgot. You got a supply then?'

How could Manolo talk about blowing up the dam when his own family lived right in the path of the water?

'Las Hoyas,' Manolo said. 'That's where we'd put feelers out. Before the war they were using dynamite to make the tunnels for the new road.'

'No shortage of *Guardia* in Las Hoyas either, in case you hadn't noticed. Why else did they make it their headquarters, if it wasn't to keep things like dynamite out of enemy hands?'

'You wouldn't need a lot to blow up the pump house,' Manolo said. 'Even less for the water-pipe. There are comrades in Las Hoyas would get us enough dynamite for that. It's a question of contacts.'

Not the dam, then. Albi sank his chin onto his knees to stop his teeth chattering, though it wasn't cold. He didn't like the thought of Manolo creeping about Las Hoyas under the noses of the *Guardia*, and then creeping back up the hill again with dynamite under his arm.

'You got a contact then?'

Manolo started to speak but the Butcher didn't wait for an answer. 'Save your breath. There's no point wasting time dreaming up fancy schemes for things we haven't got. We wouldn't be skulking up here in this bloody wasteland if we had dynamite. Think small, comrade. Think small and lethal.'

'Poison the water then,' another voice said. 'Poison the dam.'

'What with?' Manolo asked. 'You suggesting we all go and piss in it?'

Laughter.

'No, but we could chuck a few dead bodies in.'

'Fascists would do,' somebody else said.

They all started talking then, except Sergio, who picked up his guitar and began quietly strumming. Albi studied his bare toes.

'Anthrax,' the Butcher said suddenly. 'They say it's deadly if you catch it. I heard of a butcher got it in his arm and his arm turned black and he died. If sheep and cows die of it, why not wild animals like these ibex? D'you ever see anthrax round here, comrade?'

'I've heard of it,' Manolo said slowly. 'Don't know that I've ever seen it. How would you recognise it?'

The Butcher shouted, 'Hey, *medico*! How would you know anthrax if you saw it?'

Sergio stopped strumming. 'Anthrax? Dark blood oozing from body orifices. Blood not clotting. That's mainly what you'd see in a person who was already dead. I guess an animal would be the same.'

Orfice? That sounded nasty, whatever it was.

'Sudden collapse, laboured breathing – that's probably what you'd notice if the animal was infected but still alive. It's a bacillus.'

Basi luss. Strange words, this anthrack-thing had.

Manolo's voice said, 'So, if we found something that had died of it and threw it in the dam as near where they take the water off as we could get, would it be infectious through the water?'

Silence, just the fire crackling. Then Sergio said, 'Poisoning healthy people isn't a doctor's job.'

'Fuck the job.' That was Manolo again. '*Might* it work?'

Sergio didn't say anything.

The Butcher growled 'It's your duty to say, comrade. Beggars can't be choosy and we sure are beggars. We have to use whatever weapons come to hand. Would it work or wouldn't it?'

Albi heard the hollow echo that was Sergio laying his guitar down on the ground.

'First, you'd have to find your dead ibex, or your sheep, or whatever. And as Manolo said, he's never seen it; it's not all that common. And when you'd found it you'd have to carry infective material to the dam. The disease is spread by spores, the spores spread easily. They're highly infectious and they hang around for a long time. Without special protective clothing the one most likely to die would be the comrade who handled the material, and he'd probably infect his comrades so they'd die too. Whereas the inhabitants of Valbono might, but only might, ingest a minute trace of it via the water supply. In which case, some people might die. Or they might not.'

Albi was surprised. Then he was sad. He'd thought Sergio was a nice man, but here he was talking about how to poison people. Some of his cousins lived in Valbono.

The Butcher was disappointed too. 'So, you're saying it would be a suicide mission? Pity.'

They all started talking then. Albi stopped listening.

In the morning, in the Molino kitchen, he told the blind man about the anthrack plan.

'Ah,' said El Ciego. He didn't say anything more.

'They can't know about the new pill-boxes,' Albi said. He hadn't said anything last night when the comrades were making their plans, but they wouldn't be able to drop anything in the dam without being seen, not now the new pill-boxes were there.

'Oh, they know about those,' El Ciego said.

So who told them? Then he remembered, Manolo had seen them, the night he took him to the *maquis*. Only, how did the blind man know that?

When he got home his mama said she'd told his sisters he was up in his bed all yesterday evening with a fever. 'But I can't tell them that more than once.'

There were tears in her eyes. He looked at them with interest

236

thinking they were just for him, until he remembered the pot of honey.

She grabbed him suddenly by the arm and leaned close. 'I had to bottle-feed all the lambs with cow's milk to shut them up. Last night and again this morning. It's very dangerous. Somebody will hear, and they will guess.'

Albi sat on the edge of the *fuente* in the Plaza, waiting for the cattle to drink their long, thirsty fill. He stared at the water spurting out of the metal spout. Water looked as if it couldn't hurt you, but now he knew it could. If Manolo and the others carried out their plan, the people in Valbono would think the water wouldn't hurt them too, then one day they'd be wrong and they would die. Thinking about it made him cold to his bones in spite of the late afternoon sun, hot on his back. He didn't want to die.

What was this poison thing anyway, that could make the water kill people? It had sounded so dangerous, but then it only seemed to be about sheep and cows and ibex, which were not dangerous at all. Except for bulls, but that was different.

Belén came with her water jar. 'Hello Albi,' she said, smiling her gap-toothed smile. She held the jar under the *fuente* where the water came out of the metal pipe and filled up the trough and ran over the side and down into the drain through the metal grid. Belén filled her jar and carried it away on her shoulder.

The cow and the oxen went on drinking noisily from the trough. He stared at the water gurgling down into the ground. When they were little, him and Carlos, they used to dare each other to stand on that grating because the drain was so dark and scary. Carlos told him once that if he fell down one of the cracks between the metal bars he would go down down down to the very middle of the earth. Now he was half grown-up, he took supplies to secret people. He knew it was only a drain.

But last night something as simple as water was suddenly made terrifying. It kept things alive, and made the plants grow, it washed their clothes and cooled their faces, went in the pots to cook the food, and in the bread dough to make more bread. Water in the big jars in the kitchen, cool and tasting of clay. Water in the *chorreta* and the wash house, in the river, in the ponds, in the *barranco* behind their house, water in the dam. Water was the reason this village was here. Water was all of history, of the Moors coming, and before that of the hills being made, if you believed the old schoolmaster. And now they said water could kill you.

He tried to remember the long words Sergio had used. He hadn't followed what they were saying except that it was about killing people, which seemed to make them excited, those bored, dirty men. You could hear it in their voices. It was all so confusing. God said it was wicked to kill other people, but if you were in a war and they were trying to kill you, was it all right to kill them first?

29

Midsummer

'Where are you going?' Mari-Jé says, sharply.

Thursday is the doctor's weekly surgery in the old *Ayuntamiento*.

'To see the *medico*.' Alberto won't look at her, to see the glint of triumph in her eye. But then he can't quite *not* look. He raises his eyes. Mari-Jé's face is pleased and anxious both at once, but not triumphant. Shall he tell her he's only going about his in-growing toenail, or let her go on guessing?

'Good.' She turns back to the sink. 'But don't forget,' she adds. As if that is a joke.

He limps out of the room. His problem isn't forgetting. It's remembering too much.

*

El Ciego put his hands on Albi's head. 'You're tired,' he said, as if he could feel it with his hands. 'There's another message for Estrellas today. Can you manage that?'

He heard the worry in the blind man's voice. Was it worry for him being tired, or worry about the message? Carlos would never say no.

'Yes. And I'm not tired.'

'Take this.' The blind man held out a small oblong package, wrapped in white cloth bound round and round with sky-blue thread.

When he was safely away from the village he took the package from his bag and turned it over in his hands. It felt solid, weighty for it size, and when he held it to his ear and shook it there was a faint rattle.

By the time he rounded the bend of the road by the Ermita his legs were as drained as if all the blood had run out of them. He was hot and thirsty and dreaming of Mena's kitchen – of things to eat, cold milk to drink – but there was Andrés coming towards him, the scythe over his shoulder glinting in the sun. He gave him the message, right there on the track, and held out the package. Andrés seemed to go very still, then he reached out his hand and took the parcel.

Albi turned to cut across the thyme and rosemary towards the Molino meadows but Andrés called him back.

'Aren't you going to the house? Mena would like to see you.' His eyes crinkled at the corners when he smiled. 'Put your sheep in the corral and go into the kitchen. We so rarely see friends up here.'

Friends, Andrés had said he was a friend. And there might be food… Suddenly the whole day looked much more cheerful. He ran down the track towards the farm and there was Mena in the yard. Mena who Sergio said had been going to be a doctor, feeding the chickens instead.

And then she fed him on bread and honey in her kitchen. After that the thought of spending the whole day up on the *Meseta* on his own and the long walk home didn't seem so bad after all.

*

The tap-tap-tap of a stick. Alberto looks up, his mind jumping as always to El Ciego, but it's Mari-Cristina standing at the door of the waiting room, frail and uncertain. Of course it is. El Ciego is long dead. He gets to his feet and calls out a greeting as he hobbles to help her over the step. Side by side, they sit against the wall and chat about this and that, and what the weather is doing, which Mari-Cristina can't see but she has strong opinions about it all the same. He tells her the doctor is a locum today, nobody they know. They talk about their children and grand-children, and how Mari-Cristina's family want her to get her cataracts done but she won't. She's scared of doctors, she says.

You and me both, Alberto thinks, watching her face, her sightless stare.

*

There was one small stone building on the Molino lands up at Estrellas, but nothing inside it except shade from the sun. A line of poplars grew along the trickle of a stream that bordered the broad meadow. Seated with his back against the grey rock that stuck up in the middle of the meadow Albi could see all round, from the poplars on his left to the shoulder of open hill on his right, from the barn in front of him to the edge of the pine trees behind him. The pines grew thickly all the way up the slope above the meadow and he couldn't see the Torre from here, or even the ruined Ermita, but beyond the barn he could see all the way to the horizon, blue and distant.

In the middle of the day, when it grew hot, he could have retreated inside the building. But that would stop him seeing and hearing, so he sat in the shade of the big rock instead, moving round it as the shadow moved. He kept a pile of stones beside him and if a sheep wandered beyond the Molino land, he shouted and threw a stone. Sometimes just shouting did the trick.

He watched, and dozed, and looked at the birds and the little things moving among the stems of the grass, the ants and beetles and things with no name. Or he practised catapult shots at a stick he'd pushed into the ground a distance away. He took his cup from his bag and squirted some milk from one of the goats into it and drank it down. The milk was warm, it wasn't refreshing. He sat back down again in the shade, and when the flock lay down to rest he lay down too, and slept for a bit. But his ears always listened, like a dog is always listening. The bells told him what the sheep were doing.

This is what it's like for El Ciego.

He closed his eyes again and let the sounds tell him things. What shape was the world? He could hear the heat, not just feel it – the buzz of flies looming close and away again, the soft whistle of the wind in the pine trees – but mostly he could smell it.

He was so busy smelling the smells with his eyes shut, his mind didn't notice the footsteps until hands came over his eyes. He jumped away. It was the *Guardia*! It was the *maquis*. It was the blind man. Though he knew, really, the hands were too small and too gentle, even before he saw it was Mena.

241

She was laughing at him. 'Did I make you jump?'

'What are you doing here?' he said, to hide his embarrassment.

'I brought you some dinner.'

He stared. Had she forgotten she'd already fed him on bread and honey this morning?

She lifted the red and white cloth off the top of the basket and spread it out on the rock as if the rock was a table. She broke some bread in two and put the larger piece on his side of the cloth, and the smaller on her side. She took a lump of fresh white cheese out of the basket and cut it in two with a knife: smaller piece on her side, larger on his. And then she put four big strawberries on his side of the cloth and laughed at the look on his face.

'In exchange,' she said, 'I want you to tell me the names of the birds.'

He was dismayed. He knew only three birds by name, cuckoo, woodpecker, and vulture. And the yellow and black *cerisero* that liked cherry trees and sang the same word, almost: *cerisero, cerisero.* Four names.

'You really don't know any others? What's that bird singing now?'

He listened. 'It's like a canary. Only it isn't.'

Her eyes widened. Then she laughed. 'That's a nightingale, silly. Even I know that one.'

All this talk of birds. He humoured her, but it was hardly important when there were so many more important questions. Are you really going to be a doctor? Can you really poison people by putting a dead animal in the dam? He didn't ask. He didn't even ask if she knew a man in Valencia called Sergio who was going to be a doctor. He wasn't supposed to know Sergio himself.

*

The doctor is young, female, and kind. She inspects Alberto's toe-nail and puts his canvas shoe back on for him; promises a visit from the chiropodist; sits at her desk to make a note on the computer. He studies her slender back. Why does she remind him of Mena?

She turns and looks him in the eye. It's her eyes. Behind the glasses her eyes are darkest brown, like Mena's eyes.

'Is there anything else you'd like to talk to me about, Señor Álvarez?'

His first instinct is to hide. Has Mari-Jé been talking? But the girl leaves the question hanging, and smiles as if it is innocent after all. His second instinct is that she's a stranger: he will never see her again, most likely, and there *is* something she might help him with.

'Can you do anything for bad dreams?'

Mari-Jé is coming up the street with the bread. 'Well?' she says.

'Well what?'

'What did he say?'

'She. It was a locum. The chiropodist is coming on Tuesday – she's made me an appointment.'

He enjoys the confusion on Mari-Jé's face, until she shuts her mouth in a tight line and walks off. The set of her shoulders makes it clear she knew she was right all along and he's just confirmed it. He turns his back on her and limps down to the *fuente*. No point trying to walk anywhere today, not when his foot is so painful. Hopefully the chiropodist will be more effective than anything else the sweet young *medica* was able to offer: a prescription for valium and the suggestion he might like to see a counsellor, that was all she'd come up with. So that's that then.

He pulls the prescription out of his pocket and screws it up. He drops it into the drain by the *fuente* but it lodges between the bars and he has to push it through with his stick.

What good are pills and talking?

*

243

Miguel cut the hay for them. Albi helped his mama turn it, and rake it, and bring it home in the panniers on the mule. School had closed for the summer and Carlos was on the loose, but Albi was much too busy loading up the mule and trudging home with the sweet green hay to run free with Carlos.

The day after the hay was safely stacked, on the *solenar* and in the back attic, he went down to the Molino again. Perhaps El Ciego would send him to the *maquis* today, or to the Torre. But there was Joaquín coming out of the Molino like a mole coming out of its tump, all unfamiliar in the bright morning. The dew was still sparkling on the grass and on all the spiders' webs pegged out to dry, but Joaquín had a scythe over his shoulder. By the time Albi was penning the sheep in the corral to go upstairs for his breakfast, Joaquín was walking steadily through the long grass, swinging the great gleaming blade from right to left, right to left. Swish. Swish.

El Ciego appeared in the doorway with a pitchfork and told Albi to go out and turn the hay for Joaquín.

He was sick of hay.

Joaquín walked steadily, up and down the big meadow. With every swish of his blade a fresh slice of grass toppled on the suddenly naked ground. Albi walked along the flat swathes of cut grass, fluffing them up with the pitchfork so the sun and wind could do their work. The grass was shiny on the ground but when he fluffed it up it stopped being shiny. The heat came up and the sweat came out. Dust and seed-heads stuck to his damp skin. Would he get dinner, then, instead of breakfast, if he was here all day? But it was early yet. Joaquín passed him, up and down, up and down, getting further and further ahead. He worked steady and fast, the big man. Did he even know he had company? He finished scything when Albi was only a quarter of the way across the meadow.

He watched Joaquín go in through the cavernous doorway of the mill, as if that was it for the day, but nobody called him for dinner. He looked up at the sun and saw it was still a long way from reaching the top of the sky. Didn't the blind man say he would agree a price if he wanted extra work doing? There'd been no mention of it in the corral this morning. He felt very lonesome working there all by himself in somebody else's meadow.

Then Joaquín reappeared, carrying another pitchfork, and began to fluff up the next row. He drew level, and went on by. Albi worked faster but he couldn't keep up, no matter how hard he went at it. Joaquín came back along the next row and Albi still hadn't reached the edge of the field. He glanced up as Joaquín came close. The big man was looking at him with his mouth hanging open, same as usual. He gave a sudden lopsided grin as he went past and leaned across and clawed a section of Albi's row into his own.

Albi hesitated, looking at the gap Joaquín had made. Was that supposed to be a joke? He could see the big man's shoulders shaking but no sound came out and he didn't look back. So Albi hooked back a wadge of grass out of Joaquín's row to fill up the hole in his own.

When they'd finished the field Joaquín beckoned with his great clumsy forefinger and they went into the Molino. The blind man had cooked them eggs and new potatoes and green beans so fresh and tender they melted in his mouth. After they'd eaten, El Ciego went off with a sack of bread for the garrison, and Joaquín lay down on the narrow bed against the kitchen wall. In a moment he was snoring. Albi waited, but El Ciego didn't come back so he lay down on the cool red tiles of the floor and slept.

The sun was sliding downwards when they went out again to load the hay onto the Molino cart and carry it into the mill. El Ciego led the mule slowly round the field while Joaquín and Albi pitched the hay up from either side.

It was a long day.

*

Alberto goes downstairs to feed the sheep. His toe is much less painful since the chiropodist. All the same, the sound of his own feet shuffling in his slippers makes him think of Papa.

In the back stable, he cuts the strings on the hay-bale and puts the penknife back in his trouser pocket: if he doesn't do that straight away he knows he'll forget where he's put it. He grunts, annoyed at himself, but surely that isn't what Mari-Jé meant? Not that sort of forgetting. He pulls both strings out of the bale and hangs them over the nail along with the rest. This is the last-but-one bale – better remind Raul to bring some more. That makes him snort, that Raul should have forgotten. He breaks open the bale and carries a slice into the pen where the sheep are waiting.

The fragrance of summer grasses hits him as he loosens up the hay. He lifts it to his face and breathes it in. Herbs and sun and summer pasture. And like a black flood filling his senses, the iron smell of blood.

He jumps back, dropping the hay. Stares at it, unseeing, then the sheep come pushing and nearly knock him off his feet. He shouts at them. Bends awkwardly and scoops the hay up in his arms. Breathes it in, just enough to check... but no, the dried grass smells only of summer.

'What's the matter Alberto?' says Mari-Jé's voice at his back so that he jumps again. 'I heard you shout.' She looks down at the sheep and narrows her eyes. 'Five? What happened to the other one?'

30

Fire and Water

There were days when Albi was so tired all he wanted to do was lie in the shade and go to sleep, but he couldn't, not with all the things he had to do for the blind man. Not just the visible things, like making the hay out in the middle of the field where everyone could see, but the invisible things which nobody must know.

And whose eyes might be looking? El Caballero, with his henchman Jesús? The *Guardia*? The inquisitive priest with his big black hat, roaming the village with his awkward questions? *Why aren't you in school? Where are you going? How long have you had that cough?* He was scared of the priest. Inma coughed a lot.

Worst of all there was Carlos. Carlos who was his friend, but now his company was dangerous, and there would be no school to keep him out of the way until September.

'Be careful, lad,' El Ciego said. 'Not a whisper must pass your lips. Understood? Let everyone think you're the same boy you used to be, who goes nowhere and sees nothing.'

He touched the blind man's sleeve to let him know he'd heard, but he couldn't keep out of Carlos's way for ever. If Carlos insisted on coming with him, he wouldn't be able to do the secret things. What would happen then?

He hurried his morning jobs at home so he could be down at the mill before Carlos was even out of his bed, but Carlos lay in wait for him when he came out again. That day it didn't matter, there was no message and the blind man had told him to graze the river meadows. The day after, when he heard the *Guardia* on the sentry post shouting at someone to bugger off, Albi had things in his bag and *the wind will be blowing from the south tomorrow* inside his head. The words in his head he could have

247

kept a secret, but what about the six buttons on a loop of twine, and the cotton reel with a needle stuck under the red thread? That would surprise Carlos. And what about the loaf of bread and four hard-boiled eggs that weren't his to share? He turned back quickly and went along the *acequia* above the mill where the trees would hide him.

'Where were you yesterday?' Carlos said next morning, jumping out of the bushes on the Molino track.

Albi waved his hand in the wrong direction. 'Up there. Were you looking for me?'

Each time he came back from the secret valley his bag was empty and he had another bit of nonsense in his head. The messages in his head were always meaningless. Who wanted to know *the whore has got her skirts up at the back*? Yesterday it was *if there is no fiesta we cannot sing*.

Well they certainly weren't doing much singing any more, these *maquis*. They were too busy arguing, should they do this or should they do that instead? Not enough guns, no dynamite, no animals conveniently dying of the poison thing. 'We have to improvise,' the Butcher kept saying – another new word, a good one or a bad one? Albi didn't know.

He longed to tell Carlos all the new things he was learning, and the new words to go with them. He couldn't talk about the things, but he could let some of the words out into the open air. One Sunday they found a dead rat, him and Carlos. It was lying on the cobbles against the wall of a house. They were very hungry and he wasn't surprised when Carlos said, 'I suppose we *could* eat it.'

Albi leaned over the corpse, inspecting it closely. That might be an *orfice* the blood was oozing from. 'I don't think we should touch it. I think it's ingested.'

'That's just what I was about to say,' Carlos said.

A good comrade would take this rat and throw it in the dam, somewhere as near the water pipe as possible. Perhaps he should do that. But maybe it was wrong, killing people, just like the Bible said. If you believed in the Bible it was easy because then you didn't have to wonder whether you ought to do things. You just did what the Bible said.

He could pretend they'd never seen the rat. Then he wouldn't have to worry about the answer.

'I've got an idea,' Carlos said, leaping down out of the tree just when Albi thought he'd got out of the village without any trouble. Now Carlos would want to come with him to the mill. Even the threat of running into El Ciego wouldn't stop him. Carlos would sit out of sight and wait for him to come out again with the sheep.

'It's a really good idea,' Carlos said. 'You'll see when I tell it to you, when you've fetched the sheep.' And he sat down on the bank, behind a bush.

Albi went in through the back gate of the mill. El Ciego was waiting inside the corral.

'Who was that with you?' His voice was sharp, edgy. There was a look on his face Albi hadn't seen before, a wary, suspicious look.

'I tried to leave him behind, señor. It's Carlos Perez. He wants to come with me and I didn't know what to say to make him go away.'

'I'll deal with this Carlos. Go up to the kitchen – there's a plate of ham for you on the table and a cup of mint tea.'

Whatever it was El Ciego said or did, Carlos had disappeared when Albi went out again a short while later.

All the long walk up the hill the sun beat down on his head like a hammer. In weather like this a fork of lightning could set the countryside on fire; the rosemary, thyme, and juniper were dry as tinder waiting to feed a spark.

What would he do if there was a fire? Where would he hide?

In the river, perhaps, if he could get to it in time. The dam would be better, if the *Guardia* allowed it. Probably they wouldn't try to stop you if the land was all on fire, they would be too busy jumping in the water too. He stared down at the piercing blue-green sheet of water, glinting in the sunshine. It was too far away, anyway. He'd never get down there in time. He turned his back and trudged on up the hill, wishing he was safely down in the valley. He passed the old Ermita and hurried down to the Torre to find Andrés and give him the message. Mena might be there too.

He slept for a long time in the shade of the rock. The sheep grazed quietly, and rested, and grazed again. The day slid past. Far away, thunder rumbled. He slept some more.

At last the sun had gone far enough over, between its banks of clouds, for it to be all right to go home. He called up the sheep and started climbing the slope.

He was topping the rise by the Ermita when he saw the storm in front of him, sweeping up like a grey wall out of the Rincón valley and blanking out the sky. A bolt of lightning crackled down onto the horizon. He stopped and the sheep milled around him. Then the wall of rain hit him. He turned and bolted, the sheep pressing forward in panic as lightning hit the ground all round them.

'No question of it!' Andrés had to raise his voice to be heard over the pounding of the rain on the porch roof. 'Even if this blows over you won't get back to the village by curfew. We'll put your sheep in the barn and you will stay the night.'

Mena stood in the doorway, her eyes shining in the gloom. 'Oh yes, Albi! We will have such fun!'

Andrés helped him corral his flock in the outbuilding where the Estrellas animals were already safely penned. They ran back to the house through rain so heavy it splashed up off the ground like steam, and then, in the kitchen, the water ran out of them again and made great puddles on the floor.

Mena brought two blankets. 'Take everything off and wrap up in this.' She saw the alarm on his face. 'I'll go out of the room. Call me, Andrés, when it's safe to come back in.'

They sat on the settles on either side of the great hearth, watching Mena bustle about the kitchen while their clothes steamed gently on the backs of chairs drawn up in front of the fire. The room was dark as a cave with the shutters closed, just the fire lighting it, and a single candle on the table. The storm raged, safely out of reach.

Mena made peppermint tea to warm them up, and little cakes she'd baked that afternoon. She peeled potatoes, and stirred the mutton stew simmering over the fire.

Albi heaved the blanket up around his shoulders. A bad thought had come to him: the storm was so loud you wouldn't hear the *Guardia* coming. He glanced round at the door to check the big bar was across it.

When he turned back to the fire, Andrés was watching him. 'The *Guardia* will stay snug in their garrison tonight. Too much danger of landslides on the road.'

Mena sat down next to Andrés on the settle. She smiled at Albi and his heart lurched. Such a warm feeling, it gave him, tasting of peppermint. Or was that just the tea? She saw his cup was empty and got up to pour him another one.

Andrés started telling stories about the house. It had been a monastery once, just like Papa said, but the tower was even older. The Templars built it.

'Who?'

'Don't you know about the Templars?' Mena said. 'They were Christian Knights. They built fortified resting places like this for pilgrims to stay in, safe from the *Moros*, on their way to the Holy Land.'

He pictured the *Moros* attacking, and the warriors fighting from the top of the tower. That sort of time had come again, only it wasn't the *Moros* now but men who were Spanish, the same as they were, and that felt like the world ending. He shuddered, and pulled the blanket tight about him.

'Mena doesn't like the tower either,' Andrés said.

He saw the look Mena darted at Andrés, as if to say *not in front of the children,* so he asked what was inside it, but his voice came out small. Whatever the war had been about, it was nothing he'd done, and where would he sleep tonight? Where would Mena and Andrés sleep? Would he be all on his own in this big house, and the tower there, all strange and forbidding and full of dark history?

'Nothing,' Mena said. 'There's nothing in the tower. It's just a storage place. We'll show you in the morning. Andrés, where's the pack of cards?'

They played a new game Albi didn't know but he learned quickly. Mena looked at him proudly, as if he was her pupil and she was his teacher, but he'd rather be like Andrés, who put his arm round her and kissed her cheek. It made him sore inside, seeing that.

After supper Andrés began to sing. His voice was rich and deep, though he was not a tall man, and only slightly built. Albi looked at his shining black hair and his sun-flushed cheeks and wished he was Andrés. And then he looked at Mena and saw she was gazing at Andrés too, and that made him wish it all the more.

The storm had gone quiet, though the rain was still dripping off the roof and splashing on the ground outside. Now there would be no fear of fire running among the juniper bushes and licking at the trees and killing animals – and boys if they got trapped.

Mena made up a bed for him in the *alcoba* of the parlour, where Andrés used to sleep when he was a boy. The bed wasn't just blankets – it had crisp white sheets, turned down as if to let him in. And the mattress wasn't hard wool like at home but feathers, and it had been shaken till it was soft and billowy. As soon as he lay down on it he fell asleep. He slept until morning as if he was a king in a palace and not a shepherd boy.

31

Middle Class

All that night, in the strange bed in the unfamiliar room, he'd dreamed of fighting men up on the tower firing arrows at bad men down below. But now, in the morning, the sun was shining. The world was bright and new, and there was a joke-bird perched on the battlements and shouting *poo-poo-poo*, first in one direction, then the other.

Mena laughed at him because he didn't know the name of even this bird. '*Abubilla*,' she'd said, digging him in the ribs. 'Can't you hear it? Bu-bu-bu? Abu, *abubilla*.'

He ran the word over his tongue. *Abubilla*. A good word for this bright bird with its crest and its long fine bill, bob-bob-bobbing as it bu-bu-bued. If you have words for things, then you begin to see them.

Some things don't need words to see them. He didn't need words for the tower, when Andrés and Mena showed him inside. It was just a big empty space with a narrow staircase winding up, and floors like platforms at different levels for storing things: sacks of corn, a big pile of hay, bundles of fleeces. All of it ordinary, but Mena said suddenly, 'Let's go outside in the sun.'

Andrés laughed at her. 'Mena the doctor is afraid of ghosts.'

Mena the doctor. So it was true, what Sergio had said.

Outside in the sun again, Mena shaded her eyes with her hand. 'This land is full of ghosts.'

Albi looked where she was looking, at the wide view that stretched away below them to the blue curve of land meeting the sky. Ghosts, and real people too. Sergio, who was real and knew Mena, was hiding out there in that huge landscape, not very far away, and she didn't even know. Albi didn't say anything in case it was a secret from Andrés, Sergio knowing Mena.

'So many wars,' Andrés said softly. 'So many wars have passed through this place, all forgotten now.'

Mena turned back towards the house. 'Maybe that's what ghosts are – the forgotten stories haunting us.'

It was late morning when he got home and the sun was high. Following the sheep into the house he went blind in the sudden shadow.

'At last!' said Mama's voice somewhere close, making him jump. '*Madre mia,* Albi! Where have you been? I can't keep making up excuses!'

She'd let his sisters think he'd been caught in the storm, she said, and anybody who'd heard the noise the lambs were making all night or heard the racket the ewes made coming back to them just now… Well, she hoped they'd thought the same thing.

But it was true! He *had* been caught out in the storm.

His mama's face said she didn't think it was enough. He followed her upstairs. On the *solenar* Papa gave him a keen look and went back to whittling the walking stick he'd promised Felipe Moliner.

It was strange being out on the *solenar* in the morning when it wasn't a Sunday, but the Molino sheep were safely back in their pen at the mill and El Ciego had told him to get his flock home to their lambs before their udders burst. It was late enough for the *Guardia* not to take any notice of him coming back into the village, the blind man said, and his parents needed to know he was safe. His mama had already been down to the Molino that morning, looking for him.

The sun spilled hotly across the *solenar* floor and the sweet scent of stacked hay filled the air. He looked out over the balcony rail at the shimmering leaves of the poplars. Morning sounds drifted up from beyond the wall of their corral: somebody chopping wood; Francisco next door shouting across the terraces to his wife; from beyond the poplars, the sound of hammering. The stream in the *barranco* had woken up again with the rain.

Papa didn't ask any questions, and Albi was grateful. He'd have to work out which bits were all right to say and which bits he shouldn't, and Mama was cross enough without him saying anything at all. He sat down on the little chair and La Gatica jumped onto his lap, curling up in a purring ball.

'Here,' said Papa, tossing a tangle of string towards him. 'If you're going to just sit, sort this out. And if you're not taking the sheep out again today you can help me in the *huerto* in a bit.'

'Oh! I was going to look for Carlos.'

Papa withered him with a look. Albi didn't mind, really, because he shouldn't talk to Carlos about the Torre de las Estrellas, something might jump out of his mouth before he could stop it. He began to unravel the string, Gatica helping now and then with a lazy swipe of her paw until he had to push her off his lap. Mama went into the house and soon her broom was banging about in the kitchen. There were scraping sounds as chairs were dragged across the floor.

'So you got a bit wet last night,' Papa said, squinting at his whittling, not looking at Albi. Papa had lost another tooth this morning and it made him look lopsided.

'I stayed in the Torre.'

Papa paused, staring down at his hands, then went on whittling. 'Did you now.'

Albi watched the blade of the penknife shave off slivers of wood. He'd burst if he didn't tell somebody. 'Papa, did you know, there's nothing inside the tower? Nothing at all except some bags of corn and a big pile of hay.'

'They showed you inside the tower, did they?'

'And Papa, they have a whole room full of books, from the floor up to the ceiling!'

Papa wasn't impressed by that, but he did want to talk about the tower because it had been built against the bloody *Moros*, which should be an example to them all. He talked about the Moors as if they were just a little while ago but Mena said the tower was very old. Hundreds of years old, she said, more than six hundred. How many generations would it take to measure out six hundred years?

'It wasn't Andrés's family, lad. Three generations, that's all they've been at the Torre for.'

Mama came onto the *solenar* with her broom and started sweeping out the corners briskly. The dust made Albi sneeze.

'Time we got some work done,' Papa said.

Downstairs in the passageway he put his head close to Albi's. 'No need to spread it around you've been to Estrellas,' he said, as if even Mama shouldn't know. Then he said out loud, 'As you're here you can help me irrigate.'

'But Papa! It rained.'

'Not here it didn't much. Four drops and a lot of noise. That *huerto* needs a good soak.'

Albi opened the wooden gate to let the water from the *acequia* into their garden. Water was a powerful thing. He had to be quick with his mattock, letting it into each section of the garden, then shutting it out again before it broke down the earth ramparts or washed away the seedlings.

Papa hopped round the *huerto* telling him where to let the water go next. Then they stood in the sun while they waited for each plot to fill up to the top of the earth banks.

'Andrés's great-grandfather was the one who bought the farm,'

Papa said. 'The books would have belonged to him. He wasn't from round here. Valencia, that's where he came from. That's enough for the lettuces. Carrots now.' He swung himself over to the next section. 'Good masters, the Velasco family. Always treated their workers well.' He balanced on the earth rampart, his wooden leg sinking into the soft black soil while Albi broke down the ridge with his mattock and let the water run in among the carrots. The sun was hot on his back, the cool slickness of the mud squelched up between his bare toes.

'Steady, lad. Keep it tidy,' Papa growled. 'D'you remember going there with me once?'

Albi stared, until he realized Papa was talking about Estrellas.

'Bank the lettuces back up again, lad. Bank them up. I took you up there to fetch cider apples, with the mule. You don't remember?'

A hazy memory swam slowly to the surface. That feeling he'd had all the time that Estrellas was somehow familiar. But when the memory finally surfaced it felt like a different place altogether, because the picture his mind made was full of people. He remembered a row of men sitting on a bench along a house wall, passing a wineskin from one to another, and him on his papa's knee, watching the children running around but too shy to join in. When he thought about it carefully, yes, he could just remember the same table and bench that were there now, under the vine. And the flagstones of the patio.

'Tomatoes, lad. Wake up.'

So where had they gone, all those people?

Papa went through the names like a list. Andrés's uncle, Pedro Velasco Ruíz: died three years ago. Andrés's two brothers, Raymundo and Fernando Velasco Ibañez: gone to Valencia. Another uncle, Manuel Velasco Ruíz still lived in the village. There were cousins living in Las Hoyas, another branch of cousins in Escucha. The names were musical, like the sound of the water running across the *huerto* and the stream running in the *barranco* below. This was what people talked about in this village: the names, and the patterns they made. Who was family with whom, and when they were born and when they died. Papa reeled them off like something he'd learned in church.

'Estrellas was like a village. In the old days…' Papa pointed with his crutch at the marrows, Albi let the water in, rippling brown and muddy under the big leaves. 'In the old days the Velasco family paid their workers well, gave them rooms to live in so they could have their families with them. He'd made a lot of money in Valencia, the great-grandfather. And then he came to live all the way out here and they never went back to the city. Not until this war came.'

Albi knew that bit. When the war began, Andrés's two brothers went off to Valencia, same as Andrés did the following year, but then he came back with Mena. One of the brothers was a clerk in the Republican government, the other was in the Republican army. The brothers' wives had taken their children and gone back to live with their parents, one in Las Hoyas and one in Montesanto, until the war was over. That's where they were still, because Raymundo had gone to France and nobody knew what had happened to Fernando, and perhaps the war was over but perhaps it wasn't really.

'That'll do for the tomatoes,' Papa said.

They moved on to the beans.

'The Velasco family used to be middle class,' Papa said, bending awkwardly to pull some weeds from around the bean plants. 'Now they're no better than us.'

'Where did Señora Teresa come from then?'

'Oh, somewhere else,' Papa said. That careless phrase, *de fuera*: not from here, so not significant. 'They have a habit of it in their family, bringing their women back from somewhere else.'

Like Mena. Albi thought of Teresa in the wash house, rubbing shoulders with the other women, her hands red from the cold water just like theirs, and Mena beside her. Perhaps his papa was teasing him. Why didn't the Velasco family have servants if they were so smart, like El Caballero had Inés to be his housekeeper? He itched to ask but Papa was glaring down at the muddy water, filling nearly to the tops of the earth banks, and he wouldn't like being asked, not if El Caballero came into it.

He waded back to block the water out of this section.

Papa said 'They lost all their money, I suppose. In the end. The farm is all they have left. Same as us.'

Only they weren't the same as them, Albi thought, when the irrigating was finished and he was walking up the track to shut off the sluice on the *acequia principal*. Andrés still had a lot of land and buildings. And a truck, even if he had no petrol for it. And there was the uncle who had land in the village but no sons or daughters of his own to leave it to.

The bell started ringing for the daily Mass. As he came down past the church a group of women was climbing the steps, but when he got home his mama was in the sheep pen milking the goats. Papa would not be angry, then.

32

Family

The weather stayed hot. The sentries took off their jackets and rolled up their sleeves, and some of them teased the girls who passed by carrying baskets of lettuce and tomatoes from the *huertos,* and onions, white and gleaming, the sun shining through their hollow green leaves. The girls tried not to smile. Even Albi could see it was a game. But when the *Guardia* with the curly hair called after Ramona and she laughed – it wasn't a game then.

The *Guardia* still had their guns, their rifles near at hand, their pistols in the holsters on their belts. How could she pretend that didn't matter?

She caught his eye and tossed her head. 'Don't give me that look. You're getting as bad as Papa.'

She stopped to take a stone out of her shoe. Albi stopped too, to make sure she didn't do any conniving, but it troubled him. However brave Papa might have been once, he didn't want to be like Papa the way he was now. He looked up at the intense blue of the sky, at the old moon sliding downwards as if it was about to fall into the white cliff.

Ramona walked off and he ran to catch up. The factory was closed on Saturdays so people could harvest their crops and the *huertos* were full of people.

Albi stood in the shade sharpening his sickle with the whet-stone. His sisters and his mama bent over their weeding as they moved steadily up and down the rows of onions. The cracked church bell rang out for the daily Mass and Mama straightened her back to listen, but all she said was, 'Tie up those tomatoes for me, Pilar. Inma, those lettuces need thinning.'

He started cutting grass to carry back for the cattle in the byre. Over the hiss of the blade he heard his aunts and uncles and cousins, their voices rising and falling on nearby terraces as they hoed and mowed and weeded, just like them. Beyond them, other families were doing the same. They were all connected by the stories they shared as well as by blood. Even Andrés and Mena who were not related to anyone here – even they were connected, by the stories.

He put the scythe down and tied the cut grass into a bundle.

Now the *Guardia* were here and making the newest bit of the story. But they didn't share it because they were on the other side looking in, with their guns and their threats and their thefts.

He lifted the bundle onto his back.

He'd rather be a prisoner in his own village and belong, than be one of those outsiders telling people what to do.

At dinner-time they went back to the house to eat, and rest a little through the heat.

'Where the devil have you been,' screamed the *abuela,* when Albi took her the bowl of soup. 'Thought you'd up and leave me, did you, you dirty little sod?'

He hesitated, shocked. She'd never called him that before.

Then Mama was there in the *alcoba* beside him. 'I'll feed her. Go on – you go.'

He went back to the cool of the kitchen and spooned thin soup into his bowl.

'That's enough, Albi,' snapped Pilar. 'Mama hasn't had any yet. Nor Papa either.'

'Where *is* Papa?'

Pili shrugged as if she didn't care. She held out her hands, all black from the tomato vines. 'Look at the state of my skin! And I was going to finish embroidering that white blouse later!'

Ramona threw down her spoon. 'What kind of a life is this? Slaving all week in the factory, slaving all of Saturday in the *huerto.*'

'Exactly,' said Pilar.

Inma coughed a long cough, and then she said nothing at all. Albi sneaked a sideways look at her, but he didn't know what she was thinking any more. Inma and her silences – she wasn't the way she used to be.

'As soon as I get the chance I'm off,' Ramona said. 'I'm not going to fester here all my life. I'll go and live in town and nobody will stop me.' She gave Albi a hard look as if daring him to tell Papa. He stared back, horrified. How could she even talk about it? El Rincón was their home.

Anyway, which town? Las Hoyas? He looked away, staring at the wall instead, and didn't ask. The wall started to go wobbly.

He brushed his face as if he was just rubbing the sweat off. If Pilar went to be married she wouldn't be here to argue with Papa any more, and that would be better. But if Ramona went away to live in a town and Manolo stayed up on the *Meseta* being a *maquis* they would be so very few left, Mama and Papa and Inma and him. And the *abuela*.

At curfew, when they finally came back from the *huerto,* they were all tired and bad-tempered. It had been such a long hot day. Albi sat in the shade of the corral, stroking his speckledy hen and listening to Papa and Pili arguing upstairs – Jesús, again, Jesús the outsider. Papa winning because he always shouted loudest.

'Of course we can't trust him, you stupid girl! El Caballero only employs him because he has no family here. Can't you see that? He's the answer to a money-lender's dream! No family means no strings for people to pull!'

The *abuela* started shouting too. Albi shut his ears but he couldn't shut his thoughts. Even Mama had started saying *we don't know anything about him, Pili.* Why did they give their permission at the beginning, then? He heard the thump that was Papa hitting Pili, and then the door slamming and, from the *solenar* above him, the usual weeping.

'You've forgotten,' Inma said as they sat in the kitchen after everyone had gone to bed. 'Papa always did mind about Jesús being *de fuera*, but not so much at the beginning when Don Fernando brought him here to be foreman in the factory, and Pili worked in the packing-room. Jesús became her sweetheart and then he asked her to marry him.' He fidgeted on his stool, he knew all this already. 'It was Don Fernanado's connection with Jesús that led Papa to think he was suitable.'

Albi looked up in surprise. He hadn't realised Jesús came from a better family.

'No, Albi! His father was Don Fernando's chauffeur in Zaragoza. He was a *servant.*'

Anyway, he knew the next part of the story. Jesús started working for El Caballero, and Papa stopped being pleased about the betrothal. When the war started and El Caballero and Jesús ran away together to Bilbao, Papa said it was just as well as he'd always had his doubts about the marriage. But now Jesús was back and Papa and Pili were fighting, even more than in the old days, which was always quite a lot because she was very annoying.

Next morning, Mama was in the bakehouse and Ramona and Inma had already left for work, but Pili for some reason was still in the kitchen and the fighting erupted again. Albi opened the kitchen door quietly to slip out of the room.

'You should be grateful!'

He turned back in surprise but Pili wasn't saying it to him.

'It was Jesús who told them to leave us alone, you fool.'

Those were terrible words to say to their papa.

'You interfering little bitch!' Papa threw down his crutches. '*He* should keep his nose out of our business, and *you* should have more respect.' He pushed his sleeves up over the muscles in his arms.

Albi hovered in the doorway. *Please, Pili. Please don't say anything!*

'Respect, Papa? Respect *you?*'

He slipped out onto the landing.

'I know what happened in La Selva, Papa.'

La Selva was the forest where Papa was working the day the war came and swallowed him up. But Papa didn't hit Pilar. He went limp like a plant in the hot sun.

Pilar saw Albi hesitating on the other side of the door. 'People tell you lies, Albi. In this house even the people who should love you tell you lies. It may be what you want to hear, but it's still lies. Remember that!' She flounced past him and down the stairs.

Papa coughed uneasily and dropped onto the nearest chair. 'Women!' he said. 'Can't live without them but you'll find out for yourself one day – they're crazy, every one of them. But that one especially.'

Albi nodded, and closed the door behind him.

If Pili married Jesús she would go and live in another house and then the fighting could stop.

Albi sat with his papa in the stable mending harness (even though it was a Sunday and against the law), and wondered if he should try to persuade Papa to let Pili go. After all, not everyone thought El Caballero was a bad man, and he did lend lots of people money. Wasn't that a friendly thing to do?

Papa looked up from under his shaggy eyebrows. 'Lend. Not give, Albi.' One of the shaggy eyebrows pivoted upwards as Papa drove the needle through the leather strap. 'Lending means interest. Didn't they teach you that in school?' Then Papa – who couldn't remember anything he'd learned during his three years in school and who didn't deal in money but only in things – gave him a lesson in sums: twenty per cent, and compound interest.

'But Papa, how can people pay him when they don't have any money?'

'Simple. El Caballero lets them pay him with goods, same as El Ciego does, but you can be sure when he sells the goods on in his shop the price will be at least double what he counted it as against the loan.' He leaned over and peered at Albi's stitching. 'Keep it even, lad. When the war started and he ran away to Bilbao we thought we were rid of El bloody Caballero, and Jesús too. Didn't expect either of them to come back.' He paused, squinting at his needle to re-thread it. 'During the war El Caballero made a packet supplying the Fascist garrison. But then the soldiers come to El Rincón and he smells opportunity like a dead man's fart, wafting all the way to Bilbao. So back trots our little José-Pablo like a bantam cockerel. Opens up his house again, dusts out his shop. Before you know it, he's back where he left off with the money-lending.'

He pursed his lips and pushed his needle through the thick leather as if that was the end of the story. 'How many people in El Rincón do you suppose were glad to see him run away in '36? I'll tell you. Every single man and every single woman, lad. That's how many. There's not a household didn't owe him money.'

'Us too?'

'Of course us too. We thought we'd seen the end of all of that when he went. But oh no, back he comes again, with his bloody henchman and his little book, all the old debts even bigger now with two years of interest added on, and the new debts are going in there too. What do you think Jesús does for his wages? He collects the debts, of course. El Caballero doesn't do his own dirty work.' Papa stabbed down with his needle, through the old holes. 'And he's got both hands in the pockets of the garrison, just as you'd expect. The priest is in on it as well. How else do you think *that* old bugger keeps so much meat on his bones?'

'Do we still owe El Caballero money, Papa?'

His papa said nothing, but he looked so fierce Albi had his answer.

33

Abuela

Albi came upstairs from feeding the cattle at the end of the afternoon. The girls weren't back from the factory yet, curfew was still a little way off and all was quiet in the house so he went through the kitchen to see if the *abuela* was asleep.

She was lying in the bed like a husk a squirrel has left behind. He knew at once she was dead, even though her eyes were closed as if she was only sleeping. He stood in the archway, looking at her lying in the shadows, her empty mouth fallen open, her white hair escaping from its pins as usual.

'Mama. Mama!'

But his mama wasn't in the house. His papa shouted up from the corral, 'What is it?'

When Papa saw the *abuela* he stood there on his crutches and the tears made runnels down the dirty stubble of his cheeks. He kept saying, 'Mama,' which was a name he hadn't called her for a very long time. And then the girls and Mama were suddenly in the house, and the tramping up the street was curfew starting.

All night long, the candles and the prayers. The *abuela* all washed and polished and neat, as she hadn't been in years, lying on her back in the narrow bed in the *alcoba,* on clean sheets, her hands crossed on her withered chest. Her quiet face in the precious candle-light, hollows dark around the fallen mouth, looked as if she had never shouted obscenities or loved to win noisily at cards.

Albi stood behind his sisters and his mama as they sat on their upright chairs with their heads bowed as if they were praying. Papa sat on another chair a little apart, half turned away as if he didn't know where to put himself, as if he was half in the circle and half outside it. He certainly wasn't praying. Albi didn't know what to do either, so he lay down on Inma and Ramona's bed and slept.

He woke in the night and they were all still there, Papa on the edge of the group. He slept again. Nobody chided him.

The bell rang in the morning for curfew ending. The sun filled the valley with the first golden light of the day. Now that curfew was over they could fetch Papa's brothers from their houses, and his sisters from Las Rocas and Valbono.

'And the priest,' Mama said. 'We have to tell the priest.'

266

The morning grew and they were still arguing, and none of the uncles and aunts and cousins had even been told.

'Ramón – you can't.'

'Woman, it's *my* mother we're talking about.'

'Ramón, you know how she'd have felt about it. Before.'

'Well,' said Papa. 'Doesn't say much for your God, does it. Condemning her to the *after* she's had.'

Mama didn't answer. She had an obstinate look on her face.

'Where are you going, Albi?' she said, sharply.

To feed and water the beasts, of course. To take the sheep down to the Molino. The same things he always did. But the girls hadn't gone to the factory this morning, they'd put on their black clothes instead, all creased from the chest and smelling of camphor.

'What are you thinking of, boy?' Mama turned on Papa. 'See what a lot you have to answer for, Ramón!'

'Not today, Albi,' Inma said quietly. 'Today we have to fetch the priest and bury *Abuela*.'

'But El Ciego will be expecting me.' He looked to his papa for support.

Papa stared at the floor, trembling as if he might fall. Then he lifted his wooden crutch, shifted his grip to halfway down the shaft, and flung it with all his might at Inma.

Nobody moved. Nobody made a sound. Papa had thrown his crutch *at Inma.*

She stood up. 'Papa, whether the priest is involved or not, *Abuela* must be buried. In this heat you know she must. And the priest has the key to the cemetery. So what do you suggest we do?' She bent and picked up Papa's crutch and gave it back to him. Albi watched, wondering how she could be kind to someone who had just tried to hurt her, but her face was closed off. She put her hand on Mama's shoulder. 'What happened when Pepe Diego died, Mama?'

'The priest said the Church must bury him. There is no

267

other way now, whether we like it or not. Since they made it the law.'

'So,' Inma said, 'we don't have any choice, Papa.'

Papa shouted, 'It's my mother we're talking about. I am the eldest son! I want no meaningless mouthings from some outsider telling us she died without the last sacrament!'

Pilar kept quiet, which was just as well. There were tears running down Ramona's cheeks and dripping off her chin – Ramona who never cried. Albi turned his gaze back to the *abuela*. She looked a long way away, lying on her back on the bed. Perhaps she was rotting already. He thought of how quickly the maggots come, writhing thin and tiny like a mass of cut white threads in the anus of a dead sheep, growing fat and wriggly hour by hour till they spill out of the big holes they've made. There was no time to waste. If only they'd all stop talking and do something.

Inma said, 'Papa, we haven't even told your brothers yet, or Aunt Ana or Aunt Isabel. Surely you have to decide with them what's to be done?'

'Bah!' Papa pivoted on his wooden leg and plunged out of the room. His crutches and his peg-leg thumped unevenly down the stairs and out into the street.

When he'd gone, Pilar put her arms round Mama.

Ramona sniffed and blew her nose on a corner of the apron she'd put on over her black clothes. 'Let them decide between them, Mama. No point us getting on the wrong side of Papa. Let them do the deciding and if they don't agree, *they* can fight him.'

'But I made her a solemn promise. She wanted her immortal soul to rest in peace. I know she did. And I promised her!'

Ramona caught Albi's eye. Mama might well have promised, but it was a long time since the *abuela* had worried about her soul.

He went downstairs to feed the animals. They still needed to be fed and watered, whatever else was happening in the house.

The priest came while Papa was still out. Albi heard the swish of his black soutane in the street and the whisper of his sandals sneaking up the stairs. He hid in the byre with the oxen and listened as the priest talked to Mama in the room over his head but he couldn't hear what they were saying, only the murmur of their voices.

When Papa came with the uncles he told them the priest was still there.

'What? She invited him in?' Papa shouted, but the uncles held him back. They huddled in a corner of the byre, whispering. *No point looking for trouble, Ramón. Not when trouble is quite so anxious to come looking for us.* Glancing at the ceiling as if they might be able to look straight up the priest's black skirts in the room above. Papa argued, but it was difficult to argue in a whisper, even for an angry man.

'She's got to be buried, there's no other way for it,' Uncle Pedro said at last, and the other uncles agreed. They turned their backs on Papa and climbed the stairs with their caps clutched to their chests.

Albi stood behind his mama's chair in his stiff, uncomfortable best clothes that smelled of the chest they'd been put away in. The priest made his murmurs and gestures over the *abuela* under Papa's hostile stare. The grave-digger had gone up to the cemetery to start digging. It was a hot day to dig a grave. The flies were already buzzing round the *abuela*, even though they had closed all the doors and shutters and laid sprays of mint and lavender on the bed to keep the flies away. The room was full of people. The candles in the *alcoba* made the air very warm and the faces solemn.

Albi shifted from foot to foot. He wanted to be outside, not cooped up in here. Pili frowned at him to stand still. He tried very hard not to move, just his eyes looking round the room in search of something to think about. Up close, the priest's fleshy face was gleaming and folded in the candle-light, like an old animal that has fed well all summer. He looked stern, staring through his little spectacles at his black Bible, but maybe he was just avoiding Papa's glaring eye.

Albi was nervous in case Papa started shouting, but he didn't. They were waiting for the married aunts. One cousin had been sent to Valbono, another to Las Rocas, to fetch them. It was a long hot walk to both places.

Aunt Isabel sent a message saying she'd hurt her leg and couldn't come.

Aunt Ana arrived at last, out of breath and red-faced. Albi was glad it wasn't him who'd had to do the fetching. He was pleased to have a day off from walking in the heat, even if he was bored. Even if he had to wear these tight clothes, so scratchy and unfriendly. He wondered how long he would have to wear them. When the *abuela* was put in the ground would he be able to put his ordinary clothes back on straight away, or would they make him wait until tomorrow?

The priest stood up and made his holy noises, recommending the *abuela* to God. First in the *alcoba* he did it, then going down the stairs, and out into the street, and all the way up to the cemetery. But Papa turned back at the cemetery gate. He hobbled back down to the village and spent the rest of the afternoon in the bar.

'How could you, Ramón?' Mama said when Papa came home at last, hounded out of the bar by curfew. 'Your own mother!'

'Aha,' Papa said in a slurred voice. He had a black eye starting, and he'd lost another tooth. 'I'm glad you finally remembered she was *my* mother. Not yours.'

Mama wasn't the only one who was angry now. Two of the uncles had gone to the bar to tell Papa to stop disgracing the family and go home, and there'd been a fight. If the neighbours hadn't pulled them apart and calmed things down, how would it have ended? A man with only one leg can't win a fight with two men with four whole legs between them. Not to mention the three cousins who came and joined in the fighting too.

Papa couldn't get up the stairs, he was staggering so much. Inma and Ramona had to come down and help him. They tipped him onto the bed in the front bedroom and went to help Mama. In the *alcoba* the bed was stripped bare and naked. You could still see the dent in the mattress where the *abuela* used to lie.

'So small,' Ramona said, stroking the place.

Pilar said, 'I shall have the *alcoba* now. It will give me more privacy.'

How strange. They would have a bed each now, only Papa and Mama still sharing. But Mama said, 'No, Pilar, you will not. I will be sleeping in that bed. You can go on as before.'

It surprised Albi how much he missed his *abuela*. As if, by dying, she'd gone back to being the way she used to be instead of the strange old woman she'd become.

If he died would people remember him as grown up as he was now, or as he used to be when he was little?

She wasn't in the cemetery on her own for long before another hole was dug in the sandy soil, another procession climbed the track behind the glossy priest, and Old Jaime went to keep her company. But Young Jaime didn't fight his little wife, Belén, over it, and he didn't go to the bar afterwards. No brothers and cousins fell out and had to be separated by neighbours before they killed one another, and his family wasn't shamed.

34

Books

Albi leaned his head into Amapola's sweet-smelling hide, soothed by the rhythm of the squirting milk. He closed his eyes.

'Have you told him, Albi?'

He jumped, spilling milk out of the bucket.

Mama gazed down at him, twisting a cloth in her hands. 'Does he know yet?'

'Who? Does who know what?'

'Manolo. About *Abuela*.'

He frowned into the bucket. She wasn't supposed to do that. They must never speak of Manolo, here in the house or anywhere else there might be ears to hear. He couldn't tell her that he hadn't seen the *maquis* since the day the *abuela* died, but if he didn't tell her she would think it was his fault Manolo didn't know yet, so he said 'Yes,' and hoped that would be the end of it.

'Was he sad?'

'Very.'

Mama waited a moment. Then she nodded and went away.

*

'*Tío? Tía?*'

'It's Santi,' Alberto says. She hadn't heard him call. He knew it! She *is* going deaf.

But even Mari-Jé hears Santi's trainers running up the stairs. The door bangs open and he bursts into the room. Short as Santi is, the ceiling always feels lower when he is in the kitchen. He looks from one to the other, his smile fading. 'I'm going to Montesanto for poultry feed. Do you want anything?'

The air hangs bleak and empty over the table. Alberto looks

down into his coffee. Mari-Jé always wants something in town, but she doesn't say a word either. He lifts his eyes and sees the look she gives Santi: *he's being tricky again.* As if it's a conversation they've had before and Santi is on her side. He drops his eyes again, clasping the cup between misshapen hands that do not seem to belong to him. He hates being old.

'*Tío*, why don't you come with me?' Santi says, as if the idea has only just occurred to him, and immediately Alberto is trapped. If he says yes, he's giving in to Santi trying to humour him out of being difficult, which would put Mari-Jé in the right. If he says no, that's just him being difficult. And it wasn't even him making the argument. It was her, going on again about funny turns, and doctors.

'It would do you good to get out, *Tío*. And you too, *Tía*. Why don't you both come with me?'

Mari-Jé's eyes light up. She loves the idea, probably was only waiting to be asked. So what does he do now? He'd much rather dig his *huerto*. And what about the sheep? They need to go out. But if he says so, how will she interpret it?

'Go on, *Tío* – *Tía*'s up for it.' Santi's hand comes down on his shoulder. 'And those poor old sheep would be glad of a day inside resting their poor old legs. Besides, there's been a heavy frost, they won't miss much. Come with us, *Tío*!'

Mari-Jé starts bustling about as if the matter is decided. As if they'd only been talking about the weather when Santi came in. 'I could go to the supermarket. And… Would we have time for me to get my hair done? If María can slot me in?'

Santi shrugs and grins. He's in no hurry, obviously. Behind Mari-Jé's back, as she gets on the mobile to María, he gives Alberto a searching look. *Has she been getting at you again?* the look seems to say, as if he's on Alberto's side after all. 'You'll come with us, won't you *Tío*?'

He feels his resistance melting.

'Here – you can wear your new cardigan,' Mari-Jé drops the

273

olive green garment into his lap as she goes past to the little mirror by the sink. She stretches her lips and applies lipstick and the words come out distorted: 'Lunch will be on us, Santi. Casa Diego's?'

Santi looks more than willing. *It's not right though*, Alberto thinks as he pulls on the cardigan, all soft and new. Santi should be going about with people his own age, not oldies like them.

*

No messages for the *maquis*. None for Andrés either, but El Ciego sent Albi up to Estrellas just the same because the grass all round the village had been grazed to nothing.

For days now there had been a lot of to-ing and fro-ing of *Guardia* trucks, speeding backwards and forwards up the dirt road from Rincón onto the *Meseta*. Albi watched the little black dots trailing plumes of dust as they crisscrossed the *Meseta*, white dust in some places, red dust in others, as they drove up and down cart-tracks.

'The *Guardia* like to travel for their summer holidays,' Andrés said, but Albi couldn't laugh. Not when he had to walk home all alone and never knew where he might run into them.

'It's got too dangerous for you-know-who to stay you-know-where,' El Ciego said next morning. 'That's why you haven't seen them for a while. There's a new place, further away.'

Albi stared up at the dead eyes. How did the blind man know? Who had told him?

'Place called Barranco de las Carrascas,' the blind man said. 'It's near Las Rocas.'

'I know it,' he said. Papa talked about it. It was full of wild boar and *cabra*, that valley, good for hunting. To go there you had to cross the ridge called La Peña at the back of El Rincón and walk to Las Rocas, where Aunt Ana lived. Then from Las

Rocas you had to cross the next ridge into the *barranco*. But the path down into the *barranco* was narrow and dangerous – it wasn't a place to go to graze your sheep, there was too much rock and not enough grass. It was too steep for a mule, so no good for firewood, and the stream was too small for fish. At the bottom end, where the valley tipped itself into the river, the cliffs stood guard on either side like castle walls. There was no way round them, unless you climbed into the fierce water running through the gorge and swam upstream. Nobody would bother with it now that hunting was forbidden.

But if anybody really wanted to, there was a single path from the village, skirting along the base of the cliffs and up over the top. He'd climbed up there once, last summer before the soldiers came, when he'd been sent to spend a few days with Aunt Ana to keep her company after her husband died. Where the path crossed over the narrow backbone of rock you could stand and look down on three sides at the green river far below, passing through the throat of the gorge.

Or you could look down, if heights didn't make you feel dizzy and sick. He didn't like that place and the thought of going there again slid down his back like ice.

'Yes, yes,' the blind man said, sitting safely in the kitchen of the Molino. 'We know you can get over into the *barranco* from Las Rocas but we have to think of a good reason for you going there. Las Rocas itself isn't difficult, you could always say you were there on an errand to your aunt. We could even get you a temporary permit. But we'd still have to have a reason for you to climb over the cliff and into the Barranco de las Carrascas.'

Albi chewed on his bread and thought about it. There was one thing the blind man might not know, if nobody had ever told him. From the crags above Las Rocas, if you stood with the sun behind you and looked up the Barranco to your left, away from the river, the ruined Ermita de La Virjén de Las Estrellas was perched on the skyline. That meant the upper end of the *barranco* must be quite close to the Torre. If anybody stopped him he could say a sheep had wandered off the last time he was grazing at the Torre and he was looking for it. It was the excuse he'd been carrying in his heart all summer when he was where he shouldn't be, like a note in his pocket. He hadn't needed to use it yet, but he could only use it once. It would arouse suspicion if he kept losing sheep.

He hesitated. If he kept quiet maybe he wouldn't have to go.

If he kept quiet, he'd be a coward. He told the blind man his idea.

'Good,' El Ciego said. 'That's much better. In that case you don't need to go to Las Rocas at all. Climb down into the *barranco* from Estrellas. That's what you'd be doing if you'd lost a sheep, you'd be going from the Molinos land. You don't even need another permit.'

*

All along the road from Valbono to Montesanto icicles hang deep and brutal from every rocky ledge. Santi drives even more erratically than usual, stopping to take photographs on his phone. They drive in shadow, the low sun not clearing the cliff-tops along this narrow road, the pine trees sombre.

Santi was right, it does feel better to be out. Alberto sits in the front passenger seat, enjoying the passing scenery as he listens to Santi's chatter. Mari-Jé in the back seat joins in from time to time, but she can't hear well enough to follow much. The truck climbs steadily. They pass under the buildings of Los Perales, perched on the ridge. Deserted now. A lonely place, there's no other building for miles.

'They used to hide the *maquis* at that place,' Santi says, seeing him looking. 'For years after the war ended. Papa says the *Guardia* knew what they were up to but they never managed to catch them at it. They couldn't beat it out of them either.'

276

Alberto peers up at the sandstone walls, the once-proud roof, the corral with its fine stone arches. Only a day's walk from El Rincón but not people he knew. Or maybe they weren't entirely unknown, maybe his *maquis* used to come here. He'd had no idea, really, what lives they led when he wasn't with them.

A fox crosses the road in front of them – a big grey-brown fox as surprised to see them as they are to see him – and the conversation moves on.

*

Albi was very tired by the time he got to the Barranco de las Carrascas but he couldn't stay long, not if he was to be home by curfew. Mama would be angry if he stayed out another night. He made his way down the *barranco*, jumping from rock to rock, the goats and sheep sending stones slithering into the valley below. He could see from here that the bottom of the valley was overgrown and empty, but even if it wasn't they were making enough noise, him and his animals, for anybody hiding to know he was coming.

The *Guardia* too. He glanced fearfully up at the trees growing along the tops of the high rock walls on either side. The trees looked calm and peaceful like they always did but, like always, he had the bad feeling of being watched.

He got down to the stream and stood still, listening. Nothing. Just the wind in the pines, and the muted sound of the water at his feet, running narrow in its dried-out bed. This valley would be full of wild boar, now that hunting was forbidden. The thought made him nervous. Walking downstream he pushed through brambles and briars and thorny scrub, afraid to make a noise in case the *Guardia* heard him, afraid to be silent in case a boar didn't hear him until he fell over it.

After a while he thought any *Guardia* would be too far away to hear, whereas the boar might be very close indeed. He started making lots of noise.

Everything was dry and brittle, the long grass yellow as straw. One night of rain is soon forgotten in a drought. If fire came the boar and the ibex would be trapped. So would any men. Albi shivered. He didn't like this place. He put the thoughts away and whistled to La Perrita.

As if it had been a signal, an answering whistle came from somewhere above him.

He stopped, startled. Stared up at the blank rocks, at the bright pines growing along the top of the ridge, a thin green line wedged between the white rock and the empty blue sky. The whistle came again, closer this time. And then Manolo's face bobbed over a ledge of rock above him.

'Hello, little brother. I heard you a mile off.'

*

The winter sun shines in through the window of the low-beamed dining room at Casa Diego's. In its pale glare the olive oil bottle casts a green blob on the white tablecloth, the three glasses of wine glow red, and Mari-Jé's new perm is brassy-bright.

A man Alberto doesn't know comes in and sits at the table in the corner. He nods at Alberto and Mari-Jé but Santi he addresses as an old friend, as everybody has today. Santi likes this town. You can hear it in the way he talks, even before he declares he wouldn't mind living here. His politics are skin deep, Alberto thinks. Montesanto is a right-wing town and always was. When the soldiers arrived here at the end of '38 the people offered to man the roadblocks to prevent their Republican neighbours leaving, and they murdered the communist mayor themselves to save the soldiers the trouble. Santi is just a romantic, he thinks, watching Mari-Jé's face as she flirts with the boy.

Diego's daughter comes to take their order, standing to attention as she reads the choices out of her notebook. Felipa and Santi know each other from college, it seems, when he was a boarder in the town. It's clear she's sweet on him. She blushes as Santi teases her, sudden dimples transforming her face when she smiles.

It's obvious Santi is keen on Felipa, too. Now there's a surprise. All the girls he might have for the taking and this plain little bird is the one he's soft on? Alberto catches Mari-Jé's eye. She smiles, and shakes her head slightly for only him to see.

The room fills up, mostly working men eating alone. On their table a big plate of salad glistens bright and glorious in the shaft of sun. A day of icicles, and they eat fresh salad!

Now Felipa is bringing them the first course. Alberto looks down at the plate of cured meats in front of him. That would have feasted a family for a week, once, but he finishes it in ten minutes, even with his unhappy old teeth.

For the second course, Alberto and Santi have chosen the fish, Mari-Jé the chicken. The plentiful flesh goes down their gullets. The wine goes down too, until Mari-Jé's cheeks are pink – she's not used to drinking in the daytime any more. Alberto feels his thoughts softening. Is it the wine, or is it the company? Felipa comes to the table. Her cheeks are pink too, but not from alcohol. She pulls the notebook from her apron pocket, reads the list of desserts. Crème caramel, blackberry tart, ice cream, fresh fruit. When I was a boy… he thinks.

When I was a boy – what?

He looks at Santi, who is in a strange mood today, unusually reflective as he talks to Mari-Jé about his plans, or the lack of them, and how his parents want him to go away and make his life in the city. 'But I don't want to, *Tía,*' he says. 'I love this life.'

Alberto's heart swells. He hadn't realised Raul was planning to sell the rabbits until Santi said his papa doesn't want him to be tied to a rabbit shed.

I love that boy! The thought comes suddenly as he looks into the fresh young face with its high cheek-bones, the mop of black hair. Better than his own sons, he loves him. Though the fact is not to be admitted. Not to anyone, ever. A secret.

The hot days. The dry days. The days of the longest walks of his life. Albi's feet hardened and cracked like an old man's feet. Such a hunger on him, all the time, as if he could never catch up with his own body, no matter what he got to eat.

The days he was sent to the *maquis*, if Mena invited him in as he passed the Torre at Estrellas he had to say no, though it made his stomach hurt with the craving of it all the long way down into the *barranco*. The day would slip away too soon and he was scared of not getting home by curfew. He couldn't afford to dally in Mena's kitchen when he had a message for the *maquis*.

The days he had a message only for Andrés were the best days. Those days he didn't have to walk so far, and he ate well too, even though Mena's garden was suffering in the heat like everyone else's and Andrés was worrying their spring might dry up.

Drought or not, Mena always greeted him as if she had no worries at all. She sat him down at her table and served him food. And Albi accepted what she gave him and wondered at it, now Papa had told him she was middle class. He was conscious of the weight of the great house all around him, the middle class house. A house with white sheets and feather mattresses, and a special room full of books. (He needn't think about the tower. It might be an old castle on the outside but inside it was only a store. And anyway the door was kept locked when he was there. 'To keep the ghosts inside,' Mena said, turning the key and putting it in her apron pocket. Andrés wasn't there to laugh.)

One morning when he came into the kitchen there was a book on the table. Mena was busy at the fire making the omelette and the book was lying by itself, all secret and quiet. It had words on the cover but not ones he recognised. He ached to know what was inside. He glanced over at Mena but she had her back to him. Very gently, he lifted the cover and peeped. Turned one page, then another. The book was full of pictures. Bright, beautiful paintings, every one of them of a different coloured bird.

'Your hands, Albi!'

She hurried over, wiping her own hands on her apron, flustered as he'd never seen her before. She slid the book away and showed him the smudges his fingers had made on the pages. He put his hands behind his back and his face went hot. Then he did the normal thing – he spat on his palms and rubbed them briskly together before wiping them on his trousers.

She placed the book on the far end of the table. 'That won't do, Albi. Have your omelette first and I'll show you the pictures after.'

He ate his food but it had no taste to it. It felt worse than Pilar being jumpy about him touching her sewing, because he really wanted to see inside that book. He finished the omelette and pushed the plate away and still he felt bad. Even when Mena came and sat beside him, after carefully wiping the table with a cloth and brushing away all the crumbs. A strange sad feeling filled him up, though Mena sat so close he could feel her warmth through his shoulder, and the rise and fall of her breathing. She thought he was dirty.

She opened the book and turned the pages carefully, one after another. She pointed out the birds they'd seen in the meadow, but she thought he wasn't good enough. She ran her fingers along the words but his eyes were blurred and he couldn't see them clearly. 'See,' she said, 'this is the Spanish name, and this is the Latin. Latin like in church, Albi.' He kept his face turned away so she wouldn't see he was nearly crying. 'This is a good one,' she said, running her finger along the word on the page, under the picture of a big grey bird with a barred chest. '*Cuco*, or *cu-cu*, those are its Spanish names. You know that one! *Cuculus* in Latin.'

He was surprised into looking. Of course he knew that one. So much noise it made, telling them summer had come, but he didn't know it looked like that.

'It's an easy one to read, too,' Mena said, tracing her finger underneath the writing. He looked at her tapered fingers with their short clean nails, and the bad feeling came back. She was middle class. 'C-U-C-O,' she spelled out, pushing the book towards him. Without thinking he put out a hand to steady it.

He felt her tense. He put his hand under his thigh and pressed it down on the chair.

'I should be going,' he muttered, but Mena said, 'Look: here is a *C*, here is the *U*, another *C*, and an *O*.' And then she made the sound of each of them and he knew she was trying to make up for hurting him, so he said it after her, trying to say sorry too without saying it in words, staring at the pattern on the page until the letters began to be familiar again. He heard the old schoolmaster's voice in his head, the sound of chalk on the big blackboard, the squeak of chalk on the slate in his hands, and stopped holding his shoulders so stiff. He let himself feel Mena's warmth flowing into him.

But she thought he was dirty.

It was only ordinary dirt, too, like he always said to Pili. Sheep-grease and dust-dirt. Not tar from the chimney, or oil, or anything bad like that.

Mena said, 'Isn't it a wonderful book? I found it in the library here.'

Library? What was one of those? Before he could ask, she turned another page and there was the poo-poo-poo bird – the *abubilla* – just as he'd seen it on the battlements of the tower, with its crest half up and its slender beak open. Only in this picture he could see that the bird was not just pinky-brown, it had complicated black and white patterns on it as well.

She turned the pages back the other way. Owls. Whole pages of owls.

She turned more pages. *Perdiz*. He looked at the picture of the partridge and saw it there in all its lovely markings, like the real ones running among the bushes, or wilting, sad and beautiful, in his snares. If he was lucky enough to catch one. He looked at the picture and the bird in it was alive. He longed to trace the curves and lines of its markings with his finger. He longed so much that he had to sit on his hands even harder to stop them jumping up all by themselves. Mena read the Latin name, and then the words that said where partridges live and what they eat, and what sound they make.

She turned another page. It was the black and yellow bird that came to the poplar trees, the one that made the lovely fluting call. '*Ovopéndula,* latin *oriolus oriolus,*' she said, tracing her finger along the words.

'But that isn't what it's called! That's a *cerisero*. It lives in the cherry trees.'

Mena laughed. 'You have different words for lots of things here. Aragonese words. Like Andrés saying that here an *abubilla* is called *paput*, and the washing place being called a *chorreta*. They don't have the same words in other parts of Spain.'

That gave him a lot to think about, all the rest of the day, sitting in the shadow of his rock while the sheep and goats picked about in the dry grass. How could it be that different people call things by different words? How could you own books and have to have clean hands to look in them? He felt such a muddle of things, sad and bad and excited and happy all at once. He remembered suddenly how he'd slept in her clean sheets not just with his dirty hands but with his even dirtier feet, and he hadn't given it a thought. He wished he could do it all again and do it differently, but you never can. Did she find the sheets all dirty afterwards and was that why she was funny about the book? But books were expensive, he knew that. And they made him feel stupid. He could only read some words, not enough to read a book, but Mena could and she was only a girl. Well, a woman really, but then Mama couldn't read. His sisters could because they had been to school for long enough, but they never did so it didn't matter at home.

Mena had said, 'Next time you call in we'll look in this book again and learn the names together. Every time you come we'll learn some more. Would you help me do that? And every time we see a new bird we must remember what it looks like so we can look for it in the book afterwards.'

It made him feel hot and happy, the thought of learning something new together.

It made him feel hot and happy for a long time afterwards, while he waited for El Ciego to send him to La Torre de Las Estrellas again. But El Ciego didn't send him there. For days and days there were no messages at all, and when at last there were any they were only for the *maquis*.

35

Plots

Sergio called this time the dog-days of summer. It was true that down here in the *barranco*, where there were no breezes to dry the sweat off you, the *maquis* were like dogs. Nine shaggy men lying about in the hot shade of the pine trees snapping at one another.

Where had the others gone who were here last time? Nobody mentioned them and Albi didn't ask. He handed over the package. He knew what was in it, he'd secretly unwrapped it to have a look. Whatever it was – the small piece of steel, heavy, precise, well-greased – the Butcher snatched it and put it in his pocket. Manolo said something but the Butcher interrupted.

'No you won't, comrade!' They started arguing.

'It'll end in tears,' Sergio murmured, watching over his guitar.

Did he mean the package, or the argument?

The Butcher scratched irritably at his hairy chest and turned his back on Manolo. 'Hey! Albi! Can't you bring us new clothes? These lice are killing me.'

Perhaps it was a joke, but he wasn't smiling. Albi stared at the great hairy chest, the sinewy arms. Even hungry, the Butcher was a big man. He made Manolo look small and slight. Whatever Albi felt about Manolo, it hurt to think of his brother being pounded to a pulp.

'What are we waiting for, comrades?' Manolo exclaimed suddenly, looking round the others for support. 'The only action I've seen since joining you lot is snaring fucking hares and partridges!'

They started arguing again about the pump house. Manolo was still fretting about it, but every idea he came up with, somebody found fault with it. The same old story as before: no dynamite, and only one rifle, two old shot-guns and one pistol between the lot of them.

'What would be the point, anyway?' asked the Butcher.

'But don't you see?' Manolo said. 'If we blew up the pump house it's not only Valbono would lose the electric. There'd be no street lights in Rincón either. The village would be laid wide open for us. We could creep in and attack the sentries. The villagers would rise up and join us and together we'd throw the *Guardia* out.'

He sounded like Carlos.

'And what then?' the Butcher said. 'Seize one small village for one night, maybe two if you were lucky, and cripple another. But then what? Run away and leave your family to face the music?'

Albi was relieved to hear the Butcher mention that. His brother might have forgotten.

'Okay, okay. Let's bark up a different kind of tree, then.' Manolo's voice was excited, as if he'd suddenly had a new idea. He went over and sat down by the Butcher and spoke in his ear. Albi heard the word *Estrellas* – that made his mind wake up. He heard Manolo say *Raymundo Velasco Ibañez*, and then the word *government*. It must be Andrés's brother in Valencia they were talking about. The Butcher nodded and leaned closer. It sounded like more names.

The Butcher's head shot up in surprise. He stared at Manolo and said out loud 'You mean *our* Fernando Velasco Ibañez? Really?'

'Yes. Same family. This Andrés is their brother.'

The Butcher and Manolo started whispering then.

They whispered for so long Albi gave up trying to hear. Fancy the Butcher knowing Andrés's brother Fernando. La Perrita yawned and made a squeak and he laughed.

Manolo stopped talking and looked across at him. 'Sergio, take the kid for a walk, would you? His sheep could do with a change of scene.'

'See that cave?' Sergio whispered, leaning against him as they sat on a rock and the sheep fanned out over the thin grass.

'Where?'

'Under that bluff. There's a little cave, right underneath. See it?'

He squinted against the sun, into the dark shadow beneath the rock.

'There's an ibex lies up in that cave in the heat of the day,' Sergio whispered. 'Horns on him this big.' He spread his arms wide.

They crept towards the bluff of rock. The ibex rose up suddenly from under the shallow overhang and careered away, his wide horns clattering against the low branches.

Sergio grinned. 'Our secret. Don't tell your brother.'

They found a comfortable place to sit in the shade of some *carrascas* trees.

Albi said, 'You know you said you knew a girl called Carmen?' He'd been wanting to say this for so long but he hadn't liked to mention it when the others were there in case it put them in mind to visit the Torre themselves.

Sergio gave him a funny look, as if he didn't know what he was talking about.

'You know – Carmen from Valencia.'

'Carmen? Carmen who?'

'Carmen who was going to be a doctor,' he said, surprised Sergio could have forgotten already. 'Who was a student with you in Valencia.'

Sergio looked at the ground and poked it with a stick. 'That was another Carmen.'

Albi stared. One Carmen from Valencia going to be a doctor and living round here was unlikely enough. How could there possibly be two?

'I was mistaken,' Sergio said. 'The Carmen I knew lives near Teruel. Not round here at all.'

Albi kept his eyes fixed on Sergio's face but Sergio wouldn't look at him. He waited, and then he waited some more, but Sergio didn't say anything. 'Why are we waiting here?'

'Best not to know, sometimes.'

They waited some more. Tears pricked at Albi's eyes. He'd thought Sergio was his friend but friends don't lie to one another.

Or do they? Sometimes he did lie to Carlos. He knew Carlos lied to him.

The ewes drifted away, grazing quietly.

After a while Sergio stood up, so he got up too and followed him back to the others.

Under the pine trees something had changed. They all looked awake and excited, and Manolo was saying to the Butcher, 'We need more information. Hard facts, that's what we need.' The Butcher was quiet.

The sun was beginning to drop off the top of the sky. Albi stood up and said he'd better be going.

'Wait,' said the Butcher. 'A message for El Ciego.' Manolo looked up. 'A question first,' the Butcher said. 'How many people in your village have trucks?'

Albi said, 'Apart from the *Guardia*? Only one with any petrol, that's El Caballero.'

'*El Caballero*? Who the hell gets called *The Gentleman* round here?'

'The big boy of the village,' Manolo said, and his voice wasn't polite. 'Used to be the *alcalde*. Don't know if he is still. Is he, Albi?' Albi shrugged. He didn't think they had a mayor any more but he didn't want to look stupid, and anyway Manolo didn't wait for an answer. 'His parents came from the village but they went to Zaragoza before he was born and made pots of money. Then this git made pots of money on his own account and came back and bought up half the land in El Rincón. Rents it back to the former owners at wicked prices. Loans out money at extortionate interest rates. Has a shop. All the usual stuff.'

'Anyone besides him got a truck?'

Manolo looked at Albi, one eyebrow raised.

'Andrés at Estrellas,' he said, wanting to be helpful. 'He has a truck, but he doesn't have any petrol so it stays in his shed.' The Butcher began to look much too interested and he wished he hadn't mentioned it. 'The chickens are roosting in it. And laying their eggs on the seats.'

'Let's stick to working trucks, shall we,' said the Butcher. 'Apart from the *Guardia* and this Big Boy Caballero, what other lorries or trucks come in and out of the village regularly?'

Albi thought for a moment. 'I don't know.' He looked anxiously from the Butcher to Manolo.

The Butcher said wearily, 'Ask the blind man, boy. Ask the blind man.' As if that had been the answer all the time.

36

Birds

Albi made a story in his head. In it, Mena came to him in the meadow. She showed him things that come in books, like birds, and he showed her useful things like how to catch a lizard. And she let him touch her hand. He sat next to her and little by little he leaned against her. Andrés wasn't there. She let Albi be the one who looked after her, and he took her home to the Torre and she gave him nice things to eat, like honey cakes. And in the evening she let him sit beside her on the settle and put his arm around her.

No he wouldn't – she was taller than him. If he put his arm round her it would make him look smaller than he really was. Safer just to hold her hand, perhaps? She let him sit beside her on the settle and he held her hand.

Pity about Andrés.

He opened his eyes and it was the same old sheep, the same old meadow. A big white eagle flew over with a snake dangling from its beak. He could tell her about that. Next time. He closed his eyes against the sun. The sheep bells were almost silent. He slept.

Mena came walking along the edge of the meadow, only her chestnut hair visible, glowing in the sun. Then her shoulders, in a faded print frock. She was carrying the basket with the red and white cloth covering it. She climbed up the last bit of the path and he could see her brown bare legs and the faded espadrilles, and she saw him there under the tree and waved, as she always did. And it was real, it wasn't a dream.

His heart had turned over when he first glimpsed the sun on

her hair and it wasn't pretend. It turned over again when he realized she was coming to find him. But when he saw the basket his stomach turned over even faster than his heart. Perhaps she was bringing him the breakfast he might have had, if he hadn't met Andrés on the road this morning on his way to the farm. He'd given Andrés the message and then he'd had no excuse to go to the house, except for their bird book lesson, and he was suddenly shy. So he'd gone straight by without turning down into the yard. Could she really be bringing food just for him? He tried not to look too eager.

She walked across the tight-cropped grass in the shimmering heat and she looked like an angel, her hair shone so brightly. She came to him in the shade of the tree and put her basket down.

'You should have called by the house and saved me carrying all this way. It's a while since we've seen you. Have you forgotten us?'

He mumbled a reply. How quickly and neatly she sat down beside him on the grass.

She looked at him mischievously. *'Que pasa?'*

It was a joke. Of course nothing had happened, nothing ever did. He had watched an ant walk past carrying a dead ant three times its own size. There was a big green lizard without a tail hiding under that rock over there. That was all he would have had to tell her before, but today he could also tell how he'd heard the choughs flying over, though too far away to see the red legs she'd pointed out in the book last time he stopped at the Torre. And he'd seen a bee-eater, all chestnut and yellow and lovely grey-blue. It had perched in that dead walnut tree over there. And the orioles were noisy in the poplars. Birds he didn't see, once, but now he saw them everywhere. Nothing happens, but everything does if you can see it. If you can name it, you begin to see it. That's what it was.

He watched her face watching his as he told her all the things he'd seen. When he'd got to the end of his list she nodded, and then she went through the names of all the birds they'd seen between them that summer. A long list, and the last name was *chotacabras.*

'*Chotacabras?*'

'Andrés says you call them *gallinas ciegas* here.'

Blind chickens? She was teasing him.

'Funny name, isn't it,' she said. 'You only see them after dark, and mostly you hear them, not see them. *Chotacabras* and hares – we see lots of hares up here.' But he'd stopped listening, caught like a bird on a thorn. She and Andrés went for walks on the *Meseta* in the dark? But what if the *Guardia* came? What if they stumbled into the *maquis*, she and Andrés, and the *maquis* shot them?

Or… He thought of Sergio being funny about pretending his Carmen was a different Carmen. Was that why she and Andrés went walking in the dark? Did they all know each other, and making him take messages separately to Andrés and to the *maquis* was El Ciego pretending they didn't?

Maybe El Ciego didn't know.

She went on talking about birds. She didn't seem to notice he'd gone quiet. It wasn't that far from Estrellas to the place in the *barranco* where the *maquis* were hiding. And the Butcher had talked about Andrés's brother as *our Fernando Velasco Ibañez,* as if he knew him. Albi's heart clenched up like a fist, but Mena looked so calm and untroubled he couldn't say anything. He had to swallow them down, all the things he wanted to ask. The friendliness had drained right out of the day.

She started unpacking the basket.

'Peaches!' He was startled into speaking.

'Haven't you seen the tree? On the end wall of the house, in the old corral?'

There weren't any peach trees in El Rincón. Papa said it was because of the spring frosts rolling down the hillside. She put one of the peaches on Albi's side of the cloth. He eyed it suspiciously.

Next to the peach she laid a thin slice of ham. That was quite friendly.

On top of the slice of ham she placed a small wedge of cheese.

'Eat up,' she said. And she smiled at him.

So he did.

'Tell me all the bird names you can remember,' she said, when he'd finished eating. She settled herself against the tree as if she could stay a while yet. Mena who might know Sergio and might not, but perhaps it didn't matter. So he went through all the bird names he had in his head. And then she went through hers. When they got to the end of what they knew, and Mena had packed up her basket again, she leaned over and ruffled his hair and told him he learned very quickly. The last of the sad feelings flipped like a fish and swam away. It made him feel very proud, her saying that. Prouder than he'd felt since day the old schoolmaster said he was good at sums.

Ramona jumped backwards as another flight of black arrows went screaming past the *solenar*. 'Ugh! These birds! They'd take your head off if you leaned out too far.'

Albi, sitting on the floor of the *solenar* with La Gatica across his knees, said, not really thinking, 'Those are swifts.'

Ramona looked down at him and frowned, and then he *was* thinking. He was thinking fast and anxious.

'*Swifts*?' she said. 'And how would you know?'

'The *Valenciana* told me.' It was safe to say that. The Molino lands were next to Estrellas, after all, and Ramona knew the blind man was sending him up there to graze the flock.

'Oh, *the Valenciana*, was it?' she said, her voice mocking. 'I thought it was going to be another of those things you claim you learned in school.'

'No. She told me.'

Ramona narrowed her eyes again. 'You should keep the space in that head of yours for more important things than the names of birds.'

She sounded like Papa, the way she said that. Did she do it on purpose? And then he thought she knew something she wasn't saying. Did she know about the messages? He stared carefully at La Gatica's head and pretended he was looking for a flea.

Joaquín was on the stairs. No lopsided grin today, he brushed past and didn't look at Albi, as if he was upset, or maybe angry.

In the kitchen, the blind man was waiting for him with a message for the *maquis* and an egg frying in the pan. El Ciego didn't say much. He looked different too.

Albi closed his eyes and made sure he'd got the message fixed. *Between nine and twelve on Thursday.* Then he concentrated on the egg. It went down very quickly. He wiped the yolk from the plate with the last of the bread and glanced round, but El Ciego was feeling along the top shelf with his back to the room, so he lifted his plate and quickly licked it clean.

El Ciego came to the table and held out a candle. 'Take this to them as well.'

A candle? No point asking what use one candle would be. He put it in his bag along with the ham and the hard-boiled eggs and did up the strap.

'Now – something I must say to you,' the blind man said. 'Come.'

Albi followed him down the stairs and through the corral, straight past the sheep in the pen. El Ciego went outside and led the way round to the front of the mill. He leaned down and put his mouth close to Albi's ear. 'If ever you need to hide, hide here.'

Hide from Carlos, did he mean? All he could see was nettles, growing thickly on either side of the mill-leat. 'Where?'

The blind man knocked at the nettles with his stick. 'See the place where the water comes out?' he said, staring at nothing.

Behind the nettles, at the bottom of the wall, there was a low arch where the leat came out from under the mill. Not in there – surely the blind man couldn't mean in that tunnel? He'd have to crouch like a rat, it would be dark. He might get caught in the giant cogs that drove the millstones and if somebody opened the *acequia* while he was in there he might be drowned instead.

'*Sí*, señor,' he said. He'd rather die than hide in there, but the blind man couldn't see his face and it was better not to argue.

'What's cooking?' he asked, sidling up to the boys who were leaning sullenly against the *pelota* wall. Before they had curfews, he used to run about with them after he'd finished his jobs, no matter how tired he was. These days he had to catch up with them as best he could.

'Nothing,' Carlos said. 'Nothing at all. Bloody *Guardia* have stopped us swimming now.'

'They think the whole bloody river belongs to them,' Rafa said.

Yeah, they do, the others agreed. *Bloody Guardia.*

'They said we'd poison the fish,' Rafa added.

Albi felt as if a cold shadow had dropped down on him, remembering the anthrack plan.

'This whole village has been turned into a prison,' Rafa said. 'If you haven't got a permit.' He scowled at Albi.

El Ciego was Rafa's uncle. Perhaps Rafa wanted his job. Albi looked away.

Later, when they were on their own, Carlos said 'I should be the one looking after the Molino sheep. Then I could have a permit too and we could go out together. That would be good, wouldn't it?'

Albi was alarmed. What if Carlos went to see the blind man and made an arrangement?

If he did, or if Rafa said anything, El Ciego didn't mention it. Albi went on looking after the sheep and goats, and taking messages, and coming back too late to join whatever the other boys were doing. It was important, carrying messages, but he did mind being left out. He minded a lot.

He stooped over the verges, pulling greenstuff for the rabbits, watching the boys tumbling about on the edge of the village and being shouted at by the sentries. He passed them playing football in the streets when he took the beasts down to the *fuente* to drink in the late afternoons; he had too many jobs, he couldn't join in. They always called to him, but he knew they'd forget him as soon as he was out of sight. He was smaller and younger than most of them but they were still children, those others let out of school. And what was he? The in-between one. Not yet an adult, not quite a child.

37

Collaborating

Mari-Jé clicks her fingers near Alberto's face. 'You're doing it again.'

'What?'

'Gawping into space.'

'I wasn't gawping, I was dreaming.'

She gives him the eye. Her expression is almost hostile. 'With your eyes open?'

He shrugs. 'Daydreaming, then.'

He is on the verge of telling her. For just a moment he very nearly does. But she starts speaking again.

'We need to talk to the doctor about this.'

'Talk about what?'

She frowns, but he isn't trying to be difficult. He's giving her the chance to not say the thing he's afraid she is about to say.

'You've always been distant, Alberto, always remote, but these days you're so wrapped up in your own world. It's very lonely in this marriage.'

He stares in astonishment. Her voice is so sad, so unaccusing. So full of loneliness. He looks down at her worn hand on the table by her plate. The fine skin is freckled with age, the wedding ring sits loose on her finger. He puts his hand over hers, hearing the echo of the girl she used to be when he first knew her. Such a pretty girl, he couldn't believe she should be attracted to him, all those years ago when she was twenty and he was thirty-five. He squeezes her hand, remembering how it felt to discover he could love a woman and be loved in return and his gratitude to her for that, back then when they were young.

Mari-Jé turns her hand over and squeezes his. 'They can give you drugs you know. To slow it down.'

He pulls his hand away. She's talking about Alzheimer's, not about him at all.

'Bernardo says—'

He gets to his feet. He knows what she's up to. He picks up his cap and goes out down the stairs. Collaborating, that's what she's doing. Collaborating with Bernardo, against him.

*

A new word. A whispered word, sprouting everywhere like a fungus in the streets wherever neighbour stopped to whisper with neighbour.

Collaborating.

Collaborating was a bad word. Like fraternising. But who was doing it? Something stopped him asking Papa. He asked Ramona instead, in the privacy of the *huerto,* while they weeded the lettuces on a Saturday afternoon.

She gave him a funny look. 'Don't you know?'

'Know what?' But he knew what was coming, even though he'd never thought it in the words Ramona used.

'The blind man is milling the grain the *Guardia* steal from the villagers. He makes it into bread for the *Guardia* to eat and they pay him good money to do it. That makes him a collaborator, Albi.'

He stared back at her defiantly.

She rubbed her nose with the heel of one soil-encrusted hand. 'A mill always makes money, in good times and in bad.'

'So?'

'So. It makes people jealous. And then they say jealous things.'

'But the *Guardia* order El Ciego to make the bread. He's only doing it because they make him.'

'Oh yes,' she said, looking at him in that funny way again. 'So he is.'

They were only halfway through the lettuces but Ramona stopped weeding and stood up. She pressed her dirty hands into the small of her back as if it was hurting and stared out over the terraces towards La Guadaña, hazy in the heat.

'What a life,' she said.

Two days later, he watched the blind man walking along the path on the opposite bank of the river in the direction of the garrison. He had a sack of bread over his shoulder and he was walking slowly, tap-tapping hesitantly with his stick as if he was afraid of losing the path. That was odd.

All round Albi the sheep chomped loudly on the grass but the blind man wouldn't hear them over the noise of the river. He couldn't know Albi was there, watching, but he would know somebody might be. It was a trick, that's what it was. A story within a story. El Ciego was letting other people think he helped the *Guardia*, and he was making everyone think he was just a blind man who couldn't see.

It was so convincing Albi almost believed it himself.

Carlos's eyes glinted as he looked back over his shoulder. 'Hear that?' he whispered.

A scuffling sound came again from the far side of the bushes. Then grunting.

Albi crept closer. It might be a wild boar, they should be careful. But Carlos had his spying on the *Guardia* look, his blue eyes excited and the tips of his ears flushed pink.

A mewling came from the bushes now, like a cat being smothered.

He peered through the leaves. A man was lying face down on the ground. A big man, making the grunting noise. Carlos edged closer so he did too. Something was not right and his heart was frightened. It could be Joaquín. Joaquín might make sounds like that, not quite human.

Carlos looked round at him and mouthed, 'Jesús!'

Startled, Albi turned his eyes back to the gap in the leaves but all he could see was the curve of a back in a blue shirt, humping up and down. Jesús had been wearing a blue shirt like that this morning. Well well well. And if that wasn't a cat then there must be a woman there too, but why would Jesús be fighting with a woman in the bushes?

Carlos wormed a little closer so he followed. His sister would want to know about this! And his papa.

The noises stopped. Jesús and whoever it was had moved and he couldn't see them any more, only the patch of bruised grass they'd left behind. There was a rustling and a whispering, the striking of a match. He smelled the slow fragrance of tobacco burning. Real tobacco. And then, quite clearly, he heard Jesús's voice, talking ordinary, and the murmur of a woman's laughing reply. He ducked his head, disgusted. How could that slut fight with Jesús one minute and be laughing the next?

On the other side of the bushes Pilar's voice said, 'Best be getting back then.'

Pilar? *Pilar* wrestling with Jesús? He shrank down. It was all the wrong shape. He couldn't make a thought out of it. Then the realisation she might be coming this way hit him. He hid his face in his arms. Please God, don't let her catch me! Please let them not come this way.

The footsteps moved off down the slope. He lifted his head, but when he saw the look on Carlos's face he knew for sure it was all wrong.

'They were *doing* it,' Carlos whispered, his eyes glittering. 'They were doing it! Your sister and Jesús! And on a Sunday too.'

All the way home Carlos was like a cricket tied on a cotton thread. He didn't walk or run, he jumped, bouncing off the trunks of trees, bounding up on rocks and leaping off, his eyes flashing, his mouth grinning all the while like a crazy new moon. He kept looking at Albi sideways, as if they shared a secret.

Albi trudged along the path, his feelings all muddled. He knew perfectly well what Carlos meant by *they were doing it* – the other boys talked about that stuff all the time – but the idea didn't fit what he'd just seen. Sheep didn't look as if they were fighting when they were *doing it*, they looked bored and then it was all over. Rabbits too. Dogs always looked funny, the way they grinned, and went round afterwards stuck together and still smiling. But people? People were supposed to be different. And *Pilar,* who wore skirts and petticoats and dreamed of nylon stockings and gold wedding rings, who sewed white things for her trousseau and wanted to get married in the church. How could Pilar lie on the rude bare ground like that, fighting and making strange noises, and then sit up and talk as if she'd just been to the village shop? It didn't make sense. But the funny way Carlos was looking at him made it obvious he hadn't dreamed it.

What had they actually been doing, then, Jesús and Pilar? What was *doing it*, if you weren't a sheep and you weren't a dog, or a beast or a horse, but a man, and with a woman? All those skirts and petticoats hiding things, that funny underwear flapping from the washing-lines across the streets but not leaving you any the wiser. He trudged after Carlos, who was springing up the path like an ibex, whereas he felt cross and muddled and for some reason very sad. He thought about Mena and his feelings went hot. She and Andrés surely didn't do things like he'd just seen. But everything was turned upside down as if he didn't know anything after all. It made a taste in his mouth, and a strange sly excitement that he didn't want to notice he was feeling.

That night he watched Pilar from under his lashes. She was the same Pili as usual. A bit tetchy, tossing her head a lot, not really seeing him at all except to tell him off. Talking to Mama as if nothing out of the ordinary had happened today. Jesús had sounded fierce in the bushes but Pili didn't look as if she'd done anything she didn't want to. Rather, she looked pleased with herself, even when she slapped him for sitting on her sewing. Well, why had she left it on his chair then? He jumped up quickly. As she bent to pick up the embroidery he looked down and saw there was a tiny dead leaf stuck in the back of her dark hair.

Albi picked away with the adze, shaping the inside of the wooden trough, and all the while his papa leaned over him, getting in the way and keeping up a flow of advice. He knew all this. Really Papa might as well be in Julio's bar, all the use he was being. But there'd been four off-duty *Guardia* in the bar, drinking, and Papa had left Julio to entertain them all by himself.

Papa hopped out of the way as Albi came round the other side of the log, which was nearly a feed-trough now. The sharp blade of the adze bit into the wood and flat chips flew. It was calming work.

'Your poplar wood, now,' Papa said, not being calming at all, 'that's the peasant of the timber world. Quick-growing, straight, serves a purpose. But it won't last as long as your pine. When do you cut pine for timber?'

'On a waxing moon, Papa.'

'That's it, that's it. But for firewood, cut it on a waning moon, and prune your vines. That's your trees that keep their leaves in winter, not your oak or your walnut. Now those are the kings of trees. What timber for clogs, Albi?'

'Alder,' he said, not having to think about it. He stopped listening and let Papa rattle on. All Papa could do these days was talk. Other people had to do the doing. (Unless it was a matter of drinking. Papa was still good at that.) He knew all this stuff. He'd heard it all his life, of course he knew. But he hadn't known until yesterday how men and women could do it out in the open like animals and the woman doing it could be his own sister. There was no room in his head for waxing and waning moons and the uses of timber. And anyway, wasn't *doing it* collaborating, if it was with Jesús?

'You can stop now,' Papa said. 'Get the mule watered. You can finish the trough next time you get back early.'

He didn't tell Papa about Pilar, he didn't tell anyone. Not even Manolo, the next time he took a message to the *maquis*. He was afraid Manolo would creep into the village and kill Jesús, if he ever found out Jesús was *doing it* with their sister.

Two *Guardia* came along the street, one with a sheaf of papers, the other with a hammer. Albi squatted with his back against the wall, waiting for Papa to come with him to the *huerto* with the mule. He watched them pin the notice to a stable door below the church.

Papa poked his head out of the bar as they walked away. 'Go see what it says,' he hissed. Albi slid up the street.

A special Mass, the notice said. Tomorrow night. Followed by a dance in the Plaza. Curfew delayed until midnight.

'You sure you read it right?' Papa said.

Jaime came out with a beaker of cider in his hand to see what was going on. 'What the hell are they up to? It's a year since the bloody soldiers came. Is it supposed to be some kind of celebration?'

Papa shrugged. 'More like divide and rule, lad. You'll see. They think they'll get some of us on their side, and then the real trouble will start.'

Real trouble? Didn't they have real trouble already, now that Papa was having a war with his brothers as well as with Pilar? Something about land, after *Abuela* died, something bad enough to make the uncles stop drinking in this bar. Their family divided.

The longer the bell tolled the longer Papa sat on his chair on the *solenar*, his wooden leg unstrapped and lying beside his crutches on the floor.

The girls and Albi sat on the other chairs waiting, waiting, pretending they weren't. After the bell, the special Mass would happen but they weren't going. And after that, the dance, but Papa said they were none of them to go to that either. Glaring at them all.

The bell stopped and still Papa sat sucking on his empty pipe, staring over the *solenar* rail at the darkening sky. He's going to sit here all night, Albi thought in a panic. Ramona fidgeted. Nobody said anything.

Papa picked up his leg and started strapping it on. 'Think I'll go to Julio's.'

Yes! Albi kept his eyes down, staring at the floor by his feet. It would be easy to sneak past Mama, once Papa was out of the way.

'You'll come with me, Alberto.'

He scowled at his sisters as he followed his papa. Ramona stuck out her tongue.

'You stay here,' Papa said, hopping over the step into Julio's bar. 'Where I can see you. Keep an eye open for your sisters and tell me if they sneak out.'

He sat down on the step with his back to the smoky room. It was strange to be out after dark again and to hear chattering and laughter in the night-time streets. He leaned his head against the doorpost, listening to the patterns the voices made, everybody relaxed because the *Guardia* were safely in the church. Then his ear caught another sound: distant, in the next street perhaps, the strum of a guitar. That great shiver of sound but not like Sergio playing, this was a tune he knew. And then… Yes! Tomás's rich bass, singing the familiar words. It was so long since there had been any music in these streets. Maybe the dance really was going to happen.

He glanced over his shoulder at Papa with his crutch propped under his armpit, chopping the air with his free hand, 'And I'm telling *you*…' Albi slipped out into the street. Excitement was in the air, voices rising. He ran down to the wash house but the other boys weren't there.

He found them leaning on the wall of Mario's corral, waiting to see if Mario would bring his gramophone out tonight, the way he used to in the old days whenever they had dances, playing his three records over and over, all night long: Louis Armstrong and Duke Ellington and Benny Goodman.

But that was before.

'It's not allowed any more. It's too American now,' Rafa said. 'There's a new law.'

All round the Plaza the *abuelos* sat on their chairs, leaning on their sticks and chattering. Ramona was standing with her friends by the *pelota* wall. If Pili was anywhere, Albi couldn't see her. Or Inma. He didn't see Mena and Andrés either. Perhaps they were safely up at Estrellas.

He tried not to think about what they might be doing up there, all on their own in the dark.

A cheer went up as Mario came out with the old card table. He went into the bar and came back with the gramophone and wound it up.

'He might have got some new records,' Carlos whispered. 'Up to date ones.'

They watched Mario put the arm over and carefully lower the needle onto the record. It was Duke Ellington – the same old one. Groans from the *Ayuntamiento* wall where the young men were standing.

A few of the younger married couples drifted out into the middle of the Plaza and began to dance. The *abuelos* tapped in time with their walking sticks, the unmarried girls gaggled along the *pelota* wall and the young men along the wall opposite pretended they weren't looking at them. The talking and laughing nearly drowned out the music.

Albi watched the little boys playing in the Plaza under the streetlights, all of them being bullfighters but nobody willing to be the bull. It made him smile. When they were small, he and Carlos were always the bullfighters, they always made Pepito be the bull. Was Pepito remembering that too? But when he glanced along the row to catch his eye, Pepito wasn't the innocent little boy he used to be. He looked thin and grey and old already, even though he was only half-grown.

A hush fell, the children rapidly shushed. Some *Guardia* were strolling down the lane from the church. Even in civvies everybody knew who they were. Albi saw the curly-headed one with the big smile and ducked his head, not wanting that smile to come anywhere near him. Especially if Carlos and Rafa were watching.

Nobody spoke. The record went on playing, scratchy and lonely, but the dancers had melted away. The *Guardia*, immaculate in their black trousers and white shirts like another kind of uniform, walked in a big group right into the middle of the Plaza. They looked about them grinning but nobody grinned back and after a while they drifted into Mario's bar. On the gramophone, the music ended and the record went round and round. Still nobody said anything out loud.

Mario's son came out and wound up the gramophone and put another record on. Benny Goodman. A sigh went round the

Plaza. Under the safety of the music the talking started again, quietly at first, then voices rising. Two couples came back out to dance. Three more followed. Rock-rock went the Comandante on his heels in the doorway of the bar, bending his head to hear something El Caballero said, but his eyes never leaving the Plaza. Two of the *Guardia* came out of the bar and stood by the tables, their white shirts glowing eerily under the streetlights as they raised glasses to invisible lips. A moment later there were three of them there, then five. The noise level in the Plaza dipped uncertainly, and rose again. The girls by the *pelota* wall giggled into their hands.

Rafa said in disgust, 'Look at those bloody *Guardia* eyeballing our girls.'

Albi had already noticed the girls looking towards the bar as if they were eyeballing them back. *Please let Ramona not be one of them.* He clenched his fists so hard his fingerails dug into his palms. The girls stayed by the *pelota* wall, the men in smart clothes sat at the tables outside the bar. The curly-haired one was among them, his big grin shining in the shadows as one of the others said something in his ear. The girls were openly looking at them now, and the men stared back. Those girls had no shame. Albi studied his bare feet so he didn't have to watch, but he could feel it all the same – the *Guardia* and the girls staring, the village youths watching, the old people tutting under their breath, and the Plaza going very quiet, in spite of the music.

Carlos dug him suddenly in the ribs. He wouldn't look up. Then he heard Rafa swear under his breath and raised his eyes. Four of the *Guardia* had walked up to the row of girls by the *pelota* wall and asked them to dance. And now four girls had said yes, but none of them was Ramona, though the curly-headed man was dancing, with Luis Irún's sister.

'She'll cop it later,' Rafa said.

The young men who had been lounging by the *Ayuntamiento* wall were standing up, straight and indignant now, staring at the

305

dancers. It wasn't fair. The *Guardia* had all the authority on their side. They had money too, and the girls knew it. When the record came to an end the strangers took their partners to sit at the tables outside Mario's bar and bought them drinks. Even from here you could feel the anger in the young men's eyes. Albi's guts went tight. There would be trouble now. But the *Guardia* behaved as if nothing was happening, and Young Mario came out and put another record on the gramophone, Louis Armstrong this time. The young men stayed by the wall and the dancers went on dancing.

They were back with Duke Ellington when Carlos dug Albi in the ribs a second time and there was Ramona, dancing with the curly-headed *Guardia*.

'Whore,' he said out loud. He had to say that word, it's what you say when your sisters do bad things with men, but *whore* is an anger word and saying it made him feel better.

Besides, it was nothing to what Papa said afterwards, when Albi told him.

After the dance Papa beat Ramona, but Ramona didn't react like Pili always did. She stood up to Papa. She took his crutches off him when he tried to hit her with them and threw them straight over the *solenar* rail, into the corral.

Papa was like a bird fallen out of the nest. He was furious, but without his crutches he couldn't do more than stand where he was or else sit down. If he had tried to hit Ramona now he would have toppled over.

Ramona folded her arms and stared at Papa, her face like stone. 'I'll fetch your crutches back for you when you promise not to hit *anybody* with them.'

She did what she said. But afterwards she hit Albi. She hit him hard with her fist. She was angry with him for telling but if he hadn't, somebody else would have. Besides, it was better for papa to take out all his crossness on Ramona and leave the rest of them alone. Albi knew Pili had been out last night, he'd seen her. And he was pretty sure Inma hadn't stayed indoors like Papa said, but for some reason Inma was angry with him too. He did mind that.

He wasn't the only one to tell tales. Rafa must have told his uncle about Ramona dancing with the *Guardia* because the blind man asked lots of awkward questions in the Molino next morning. Albi answered as truthfully as he dared, then spent the whole day worrying he was about to lose his job. But El Ciego said nothing more about it.

38

The Factory

Carlos couldn't get the words out fast enough, he was so excited.

'There were six *maquis*. Sacks over their heads – you know, holes cut for their eyes but so you couldn't see their faces?' (His own eyes feverish with the telling of it). 'Two pistols each. El Caballero came along in his truck and they shot out the tyres and pulled him out of the truck and told him to run away and they shot at the back of his legs to make him run faster. Then they rolled the truck over the edge of the road and it landed on the roof of the factory.' He paused, checking he had Albi's attention before he said the next bit. 'It went up like a bomb.'

'But you weren't there! You were in school!'

'My papa told me. He got all the workers out 'cos the *maquis* shouted a warning and gave them time to get out before the factory went up in flames.' Carlos looked wistful. 'Wish I'd been there. Papa says it was the best bonfire ever.'

'But the factory was his work! What'll he do now?'

Carlos shrugged as if the question wasn't important. 'He said it was worth it just to see the look on El Caballero's face before he started running. And that scum Jesús too. Oh didn't I say? He was in the truck with El Caballero.'

Albi hadn't been there either. He'd been on his way back to the Molino when he saw the smoke. It looked like a big fire. It was away down the valley, nothing to do with the pump house, but it scared him. He ran home past the sentries who were standing in the middle of the road watching the smoke with worried looks on their faces, as if they didn't know what they ought to do.

As he came up the Calle San Juan his parents came rushing out of the house. Jaime had just come to tell them there'd been an explosion somewhere down towards the factory and El Caballero had been shot in the leg. Albi went with them to the Plaza. The factory girls were just walking into the village, laughing and crying and talking all at once but none of them seemed to be hurt.

And Carlos had jumped down off the wall of Mario's *huerto* and grabbed Albi by the arm, already full of the story.

'We were nearly killed,' Ramona said, back in the safety of their kitchen.

Pili wailed, 'My poor Jesús! Those wicked *maquis* would have shot him too if he hadn't stood up to them. He was so brave, but what could he do, one man against ten?'

'I only saw two *maquis*,' said Inma.

Albi glanced at her. What had she guessed?

'Ten, Inma. Jesús said ten. And the *maquis* fired at them. El Caballero has a bullet in his leg to prove it. It was only luck Jesús didn't get shot as well.'

Ramona muttered 'Perhaps he ran away too fast,' but Pilar didn't hear her.

'There was such a stink of roasting mutton, Mama! That truck was full of sheep. It might so easily have been us roasting, too.'

Ramona squeezed Mama's hand. 'We were so lucky, Mama – apart from El Caballero, nobody was hurt. But the factory is quite destroyed. All that paper packed ready for collection! The lorry was due to pick it up this morning but it came too late.' She stood up and reached for the poker to stir the fire. 'I didn't see ten *maquis*, Pili. I only saw two. On the road, anyway. One big one, one scrawny little one. Scarves tied round their faces and big black beards sticking out underneath – they looked pretty silly, especially when they started laughing and dancing in the road after they'd tipped the truck over the edge, and then you should have seen how they legged it, Mama! The factory went up in flames and those two *maquis* scuttled up the rocks like a pair of ibex. You could hear them whooping and laughing all the way up the hill, all the little stones falling down behind them and the flames roaring as they took hold, and the girls screaming. There was so much smoke. We didn't see where the *maquis* went after that, we were too busy running. All that paper dust, we knew the place would go up like a bomb so we ran like crazy. And it did! It did. I've never been so scared in all my life.' She sat down suddenly on the nearest chair. 'But it *was* exciting.'

Still Inma said nothing. Albi watched her face. She knew. He pretended he knew nothing at all, the same way she was pretending. What was *knowing* anyway? Two men couldn't turn a truck over all on their own, so maybe Carlos's story was the real one. And why hadn't they blown up the pump house instead?

When Papa came in from Julio's bar at curfew there were fifteen *maquis*, and the truck had two pigs in it, and El Caballero was shot twice in each leg. Jesús only missed being wounded because he ran so fast. 'Coward that he is,' Papa added, glaring at Pili.

Ramona said, 'Only one bullet, Papa. It was only one.'

Pili jumped up. 'Papa!' she said, her mouth trembling so the words could hardly get out. 'A man can lose his leg without anyone being there to say he's lying when he makes another story out of it, but Jesús and El Caballero have witnesses. And we were there too.'

Albi sat tight and quiet on his stool. Even if his sisters had been there, what was the real truth? Because it surely was not ten *maquis,* or fifteen, but it might have been nine, two of them visible and seven of them hiding not too far away.

Pili marched into the other room and slammed the door. The talking went on without her – this happened, that happened – but it was all the same things they'd said already. He half-listened, his secret thoughts leaping about like goats. Had it been other *maquis* altogether, ones he didn't know? Something to do with Andrés's brother Fernando, perhaps? The one the Butcher knew about, who seemed to be something secret and important to do with the *maquis*? And if it was only two men, whoever they were, how could they have tipped the truck over all by themselves? Or did some of the factory men help them, just like Carlos said?

Papa elbowed him in the ribs. 'Clever, wasn't it?' he whispered, so Mama wouldn't hear as she rattled crockery in the cupboard. 'The truck didn't explode straight away, Jaime says. Good thing they'd thought to take that candle with them.'

Candle? Albi stared at his knees and another thought punched into him like a fist: the message to his *maquis* that same day he took the candle, *Between nine and twelve on Thursday*: that would have been the time the lorry was expected to pick up the consignment of paper. So it must have been his *maquis*. That was what they would have been waiting for, the paper lorry. El Caballero coming along in his truck had been chance.

The thought went down his gullet like a piece of bone. He was the one who'd taken them the message, and the candle. Did that make him the tenth *maquis*?

Uproar.

Not the villagers – they were lying low and careful in their houses, because curfew was all day long now – but the *Guardia* trucks and jeeps that came roaring into the village from other places. Nobody was allowed out of the village, even days later when curfew went back to normal times. The new jeeps squeezed down narrow streets that hadn't been built for motor cars, and sped across the Plaza and out past Luis Irún's forge, making the chickens squawk and jump for their lives. They raced back through the village and out again under the Gatehouse, and up the dirt road to the *Meseta*.

Andrés and Mena. They might be trapped up at Estrellas pretending they weren't there really.

But then he saw them in the street by the bakehouse. Just as well. The *Guardia* were everywhere, new ones added to the ones who were there already. Black figures clustered on the wall of the dam and scoured the valley on foot or on mules. They marched about the streets of El Rincón in pairs and stared into people's faces, stopping them to fire questions, but everybody had the same answer, *I know nothing*. All their neighbours watching and listening.

Then they started asking questions inside the houses behind closed shutters. Some nights there was screaming in the dark. The loneliness of the houses then, everybody listening, every family alone. And what was the point of it all, if nobody knew anything? All that seemed clear was that there had been a truck (well, that much was obvious – it was El Caballero's truck) and there were some men with their faces hidden and, yes, the men did have at least one gun, maybe two. Maybe more. The *Guardia* knew that already, since El Caballero had the bullet in a glass jar on his mantle shelf to prove it, Pilar said, and besides El Caballero was the *Guardia*'s best friend and he told them everything. But how many men and who they were: that was all confusion. In the streets, people told the *Guardia* they'd seen nothing, they knew nothing. If they were saying something else inside their houses, nobody could know.

Inside their house, when Papa wasn't there to hear, Pilar and

Ramona said plenty against the *maquis*, because there was no work now so there would be no more money. Inma didn't say anything, she just kept on knitting, and Mama went white whenever the incident was talked of.

They waited for the *denuncias* to begin. For somebody to report someone for something they'd done that made them part of the plot. Penned up in the narrow streets of the village neighbours greeted one another the same as usual, but they were watching really, and waiting. Watching waiting, waiting watching.

Only the priest kept talking. His long black skirts swishing angrily as he stopped people in the street and told them they would burn in hell if they didn't say what they knew. Albi, on his way to look for Pepito, saw the priest lecturing two girls who used to work in the factory. The priest shook his Bible, the girls cowered against the wall. Albi turned back and went the long way round to Pepito's house.

Even with a permit he couldn't take his sheep out now or go down to the Molino. He was waiting too, just like everybody else, but he didn't like to think what they were waiting for. And his sheep were very hungry.

La Guadaña: from the *solenar* its face was in shadow, but the pillars of rock along its length stood out in the light of the setting sun like statues in a church. Why was La Guadaña that shape?

He frowned, trying to make the question push the thoughts right out of his head, and stop the trembling in his hands. But he couldn't do it. Every time he tried, four big *Guardia* men stepped out from behind the question and took up all the inside of his skull. Four big *Guardia* men, crowded into the kitchen with their tricorn hats brushing the ceiling beams, dwarfing his mama and papa, his sisters, and him. That feeling of not being able to breathe, as if his bones wouldn't move up and down to let the air come into his chest.

312

The questions started easy: *Where were you? What were you doing?* Of the girls to start with, and their answers were simple; they were all three inside the factory, then they were outside it and running, lucky to be alive.

The *Guardia* started asking *What did you know? What did you say to whom?* and it wasn't about seeing or being any more, it was about the lorry due to come that morning. Who knew it was due that day? Who had told somebody else? Even though the paper was already burning inside the factory when the paper lorry came.

His heart felt as if it had jumped up into the back of his throat. As if it wasn't in its proper place at all, and if he opened his mouth to speak they would all see it sitting there in the back of his mouth. The *Guardia* would see it, Pilar would see it and she would tell Jesús, and Jesús would tell El Caballero. Mama and Papa would see it and it would make them afraid he might say something that put Manolo in danger, and trying to stop him they might say something dangerous themselves. Ramona would see it, and Inma too, and everything would go oh so wrong.

He kept his mouth firmly shut and his eyes down. He looked at all the feet: eleven brown feet cracked from the sun, in faded espadrilles and his own feet bare. Eight big boots with steel caps which would break your ribs if the large men inside them were to knock you down and start kicking. He looked at their feet, and he saw that the *Guardia* knew the lorry coming for the consignment of paper had been the real target, which meant somebody had told the *maquis* to expect it. That was about knowledge, not chance, and it was somebody in the village who had done the telling.

Are they looking at me? Are they looking? He dared not look up in case they were. His ears might be going red. Inma said his knees always went stiff when he'd been bad, that was how she knew when he'd done something he shouldn't. Were they stiff now?

313

Nobody asked him about the lorry. He'd already said he was on the Molino land down by the river all that day and it was true: the *Guardia* on the road-block above the bridge had seen him there.

Now, in their kitchen, the *Guardia* were sharp in their questioning of Inma, and then of Ramona. Pilar they were not so sharp with. Albi wasn't listening properly, he was too busy thinking of the last message he'd carried from El Ciego to Manolo and the Butcher and the other *maquis. Between nine and twelve on Thursday.* What would he say when they moved on from Pili and started on him?

But they passed straight over his head and started on Mama. *What do you know? What did you see?*

No se nada. No vi nada.

'Come,' one of the *Guardia* said roughly, as if he was ready to shake an answer right out of her. 'We know you have a son – not this one, the other one. Where is he?'

Mama stared back at him, her eyes very dark and hollow and her face grey. 'Señor, my son was forced to enlist by the Reds. He had no choice and we haven't seen him since. You know how it is. They would have shot him if he'd refused to go. For all we know he's no longer alive.'

The officer looked from Mama to Pilar. Pilar looked back as steadily as Mama did and said, 'What she says is true, señor.'

The man turned to Papa and said with a sneer, 'You we know about. You were in Julio's bar all morning resting your one good leg, I suppose?'

Such insolence in the man's voice, but all Papa said was, '*Si,* señor. That is indeed where I was.'

The officer said, soft as a rat's whisker, 'But that doesn't stop you *knowing* things, does it, Álvarez. Or telling. We're watching you, you might as well know it. We've been watching you for some time.'

Papa didn't blink. A tiny muscle working in his jaw, his

knuckles like bird claws gripping his crutches, that was all that showed how much effort it cost him not to react.

At last the four men had turned on their heels and ducked out through the doorway, one by one. The officer shouted at Papa, 'You're lucky you're not studying the inside wall of the lock up. You would be, if we didn't have bigger fish to fry.' Then he, too, ducked under the low door frame and clattered heavily down the stairs. Mama sat down suddenly on the nearest chair. Inma went to sit beside her and took hold of her hands. Albi didn't want to catch anyone's eye. He watched Inma interlock her fingers with Mama's. He saw the hem of Ramona's skirt move away.

'Can I take the oxen down to the *fuente* now?' he asked at last, of no-one in particular. 'Or are we to stay in the house?'

'Do you ever think about anything except your damned animals,' Pilar said angrily. Papa said, 'Off you go, lad.' His voice was very tired and seemed to come from a long way away.

PART THREE

39

The Pump House

The special restrictions were lifted after seven days. The crops were spoiling on the terraces and the corn was waiting to be threshed. Even the *Guardia* could see the villagers would starve next winter if they didn't get back to the fields, and the shepherds needed to take their scrawny animals out to graze.

Albi's flock pushed him all the way to the Molino, grabbing grass out of the verges, running from mouthful to mouthful. At the Molino, El Ciego and his assistant were sitting outside in the porch. The blind man looked smaller, next to Joaquín. Had he shrunk, or had Joaquín grown?

'Is that you, Ramón's boy?' El Ciego said, but he knew it was him really, same as as he knew his name. 'Let your animals loose on the meadow and come and sit with me.'

It was early yet and the machinery inside the mill was silent but even so, when Albi came back to the porch, El Ciego was alone.

'So the *Guardia* came to your house,' the blind man said. Was it Joaquín who told him these things? Did Joaquín know things really and tell them in his secret voice? 'Tell me, boy. Tell me what happened.'

He told how the *Guardia* had asked questions.

'And you? Did they not question you?'

'Only what I told you already, señor. They didn't speak to me apart from that.'

'Good,' the blind man said, as if Albi had delivered a package he'd been waiting for. 'Good. Now, we will wait for things to calm down before you take the sheep up to the *Meseta* again.'

Things didn't quieten down. The *Guardia* crawled everywhere like ants, scouring the valley, fanning out across the terraces. Some of them had dogs – big dogs, ugly and eager on their short leashes, baying for blood. The men broke down tomato vines as if the *maquis* might be hiding underneath and they knocked down haystacks. They moved along the crests of the cliffs, and backwards and forwards along the wall of the dam, and they rode their mules up and down the paths.

'As if they own them,' Albi said.

'It's all a show.' Papa was bouncing like an india-rubber ball these days. 'They're warning us.' He didn't sound afraid. The *Guardia* were still searching; that meant they hadn't found anything.

Perhaps the *maquis* had gone away. Right away, somewhere safe.

Pili stabbed her needle into her embroidery and held her tongue, but she wanted them found, these *maquis* who had shot at her Jesús, and wounded his employer. They'd destroyed her place of employment and the money that went with it, and now she had to help Mama in the house instead.

Pili worked hard all morning, washing and cleaning and mending Papa's and Albi's clothes, but in the afternoon she did her own sewing, out on the *solenar,* while Mama slept.

Asleep in the daytime? Mama?

Albi stopped in astonishment on his way past the shadowy *alcoba*, and stared at his mama lying in her bed. It was such a strange thing to see, but especially when he and Inma and Ramona had been working hard all afternoon. It didn't feel right. There was all the end-of-summer work to be done, on top of the ordinary jobs, and here was Mama only doing the bread and helping with the washing, Pili said. How long had that been going on? He knew about the milking, but here she was in bed and *sleeping* and it was still daylight. It wasn't fair.

That was a very strange thought to have of Mama, but this

was the precious time of making cheese, now that the gypsy had been again and bought the lambs off them. Albi was milking the sheep as well as the two goats and the cow, all by himself at night and again in the morning, because Mama kept forgetting to do it. Sometimes the milk stayed on the shelf so long it spoiled, because she forgot to make the cheese, too. Each time he asked she said she would do it tomorrow.

He didn't want to tell on Mama but in the end he had to.

Ramona frowned at him, and then she looked alarmed. 'What? Mama isn't making the cheese?' She sounded as scared as he felt. Then she looked cross. 'I can't possibly make cheese as well as everything else I'm doing! Pilar will have to make it.'

On the street up to Miguel's threshing yard, in the quiet of the early afternoon, the girls laid the heavy threshing board down on the cobbles and leaned against the cool wall to rest a moment in the shade.

Albi halted the mule and stood waiting. 'Is Mama sick?'

'Not sick the way you mean, Albi,' Inma said, but speaking made her start coughing and she didn't say any more.

'What then?'

'You don't need to know, Rabbit,' Ramona said.

'What's the matter with Mama?'

Ramona gave him her big-sister look. 'When God took Adam's rib and made a woman out of it he gave the woman all the difficult bits. It's nothing, Albi. Just another cross we women have to bear. Ready Inma?'

Inma nodded and bent to pick up the *trillo* again, but bending brought on another fit of coughing. Ramona patted her firmly on the back. The mule flicked her ears and looked on wisely while Albi stroked her nose. Inma coughed some more, Ramona patted.

'It's not right,' Ramona said. 'You shouldn't be doing this work, Inma. The dust isn't good for you, not to mention the fact there's only three of us doing the work of six. Not three, even – more like two and a half.' She shot Albi a dark look but that wasn't fair. In the *era,* Inma would be riding round and round on the threshing board and Ramona would be leading the mule, but it was him who'd be doing all the running about. Pilar should be here. Why wasn't she? Before he could ask, Ramona and Inma picked up the threshing board and set off up the hill. He followed after, breathing in the deep smell of mule and the hot smell of dust. The threshing ground wasn't such a bad place to be on a fine September afternoon, and Miguel's *era* was the best in El Rincón, catching every breeze. He loved the *era* really, the corn spilling out onto the hot paving, the wind blowing away all the chaff. It was just that it was better, always better, with more people. It was lonely to be only three.

That night he was woken by footsteps on the roof tiles right over his head. He lay rigid, his eyes drying out with listening so hard, but the footsteps overhead had stopped. He waited, not breathing, for the shooting to start. But nothing happened.

For hours afterwards he lay listening to the owls hooting, *tu-wit tu-wit,* not far away. Was it real owls, or people making signals?

In the morning he told Papa there'd been a sniper walking about on the roof.

Papa laughed at him. 'It would have been an owl, Albi. Have you never heard one before?'

He gave Papa the eye. Now he was ten years old Papa should be straight with him. And it wasn't a laughing matter.

Nowhere felt safe any more, not even the inside of their house. Even his bed didn't feel safe, not if snipers might be climbing about on the roof tiles just over his head. Every day he looked for them, these strangers on the roofs, but he never saw one. Whenever he passed any *Guardia* in the village or on the paths he thought, *Or was it you?* He tried not to look at their faces, not to snag against those hard cold stares with his own scared eyes. But the *Guardia* were too busy glaring at the rocks and the bushes behind which a man might hide. They weren't interested in a barefoot boy with twenty sheep at his heels and a little black dog running after.

One morning, just as it seemed the *maquis* had got clean away, the news went whispering all round the village, *somebody's shot at the pump house!* Such excitement shimmering in the air.

So they were still here. El Ciego didn't say a word and Albi didn't like to ask. The blind man sent him out yet again along the river. He could see the pump house from here. It looked untouched. Why hadn't the *maquis* done the job properly and blown it up?

40

Reprisals

After the pump house incident, the *Guardia* took the pigs in punishment. Every pig from every house.

'No, not every house,' Papa said. 'Not the ones that still have bottles of tomatoes on their shelves and apples and onions in their attics. *Those* houses will still have corn bins stuffed full of wheat, I'll be bound. Hard for them to explain why they get let off so lightly. Naming no names, but why's Martín still got a pen of porkers when everybody else's pigs have been taken?'

Albi kept quiet. In the Molino, too, there were three fat pigs in the pen, guzzling up all the mill-waste.

In their house there had been no pig to take. The corn bins

were half empty, and there weren't many cheeses. But grapes and fresh figs – those they had in abundance, until he was sick to death of them, his belly griping at night as he lay in his bed clutching his arms around himself to dull the pain.

He really could be sick to death.

As soon as Sunday Mass ended and they were released from the church, Carlos pushed through the crush and put his mouth close to Albi's ear. 'About time we did some more spying. The *Guardia* have got tents now. Did you know?'

Of course he knew. From anywhere high up you could see them, set out in a row next to the garrison like a white village for all the new *Guardia* to sleep in. Six tents. If six men were sleeping in each tent that would make thirty-six extra, in addition to the ones sleeping in the garrison. That was a very good reason not to go spying on them.

'See you after dinner, then,' Carlos said.

Dinner was hardly worth the bother of going home.

'I'm sick of figs!' Ramona said, standing up so suddenly she knocked the enamel plate on the floor.

Albi followed Carlos and Pepito followed Albi. They crept along the river bank under cover of the willows until they were opposite the garrison on the far side of the Junction Pool. A lot of busy noise was coming from there, and the smell of woodsmoke, and cooking. The deep-throated baying of a dog rose and fell in the balmy air, nearly drowning out the sound of engines running, men's voices, the whinnying bray of a mule.

'They've still got those dog-handlers, then,' Carlos said.

If the *Guardia* let the dogs out, would they swim straight across the river and grab them by the throats? Albi tried to concentrate on spying. From here, the tents were out of sight, but the thin columns of smoke from several campfires climbed steadily above the trees. There were fines for making fires out of doors if you were an ordinary person. The *Guardia* had different rules for themselves.

The smell of cooking drifted across the pool. Pork. Pork and chick peas, and red peppers in it. Possibly the same red peppers the *Guardia* had taken yesterday.

Pepito moaned, 'My guts hurt all the time. Do yours?'

'Yep,' said Carlos. He let out a long fart.

'They'll hear you,' Pepito protested, but he was laughing.

Carlos farted again, even louder

'Oi!'

On the far side of the river a man was standing at one of the upper windows of the garrison. Even from here Albi could see the green braces over the man's undershirt and his big droopy moustache.

He ducked down. When he peered through the leaves again the man had disappeared.

Carlos crouched next to him. 'Anyway, what could he do about it, even if he did see us?'

The man might do lots of things. He might let the dogs out. Albi opened his mouth to argue, but the *Guardia* was at the window again, one hand raised level with his shoulder.

It took him a moment to realise that sharp dry *crack* had been a gunshot. The man had fired at them! Not up in the air, straight at them. Albi dropped to the ground, wondering if he'd been hit. But nothing hurt, his legs were still working. He backed quickly out of the bushes and scuttled after Carlos. Up the bank they went and into the trees, as fast as any rabbit, through briars and brambles until they burst onto the track. They raced uphill towards the village and only stopped when they were in sight of the sentries on the check-point by the gatehouse.

Carlos grabbed him by the arm, panting so hard he could barely speak. 'Listen! We won't tell…anyone. Don't say…we ran away.'

There was no sign of Pepito.

Albi walked home alone, his heart still pounding and his thoughts all jumbled up. That man had wanted to kill them.

They were going to be in big trouble now, him and Carlos, and not just for making the *Guardia* mad. Pepito was weak-chested. He couldn't run fast and they'd left him behind; he might be lying dead in the bushes. Albi went indoors and crept upstairs to hide in the attic.

When curfew time came at last he heard Inma's voice in the kitchen, worrying that he wasn't in the house. He had to go downstairs then. They laughed at him for being up in his room and nobody knowing he was there. He sneaked a look at their faces and saw they didn't know.

In the morning, there was Pepito at the *fuente* looking his usual scrawny self. 'You might have waited,' was all he said.

'I hear your friend Carlos was up to mischief yesterday,' Papa said. Albi looked up from treading grapes in the zinc trough, feeling as if his heart had stopped beating. 'Taunting the *Guardia*, I heard.'

'What?' He turned his eyes back to his feet, all purple from the grapes. 'What did he do?'

'Only crept right up to the garrison and fired his catapult at the shutters until the Comandante took a pot-shot at him with his pistol. Crazy boy! They might have loosed the dogs on him. What the devil did he think he was doing?'

Albi grunted, trying to sound as if it was nothing to do with him. Was this another time he didn't know about? Carlos had run away so fast it was hard to believe he would have gone back after.

'Good thing he was on his own,' Papa said. 'You keep away from him. That boy is trouble.'

Pilar came out onto the *solenar* with the broom. 'What's Albi doing, treading grapes, Papa? Food before wine,' she said, talking in riddles. 'Food before wine.' She banged about with the broom

326

as if she was cross. Albi shut his ears and went on trampling. He didn't mind this work. The grapes were cool against his skin, squelching up between his toes. When he opened his ears again Pilar was still nagging. 'The Martíns, Papa. And Emilio Serrano. *They* were allowed to keep everything.'

'Arse-lickers the pair of them.'

'But Papa, you don't have to *be* like them. All you have to do is keep quiet!'

Albi shut her out again and tramped backwards and forwards along the short trough. Troublemaking was a kind of brotherhood. It had its own words, like badges: comrade, *maquis, resistencia.*

It was such a whispering word, *resistencia.* A good word. But reprisals was the bad word that followed after it.

In the dead of night Miguel was taken from his house for questioning. Afterwards he had welts across his face and he was limping, but at least he was alive and wasn't in the lock up. Papa said it was a reprisal. He didn't say what for.

A few days later the *Guardia* seized Ovidio from his house and took him away to the prison in Las Hoyas. When he got out, (if he ever did, Papa said), how would he live? The *Guardia* had taken all his sheep and goats, and his draft animals too.

In their house it wasn't the *Guardia* who took the oxen. Papa sold them. It wouldn't be the *Guardia* who would take the cow. When her milk dried up, as it surely would before long, Papa said they would kill her themselves and salt the meat. 'And we will hide it from those thieving bastards.' He swung himself across the *solenar* to his chair and dropped his crutches noisily on the floor beside him. 'It's a system, Albi. A black-market system, for taking what isn't theirs and selling it on.'

'That's not true, Papa,' Pilar said. 'The *Guardia* take no more than they need to feed themselves.' She didn't add *Jesús says*, but he could feel the two words hanging in the air.

'Of course they're not eating it themselves!' Papa roared. 'Of course they're making money out of us. Ask Cousin Javier, he'll tell you. It was the same in the army in Morocco.'

'I don't believe you.'

For a moment, Papa stared at Pilar. Then he lunged and grabbed her by the arm and shook her so hard he nearly fell off his chair. 'Look at him girl! Look at that fat bastard you call your *novio*. Do you not see how he's making money out of all this? How else do you think he keeps all that flesh on his bones? It's a system! The *Guardia* are in on it. El Caballero is in on it. Bloody Jesús is in on it. How can you not see this?'

Pilar winced, but she stared back at Papa as if she wasn't scared.

Albi was. He was very scared. He wanted her to be quiet, and for Papa to let go of her. He wanted Mama to make him stop. But she just sat there, her face somewhere else.

Papa jerked Pili closer. 'You'll treat me with respect, girl, if you want to go on living in this house.'

'Respect? Why should I respect *you*, Papa? Tell me that.'

That was a very bad thing for Pilar to say. Mama would surely scold her now, but she didn't seem to be listening.

The world was falling down, and not just in their house. The *Guardia* were rattled and angry but they were still there and nobody was fighting them, they were too busy fighting each other behind closed doors

Even their mama was.

They heard her from the kitchen, her voice coming from the front bedroom. 'All the trouble we've had since you lost your leg. And for what, Ramón? For what?'

'That's not fair,' Albi said to Ramona. 'Papa was fighting the enemy.'

Ramona snorted. 'The only enemy Papa was fighting was himself.'

This house was a mad house, this house of women.

Mama came out of the bedroom. She didn't say anything to anyone. She went and lay down on the bed in the *alcoba* and turned her face to the wall, even though supper wasn't made yet. Inma had to make it.

Afterwards, when Papa was alone in his bed in the front room, snoring away the wine, the girls sat out late on the *solenar*, wrapped in their shawls against the cold night wind. They talked softly, their heads close together. Albi sat down near them and tried to join in, but it seemed to be women's talk: they dropped their voices so he couldn't hear the words.

He got tired of trying to listen. He went up to the attic and lay in his bed listening to the silence outside. Were the *maquis* still up there, up on the Meseta? How were they managing without him all this time? There were no messages. Maybe the *maquis* had gone away now, and Manolo too. Would that mean he was safe?

He saw El Ciego every day but the blind man said nothing, and he couldn't ask.

The extra *Guardia* trucks went away again, the team of dog-handlers with them. Maybe the curly-headed *Guardia* who'd danced with Ramona had gone too – that would be good. But when Albi came past the church with Ramona, carrying the heavy two-handled potato-basket between them, there he was at the top of the steps, standing with his thumbs hooked in his belt and his boots gleaming, as if this was his village and he belonged in it. The man winked at Ramona and raised the four fingers at his belt like a secret wave only she could see. Albi hurried her past, but he knew from the way the basket knocked awkwardly against his leg that she was looking back over her shoulder.

He heaved the handle on his side harder. 'Papa would be so cross if he saw you looking.'

She tugged back. 'Well don't you go telling, then. Rabbit.'

329

He walked faster to annoy her, but she walked even faster till he had to jog to keep up.

He could be at Estrellas now, this very minute, not stuck doing a job with his sister. He'd seen Andrés and Mena on the road this morning, he knew they were going there again. It could be just him and Mena in the kitchen. She might feed him on honey and little cakes, and they could look at the bird book again, if only the blind man would send him with a message.

But there were no messages. Maybe there never would be again, seeing the sisters he had. Perhaps he should tell the blind man it was Manolo who blew up the factory. If it was.

Mama never made the supper now, she stayed in her bed instead. She didn't do the washing, either, or iron her clothes. Ramona did it for her.

'This whole village is going to rack and ruin,' Ramona said, banging the iron down on the table. She wasn't talking about Mama. 'Fetch me the other one, Albi.'

He fetched the iron that had been heating by the fire. Ramona turned Mama's blouse on the blanket. It was sad to see it all empty without Mama in it and Mama not even doing the ironing of it.

He leaned on the table. 'But when the *Guardia* go away the village will be a good place again.'

'Don't kid yourself. The *Guardia* are going nowhere. And besides, they're not the problem. Not really. I've had it up to here with living like rats in a rubbish dump. First chance I get, I'm going to the city.'

He watched the iron go in and out of the material. What city? But he said nothing, breathing in the lovely hot smell that was Mama: soap, cloth, and sunshine. How could Ramona go somewhere else when this was home? He would mind if she did.

When he looked up, she was glaring at him.

'Don't you go breathing a word of that to Papa, Rabbit.'

41

The Prisoner

Late October brought heavy rain and the *acequias* were closed for the winter. It was quiet with no water running in the ditches. All the excitement over the factory had made it seem big changes were happening, but in the end everything was the same as before. Just the flocks passing through the streets with their bleating and their musical bells, and the bigger, slower bells of the cattle drinking at the *fuente,* and the steady drip-drip-drip of rain off the roofs.

But then one afternoon something was different.

Albi noticed it first on his way home from the Molino when he passed the sentries on the barrier aboved the bridge. Even in the rain they looked alert and excited as they waved him through. The knot of people standing on the corner of Calle San Juan stopped talking as he went by and looked at him the way they did the time papa was in the lock up. He started to run, the sheep running after him.

He paused at the front door and the sheep cantered past him into the house, heading for their pen. Was that his papa's voice coming from Julio's bar, or was it coming from the lock up? He could see from here that the door of the bar was firmly shut against the rain and he knew better than to go looking for his papa without good reason. All the same, he had to make sure. He ran up the street and stood by Julio's door, listening. He could hear several voices inside but not his papa's. Anyway, there was no guard outside the prison on the other side of the road, so the lock up must be empty. He crept up to the tiny window and peered in, to make sure.

The prison was black as pitch inside. The rain pouring off the eaves and drumming on the cobbles drowned all other sound.

As he turned away a slight movement caught his eye. He paused. Another movement, and suddenly there was Manolo, dark and overgrown, holding on to the window bars and whispering, 'Albi! Get me a mattock!'

A mattock? He stepped close to the window, shocked to silence by the fact that Manolo was still here in the village when he should have got clean away. To Las Hoyas, to Valencia – maybe even to France, but somewhere safe a long long way from here.

'A mattock. Quick, before the sentry comes back. And don't breathe a word to anyone.'

He hurried to the corner and looked up and down both streets. Nobody. Behind the door of Julio's bar the rise and fall of a stranger's voice: the *Guardia* who should have been on duty outside the lock up, no doubt taking advantage of most people being safely indoors to sneak out of the rain himself. Albi ran down to the house and along the passageway to the back stable where the sheep had put themselves in the pen. He shut the gate on them, ignoring their expectant looks as they waited by the empty manger. He lifted one of the mattocks off the wall and ran quickly outside. His sisters' voices drifted down from the kitchen.

He sauntered up the street with the mattock over his shoulder as if he was going out to dig in the rain. The *Guardia*'s voice was still audible inside the bar, talking to Julio. Albi checked over his shoulder: still nobody in sight. The rain gushed off the overhanging roofs, everybody's shutters were closed. He stepped up close to the prison window.

The rain had eased by the time Albi took the mule down to the *fuente*.

Carlos called from the wash house, 'Hey! Rabbit.'

He went over, keeping one eye on the mule.

'Did you hear what's happened?' Carlos said.

Albi saw at once how puffed up Carlos was with the news, sitting in the middle of the row of boys on the parapet of the wash tank, swinging his legs. The water in the shadowy tank smelled cold and black.

Carlos said, 'They've caught one of the *maquis*. Didn't you know?'

They all of them looked excited, as if catching the *maquis* was suddenly a good thing. Albi tried to make his face the same as theirs. He joined in the talk, but his mind was racing. They couldn't know who it was or they would surely be talking differently. Wouldn't they? He looked from one to another. And then another thought slammed into his head. Did Mama know?

It was like Christmas Eve or the night of the dance all over again, because there was no curfew. *To celebrate*, the *Guardia* said, as if in the end the villagers had somehow helped them catch the prisoner.

By late evening the *Guardia* seemed to be everywhere. In uniform, but behaving as if they weren't on duty, laughing and slapping shoulders, and drinking in both bars. The priest was in the Plaza in his long black coat and his wide-brimmed hat, talking to El Caballero in a doorway. And there was Jesús going into Mario's bar, which was very crowded, everybody shouting. Angry shouting or excited? You could never tell in this village.

Albi ran to keep up with the other boys. They went up to Mario's and crowded in the doorway until somebody told them to bugger off. Then they ran back to the wash house, because it had started raining again and at least in the wash house they could get out of the wet without anybody telling them to go away. They sat in a row on the wall of the tank, drumming their heels loudly and watching the rain come steadily down.

'He'll be shot,' Rafa said.

'He will,' Carlos agreed. 'He'll be dead as mutton before the next curfew.'

A little mewing noise forced itself between Albi's lips. He clamped his mouth shut and dropped his chin on his chest.

'Do you s'pose it's the same one as blew up the factory?' Pepito asked.

They started arguing about whether it was or whether it wasn't. Nobody seemed to notice Albi wasn't joining in.

After a while the rain stopped and the night was full of the sound of water gurgling. Carlos jumped off the parapet. 'Let's go and see the prisoner,' he yelled, and the others leapt down and raced after him through the streets like a pack of young dogs. Albi went with them but only because they'd think it odd if he didn't.

There was still no guard outside the lock up. The others took turns looking in through the tiny window but it was too dark inside to see anything.

'He isn't in there,' Rafa said. 'That's why there's nobody on guard.'

'Maybe they've already shot him?' Pepito suggested.

'Nah,' said Carlos. 'We'd have heard the shots.'

They wandered off and Albi followed. He felt sick. If the *Guardia* had taken Manolo away already, did they find the mattock inside the prison and guess who had given it to him? Was Rafa right that they would shoot the prisoner? And how was it nobody else seemed to know who the prisoner was? But he hadn't known it was Manolo at the beginning, either. Not until Manolo spoke and it was his voice.

At last the boys settled down to a game of cards in Carlos's stable, passing round Carlos's papa's wineskin, and Albi could say he was very tired, he had to go home, even though they would call him *baby rabbit*. He walked quietly away through the empty streets listening to the voices coming from behind closed shutters: lots of people were in their neighbours' houses, making the most of there being no curfew. In Mario's bar they were singing lustily as if they were celebrating. Surely some people minded that one of the *maquis* had been caught?

He didn't want to go home. Everything felt sad and he was

afraid to see his mama's face and her not knowing it was Manolo. Or worse, her knowing. So when he got to Julio's bar he slipped through the open door. Here too it was very rowdy, lamplight and noise spilling out into the street. His papa saw him and waved. There were five *Guardia* in the bar now, not just the sentry, and they were drinking with everybody else. Everyone seemed excited, even Miguel, and José Iranzo too, and Papa's friend Tomás, and Luis Irún. And Papa.

Albi leaned by the door with his back against the wall. He wanted to cry. Even Papa was celebrating. He couldn't know, then, who the prisoner was.

Valentín's voice said, 'Just as well. Trouble-makers the lot of them,' and Tomás shouted, 'Shut that door, Albi. There's a draught fit to freeze the bollocks off a cow.' He did as he was told. The pitch of noise rose even higher, and then Luis started singing.

He stood against the wall and gulped back his tears. Nobody cared except him. He looked at his papa's face, bright and boozy and loud.

Something vibrated in the wall at his back.

Again. He felt the *thwack* of a mattock against a wall of rammed earth on the other side of the street. So Manolo *was* still in the lock up. He held his breath and listened with all of his body. *Thwack.* The singing in the bar got louder. *Thwack, thwack.*

They sang. How they sang. Whenever one song ended someone had already begun another. They bought drinks for the *Guardia*. They raised their glasses in toast after toast, and the *Guardia* laughed a lot, their voices getting slurred like everybody else's.

'That was a bad day for you all, the factory being blown up,' the red-faced *Guardia* said. 'Somebody's going to pay for that, now we've got the ring-leader.'

There was a sudden dangerous silence. Did Albi imagine it,

or did heads turn towards his papa? But at that moment Miguel stood up saying he needed another drink. He stumbled as if by accident into José Iranzo, who fell into Uncle Pedro, who fell on top of José de la Viña, who was playing cards. And José de la Viña jumped up and thumped Uncle Pedro, and Albi's papa too, for good measure, and Uncle Pedro thumped Papa as well (probably because he'd been wanting to do that for a long time). After that they were all fighting and shouting, and the *Guardia* were trying to separate them and calm them down.

And then they were making it up again, just as noisily, which required drinks all round. Did Papa really wink at José de la Viña? Albi was knotted up with terror, and with hope. If he strained his ears he could hear the thwacking of the mattock against the thick earth wall of the prison, but the looks on the *Guardia*'s faces said they hadn't heard, they were too busy thinking they'd had two successes in one day – the capture of one of the *maquis*, and the winning of the villagers' approval.

The *Guardia* nearest Albi said to Valentín, 'It's a disaster for the village, isn't it, the factory being closed,' and Valentín answered, 'It is that. To be honest, those bandits make a lot of trouble for the rest of us. Let's hope they bugger off now the ring-leader's been caught and leave us responsible citizens in peace.'

Albi stared at Valentín. At his back, out in the dark, the *ring-leader* was valiantly thwack-thwacking at the wall of his cell. Valentín looked up for a moment as if he heard it too and Albi's heart missed a beat. But Valentín opened his mouth and pitched into another song and everybody else joined in with gusto.

'Out!'

Caught behind the door as it slammed open, Albi couldn't see who it was shouting but the singing stopped. The *Guardia* scrambled to their feet and stood to attention. He couldn't see the gun but the eyes of the men in the bar, all staring at the door, told him there was one. The five *Guardia* slunk out of the bar, heads down, faces averted.

'And you – cut the singing and stay where you are. You're all under arrest.'

The door slammed shut.

Nobody moved, nobody said a word. Albi was shaking so hard his teeth rattled. They wouldn't all fit in the prison. Outside in the street the harsh voice was still shouting. Commands, it sounded like. If Manolo had got away they might catch him any minute. And what would happen when they found the mattock? Would they be able to tell whose it was?

The *Guardia* didn't mention a mattock when they flung the door open again, hours later, and ordered them out of the bar, jabbing with the muzzles of their guns to make them hurry. But there for everybody to see was a jagged hole in the lock up wall big enough for a man to crawl through.

Albi couldn't see the mattock and anyway he didn't look very hard – the *Guardia* were shouting and waving their guns in the air and he was running for the safety of home, leaving his papa to stagger down the street behind him.

To the *Guardia*, it looked like a trick, even though the singing in Mario's bar had been just as loud. That was where El Caballero liked to drink, it wasn't the left-wing bar. The *Guardia* with their sore heads and their hot embarrassed ears didn't care who drank where, they wanted everyone punished. Curfew was from four in the afternoon until eight in the morning now and nobody could leave the village, even if, like Andrés, they had farms outside the village walls. They had them all trapped like hens in a coop and the questioning started all over again, stopping people in the street and searching them as if they might have the prisoner hidden in one of their pockets. They marched into houses and tipped over the beds, they thrust furious rifle butts deep into the grain bins while the people of the house watched in terror, because who knew where the prisoner might be hiding without them knowing, whoever he was?

But when the *Guardia* weren't there to hear, the buzzing was like a hive full of bees: *Who was it? He got away! Clean away!* As if everyone was excited about it, whatever they pretended. And pleased.

'El Caballero is furious,' Pilar said, out on the *solenar*. 'He says when they find the prisoner he'll be shot.'

Albi shivered, but of course she didn't know she was talking about their Manolo. Nobody seemed to have guessed that, not even the *Guardia*. Or that he was the one who'd taken Manolo the mattock to break down the wall.

'El Caballero is still in bed,' Pili said. 'He's got his leg in a splint with a cradle over the top to keep the blankets from pressing down on it.'

Jesús must tell Pili such a lot of things.

'El Caballero says this is what comes of the *Guardia* fraternising with the villagers. He says it's got to stop, and Jesús agrees.'

'You make it sound as if El Caballero is Jesús's puppet, not the other way round.' Ramona said.

'Huh,' said Pilar. 'And you sound just like Papa.'

If Ramona was like Papa she wouldn't talk to that grinning *Guardia* the way she did. Albi bent his head over his whittling and tried not to think about anything at all.

A new rumour slid from mouth to mouth. Albi heard Luis Irún outside the stable window, murmuring to Geronimo Gonzalez, 'Couldn't have been Ramón's Manolo, could it?'

He froze. The mule snickered, and craned to grab a mouthful of the hay in his arms.

Geronimo Gonzalez murmured back, 'No no, it was a stranger. Definitely a stranger. No one recognised him.'

'Might still have been Manolo who burned down the factory,' Luis said. 'I know the *Guardia* are saying they caught the right one, but they might be mistaken.'

They muttered some more, then Luis went up the street, Geronimo went down. Albi climbed up and dropped the hay in the manger.

He waited all day, but nobody said a word about it in their house, not even Pilar. Perhaps they hadn't heard.

By the next morning the gossip favoured it being a stranger.

Carlos said, 'That *maquis* was big as a fighting bull. He broke the wall down with his bare hands.' As if he'd seen the prisoner with his own two eyes.

Albi nodded. 'See you,' he said. 'Got to go.'

He hurried home. Had it been the Butcher in the prison and not Manolo? Had he risked everything for the Butcher?

In the stable, Papa fizzed like a flagon of cider that had been shaken up. His moustache was fluffed up with the things he might say, but all he said was, 'Less we say, safer we stay.'

On the fifth day gossip flew from mouth to mouth like flies between corpses.

Carlos found Albi by the *fuente*. He said he shouldn't tell really but he would burst if he didn't because he'd known all along it was Manolo only he couldn't say so because it was him who'd smuggled in the iron bar to make the hole in the wall.

Iron bar? Carlos said it so proudly Albi nearly believed him.

'Did *you* know, Papa,' he murmured later, when he and Papa were in the byre and nobody else was near. 'Did you know the prisoner was our Manolo?'

Papa leaned in close. 'Course I did, lad. I saw them taking him in there. But don't tell your mama. I never told her I'd seen him, like I wasn't going to tell you. You've found out soon enough.'

Albi went upstairs. Pilar and Ramona were both talking at once. *Our own brother! Dropping that lorry on the factory. He nearly killed us!*

'But he didn't,' Inma pointed out. Albi was glad she'd said it

339

first because he was bursting to say the self-same thing. 'Even if it *was* Manolo who blew up the factory, he waited for us all to get out of the building first.'

'Him and that other one,' Ramona said.

The mysterious *other one*. Was it the Butcher? It couldn't have been Sergio because people would have seen his glasses. It couldn't have been Toni, because his beard was fair. But then, surely it couldn't only have been two men, either, tipping a truck. Even the Butcher wasn't strong enough to do that. If Albi went to the Barranco de las Carrascas now, would he find them all still there and the Butcher with them, sitting in the rain? Manolo, too, perhaps? Or maybe Manolo had got away now, like he should have gone before.

He listened to his sisters talking. They knew nothing at all. Not even Pilar, who thought she knew everything. She didn't know about the secret places, or about the Butcher. She didn't know about the strange messages to La Torre de Las Estrellas. Albi knew all these things. When Pilar said, 'Somebody must have told them the paper lorry was due. There'll be retributions when they catch the culprit, Jesús says,' he knew that meant him. He was the one who told. But he didn't know what *retributions* were, and he was afraid to ask.

His sisters were whispering now. He couldn't hear what they were saying but he could tell it was about Mama, because Mama was in her bed even though it was only the middle of the afternoon. She'd looked at them as if Manolo would be sitting safe in their midst right now if it hadn't been for them, and got into her bed and turned her face to the *alcoba* wall.

Papa shouted at Mama when he came in, standing over her and yelling till the spit ran down his chin. Then he crashed out of the house again and went back to the bar. Like a bolt of lightning, Albi understood: he wasn't the only one who was afraid that Mama loved Manolo best. But now that Manolo was a hero and couldn't come back to the village ever again, not unless the

340

Guardia and the soldiers and El Caballero all went away, he and his papa were probably better off. Mama would stop pining soon and then they would go back to being the way they used to be, before Manolo came back from the war.

42

Confessions

In the Molino kitchen, Albi peered into the blind man's face trying to tell what he was thinking, now the curfew was back to its usual times and they were allowed out of the village again. He wanted to know, was it a good thing or a bad thing that Manolo had done, blowing up the factory and then escaping from the prison? But El Ciego looked the same as he always did as he pared slices off the ham-bone with his long sharp knife. His face was expressionless as if he didn't have feelings, only thoughts, and Albi couldn't read it.

There were no messages. That made him agitated, because maybe the blind man didn't trust him any more, but he didn't ask. Every day El Ciego sent him to places not far from the village where there was no grass anyway because of all the other sheep.

One afternoon Albi came home and the byre was empty: no Amapola to take down to the *fuente,* just a pile of dung in the straw. He wept until the snot ran down and he had to wipe it away with his sleeve. Papa must have known. How could he not have said?

There would be meat now.

He stopped crying. His lovely cow would leave them one last

good thing. He heard Papa coming in from the street and went out into the passageway.

'Oh there you are.' Papa didn't sound pleased to see him.

'Amapola?'

Papa's eyes shifted away.

'Was it Miguel did the killing? Is there a lot of meat?'

Papa turned to go up the stairs, lifting his shoulder as if to fend off questions. 'Meat? There is no meat.' He paused on the corner stair and looked back. 'Stop that noise, boy. You're too old for that.'

He held up the hank of wool for Inma. 'Papa should have told me.'

Her hands moved fast around his, winding, winding, the ball growing, growing.

'And anyway, why isn't there any meat? Was he just saying that because it's all hidden?'

She glanced up at him, and away. 'He sold her.'

'*Sold* her? Who to?'

'El Caballero.'

He thought one thing. And then another. He watched Inma's hands going round and the ball getting fatter. Even Papa could change his mind, then.

'So there's money now?'

'Not for money. He was under pressure, Albi. To settle a debt.' Her hands stopped in mid-air. When he looked up her eyes were on his face. 'It wouldn't have been much money, sweetheart, even if he'd sold her for *pesetas*. Or much meat if he'd kept her. She was only fit for glue.' She turned her head away to cough. Her shoulders were so thin.

'You've been coughing such a long time,' he said, when the fit passed and she started winding again.

'It's the dust in the factory.'

'But you don't work in the factory any more!'

'It's still inside me. In my lungs.'

He squinted at her face, so pale in the dying light of the fire. The summer sun had faded quickly on her skin. She seemed tired all the time, and there were dark circles round her eyes. All the things he couldn't talk about and this was another – Inma coughing.

She wound the end of the wool onto her ball. 'Don't look so worried, little one,' she said, and tousled his head.

It made him think of Mena when she did that.

Mena. Was she going up and down to Estrellas again, now they were allowed out of the village? The *Guardia* were still angry and that was Manolo's fault, he was the reason they were driving their trucks around on the *Meseta* making sure nobody stayed up there at night.

He didn't see her in the village and there weren't any messages. The blind man didn't say why, only that it was better to keep close to the village for a while longer. Albi was glad, really. He didn't have to walk far with the flock, or carry anything more than bundles of firewood or food for the rabbits. But no Estrellas meant no little cakes and no bird book either. No way of knowing that Mena didn't hold it against him, that he was Manolo's brother.

But then, one morning, there was Andrés's cart, rumbling up the road behind him and Mena was in the cart too. Albi called the sheep out of the way to let them pass. Mena waved and she was smiling. His heart lifted like a sudden bird – she wasn't angry with him. He waved back, but he saw how the black mule had gone shabby. The cart was spattered with mud from the *Guardia*'s trucks passing on the dirt road and Mena was as thin as the mule, sitting there in her overcoat in the rain.

The rain. The autumn rain, bringing winter closer. And Mama, who'd stopped doing so many things, didn't put bowls under the drips in the attic either. Albi had to do it, and sometimes – when the drip moved and came out in another place – his bed got wet and he had to sleep on the floor.

El Caballero stood square in the archway of his big front door, staring through the smoke that curled upwards from the cigarette in his hand. Jesús loomed at his shoulder.

Albi was scared. He didn't know why Jesús had stopped him on his way to the Molino this morning, telling him to put his sheep back in the corral and come down here instead. He looked down at El Caballero's trousers. You couldn't tell just looking which leg was the one that got shot.

'Small for his age, isn't he?' El Caballero said, as if Albi was a calf he was buying in the market and he was quibbling over the price. 'What can you do, boy?'

Albi thought for a minute. 'I can chop wood,' he suggested, caught between wanting not to be of interest and not wanting to seem a child.

El Caballero's eyes narrowed. He nodded to Jesús. 'Give him the axe. See what he can do.'

And right there in the road for everyone to see, Albi split logs for El Caballero. How his papa would beat him when he found out!

And El Ciego? What would he do? Would the blind man think he was saying things he shouldn't while he chopped logs for El Caballero? Albi felt sick. He wasn't trying to miss with the axe but the big blade glanced off the knotty wood. He took another swipe. The blade caught the wood awkwardly and wrenched the handle right out of his hands.

'Stop, stop!' El Caballero straightened up and turned away. 'Stop him, Jesús, before he breaks the fucking axe. He's just a kid. He won't do.'

Jesús grabbed the axe. 'What the hell are you playing at?'

He smelled of garlic and real tobacco. Albi felt his eyes filling. He didn't want to work for El Caballero but he hadn't made such a mess of it on purpose.

'I gave you one good chance,' Jesús said, his single eyebrow furrowing fiercely from one side of his forehead to the other. 'I won't give you another. Throwing it back in my face like that!'

Albi stumbled home, rubbing the tears roughly from his cheeks as he went narrow in the shadow against the wall, willing nobody to see him.

That afternoon, Papa found him in the byre and cuffed him fiercely round the head. 'What were you doing chopping El Caballero's wood, you little fucker? And in the street, too!'

Albi tried to duck, clasping his hands over his hot, sore ears.

Later, on the *solenar*, Pilar slapped him twice, once on each throbbing ear. 'Wasting the chance I gave you.'

He jumped out of reach and glared. 'I didn't want it! I didn't want to work for stupid old Caballero anyway.'

'Stupid boy, more like! He'd have paid you in cash. Not in rancid bacon like stupid El Ciego does. Cash, Albi. Don't expect me to put myself out for you again because I won't.'

She flounced off into the back bedroom.

He sat on the stool in the corner of the *solenar* and nursed his sore places. Not El Caballero or Jesús trying to get him off the blind man, then. Pilar.

He watched the setting sun flush the face of La Guadaña. His heart had been beating over-hard all day, ever since Jesús had hoisted him off this morning. He hadn't told the blind man why he was late. What would El Ciego do when he found out? Would he beat him too? Would he say that was the end of being his shepherd? The light on the cliffs went darker orange, then it went pale. Each tree growing on the ledges of the cliffs stood out sharp and green and distinct. His head was sore but if he sat very still it didn't hurt quite so much.

He sat so still and quiet for so long that everyone forgot he was there.

43

Young enough to be useful

'Get your shoes on,' Santi says. '*Tía* wants to go to the butcher and you could do with an outing. I'll run you both over to Valbono. After the butcher we can call in at Casa Pilar's for a coffee.'

'I'll have to find your *Tía* first,' Alberto says glumly. They had words again this morning, he doesn't know where she is.

Santi laughs and pulls out his mobile. In a moment he's talking into it – she is in Mari-Cristina's house. Not lost at all.

In ten minutes they're on the road, diving round bends and swooping along the river, Alberto hanging on to the seat belt with both hands. Santi's been watching too many car rallies on the telly. He does slow down through the echoing narrows of El Portal, though. They pass above the old factories, just visible in the trees below the road.

'How's that bitch doing?' Alberto asks.

'Great, *Tío*. Great. Pups are growing fast. You'll have to come up and see them.'

In Valbono, they climb out of the car in the Plaza and Mari-Jé props herself against the door, fanning her face. She's laughing, but she does look a bit green.

'Maybe not so fast on the way home, eh, Santi? Life is short enough, without going over the edge.'

'Sorry, *Tía*. You should have said.'

Valbono is quiet. Just as quiet as Rincón. Santi leans on the bell of the butcher's shop until Julia sticks her head out of an upstairs window. '*Hombre!*' she says when she sees Alberto and Mari-Jé. 'How are you both?'

She comes down and opens up. The shop is cold inside, the different types of sausage laid out neatly on the gleaming trays in the glass cabinet, the cold-store humming at the back of the shop. Julia fetches a leg of lamb and slices it thinly on the band-saw. How things change, Alberto thinks, watching her and remembering how Papa produced that knife from his boot, the time Miguel came to kill the pig.

*

If the blind man heard about Albi chopping wood for El Caballero, he didn't say a word. But still there were no messages, none at all. The *maquis* might have gone away to another place altogether but there were no messages to Estrellas either.

Albi went every day to the Molino, same as before. Late autumn sunshine had brought a flush of grass. Every day El Ciego told him where to go with the sheep. *Graze off the terraces of La Granja,* he might say, or *Graze Bernardino's lands*, because families had started closing up their houses and going to the cities in search of work. Or he said *Go up on the Prados below La Guadaña*. Or simply, *Graze the meadows here*. Not a word about the *maquis*. Albi wanted to ask, but one glance at that hawk-face and the question dried in his throat.

One rainy morning as he climbed the stairs to the Molino kitchen, his bare feet silent on the cold stone, he heard the murmur of voices from the other side of the closed door: a rumble he didn't recognise, and nearer to the door, the blind man's voice replying, 'A coincidence, I think. But I've been playing it safe ever since.'

That rumble again, the words too indistinct to make them out. Albi stood very still, afraid to knock on the door and reveal himself. He could hear from El Ciego's voice that he was sitting at the table with his back to the door. The other man must be in the chair by the fire.

El Ciego said, 'He's still young enough to be useful. For another year perhaps? No more.'

They were talking about him. He strained to hear what the other man was saying. Walls have ears, people kept saying, but they didn't. He couldn't hear through these walls, or even through the door. But if they caught him listening he would be in trouble just the same. He turned and tiptoed hurriedly down the stairs and stood under the eaves at the back of the Molino, trying to keep out of the rain.

He waited, and then he waited some more. If he'd heard anybody leaving he would have peeped round the corner of the building to see who the voice belonged to, but he heard nothing. Who could the stranger be? Nobody in El Rincón had that voice.

It must be one of the *Guardia*.

The thought hit him so hard he slumped against the wall. It must be. There were no other strangers in the village.

He had to go inside at last or El Ciego would hear through the window that his sheep were already penned in the corral and would wonder why he hadn't come up to the kitchen, stranger or no stranger. Albi climbed the stairs, his legs unwilling, his heart in his throat. The door to the kitchen was open, the room was empty except for El Ciego sitting at the table.

Another thought came as he sat at the table and the blind man got up to cut the ham with the long knife that sliced through meat like a sword. Perhaps the stranger on the other side of the door had been Joaquín. Joaquín, when he wasn't pretending that he didn't talk, might sound like that.

And how was it the *Guardia* hadn't taken that knife?

'Take the path to the waterfall as far as the mule path that goes up to the *Meseta*,' the blind man was saying. 'Go to the place where you used to go in the spring.' He held out a packet of sliced ham in one hand and four hard-boiled eggs in the other. Albi put them in his satchel. The blind man gripped his wrist hard so he should understand he was taking the food for somebody else, not for himself. As before: not so much food as to arouse suspicion but enough to satisfy a hungry man, or even several hungry men.

Still young enough to be useful.

He looked up at the harsh face with its chalky eyes and a chill weight settled on his guts.

'Tell them,' El Ciego said, his claw-hand releasing Albi's wrist and gripping his shoulder instead, which meant *listen carefully and remember*, 'Tell them *The path to the moon is closed for the winter. Come down from the stars.* And leave the black-faced ewe with them.'

The secret valley looked different in the rain. The magic had gone out of it. No flowers now, no bright tender grass, no sun and delicious shade. Just water dripping off every ledge, and the mist so low that the valley below and La Guadaña on the far side had disappeared.

He started to walk up the valley from the bottom end. The sheep ambled after him. What did they think about it, coming here again after so long, and for what? There wasn't much grass underfoot. 'Won't the *Guardia* think it odd if I take the sheep up there to graze so late in the year?' he'd dared to ask before he left, but El Ciego said 'They're townies. They don't know a sheep's snout from its arse.'

Soaked to the skin and shivering in the bitter *Meseta* wind, he hardly noticed the cold in his nervous excitement. In a little while he would find out whether Manolo was still here – the Butcher, too – and they would tell him who had really been at the factory that day, and what happened after Manolo escaped from the prison. He scrambled over the terraces, the sheep and goats jumping up the walls to either side of him, La Perrita with her bright red tongue hanging out of the corner of her mouth, panting happily at his side. *Leave the black-faced ewe with them*: that surely meant the Butcher, at least, was still here.

But there was nobody at all. He walked from one end of the valley to the other, then back again. He found a broken boot (so careless, these *maquis* – Manolo liked to say they were townies, like El Ciego said of the *Guardia*). He found the dead ashes of a fire. The ash told him they had been here not so long ago. There was nothing else, but even the little there was told him something: if Manolo had been with them, the last time they were here, he would have made sure the boot was buried and the ashes dispersed. Albi stood looking down at the old fire and wondered if he ought to do these things for them, but his feelings were too mixed up to know the answer. He sat for a long time on one of the rocks nearby, to give the *maquis* time to come to him like the first time he'd brought Manolo here. But nobody came. He got up and kicked the ashes half-heartedly into the scrub. He was beginning to understand what people in the village meant when they said they wished these *maquis* would bugger off now and leave them all alone.

A thought came to him as he climbed out onto the *Meseta* at the top end of the secret valley. Las Cabreras. That was where Manolo might be, with the *abuelos*. All the *maquis* could be there, eating his *abuela's* bad cheese and laughing. Sleeping in the deserted beds upstairs, perhaps. Even that stinking house would be better than being stuck out in this rain.

He paused, looking round him at the *Meseta* disappearing into the nothingness of the mist. It was hard to tell how late in the day it was when he couldn't see the sun but it couldn't be mid-day yet. He did have time, if he was quick. He could leave the sheep to graze here in the secret valley with La Perrita guarding them. If a truck came along the track to Las Cabreras, or if the *Guardia* came by on mules, a boy could hide more easily than a flock of fifteen sheep. Especially in this thin, trailing mist.

As soon as he'd had the thought he couldn't put it away again. Las Cabreras was surely where Manolo would be hiding.

There was another thought tucked round the back of that one.

All summer he'd been trying not to think about the secret he knew but Mama didn't, about the *abuelos*. But if he saw them again and they were all right – if the *Guardia* hadn't hurt them and the *maquis* had helped them – then he'd be able to tell his mama the *abuelos* were well and her face would get happy and she would go back to being his proper mama again. So he turned away from the valley and home and set his face to the invisible horizon where Las Cabreras nestled.

Dull rain was falling from a heavy sky, the mist drifted across the bare grey *Meseta*. He would have to follow close to the track in case he got lost and run as much of the way as he could.

At Las Cabreras there were no sheep grazing by the *fuente*. The water tumbled out of the end of the stone trough as usual, onto strong, green grass, but he could see no signs of sheep or goats, only the fat cloven prints of a wild boar and the tell-tale marks where it had wallowed in the mud. He hurried along the cobbled lane between the houses. *Abuelo*'s few sheep would be safely snug in the byre on a day like today. The shutters of their house would be closed tight against the rain, they would be sitting by the fire and talking of old times. He ran past the deserted houses, past their dead eyes and their barred gates, to the big gate at the end. But even before he got there he could see there was no smoke coming from the chimney and the gate was barred. Barred, and there was a padlock too.

He stood, trapped like a rabbit in the dead-end alleyway, his mind racing and his ears straining. Barred and padlocked *from the outside*.

There was no movement anywhere, except for the dripping of the slow rain. No shadowy *Abuelo* moving about in the mist. Not a sound of a sheep or a dog from the corral, or from the lean-to, or from any of the outbuildings. Not even a cat. But Manolo might still be here. Hidden in the house, the padlock on the outside of the gate a trick to make the Guardia think there was nobody there. Manolo might be in the house, listening from behind a shutter.

Albi knew what he had to do. He whistled as if he was whistling for his dog, though he had no dog with him. He whistled and he waited, and then he whistled again.

And then he ran. He didn't want to be trapped in the alleyway if the *Guardia* came suddenly. He ran out of the lane and turned to his right, to take the shortest way back to the track. As he did, he saw something he hadn't seen on his way in from the other direction. There were wheel-marks in the mud. And they were fresh.

All the long way down into the Rincón valley his thoughts fell over themselves as he tried to work out what to do. The answer kept coming out the same. Nothing. He couldn't tell the blind man he'd been to Las Cabreras in case the blind man was angry. He couldn't tell anybody at home, except perhaps Papa, and what would be the point of telling him? Papa wouldn't be able to do anything. He'd only say what Albi knew already – *Don't tell your mama.*

Only, maybe Papa knew already and hadn't told him?

He hurried along the path, this new thought whirling round his head and setting all the others flying up again like fallen leaves in a sharp wind. People didn't tell him things. How was he supposed to know what to say and what to do and who to be if they didn't tell him things? *Still young enough to be useful.* Was that all he was?

He penned the Molino sheep and separated his own ready to go home. Then he climbed the stairs to El Ciego's warm kitchen, his story ready in his mouth: the secret valley had been empty, he'd grazed the ewes and come straight back. It was true and it wasn't true, both at once.

The blind man was sitting with Joaquín in the shadows beside

352

the fire. Nobody else was there, though Albi looked round the room carefully to make quite sure. He sat down but he knew he mustn't say a word until, sooner or later, El Ciego would send Joaquín on some errand, and then he could tell the things he needed to tell. But El Ciego didn't send Joaquín anywhere and at last Albi had to go or he would be late for curfew. As he stood up, no story told (whether it was true, or only nearly true), he kept his eyes on El Ciego's face, but the blind man's expression didn't change. He only raised a hand and said as he always did, 'Till tomorrow.'

So what was the point in all that?

Albi walked slowly up the steep lane into the village, past the stares of the two *Guardia* on duty at the sentry post. He was tired and wet and it all seemed stupid, and the sheep were tired and wet, and hungry too. And anyway, why weren't El Ciego and Joaquín coming back to the village for curfew?

Next morning, when he got to the Molino, El Ciego was waiting in the corral. 'There is no wall that does not have ears,' he said softly, leaning over the rail to prod the backs of the nearest sheep in the pen. Albi shot him a startled look but El Ciego couldn't mean him. Was it a message? Or did the blind man mean Joaquín, and that he might be listening right now?

'So you didn't find them,' El Ciego said. Albi didn't know if he meant the *maquis* or the *abuelos*, but the blind man didn't wait for an answer. 'Today you will graze by the river. Bring me back a bundle of rabbit food – I've got three rabbits to feed.'

The *Guardia* had taken nearly all their rabbits at home, but El Ciego had rabbits now when he'd had none yesterday.

Albi sat huddled by the river. It was damp and very still, only the river moving with its complicated talk. At least the rain had stopped. Did El Ciego know he'd been to Las Cabreras when he wasn't supposed to? Was that why there was no message today? No parcel of food either.

If somebody goes missing, especially two people, shouldn't you tell someone? But who should you tell? In the old days you would have told the *Guardia* but it wasn't like that now. How could you tell them somebody was missing if that person wasn't supposed to be in the place they were missing from?

*

'Coffee?' Santi says, when Mari-Jé has bought enough meat to last them a month and they've stowed it in the car.

In the restaurant which once belonged to her mother, Alberto's niece greets them from the kitchen doorway. Concepción can't talk for long – there's too much to do – but her husband Juan is in the bar, he will serve them. 'They've started work on the Montesanto road at last,' she says, laughing as she wipes her reddened hands with the tea-towel. 'We're run off our feet with all the workmen. Can't complain though.'

They sit at the table under the TV and Juan brings them coffees, and one for himself. Juan is squarely built, with a voice to match. He teases Mari-Jé, and Santi teases him, and Alberto sits quiet, looking through the window at the slice of sky, colourless in the late-winter light. The last time he sat at one of these tables with Jesús was the year he died. The TV was booming then, same as now, the bar was empty. It was just the two of them, and Jesús said out of the blue, 'It wasn't only bread El Ciego was supplying to the *Guardia* all that time.' Jesús, stooped and balding, stirred the sugar slowly into his black coffee and sucked the spoon. He raised his eyes to Alberto's face. 'Didn't you know? But you were so close to him – did you never guess?'

Alberto said nothing. After all these years he'd grown familiar with Jesús but never quite at ease. He turned his head and looked out, over the bright geraniums on the windowsill, to the sliver of Valbono sky. From the alleyway came Pilar's voice scolding, a grandchild's petulant reply. Alberto looked back at his brother-in-law and wondered whether he wanted to hear what was coming.

Jesús gazed down at the glass clasped between his heavy hands. 'I always thought, myself…' He paused, the shallow breath rasping in his chest. 'I always thought… he was playing… a double game.' He looked at Alberto from under his heavy brows. 'Always wondered… how much you knew. … But then, you were only a kid.'

And you? Alberto thought. What double games did you play? But Jesús was on the winning side, the question didn't apply. He looked away.

That was all they ever said about it. Within six months Jesús was dead.

A dry sob convulses him. Perhaps he made a sound, because they are all looking at him – Mari-Jé, Santi, Juan. But he is on his own in the past and they can't reach him.

44

Walls

Ramona said, 'But Pili, that would be dangerous, Papa might knock it out of you!'

He stepped out onto the *solenar* and the girls jumped apart and stopped talking. What were they doing out here where the night was the way it was before the summer, the cold dark wind and the world all secret? He sat down on a low stool and waited to find out.

'Albi, you shouldn't creep about so,' Pilar said, as if he should push his bare feet into his boots just so she might hear him coming.

She pulled her shawl tighter around her plump shoulders. How was it she stayed plump when the rest of them were so scrawny? She must be eating in El Caballero's house, all those times she went creeping off to see Jesús while Papa was safely in the bar.

'She may never get married now,' Pilar said. That would be Margarita-next-door. Mama was in her bed and everything was all wrong but his sisters were sitting out here in the dark pretending they were talking about nothing more important than what would happen if Margarita's *novio* didn't come back. He stopped listening. Did Mama listen to her friends over the laundry and in the bakehouse? Did she still talk to them? And what was it his sisters hadn't wanted him to hear just now? All this secret talking. That day in the bushes back in the summer, he'd kept that secret inside him such a long time but now it wanted to jump out and join the other secrets that were hanging in the air, just out of his hearing. It wanted to jump out so badly he *had* to let a little bit of it out, though he waited until later when it was only him and Inma left in the kitchen.

'Pili lets Jesús kiss her,' he said, as if he were only saying *Pili has black hair*.

'Albi!' Inma's hands were suddenly still. 'You must never say that again, not even to me. Whatever you think you saw, forget it. Pili has enough trouble already. Take care you don't get her in any worse.'

What trouble did Pili have really? She seemed to be doing all right to him. Plump Pili. All she had to do was not make Papa cross. That wasn't so difficult, surely? He stared at Inma in the shadowy firelight, willing her to say more, but she kept her eyes on her knitting. When she next opened her mouth it was to tell him to be sure to take the potato peelings down in the morning, to the few remaining hens.

He tried to do what Inma said, but he couldn't. He couldn't look at Pili without thinking about *that*.

356

Then another bad thought came. The *Guardia* must have known the *abuelos* were living at Las Cabreras even though they weren't supposed to, and now they must know that they'd gone. It would have been a *Guardia* truck that left those marks in the mud. If they knew, then what did Jesús know?

If Jesús knew, didn't Pilar know too?

If Pilar knew, how could she still be nice to Mama, as if the *abuelos* were still alive and only needing to be found? And why hadn't she made sure somebody went looking? He knew how it must have been. The *abuelos* would have gone out and locked their house and they would have walked onto the *Meseta* and lain down under the stars to die. Or *Abuelo* did, carrying *Abuela* in his arms because she was dead already. That was what *Abuelo* said they wanted, to stay at Las Cabreras until they died. The foxes and the vultures would have picked their bones clean, carrying off thigh bones and arm bones so that nobody would ever know. All the little bones would bleach and fracture in the frosts and then in the hot dry winds of summer until they disappeared, same as a dead sheep disappears. But not the skulls, and not the big bones of the hips. Sheep leave those bits of themselves like flags, however fast the rest goes. The staring skulls lie about among the thyme and rosemary bushes gazing emptily at the sky. It would be the same for people.

He dreamed of bones. Of *Abuelo's* skeleton collapsing like twigs around the smaller skeleton encircled in his bony embrace. He dreamed of vultures, fat and slick on human grease. Of foxes, their fur bloodied from pushing their faces deep into cavities. When he woke his throat was painful with mysterious grief. In his heart, he realised, he'd buried the *abuelos* long ago, back in the early summer. Better to be dead than have the *Guardia* come visiting.

News of another death came all the way from Zaragoza: Don Fernando, the old gentleman Papa called a Capitalist Pig.

Broken-hearted by the destruction of his factory, the women in the Plaza said, shaking their heads. Albi ducked behind the mule and strained his ears to hear more, but it wasn't interesting.

The church bell began its slow toll as he trudged along the mule path in his new boots, but he didn't stop to listen. Don Fernando meant nothing to him, unlike these boots, so hard and unfamiliar on his feet. Boots which used to belong to Old Jaime but Old Jaime hadn't worn them much.

The sheep ambled after him on neat feet that never had to wear boots to keep out the winter cold. Between their bleating and the harsh crunch of his feet on the stony path, he could barely hear the distant bell clanging for Don Fernando. He would be in the ground in Zaragoza by now. What was left of the *abuela* in her own little hole in the cemetery, and Old Jaime in his? Would there be maggots still, even in winter? And ragged bits of flesh, and hair? Or only bones, like the bones of his *abuelos* up on the *Meseta*, picked clean by vultures? The questions hurt him inside his chest.

He looked up at the vultures carving slow circles in the high blue arc above him, so wild and free. But were they really free, those pickers of bones, or were they hungry like him?

He walked through the village with his flock, hearing the whispering rustle through the streets. *El Caballero.*

Outside the bakehouse, by the *fuente,* by the church steps, the words running like a partridge between juniper bushes, *El Caballero, El Caballero.* Like water nosing along a dry *acequia* – *El Caballero, El Caballero, El Caballero.*

And then the single word, *Jesús.* One person said it, and everyone went quiet.

Albi saw the faces turn away, the blankness of the backs of heads. The murmuring began again when he'd gone past. What had happened now? He tried to look unbothered as his new boots hurried him loudly home.

They were all in the kitchen, even his mama, and Papa was swinging about the room, knocking things flying with his hasty crutches and not always by accident. Albi looked from one face to another, waiting for someone to tell him.

El Caballero was going to rebuild the factory, that was all. Albi made his way to his corner by the fire, trying to keep out of Papa's way. Wasn't it a good thing, the factory being rebuilt?

Apparently not. Papa should sit down, before he broke something.

Papa didn't sit down. He hopped about the kitchen until he came to a halt beside Pilar at the little table, Pili sitting with her head bowed over her sewing, as if Papa wouldn't see her if she sat small enough, and quiet. Papa was quivering, every sinew like a cord pulled tight. Albi stared at Papa's hands, tense on the crutches, and willed him not to hit Pili. *Please don't.* Had he whispered it out loud? He put his hand over his mouth to hold the words inside.

When Papa spoke, the spittle flew, his head shook with rage. But all he said was, 'Fucking Jesús.'

Mama put her hand on Papa's arm in the way only she could, which seemed gentle but felt hard. 'Sit down, Ramón. Before you break something.'

She sounded like her old self. Albi looked up in surprise, but her hair was still hanging down her back in an untidy grey plait.

Anyway, even if she wasn't her old self properly, she must be feeling better.

Ramona stirred the embers and put another small log on the top. If Mama saw that she would be cross, but she'd gone to bed, and Ramona heaped the embers up round the piece of wood so it could burn quietly and not be too obvious. 'Well?' she said, her eyes glinting in the firelight. 'What do *you* think, our Inma?'

'Why? What did Jesús do?' Albi asked.

Ramona ignored him. 'So – is it a good thing or a bad thing?'

Her eyes were fixed on Inma's face, but she was smiling as if she knew the answer already.

Inma hesitated. She was sitting very still tonight, her hands – usually so busy – were clasped in her lap. She sat upright like a woman in church, her sturdy legs crossed at the ankles and tucked back under her chair. How strange it was that Inma's legs stayed sturdy even though the rest of her had got so thin. Albi raised his eyes to her face and willed her to look at him so she would see he didn't know what they were talking about and tell him, but she went on staring at the fire.

'I don't think El Caballero is necessarily a bad man,' Inma said at last. 'But he is very clever, and what's good for him may not be the same as what is good for the rest of us. If El Caballero wants to rebuild the factory it might not be a bad thing. But it might not be a good thing either.'

Ramona tutted. He looked from one to the other but he couldn't read their faces. He wanted so badly to know what the answer was but they were talking to each other, not to him, and in a minute they might start thinking about walls and ears and send him to bed, so he sat very small on his stool as if he wasn't really there.

'If Jesús is going to be the new manager we can surely hope to get good jobs there,' Ramona said.

'If we get any jobs at all, good or bad, people will assume it's because of our connection to Jesús.' Inma broke off and cleared her throat long and hard. When she talked again, her voice was husky. 'That's why Papa is so angry. It isn't only about him not liking El Caballero and Jesús. Because of Pilar, we're connected. To Papa it feels like contagion.'

Albi went up to his bed. Contagion. That was one of the priest's words when he cornered people in the street and talked in his deep teacher's voice for everyone else to hear, *This is not the middle ages so why are you people living like pigs? No wonder contagion is rife.* After the priest thought up that word it seemed to give him permission to walk right in at people's front doors uninvited. Anyone who coughed must go to a special place, that was what the priest was telling people.

He lay shivering in the cold blankets, waiting for the bed to warm up.

The priest said people who cough can die of their sickness and make other people get sick and die too. Maybe it was the same anthrack-thing that Sergio knew about. The one the *maquis* might have used to poison the dam, only they didn't. But the priest made it sound as if the coughing people were somehow wicked.

Albi hated the priest. Inma was a good person, but she coughed a lot.

Smoke was furling from the bakehouse chimney as he went down the street towards the gatehouse with his flock. Women's voices drifted out through the open shutters.

Cristina appeared in the bakehouse doorway as he went by, her apron covered in flour. 'Albi! I was just coming to your house to fetch Inmaculada. '

Something about the look on her face frightened him. 'What is it?'

'It's your mama. No, no, she's not ill, but… ' She spread her hands helplessly. 'Come and see what I mean.'

He left his sheep milling in the street and hurried after her into the bakehouse.

The air inside the long low room was very warm. Roberto was the only man in there, stripped to his vest and glistening with sweat as he stoked the big oven at the far end. It all looked normal – the women busy making bread at the trestle tables along the walls, small children running about. There were always a lot of young children in the bakehouse on cold days.

He followed Cristina down the room, conscious of the

glances flicking his way, the shift in the sound of the women's voices as they noticed him. He couldn't see his mama. Then his eyes adjusted to the shadowy light and he understood why Cristina had wanted to fetch Inma. Mama wasn't standing at the table, up to her elbows in flour like the others. She was sitting on the low bench against the wall, very still, her hands folded in her lap. As if she was praying, perhaps, but her eyes were wide open. There was no expression on her face. She stared into space, unblinking, and on the table in front of her the dough lay in a slack heap, spreading out sideways, though all around her the other women were shaping their loaves ready to go in the oven.

'She's been like that all morning,' Cristina said in a low voice, leaning close to Albi so Mama wouldn't hear. 'She says she isn't sick and she hasn't got a pain anywhere but you'd better fetch Inma to make the bread or you won't have any in your house today.'

'Tell her to hurry,' Pepito's mama said, 'or she'll miss the fire. Roberto doesn't hang about for anyone. You know what he's like.'

'I've got stock waiting to be fed, that's why,' shouted Roberto from the far end of the room. 'Run, Alberto. Go fetch your sister.'

At the end of the day, when he came back to the house, he went straight up to the kitchen before he did his jobs.

Mama was there, sitting on a chair. She was peeling potatoes and she wasn't staring blankly any more. Inma gave him a special look from behind Mama's back. The look said, *Don't say a word.*

He went back down to the stable and took the mule to the Plaza to drink. A weight had lifted off his shoulders. Mama was better, then. That was good.

The next morning Inma went with Mama to make the bread, and every morning after.

Papa's three brothers had come to the house to talk to Papa. *A serious talk, Ramón*, they'd said, Pili hearing every word from the back bedroom where she was sorting her enamel chest. She'd stopped arranging things so she could listen.

Out on the *solenar* that night, in the freezing dark, she told her sisters. And Albi. 'A serious talk, they said. About land.'

Ramona said, 'Was it about the far *tierras* again?'

'Yes. They said it was right Papa had the use of that land when *Abuela* was alive because Papa had the cost of keeping her, but it's different now. They said he's got the house, and he can't work the land anyway, and Manolo won't be coming back to Rincón any time soon, perhaps not ever. And Albi is only a boy.'

'What? I'll be a man soon!'

'They said, *We have five grown sons between us. That land should be ours.* I heard them,' Pili said. 'They didn't know I was there. There was a huge argument and then they left. Papa said they were never to darken his doorway again and never again to consider themselves our family.'

Now they would be like the Flórez family. Nobody talking to each other, one brother sliding away when he saw another brother coming down the street, the wives fighting over the laundry and in the bakehouse. Would he be allowed to talk to his cousins now? Would they talk to him?

The dirt could hardly have settled on Don Fernando's grave, far away in Zaragoza, when the hammering and clattering began on the site of the ruined factory. The sound carried faintly all the way to the village. El Caballero strutted about looking important, when he wasn't going off in his new truck to fetch building materials from Las Hoyas, and Jesús rushed on his motorcycle up and down the road between the village and the factory, spewing black smoke.

Every night, in the kitchen, Papa growled a list of names of the men who'd gone down to the new factory to do the work.

Every morning a few more, Papa and Tomás standing by the gatehouse, counting.

No, not counting. Albi walked past with his sheep and saw them there: Papa wasn't counting. The list was in his head, and it was names.

'We know who the enemy is now,' Papa said.

So many enemies. There was another war happening, not in Spain. The Germans were going to win it. In the Plaza, Martín said 'The Generalissimo is staying well out of it,' as if General Franco had privately told him so.

In the privacy of their stable, Miguel told Papa that Republican fighters were going to France to help resist the Germans.

When Miguel had gone, Albi asked what it meant. Papa gripped his shoulder. 'It means, lad, when we've helped France win they'll send their army here and drive that bastard *Generalissimo* out.'

There *was* still hope, then. That's what papa was saying.

If that was true, why were people helping El Caballero re-build the factory? When the French army came, El Caballero would be on the wrong side.

'Walls are going up in people's houses,' Carlos whispered, 'where no walls used to be.'

Albi saw a flicker pass across Rafa's face. It was as if Rafa had walked off. He hadn't – he was still sitting there on the bench at the back of the empty wash house – but his face had gone shut.

'The *maquis* are hiding in the village,' Carlos said. 'My papa says you never can tell which houses.'

Rafa stood up then and really did walk away, without saying a word. Albi watched him go. Yesterday, Carlos's papa had taken a job at the new factory. He was going to work as a carpenter for El Caballero.

'What can you do?' Carlos said, shrugging. 'We need the

money.' But how could he also be talking about walls in houses and the *maquis*? Albi wanted to walk away too, like Rafa, but if he did Carlos would only run after him.

'Anyway,' Carlos said, sitting on the parapet of the wash tank and thudding his heels against the stone as he watched Rafa walk across the Plaza. 'What's the point in making trouble? That's what my papa says.'

A week later and Albi was carrying messages again, so he was trouble. Carlos's papa would think so, and so would the *Guardia*, before they started torturing him. All the same, he was glad. It meant the blind man still trusted him.

The messages were all for Estrellas, there were none for the *maquis*. They were about whores, and wild boar hiding in the streets of Las Hoyas or Escucha. And numbers again. *Two days hence four four one*. Or, *Sunday five four one four*. What did it mean, and did it mean Mena wasn't safe?

But he knew she wasn't. How could she be, with the *Guardia* roaming about?

Up and down the steep dirt road Albi climbed, in the shortest days of winter, the sun bright and brash when the weather was good but the shadows chill, and night coming early. Andrés and Mena were up at Estrellas every day. The messages about whores and wild boar stopped but the numbers ones went on the same, all of them for Andrés. There was nobody to take them to in the secret places where the *maquis* had lived in the summer with the ibex and the wild boar, Albi knew because he'd been again to both places to look. Not that El Ciego had told him to. He just went. Long before the snows came, the *maquis* had disappeared.

The numbers in the messages were like a code, but what could Andrés do with them, up here on the *Meseta* where there was no electricity? There was no telephone, like El Caballero had in his house and the *Guardia* in their garrison. No neighbours for

Andrés to tell, and the huge distances so empty now the *maquis* had gone.

Albi puzzled over the words and the numbers, trying to see shapes in them. Then there was a message which was only words: *The pigs are all snug under the stairs.* He thought he understood that one.

All this risk and effort. He sat in the stable with his papa stitching a nosebag for the mule and wondering what two people on a lonely hilltop farm or half a dozen men in hiding could actually do. Even nine men had only destroyed jobs and nearly killed a lot of people who were on the same side as them. What good had it done, blowing up the factory, except give El Caballero the opportunity to build a new one? But the paper had been for banknotes. Perhaps, after the old factory was destroyed, the people in the towns had stopped having money. Perhaps the townspeople were like people in the country now and had to buy things with other things they already had.

The new factory was going to make woollen cloth. That sounded safer. Maybe it wasn't so bad, then, that Carlos's papa was helping to build it and Jesús was going to be the new foreman. Albi looked at his papa and didn't like to ask. His papa was buzzing like a fat summer fly, for all that he was skinnier than ever. 'The *maquis* are creeping back into the village,' Tomás had said to Papa yesterday, right in front of Albi. 'Bad weather coming.'

After Tomás had gone Papa glared at Albi and said, 'Don't ask, don't tell.'

Maybe it was more than just the weather. Maybe the *maquis* had A Plan, and his papa and Tomás knew about it.

45

Fog

'This is a nonsense!' Mari-Jé says. 'I might be younger than you but I've got ears, I can remember. All those stories people told, I grew up with them. They didn't stay silent, you know, just because *you* chose not to speak about it. Don't you think my parents talked to us kids about the things they'd been through? And our uncles and aunts, and all the neighbours.'

'Stories change with telling,' he says. 'And you weren't there.'

'You were there and you don't say anything at all.'

But he isn't listening. He's thinking of all that chatter chatter in the streets every August, the voices like birds in the trees. Of course he hears them, the old stories. Going round and round, distorting as time passes. *My abuelo did this, my abuela said that.* It goes on and on. Carla with her film crew. Coming at Easter, Santi says, to make their documentary. So what is it going to say, this documentary?

He turns his back on Mari-Jé and goes out.

Her voice follows him down the stairs. 'You don't own the past, Alberto!'

*

Carlos came aross the Plaza while Albi was watering the mule. There was something different about him, as if he'd grown even in the last few days.

'That's it for school.' Carlos leaned against the trough of the *fuente* and picked at his dirty nails. 'I've got a job in the new factory. I'll be bringing money home now. Proper money.' He looked at Albi sideways out of his pale blue eyes.

Albi stared down at the mule's muzzle sucking up water from the trough, at the way the tender hairs lay on her lips with bubbles of air on them where they were under the water, and bubbles of moisture above. 'You can't have a job in the factory, it hasn't been rebuilt yet.'

'I will have as soon as the building work starts. Sweeping, carrying bricks and stuff.'

Sweeping? Albi would rather take messages and be paid in ham. It was more important, taking messages and supplies.

Supplies was a good word. It sounded bigger than *messages* on its own. But there hadn't been any messages since the one about the pigs, and no supplies either. He didn't think there would be any more until the spring.

Spring was a long way away. The weather was dull, the rain turning to snow, icicles everywhere and nothing happening, not even in the new factory.

Strange weather came after the snow. Warm air billowed in over the cold ground like smoke, the moisture hung heavy on every blade of grass and every twig, and on Albi's eyebrows, dripping into his eyes as he took the sheep to graze above the village. The fog blanked out all the higher ground and made the world look flat. Away to his left, the shell of the *castillo* looked small and unimportant.

He had just settled himself in the driest place he could find when he saw El Ciego coming towards him, tapping his way along the path with his stick. What was the blind man doing here when he'd seen him in the Molino barely an hour ago? Albi got up and went to meet him.

The blind man said nothing until they were standing close together under the dripping trees and he could speak softly. 'You'll have to go up to Estrellas.'

'The Torre?' Albi was surprised, even though he'd seen Andrés and Mena in the mule-cart that morning, climbing the long slow bends of the road until the fog hid them.

'This is urgent.' The blind man looked different. He looked worried. 'The message is, *Tonight by the moon*. Say it back.'

'Tonight by the moon,' Albi repeated, but there would be no moon tonight, not unless this fog lifted, so what was the hurry?

El Ciego turned back. Albi whistled to Perrita and started up the rough track. The sheep came quietly, fogging the air with their breath, and Perrita behind them.

At Los Corrales, old José Irún was in the corral, making a gate. *Let people see you,* El Ciego always said. *Don't try to hide. You're allowed to be there – you have your permit saying so.* Albi called a greeting and José waved back. Under the mournful evergreen oaks, water dripped softly off every leaf. The narrow path twisted and turned, climbing the hill steadily between the trees, until it joined the dirt road from the village, safely far away from the sentry post near the *castillo*.

He climbed more quickly on the road. A truck appeared over the crest of the hill, coming down towards him. Remembering what El Ciego said he made no attempt to keep out of sight, though he called the sheep and goats to one side to let the vehicle pass. The hunched figures in the back of the truck looked out at him from under the canvas, their faces blank, their green capes shining with wet and their three-cornered hats dripping. He was careful not to look at them too hard, but they only glanced at him and looked away.

He went on climbing into the mist, up up up, the track swinging backwards and forwards in tight bends. Only him and his animals, and the fog cocooning them. The road tipped over the crest at last, and then the long, slow undulations until the road passed the Ermita de las Estrellas, perched invisibly on the very top. Up here in the fog, one false turn and he would be lost, but he had a message to deliver which could not wait.

At the Torre the heavy door was closed and locked. Only a whisper of smoke came from the kitchen chimney and there was no sign of Andrés in any of the corrals, no Mena either, just his own voice echoing off the buildings when he called their names. There was nothing to do but go down to the Molino land and graze the sheep.

He crouched against the big rock in the middle of the meadow with his sack over his head and shoulders, trying to stay dry. He kept himself warm thinking about the birds last summer, going through all the names in his head. When summer came again he would surprise Mena with how much he remembered and she would be pleased.

When he got to the end of thinking about birds he stood up and ran around to warm up. That big untidy nest in the bare branches of the poplar tree probably belonged to a squirrel. Squirrels were red, like the Republicans were red. Squirrels were better. The Republicans were trouble, in the end; trouble, and hunger, and being shut in, no better than the *Guardia*.

He took out his meagre parcel of bread and one small onion. El Ciego had come specially to tell him to go to Estrellas this morning but he hadn't brought any food. All the way up the hill Albi had been hoping it didn't matter because Mena would feed him.

The mist settled more heavily until he could no longer see the nest high in the bleak branches. The mist was dangerous, he didn't want to get lost going back. He whistled up Perrita and the flock immediately came running, as if they were eager to get home too.

He walked back to the Torre. What would he do if he didn't see Andrés now? He couldn't hear any sheep bells except for his own, and still no sound of Andrés anywhere, whistling to his dogs or calling up his cattle.

He got to the farm and knocked on the door. No answer. He tried the latch. Still locked. He hitched the sack closer over his head and shoulders. The lean-to was empty: the truck had gone. Perhaps Andrés had managed to get hold of some petrol. Andrés driving somewhere with Mena beside him in the warm cab – that was a good thought.

The undelivered message was heavy as a rock inside his chest. If he'd had a piece of paper he could have written the message on it and put the paper under the door, but that would be dangerous. The wrong person might see it. And anyway, he hadn't got any paper, only his permit. And he hadn't got a pencil.

Where were they? The buildings loomed, still and silent, in the blank white air. A noise like a dog whimpering jumped out of his own mouth and startled him back into silence. Perrita whined. She saw him looking and yawned nervously. The afternoon was as dark as if curfew was coming already. He set off up the track towards the ruined Ermita, the flock close on his heels. There was nothing else he could do.

A few kilometres beyond the Ermita Mena appeared like a ghost out of the fog, walking along another path parallel to the road, not going towards Estrellas. She was wearing a bulky old coat of Andrés's, tied with string around her middle. She was sudden and beautiful and he didn't mean to tell her, but then he did.

'I have a message for your Andrés.'

Her smile faded. 'You?' The look on her face didn't make him feel proud, it made him feel guilty. He nodded. She pulled the coat tighter around her as if she was shutting him out. 'It's you who's been bringing the messages?'

She made him sound like a stranger. As if he was *de fuera*, not somebody she knew. He nodded again, and the realization sank in – she knew about the messages, even if she hadn't known it was him that brought them. That meant he could give her this one, though she was looking at him strangely. She didn't say anything about him going back to the Torre with her either, she just held her arms tight across her chest and waited. So he told her the message.

She turned her face away. 'I'll tell him. Only in this fog…'

She sounded so tired, staring out across the blank hillside as if Andrés might be hiding from her somewhere, that suddenly he was scared.

'You'd better get back home, Albi.'

'Has he gone out in the truck?'

Her eyes widened. 'The truck? The *Guardia* took the truck back in the autumn. After the prisoner escaped they came and took it.'

The prisoner. That was a strange way to say it when it was his Manolo.

He didn't like to leave her out there on her own in the fog but he couldn't think of anything else to do, so he said goodbye and walked away up the road. When he looked back she was standing watching him. Where was Andrés? Where had she been, walking all alone, and where was she going?

The summer seemed such a long time ago.

46

Winter

Papa came home from the bar two days later, full of gossip: the *Guardia* were forcing Andrés to bring his livestock down to the village, every last one of them.

'Miguel is going up to help him drive the cattle down tomorrow. They'll have to go in the uncle's barn for the rest of the winter. Don't know what he'll do about all those sheep.'

'But all the hay and straw is up at the Torre!' Albi said.

'Try telling that to the *Guardia*,' Papa said. 'Ignorant, the lot of them.'

The weather was dull, cold, unfriendly. Mena was often in the streets of El Rincón now, carrying laundry to and from the wash house in the Plaza, going to make bread with the other women. Once, she was standing in the queue outside the shop when Albi went by. Andrés said hello to him, the same as usual, whenever they passed in the street but Mena's smile was different, as if she didn't know him. As if he wasn't Albi any more, since that day in the fog. It hurt him deep inside. Didn't she know about the *maquis* and how he'd helped them?

The prisoner, she'd called Manolo. Maybe nobody had told her Manolo was his brother.

All the colour seemed to have gone out of everything, without the promise of Mena's friendship glowing deep in his belly. It was the black and white time of year anyway, the world like a photograph. People huddled in their rusty-black clothes against the cold and the wet. The sheep were soiled from the damp floor of the pen. The trees dripped, or else everything was frost and icicles. There was no sun. He lay in his bed at night, not sleeping, thinking about Mena. He so wanted to talk to her, but if he did, what would he say? Sergio said he'd made a mistake and it wasn't Mena he'd known at the university – *Carmen*, as he'd called her. Could he have been lying? Albi tossed and turned in his bed, his body weary but his mind refusing to lie down and sleep. Why would Sergio lie about it?

If it was a lie and Mena did know him really, she might be friendly again if she knew he was Sergio's friend.

In his dreams, waking and sleeping, he talked to Mena and she understood. She smiled again as if he was special. She put her arms round him and said, *Thank you for looking after my friend Sergio all summer and taking him food and things.*

Things. He remembered the bullets and woke out of his dream. She wouldn't be so pleased about those. Probably.

All the dreams about how he would talk to Mena, but it didn't happen the way he'd imagined it.

He was out in a different place to usual, walking near the river towards El Portal. The blind man had sent him that way, to a little piece of ground the Molino owned, down near where the track to the garrison branched off the road. One little meadow with a ruined house on it: payment long ago for grinding grain into flour, from a family who had nothing left to pay the miller with except the roof over their head. He didn't like going there, it was a sad bad place, and he was walking slowly.

He came round a bend in the path and there was a figure ahead, dark against the half-melted snow. A woman, he could see by her black coat and the drab kerchief covering her hair. Her legs were neat in black stockings but she had clumsy masculine boots on her feet. When he came closer he was shocked to see who it was.

Mena looked up from the sticks she was roping into a bundle. 'Albi.'

Just, *Albi*. No happiness to the sound of it. He looked at the face turned towards him, and was shocked again. How much older she looked, close up. Not a girl after all. But all round her face tendrils of bright hair bounced out from under the kerchief, the same as ever. She was the same Mena. She gave him a small, sad smile and straightened up.

'Out with your sheep then, Albi?'

He smiled uncertainly. Why did she say it like that? He glanced behind him to make sure the sheep weren't wandering off, then back at Mena, who was looking as if there wasn't anything else to talk about now she'd said that.

'I saw a golden oriole,' he said, anxious to say something, anything, to please her, but she frowned. 'Just now I did. In those trees back there. It was really bright, all yellow and black.'

'Don't tell lies, Albi,' she said, looking at him with grown-up eyes. 'Orioles go back to Africa at the end of the summer.' She sounded disappointed. This wasn't how it was supposed to be.

'Or maybe what I saw was a handkerchief caught up in the tree.'

She bent down to finish tying the bundle and didn't reply.

He cast about inside his head for something else to say, something that would catch her attention and make her listen. 'Were you *really* going to be a doctor?'

Her head jerked up and she narrowed her eyes at him. 'Yes. I was. Perhaps one day I will be still.'

He hesitated, but he had to ask it. 'Did you know Sergio in Valencia? I don't know his other names but he has glasses and he plays a guitar and he likes to sing. He said he knew you when you were studying. Afterwards he said it was another Carmen but—'

She grabbed him by the shoulder and clamped her other hand over his mouth. 'Hush. Hush now. You *know*, Albi – there are things you must not speak of. Ever. Do you understand me?'

Her eyes stared into his, so close he could feel her breath sweet on his face. He smelled the cold earthy smell the sticks had left on her skin. He nodded and his eyes brimmed with tears. She relaxed and took her hands off him. The sheep were nosing away from them along the path, and he swallowed hard, trying to whistle for Perrita to fetch them back but the whistle wouldn't come. He swallowed again. He didn't want to go when there were so many things he needed to ask, but what can you say without using words? How can you think things if you don't do it in words?

Mena was still staring at him but more kindly now. She touched his shoulder. 'We depend on you, Albi. Young as you are. Tell the truth, but don't tell the things that don't need to be said. It's dangerous to do that. Try to forget all the things you've heard.'

She straightened up and looked at the sheep. 'You'd better go or they'll leave you behind.'

He walked away. When he looked back she was standing

watching him. Even from this distance he could see how sad her face was. He'd asked about Sergio and that had made her sad. Maybe she'd been in love with Sergio when they were students. Perhaps they'd liked each other but the war had happened and she'd had to go away with Andrés and marry him instead.

*

Mari-Jé wants to go down and walk by the river. It's the last place Alberto wants to walk just now. He would make excuses, but *I'm lonely in this marriage* echoes in his ears and he cannot say no. So they walk.

The afternoon is fresh after the rain, the river running fast and green-blue like snow melt. The poplar trees are naked in the bright sunshine, waiting like the rest of the world for the sun to give them the signal to break into bud. Another spring, and he never thought to see so many, but still he would be sad not to see another after this.

There's a couple ahead of them on the track, walking hand in hand. The boy isn't tall but the girl is tiny.

Mari-Jé sees better than his old eyes. 'It's Santi! Looks like that Felipa with him.'

Felipa from Montesanto. Fancy that.

The two young people break apart when they realise someone is on the path behind them. Santi blushes as they come close but Felipa gives a shy, sweet smile.

Santi gestures. '*Tío, Tía*. Remember Felipa?'

After the greetings and the polite exchanges, Mari-Jé says, 'Time we were getting back, Alberto.' She takes his arm and they turn and walk back towards the village.

'Remember when we were like that, Alberto? Love's young fools.'

He presses her arm close with his elbow. Yes. Now she mentions it, he does.

PART FOUR

47

Sergio

This was the dream Albi made in his head.

They had a man in their wall again. It wasn't Manolo like it was before, and it wasn't the Butcher. It was Sergio. And yes, Sergio was sick, the same as he was in real life, but not the kind of sickness which was bad. In Albi's dream Mena came to help. She spent a lot of nights in their house, helping him look after Sergio and it wasn't because she loved Sergio, she said he was only her friend.

In his dream story Pilar never found out but Inma did. She nursed Sergio, too, and even though she was plain and quiet and had thick ankles, Sergio fell in love with her instead of with Mena and they got married. In this dream, nobody noticed after a while that Sergio hadn't always lived in their house, so he could come out of hiding. Pili was too busy planning her marriage to Jesús to notice anything, and Papa didn't have to beat her any more because he'd given Pili his blessing. Ramona liked Sergio and she didn't make any fuss either.

And Mama? He wasn't sure where Mama fitted into this story so he put her in it in different places. Sometimes she was carrying food to Sergio, like she did before to Manolo, and she said she would love Sergio like a son (only not as much as she loved Albi, of course, because he was her real son). Other times Mama didn't know until the end of his dream, when Inma married Sergio, and then Mama treated him like a son anyway. Well, almost. She still treated Albi best. Whichever way Mama came into his story, she was her old self again.

He wished he'd had a brother like Sergio.

The dream story only came afterwards. Sergio was hidden behind their wall, yes, in the tiny place where a man couldn't lie down but could only sit. When the *maquis* brought him to their house in the dead darkness, hours before curfew ended, Sergio was already very sick. Papa came up to the attic to wake Albi because they needed his help.

In the basement, Sergio was lying on the floor next to the sheep pen, the two maquis who had brought him (the one Albi knew and the one who was a stranger) standing over him.

Albi hung back. Sergio might have been trying to poison the dam and got sick, like he'd talked about back in the summer. There didn't seem to be any blood, though. Wasn't that how you knew it was an anthrack – dark blood oozing from every orifice?

The two *maquis* bent to lift Sergio up but he started flailing so wildly they had to stop.

Papa said, 'Go closer, Albi. If he sees it's you he might calm down. He's been giving us no end of trouble.'

Albi said 'Don't touch him! He might be contagious!'

'Talk to him, lad. Get some sense into him.'

He'd wake everybody, thrashing about like that, so Albi stepped closer and crouched down.

Sergio grabbed him by the wrist and fixed him with feverish eyes. 'Not contagious. Sepsis.'

Albi pulled back, alarmed by the rattling in Sergio's chest.

'Please!' Sergio grabbed at the men who had brought him and held onto their trouser legs. 'Don't leave me here. Hypothermia better.'

But Papa and the two *maquis* were too busy setting about hiding him in the wall to listen.

'Go to the kitchen and get some bread and a candle and a jug of water,' Papa said.

Albi ran upstairs. Didn't they realise Sergio was terrified of being buried alive in the wall?

But Papa and the *maquis* ignored him. They put Sergio in the wall and built up the stones again, and then the *maquis* went away, through the back gate and off into the dark shadows to wherever it was they'd been hiding before Sergio got too sick to stay there.

All the rest of the long winter night Albi lay in his bed waiting to be ill. Was that blood coming out of an orfice that he could feel? He felt sick, too, but that was from waiting for the *Guardia* to come and find the man hidden in their basement.

Next morning he opened the shutter of his room and inspected himself and the bed for blood. There wasn't any, and the *Guardia* hadn't come. The sick feeling began to go away. He went downstairs and through to the back bedroom. Mama was in the *alcoba*. She didn't seem to have moved since yesterday, she didn't move now. She might have the anthrack too, the contagion could have come up from the basement and got her. The sick feelings came back in the pit of his stomach. Then he saw the blankets moving slightly, up, down, up, down. She was still breathing. She was sleeping, that was all.

He did his jobs. He went out for a while with the sheep but it was cold and sleeting and he didn't stay long. When he got back he went and sat with his rope-making near the hiding place. Whenever Sergio coughed (that horrible racking, helpless cough that was like nothing Albi had ever heard before, not even Inma when she was bad), he coughed himself. When that went on so long as to sound suspicious, he talked loudly to Perrita instead.

At last Sergio went quiet.

Albi untied the mule and took her down to the *fuente* for her evening drink. In the Plaza he strained his ears for any gossip of something bad happening in Valbono, but all the neighbours were talking about was the weather.

When he got back, Sergio was muttering loud enough to be heard through the new wall. Albi sat down with his back against the wall and pulled Perrita onto his lap. He knew what he had to do. He turned his face towards the stones and began to talk about Mena, very quietly so no one else would hear. He said he would go and find her and bring her to help. He'd thought it all out while he was down at the *fuente*. Sergio would probably be dead by now if it really was the anthrack so it must be the sep sis thing he'd talked about. Anyway, Mena would know what to do. He ought to go now, but it was too close to curfew, he would have to wait until morning.

As soon as Papa came in for curfew he told him his idea.

Papa just laughed. 'Whatever put such a thought in your head? She's a woman. What would she know about doctoring?' He frowned and put his mouth up so close his moustache tickled Albi's ear. 'Not a word to anyone. That clear? Not. A. Soul.'

Who did he mean? Mena? The blind man?

Next morning Sergio was quiet. Albi didn't hear him cough once while he was doing his jobs.

He took the flock down to the Molino. El Ciego looked the same as he always looked and he didn't ask any questions. The weather was dark and cold and sleety. Albi didn't stay out long with the sheep.

When he got home, Sergio was still being quiet.

That night Papa looked at Albi as if he was the one who was ill. 'Go to bed, boy,' he said, though the fire was still burning strongly in the hearth and his sisters were still sitting round it.

He climbed into his narrow bed without undressing and lay under the blankets, wide awake, listening to the murmur of his sisters' voices, the scrape of a chair being pulled across the floor, the wooden lid being lifted off the water jar and then put down again, a clatter of pots directly below where he was lying. At last he heard his sisters go to their room. Perhaps he slept, perhaps he didn't, but his ears were still listening, waiting for it to be late enough and safe enough to creep down the stairs.

Something caught his attention and he woke up properly. Silent as the house was, he heard the silence shift again and shudder, the ease of air displacing air as a door opened. The deliberate silences of someone moving things and trying to make no sound at all. He got out of bed and pulled on an extra jumper. He crept down the freezing stairs on his bare feet and unlatched the door to the kitchen as quietly as he could. The banked-up fire glowed dully on the hearth, the empty chairs looming like ghosts in the rosy light. He closed the door behind him and very quietly opened the kitchen door and went down to the basement. A light was flickering in the byre. He hurried down the passage towards it.

In the byre, beyond the dark emptiness where the oxen and the cow used to stand cudding in their stalls, Papa was taking the wall apart, stone by stone. A bad smell came from the wall, the smell of a dead animal that is already rotting. It must be the anthrack after all.

A sleety snow was falling. Albi went round the outside of the village, keeping away from the streets and the lights. He crossed the track to Las Hoyas, well above the road-block and the sentries, and came round behind the *castillo*. It was very dark. The castle keep loomed up against the sky to his right now, ahead of him he could see nothing at all. He crossed the open space cautiously, afraid of tripping over a boulder, until he got to the huddle of corral walls and could run like a rat in the shadows to Miguel's house.

Call twice like an owl and wait, then a third time – that is the signal, Papa had said. What was the signal at their house? Was it the same?

Almost as soon as he made the signal he heard a movement inside the house and the sound of oiled bolts being carefully drawn back. The door opened a crack. An eye peered, then the door creaked open wide enough for Miguel to reach out and yank Albi inside, closing the door behind him.

'Papa says you must come at once.'

'Wait.'

He heard Miguel feeling his way up the dark staircase without a light. It didn't feel good to be standing shivering in Miguel's house in the pitch black, the brick floor cold as death under his bare feet. He hadn't dared wear his boots for fear of being heard by the sentries. He stood on one foot and rested the other against the warmth of his trouser leg. Should he tell Miguel about the anthrack? He changed feet. Papa hadn't listened, he'd just told him to stop jabbering and move his arse. If he told Miguel, Miguel might refuse to come back with him and then Sergio would be stuck in their wall for ever. Better not say anything.

Miguel came quietly down the stairs, invisible in dark clothes.

They went back the way he had come, sliding like shadows up the alleyway and across the open ground by the *castillo*. He followed Miguel up the slope beyond the *castillo* and across the track, looking out carefully for the sentries but there was no sign of them. Perhaps they were inside their hut by the barrier.

On the far side of the track the path to the cemetery was a pale blur: the sleet had turned to snow and was beginning to settle. They hurried past the cemetery walls, then circled round through the wintry gardens until they could come in at the back of Albi's house, slipping through the unlatched door of the corral, past the few sleeping hens in the old pig pen, the line of empty hutches along the wall, and in at the back door. The sheep paused in their cudding to watch them go by. Albi led the way to the byre where a single candle cast a fitful light.

Papa had taken down the stones of the wall to reveal a twisted figure. Sergio, but not the Sergio Albi knew. Upright because he couldn't lie down. Upright, as if he was only sitting thinking, but rigid so that the grimace on his dead face was fixed as if it had been carved on a statue. But worst of all, Pilar was towering over Papa, as if he had shrunk suddenly and she had grown, with her hair all wild and her face locked as rigid as Sergio's in her fury. And Papa was raising his crutch to hit her.

The body refused come out of the hole. Albi tried to help Miguel and Papa pull the body out. It wasn't Sergio now. The terrible face looked naked without the glasses. What had happened to those?

They struggled for a while, until Miguel told them to get out of his way, they were slowing him down. He'd already told Pilar to shut up unless she wanted to wake the neighbours. He said she could start screaming again when she was ready for the *Guardia* to come and catch her red-handed hiding a *maquis*. Pilar closed her mouth, furious eyes flashing at Miguel and Papa, and at Albi too.

Even for Miguel, who was strong, and not so old as Papa, it was very difficult getting Sergio out of the wall. He'd been dead long enough to stiffen up, not long enough to loosen again.

At least the bad smell had faded a little.

Albi tried not to let his thoughts go into that black hole but they kept going there all the same. No air, rats running over your feet, cold and hot both together, and your limbs tied up like a trussed chicken by the lack of space.

Miguel grunted and pulled, pulled and grunted. The body that wasn't Sergio any more slid sideways a little. A stone tumbled and the body fell forwards out of the wall. Pilar put her hand over her mouth as if she might vomit, Papa staggered back on his crutches and nearly went down, but they could do what they needed to now. Miguel heaved, and Albi and Papa pushed, and at last they got the body onto Miguel's back. It made an awkward burden, legs and arms sticking out any old how.

'We should have left it till he'd softened up again,' Miguel muttered. 'If it had been safe to.'

Albi saw the bitter look Miguel gave Pilar from under the brim of his hat. He ran to open the door to the corral and Miguel staggered through it, away across the *huerto* and down the steps into the *barranco*. Albi thought of him crossing the stream in the dark, stumbling on boulders, sliding in the sleety snow that was coming down harder now. Making his way to the cemetery to leave the body on the track where the *Guardia* would find it in the morning. If it was the anthrack Miguel might die too. What would they do then, without Miguel to help them? Who would cut their hay and their corn next year? Unless they all died too.

'At least the body will be in the right place for burying,' Papa said in a low voice. He turned to Pilar and hissed, 'As for you, if you want to go ahead and marry that jerk you will never ever breathe a word of this. Not to anyone but least of all to your bloody *novio*. You know he'll never have you if he finds out.'

Albi stared at his sister and saw it sink in that Papa was right, she would never be able to tell. But then she gave Papa a funny look. Papa had just said she *could* marry Jesús, after all.

48

Contagion

Old Teresa opened the door to him. 'You want to speak to Carmen?' she said, as if a ten-year-old village boy could have no business asking for her daughter-in-law.

Mena appeared at her shoulder. 'Albi is a good boy, Mama, and a friend.'

His chest went hot inside at that word, *friend*, though he saw the wary look Mena gave him.

'He'd better come in, then.' Teresa turned and hobbled up the stairs. Mena nodded at him to follow.

The kitchen of this house was small, not at all like the Torre, and it wasn't dark like he'd imagined, it was bright with winter sunshine. Because the shutters were wide open, even though it was cold outside: a wooden frame with glass in it had been put in the window to stop the bitter air coming in. Through the window he could see the red roofs pitching this way and that, house after house, down towards the Plaza.

There were books in this house too. A whole cupboard of them on one side of the room. And on the little table by the chair where Teresa sat down next to the fire there was an open book with a pair of spectacles lying on top of it.

Teresa put the spectacles on and picked up the book but she didn't start reading. She stared at Albi over her little round glasses as if she was waiting. Mena told him to sit at the table but he couldn't expect her to feed him the way she did at the Torre because this wasn't her house, and anyway he didn't have far to go home. All the same, she might have given him something, if Teresa hadn't been sitting there by the fire, staring with her little beady eyes. Mena sat down at the table across from him. It was obvious she thought he shouldn't have come, but he had to tell her. If she heard about Sergio from somebody else she might not be careful what she said.

Teresa leaned over and lifted the lid off the pot, ledged in the ashes near her feet, and peered inside it. He hadn't smelled that smell for a long time. Real coffee.

'We haven't seen you out with your sheep for a while, Albi,' Mena said, and he nodded. This is the sort of thing you have to say when other ears are listening. 'We're not going out with ours today. Not with this snow. Andrés thinks there'll be more later.'

He gazed into her clear eyes and saw she hadn't heard about Sergio. Teresa had settled into her chair as if she was going to sit listening forever and he didn't know what to say. 'I've been out and about,' he said, 'but I haven't been up Estrellas way.' A warning look flashed in Mena's eyes and he closed his mouth.

The door opened.

'Albi!' Andrés ruffled Albi's hair as he went past. He sat at the end of the table and looked at his mother and then at his wife, his face grave. 'Have you heard the news?'

Mena said, 'What news?'

'They found a body by the cemetery gate this morning.'

'One of those *maquis* boys, was it?' Teresa said.

'It would seem so.'

A little noise jumped out of Albi's throat. Just the tiniest of noises, by mistake, but Mena heard it. She looked at him hard, and then she got up and fetched the pot of coffee from the hearth. She poured a small earthenware cup for Andrés, and a tiny cup for Albi. He didn't tell her he wasn't allowed to drink coffee at home.

Teresa prodded at the fire with a poker. 'Did you forget the sticks, Andrés? This fire wants feeding.'

Andrés rested his hand on Mena's shoulder for a moment and went back out. It burned Albi's eyes, seeing that.

He must tell Mena quickly, while Andrés was out of the room, but how could he say it without using words? He couldn't think of any words that were safe to say out loud with Teresa listening. It had seemed so important to come and tell her as soon as he could but he hadn't thought how he would say it.

Mena took something out of her apron pocket and pushed it across the table. He looked down – a piece of paper with a pencil on top. There was some writing on the paper. He stared at the words until they made sense and then he saw it was only a shopping list. Paraffin, it said, salt, black thread. Mena reached out and turned the paper over. The other side was blank. He looked up. She nodded at him to write.

How could he write in little words the huge thing that had happened? How could he tell her on paper, fixing it down like a stone with words of lead? Even if they burned the paper afterwards, the words would still be there. He looked up at Mena again. Her eyes were very dark, the whites of them as clear as the sunshine outside. She gave another little nod. *Write, Albi, write,*

388

the nod said. *Write this thing which is so important. Write, so Teresa does not hear.*

He thought carefully, worrying about the hidden letters in the words that might be waiting to trick him, and the wrong eyes that might see them afterwards. Worrying about Andrés coming back any minute. Worrying about writing anything at all when Mena had said he mustn't talk about Sergio, even say his name. In the end he wrote one letter and one word: *Era S.* It was Sergio.

He watched Mena read it, a puzzled expression on her face, as Andrés came in with his arms full of firewood. The church bell had started tolling for Mass. Mena screwed the paper into a ball and tossed it in the fire.

Teresa said, 'I think I will go to Mass today.' She pulled herself to her feet. 'If they've killed one of those boys he will need praying for. Shall you come, Carmen?'

Mena shook her head. 'Sorry, Mama.'

Albi listened to the sound of Teresa going haltingly down the stairs. If only she'd gone out while Andrés was getting the firewood he wouldn't have needed to write anything. He heard Teresa shuffle along the downstairs passage and out through the front door. But maybe it would have been harder to say it than to write it. Maybe it was easier to read it than to hear it. He stared at Mena. She stared back, her eyes glassy with tears. She didn't look angry at him telling, she looked stricken.

'I wanted to fetch you. I told Papa you were going to be a doctor.'

Andrés, sitting beside Mena, not seeing her face, not knowing what Albi was talking about, said cheerfully, 'Are going to be, one day. Aren't you, sweetheart?' And right in front of him, Andrés put his arm round his wife's shoulders and hugged her up close.

Mena's eyes were still fixed on Albi's.

Era S. It was Sergio. Not the body of some nameless *maquis* found lying on the track but Sergio, who had been her friend. Maybe more than a friend.

Mena said, 'Did they kill him? Did the *Guardia* kill him?'

He shook his head. Was it all right to talk about Sergio in words now? 'He was hiding in our byre but he was already sick. And then he died.'

Andrés looked from him to Mena and back again, his arm still round Mena's shoulders, not understanding.

She put her hands over her face. Tears ran out between her fingers and dripped onto the table. She was crying for Sergio, right in front of Andrés! And then she *told* him she was.

'It was Sergio, Andrés. It was Sergio.'

Andrés didn't act angry. He put both his arms round Mena and pulled her against his chest, murmuring quietly into her hair. He looked across at Albi and gave a tiny shake of his head.

Albi got up from the table and crept out of the kitchen and down the stairs. As he let himself out of the house the church bell stopped tolling.

In their house there was nobody in the dark kitchen. Nobody in the back room where his sisters slept, nobody even in the *alcoba* in the unmade bed. Nobody out on the *solenar*. He went back down to the basement. In the empty byre, the wall had been built up again. He listened with his ear against the stones. Was there somebody else in there already? But he couldn't hear anything.

In the corral, the back gate was open and there was Papa, out on the *huerto*, balancing precariously on his wooden leg and slashing at the snowy ground with his mattock as if he wanted to break somebody's head. It was the wrong weather for digging. Wherever Papa hit the ground the mattock made black wounds across the snow, the soil scattering across the white like gritty blood. Papa wasn't digging. He was venting his fury.

Albi hesitated on the steps leading down from the corral. He didn't want to turn that fury on himself but he was frightened for his papa.

Papa looked up. All he said was, 'Bloody women.' He straightened his back and wiped his forehead, stared up at the grey cliffs for a moment. 'I told them. I told them not to go.'

So that was where Mama had gone. She couldn't have the anthrack then. Was church really so bad, if it got her out of her bed? If she tied up her hair again instead of leaving it to straggle down her back like a mad woman? Teresa had gone to Mass too, even though she had books in her house and a son working for the Republican government, and she no more knew which *maquis* she was praying for than Mama did.

The expression in Papa's eyes said *he* would never think it was better, and if Albi knew what was good for him he'd stay on his papa's side and not side with the women.

And then he thought, Mama and Pilar in church – was it their own sins they were confessing, or other people's?

The snow melted away, and then came back again, and melted, and came back. The dam filled nearly to the top of the wall.

The rumours gathered like snow in a ditch, and then like melted snow they ran heavy through the streets of the village. In the bar they were still arguing about Sergio, though they didn't know his name, and they didn't know where he'd been hiding before he died. A body had been found by the cemetery gate, that was all they knew. But then it disappeared, and later the same body, or another one, was found at the bottom of the cliffs. Papa said the *Guardia* had taken the body from outside the cemetery.

'And we know what they'd have done to it before they took it up on the *Meseta* and tossed it over the cliffs,' he said, challenging Martín with a stare. 'Learned their evil habits off the bloody *Moros*, didn't they. Fucking Fascists.' He turned to scowl at Albi, sitting on the floor by the door of the bar. Albi didn't know whether the look meant *mark my words*, or *bugger off and leave me alone*. He stayed where he was.

Martín said, 'What body left by the cemetery? The poor sod

391

at the bottom of the cliffs was just some vagrant. Walked too close to the edge and missed his footing in the snow.'

'Well you would say that. Arse-licker.'

Albi shrank back against the wall. Would Martín hit Papa now? Julio was looking alarmed as if he thought so.

Martín pulled himself up very straight. He was much taller than Papa when he did that. 'I'll not stay here to be insulted. I will drink in the other bar from now on. You should watch your step, Ramón. You're walking very close to the edge.'

'Hopping, more like,' Francisco-next-door chimed in. 'You're hopping close to the edge, Ramón. It doesn't do to hop so close.' He banged out of the door after Martín, nearly falling over Albi's feet.

Julio watched them go. 'That's two more customers I've lost and Mario's gained.' He didn't sound angry, just tired.

Albi went outside. It was obvious Papa wasn't going to come for a while yet. He stared up at the clouds racing across the sky behind the high roofs. Martín and Francisco. You couldn't tell which houses held which secrets now – the men hidden in the walls, or the arse-lickers sitting on the chairs in the kitchens.

The stories grew. Francisco-next-door's pig died and some people said the *maquis* had poisoned it to punish Francisco for being friendly with the *Guardia*. Albi thought it might be the anthrack getting through the wall into Francisco's house, but nothing else died and Miguel didn't get sick.

Bernardo's sheep got out of the corral. *Must have been the maquis let them out,* the whisperers said. It was the *maquis* who started the landslide that broke down the wall of the *acequia principal*. Who made the hail so big it broke all those roof tiles. Who must have stolen all the supplies so there was nothing in either of the shops. All this bad luck that was falling on the village like snow on a duck's back.

How could the *maquis* do any of these things if they'd been

392

hiding inside the houses in the village all winter? Albi knew there was a man behind the wall of their byre again. He didn't know who the hiding man was, if it was Toni, or the Butcher (how cramped *he* would be in there), or one of other *maquis* from the summer, or a different one he'd never met. He didn't think it could be his brother because if it were Manolo, Mama would surely not be staying in her bed in the *alcoba* all the time

Papa laid one finger along the side of his nose and said, 'Least known safest.' Albi didn't say anything. He was angry that Papa was putting them all at risk, and for a stranger.

But then he thought, as long as the *maquis* were hiding in the village they wouldn't try to blow up the dam. The water was lapping to the very top, dark and sinister in the winter light, not bright blue any more. If the dam was blown up now it would destroy them all.

49

Disappearances

The *Guardia* caught Papa's friend Tomás hiding a man in his corn bin. Maybe it was a *maquis*, maybe it wasn't. There was no way of knowing because the *Guardia* had taken the man away, and Tomás too. It was three days before his wife heard he was in the jail in Las Hoyas. The bad jail. His wife behaving as if she was already a widow.

'I thought they'd shoot him for that,' Albi said. 'He was lucky.'

'Lucky?' Papa said. 'Not *lucky*, Albi. They can kill you fast, or they can kill you slow. Which would you prefer?'

That wasn't fair. He didn't want to be killed at all.

It wasn't yet morning when he was woken by banging. It took several heartbeats to realise it was on Jaime's door across the street, not theirs.

'Open up! Open up or we'll break down the door!'

Albi cowered by the window, listening. In Jaime's house there was no door at the back into another street, no door through the wall into the neighbour's house. There was only one door out and that was the one the *Guardia* were banging on, and only three windows, one above the other, and all three windows looked out over the door where the *Guardia* were waiting.

He ran down to the kitchen. Inma was standing in the middle of the room, her hand over her mouth, her eyes wide and scared. She pulled him against her. They heard the street door of Jaime's house open, and Jaime's voice answering.

When Albi went out with his sheep not long after, Jaime's house was all shut up, the shutters tightly closed.

He didn't hear the news until he came back into the village at the end of the day and Carlos pounced on him. Jaime had been taken, nobody knew where. He wasn't in the lock up because Carlos had looked, and Luis Irún said there'd been no-one in the garrison when he'd come past, the place had seemed deserted. 'Not a mule or a motorcycle or a truck visible anywhere,' Carlos said, excitedly.

'Really?' Albi said, waiting for Carlos to let go of his arm so he could go home.

The next morning Belén was collecting water from the *fuente*, same as every other day, except that her face was all white and her eyes were red.

'She's being brave,' Inma said. 'And no news is good news.'

She was right. By the end of the next day there was news, and it was bad. Jaime had been seen in the prison in Las Hoyas but then he'd been taken somewhere else, nobody knew where.

Belén locked the front door and went back to live with her

parents and her brothers and sisters in their small crowded house in the Plaza. Young Jaime's house looked mournful now, without him and Belén in it.

If there were any *maquis* still living up on the *Meseta*, El Ciego gave Albi no messages to take to them, and none for the Torre either. Andrés and Mena no longer toiled up and down to the *Meseta*, now the *Guardia* made them keep their livestock down in the village, but they were running short of hay and of grain, Papa said. Last week they'd had to pay El Caballero to bring a load of fodder down in his truck.

Albi was scared when he heard that.

He went to the Molino every day, just the same, and took the sheep out most days. There was fog and there was ice, and rain, and snow. Nothing much changed in the village. People went on looking at one another with suspicious eyes. There were neighbours they said things to, and neighbours they only said what the weather was doing. Albi took the flock out but for nothing much more than a breath of cold air and a gulp of icy water out of the river, and a bite of dead grass to eke out the dwindling store of hay. Even at the Molino the stack of hay was getting low.

All afternoon the church bell had been tolling. The sound travelled thinly through the clean bright air, all the way up the hill to where Albi was grazing the flock under the cliffs. Somebody must have died. It made him want to go home, even though everyone in their house had been all right this morning. As all right as people could be when Mama was in her bed facing the wall and wouldn't get up, and Papa got out of his bed as angry as he was when he fell into it the night before. The bell had been tolling a lot this winter with all the old *abuelos* giving up and dying because they didn't have enough to eat, or because they were too tired and too sad to go on living.

The mournful sound made him think of his *abuelos*. To lie in the cemetery, like Papa's parents, was one thing, but out among the rocks like Mama's was another. Did it matter that they hadn't been buried in consecrated ground? Did it matter if their bones got mixed up and spread about and carried off by foxes?

When he got back to the Molino, El Ciego told him the bell was for Inés, El Caballero's housekeeper. She was old and she had died. Nothing important, then.

He penned the sheep and climbed the stairs on unwilling feet, pausing on the landing to listen through the door before opening it. He'd heard them shouting before he even got to the top of Calle San Juan.

'The reason you have nothing is because you're feckless!' Pilar, the words spitting out as if it hurt her to have them in her mouth. He leaned his ear against the wood. 'Hanging on to out of date ideas while your family starves!'

He'd be better off down in the stable. He turned to go back down.

'Besides, I'd be earning good money. And I'd bring food home.'

Albi paused, all ears.

'You won't have a home to bring it back to if you take that job.'

'You fool, Papa!' She was screaming now, the whole street would hear every word. There was a crash, and the thud of Papa's crutch hitting something soft. Then Pilar's voice hissing 'You'll be shot if they find out.'

Papa hissed back, 'Not only me. I'd take you with me. Don't you forget that. Ever.'

Pilar went to live in El Caballero's house to be his housekeeper, and now she wasn't Papa's daughter any more and she was never to cross their doorstep again.

Never is a long, long time.

It was dangerous, Pilar living in El Caballero's house. At any moment she might tell the things she knew and then the *Guardia* would come in the night with their big boots and the cold metal of their guns. Albi buried his thoughts down deep but they kept bobbing up like corks in the river. Miguel and the other people in the village who didn't like the *Guardia* and hated El Caballero would think their family was on the wrong side now. El Ciego would think so too, and he'd lose his job and then Carlos would mock him. Carlos who knew too much. He'd seen Pilar and Jesús that day, he would talk. Albi kept out of his way.

Everything was wrong in their house, now they were not six but only five, and Mama in her bed all the time, so really they were only four, and Inma was still coughing. The priest might notice and come to their house. The black-winged priest with his wide hat and his fleshy face. Mama should be keeping Inma away from the priest, not leaving her to work in the bakehouse and the wash house and do the queuing in the shop – all those places where the priest might hear her coughing. How could Mama do that?

Then he wondered if Mama thought the same about him. *How could Albi do that?* she might be thinking. Because it was true, he had hidden things from her, just like Papa had.

In the morning, when everybody else was out of the house, he crept into the *alcoba* and knelt by his mama's bed. He wanted her to stroke his hair like she used to, even to say he was her Best Baby. But Mama didn't turn her face from the wall.

'She's sick, Albi,' Inma said, as though she wasn't sick herself.

Pilar stayed in El Caballero's house at night like the housekeeper Inés did before her. In the daytime Pilar was everywhere in the village, fetching water for El Caballero from the *fuente*, doing his laundry in the wash house side by side with Inma. When Inma came home, Albi glimpsed a package, neatly wrapped in waxed paper and tucked under the clean shirts, all wet from the laundry. Later, there was a knuckle of ham on the table in the kitchen, but Papa saw it. He opened the kitchen shutter and flung the ham-bone out into the street.

'I won't have any of you consorting with that whore!'

A dog carried the bone away before Albi could get down the stairs. When he came back to the kitchen Papa was still shouting.

Ramona said coldly, 'Then your shirts won't get washed for you, Papa, because where else could Inma go to wash them?'

Papa hit Ramona hard round the mouth.

Albi went to her afterwards on the *solenar* and she was crying, dabbing the blood from her split lip, but she was angry too. So angry he was scared.

'I'll kill him. I'll kill that bastard if he hits me again,' Ramona said.

Now that Pilar wasn't in their house and Mama wasn't Mama any more either, Ramona was the one who Papa hit. He hit her for Pilar leaving. He hit her for Pilar going every day to Mass, now that she wasn't in Papa's family and didn't have to do as he said. He hit her for the war being over and the *Guardia* being here. Albi was so tired of all this hitting. But at least Ramona didn't kill Papa, even though she'd said she would.

Papa was safely snoring in the front bedroom. Mama was very quiet in her bed in the *alcoba* with her face turned to the wall, and Ramona and Inma were whispering on the *solenar*. Albi crept out into the cold night air and sat quietly on the little stool. This time it was Inma crying, holding Ramona's hands and staring into her face until the crying brought on a fit of coughing.

Ramona put an arm round her shoulders. 'You're sick, Inma. You know the priest is right about that.'

The terror in Albi's stomach jumped up again. He'd been there this morning, hiding behind the front door, when the priest cornered Inma in the street outside their house. The priest used a long word that meant this coughing – another word, not *contagion*. He said Inma must go away to a sani-something to be made better.

Perhaps that would be a good thing, if they could make Inma better in that place.

'I can't go,' she'd said, 'my family needs me.'

Albi, watching through the crack of the door, saw the priest's eyes stop pretending to care.

'Nonsense! Tuberculosis is highly contagious, it's your moral duty to go. For the sake of your family, for the good of the entire village, you must not stay here!'

Contagious? Suddenly he understood. It had come. Not quickly, like Sergio said it would. This anthrack had taken a long, long time but the priest seemed to know all about it, holding that handkerchief over his face and glaring at Inma over the top of it, making it sound as if she was dirty. *Inma!* Albi wanted to run out and punch him right in the middle of his round black belly.

The priest was just trying to scare them. He couldn't send Inma away! Not now that Pilar wasn't there and Mama never got out of her bed except to go to the church, which she did every afternoon now, if Papa wasn't around to stop her. And Papa hardly ever was around to stop her because he was usually in the bar.

'How does he have the money for it?' Albi asked Ramona as he put some bread in his satchel in the morning.

She said darkly, 'Geronimo paid up at last. Papa's drinking the oxen, Albi. And when he's done that, he'll drink the mule.'

Silly. The mule was still in the stable.

Then like a rock toppling down off the cliff he realised what she meant.

Albi stood with his arms round old mule's neck and whispered in her downy ear. He told her how he loved her, she was safe with them. The mule nuzzled at his pocket though it was a long time since he'd had anything in his pocket to give her. Ramona must be wrong – Papa loved the mule too, same as he had loved the oxen. He'd only sold the oxen because they couldn't feed them any more, they couldn't make enough hay and what they made the *Guardia* took too much of it. It wasn't Papa's fault.

Such a long time ago last summer was, when he didn't know the things he knew now, when Papa was still hopeful he would plough again, and Mama was still Mama, and the *abuela* was still alive and the *abuelos* were up at Las Cabreras. Now their house felt empty and quiet. No oxen, no cow. Hardly any chickens left, and no rabbits. The flock dwindled to six ewes and the two goats. Only the cats multiplying.

'We should eat cat meat,' Ramona said, but she didn't mean it. They needed the cats, to kill the rats. Anyway, you can't eat cats.

But you can eat mule.

50

Inma and Ramona

They were on the *huerto* outside the village, cleaning up the dead tomato vines and digging over the ground ready for potatoes when the spring came properly, if it ever did. Just him and his papa. Not his mama, because she was in her bed. Not Inma, because she was in the wash house. And not Ramona because… He didn't know where Ramona was.

Would El Ciego ever give him a message again, now that Pilar worked for El Caballero? If the blind man had bad thoughts he didn't show them. He said the same things he always said these days, *Take the sheep here. Take the sheep there.* Never very far away, because until the spring came there was no grass anywhere, so today Albi had come home to help his papa in the *huerto*.

He turned the soil over with his mattock, watching the silvery blade cut cleanly into the unpromising ground and wondering where the other mattock went, the one he'd smuggled to Manolo in the lock up. You could kill a man with a mattock. Perhaps Manolo had taken it with him.

Papa grunted alongside him. Even on one leg Papa was quicker at this work than Albi was.

A movement caught his eye and he looked up. Pilar was coming across the *huerto*, carrying a package wrapped in white paper. He shot a sideways look at their papa. Papa's face had turned dark and unfriendly but he didn't stop working. Perhaps he hadn't seen her. *Chack chack chack* went Papa's blade in the dark soil. Albi didn't know what to do so he pretended he hadn't seen Pilar either. He went on working like Papa did, but out of the corner of his eye he was watching her come closer. She really was getting quite stout. The food must be very good in El Caballero's house.

'Papa, I need to talk to you.'

She sounded nervous. As well she might. *Chack chack*, went Papa's mattock in the earth. *Chick chick*, went Albi's.

'I have nothing to say to you,' Papa said, just when Albi thought he wasn't going to say anything at all.

'I think you have, Papa.'

Chack chack. Chick chick.

'Albi, I brought you something.' Pilar sounded cross now, even though she was holding out the package. His stomach rumbled hopefully but he kept his eyes down. His mattock went *chickety-chick*. 'Go and eat it over there, Albi,' Pilar commanded. He glanced up, and hesitated. She thrust the package closer. 'Please, Albi.' Her eyes were anxious.

He felt sorry then, so he did what she'd asked. In the package was a piece of cheese. He went and sat on the wall with his back to them, trying to chew slowly and savour every crumb. If he chewed loudly enough he wouldn't have to hear.

He heard anyway. Not the first bit, when Pilar was talking in a whisper, but when she shouted, 'Don't hit me! You'll hurt the baby!' he couldn't help but hear. He looked over his shoulder. He saw the sun glint coldly on the blade of Papa's mattock as he swung it up in the air, he saw Pilar flinch away with her arms up.

But Papa let the blade fall again without hitting her. Pili went away. She was crying.

What baby? She must be going crazy, like the *abuela* did when she got old in their house. All the same, he didn't like it when Papa hit people. Even if it was Pilar.

Next day, when he came in just before curfew, Inma was sitting by the kitchen fire and Papa and Mama were sitting with her. He stopped still in surprise, his heart lifting up as if somebody had pulled a string: Mama was out of bed.

But then he saw it wasn't a good thing. Mama was crying, and clinging to Inma's hand, Papa sat hunched up with his head in his hands. Inma was very still and quiet, her eyes huge in her pale face. Albi's heart shrivelled up as he looked from one to the other. Nobody spoke. He sat awkwardly on a chair. Who'd died now?

After a while, when nobody moved, nobody said anything, the curfew came with the usual marching of feet. He lifted his head, listening. Where was Ramona? He didn't like to break the silence in the kitchen by asking. He got up off his creaking chair and went out to look for her on the *solenar*.

She was in the back bedroom, on her hands and knees beside her bed, putting things into an old cardboard suitcase. One of the two that had lain under Mama and Papa's bed since the beginning of the world.

He stared in disbelief to see Ramona putting things in a suitcase.

He saw the other case was there too, standing beside Inma's bed, all strapped up. He understood then what was happening. A little mew jumped out of him. Inma couldn't go! But even while he was thinking it, and the frantic feeling was clawing its way up his throat, his eyes were telling him something else: Ramona was putting her own things into the suitcase. That was what she'd been doing when he stepped into the room, before she banged down the lid and put a commanding finger to her lips. Her eyes burned him up like hot coals. He stared back at Ramona, his heart pumping wildly. She pushed the suitcase under the bed and beckoned to him to follow her out on to the *solenar*.

He couldn't see her face clearly against the darkening light, only the loom of the rosy cliffs behind her. He wanted to beg her not to go, but Ramona was Ramona so he didn't. He wanted to tell her to stop Inma from going.

Was Ramona ill too? He wished he was little so he could cry, and even hug her, but he wasn't and he couldn't.

She looked away, out towards the evening, and then he could see her face in the last of the light, how hurt it looked, and the tears welling up and rolling out of her eyes. She stared at the view as if she was trying to swallow it down whole to keep it warm in her belly. Then she scrubbed the tears away and said, 'Don't you go telling on me, Albi. I can't stay behind, not if Inma isn't here. It's different for you. If I stay I'll end up doing everything, and anyway you know how much I've always wanted to get out of this place.'

He stood very still, impressed that she was talking to him as if he was her big brother, as if he was Manolo even. But he didn't know what she was talking about. How could she *want* to go somewhere else? She'd never been anywhere outside Rincón in her whole life, unless it was to Valbono, and you couldn't talk of Valbono as somewhere else, it was less than three hours walk away. He stared at her averted face, wondering if she was scared. She looked sad, but excited too, both things at once.

She glared, suddenly fierce again. 'Don't breathe a word, Rabbit.

403

Papa and Mama mustn't find out till afterwards.' He jumped as she put out a hand but she only touched his face. 'I'm sorry but I've got to get out while I still can. I'll come back for you one day.'

He wanted to fling himself at her and beg her not to go. But he didn't. He stood stiff and silent and looked out over the *solenar* rail at nothing in particular, and all he allowed himself was a tiny nod of the head, which he didn't mean because he didn't want her to come back for him, he wanted her not to go at all.

Albi took himself to bed. He was afraid to stay up in case he said something by mistake. He couldn't bear to see Mama so sad and knowing only the half of it, and Papa too. He thought about what it would be like to be just him and Mama and Papa in the house and he couldn't see it inside his head, the idea seemed so shrivelled and small. He didn't want to sleep because he didn't want morning to come, but he cried himself to sleep anyway.

Inma had gone, and it was a Moral Duty, the priest said. But Ramona had gone too and the priest wouldn't have called that a moral act, not if he'd known. She didn't go on the special bus with Inma. Ramona was gone so early nobody heard her slip out of the house. She went the back way, through the corral. Albi knew, because he was the one who found the bolts undone and quietly closed them up again and didn't tell anyone.

Papa was angry when Ramona wasn't there to say goodbye to Inma but Mama said she was too upset, that would have been why she'd slipped out this morning, but in the confusion of getting Inma and her suitcase out of the house they hadn't noticed. It would be why she'd stayed out of the way since.

That was one of the last things Mama said. She stopped talking after that.

He went to the gatehouse with them to see Inma onto the special bus, along with her suitcase and the six other people from the village who the priest was sending away to the sani place.

As soon as the bus was out of sight Albi fled back to the house to get his sheep, and then, late, to the Molino. He spent the day up on the Prados at the foot of La Guadaña where he could cry as much as he wanted and nobody need know.

Only when he got home again, not long before curfew, did he learn what Mama and Papa had learned by late morning – one of the *Guardia* was missing. And what mattered rather more, one of their motorcycles was missing as well. They were trying to keep it quiet because it was a scandal, Pilar said, when she came to the house not long before curfew. Papa shouted from the kitchen window that she was not to cross the doorstep. She didn't tell Papa from the street, she told Albi instead, following him down to the *fuente* and speaking in a low voice.

'So?' he said out loud.

She looked at him strangely and hurried away.

When he got back to the house he learned they had a scandal of their very own. Ramona hadn't come back. Not even after the special bus had disappeared down the valley towards Valbono, and Montesanto beyond, and beyond that, to the main road to Valencia. Ramona had not come back all day, and the other suitcase was missing too.

Did Ramona go with the *Guardia* man? Papa told Albi to tell anyone who asked, *Ramona is in bed with the 'flu*. Margarita came round with a bowl of soup for Ramona and Papa took it, and pretended afterwards that Ramona had enjoyed it.

He might have shared it, Albi thought.

After a week, when she still hadn't come back, Papa said Albi should tell people she had got better, so much better that she'd walked over to Las Rocas to stay with Aunt Ana for a while.

Did other people believe Papa when he said such things? Enough people had seen her talking to the *Guardia* with the curly hair, and she'd danced with him in full view in the Plaza. They would guess as he did, as soon as he heard which *Guardia* it was had gone missing, that Ramona might have gone away with him on the motorcycle. She would have left in the dark, before anyone was out on the paths to think it strange to see her walking there with a suitcase. Keeping to the terraces until she was far enough out from the village to circle round, as Albi had done when he went to fetch Miguel that night.

The man came from Cuenca but they wouldn't go there, that was where the *Guardia* would look for him. He must have waited until after curfew ended or the sound of the motorcycle would have raised suspicions. Or had he hidden it the day before, out on the Las Hoyas track, well away from the village? A lot of plans they must have made, Ramona and her curly-headed *Guardia*. And quickly too: they'd only known Inma was going the day before.

Or maybe it was only Albi who hadn't known until then. He thought back. Had everybody been sad and he hadn't noticed it? The old feeling filled him up again. The things they didn't tell. The things he didn't know.

Ramona and her *novio* must have gone to Las Hoyas, taking Albi's familiar route up onto the *Meseta* and over the top in the pale milky light of early morning. Passing the Ermita and La Torre at Estrellas in a roar of dust. Mena and Andrés, if they were at the farm when they weren't supposed to be, would have ducked out of sight when they heard the motorcycle, not guessing who it was. Over the great rolling plateau, two figures clinging to the machine as they raced for the far blue circle of the horizon, the sky vast over their heads, the sun rising over the rim of the world, cool and triumphant.

Now it was only Albi, and his papa in the kitchen, and his mama in the *alcoba* bed. There was no bread to eat because Mama didn't go to the bakehouse any more. Albi made the fire and then he cooked an egg over it, the way he'd seen Mama and the girls do it. It shouldn't be so difficult. But the flames were sluggish and the egg didn't set. He ate it half-raw. There was no bread to mop up the last bit so he licked his plate instead.

406

One fine spring morning he saw Andrés and Mena going up the track towards Estrellas. He'd heard they'd been allowed to take their stock back up the hill, what stock they had left after the long hard winter. The black mule was slower than he used to be when he was still a fine animal. Albi watched them go, sad there would be no more messages. Now he was ten and a half years old and had a sister working for El Caballero and a papa who drank all day and a mama who stayed in her bed, El Ciego would never say anything more than *Go here* or *Go there,* like he'd been saying for months. If Albi didn't go to Estrellas there would be no more bird book, no more little cakes and sweet cheese in Mena's kitchen.

The very next morning, without a flicker crossing his face, El Ciego said, 'You will go to Estrellas today. The message is *Three days hence five five three.'*

Albi climbed the steep track, turning the message over and over in his head. He was afraid of forgetting it after so long not having to remember. When he reached Estrellas there were no cakes, because there were no eggs, and the cheeses had all been taken, but Mena was kind to him again. She made him some bread in warm milk with a little honey in it and stood watching him eat it, all the while asking questions about his mama. 'But who cooks in your house if she doesn't get out of her bed any more?'

She sent him home with bread, and a few slices of ham.

The *maquis* surely couldn't be hiding in the village any more, now that spring had come, but there were no messages for them and no supplies. How would they manage? It was the hungriest time of year.

El Ciego gave him extra food at the end of the day to take home, as if he knew about Mama, but nobody washed Albi's clothes any more. Nobody cut his hair, or mended his shirt when he tore it on a gorse bush.

Albi emptied the piss-pot under his mama's bed. He borrowed fire from Margarita next door because their fire was always going out. Margarita looked at him kindly and said nothing but her eyes said, *I wish I could do more but I already have enough trouble of my own.* He knew that when José Cedrillas came to collect the tax from Margarita's house she had no money to pay it and José Cedrillas wrote a cross in his book against the number of her house every time. How many crosses did there have to be before Margarita's papa was put in the lock up?

José Cedrillas didn't come to Albi's house. Perhaps their house had so many crosses against it he didn't have room to write in any more. How long would it be before Papa was put in the lock up too? Would it matter if he was?

José Cedrillas didn't come but Mena did. It was strange to see her there, in the street outside their front door, very early one morning. She didn't come in but she had brought a custard for Mama, and when she went away she took the bundle of clothes she'd made him bring down to the street. Mena washing their clothes – there was a peculiar shame in that. It's a circle, he thought, trying to be proud, because who was it taught Mena to wash clothes in the first place?

What a long time ago that was. When he was still a boy.

51

Aunt Piedad

The grass was springing fast as the weather grew warmer, but not enough to keep the ewes quiet all night without hay and the hay was gone. There was none left in their back attic, none stacked on the *solenar*.

In the Molino corral El Ciego passed his hands over the backs of Albi's sheep. 'Why are they so thin?'

'There's no hay left at home, señor.'

'From now on corral your sheep with mine at night. I'll talk to your papa.'

If the blind man talked to his papa, Albi wasn't there to hear it. The next night he did as El Ciego told him and left his sheep at the Molino eating Molino hay. The sentries stared at him with a questioning look as he walked past alone. It made him feel naked. A shepherd boy without any sheep?

Aunt Piedad arrived like a hot summer wind blowing down an empty chimney and making the doors and the windows bang, though it was only March. Aunt Piedad – Mama's sister, from Teruel.

She stood in the archway of the *alcoba*, looking at Mama in her bed with her face turned to the wall.

'*Madre mia*! How long has this been going on, Ramón?'

Papa shrugged. 'She's not been right all winter.'

Albi stared at Aunt Piedad, fascinated by this aunt he didn't remember. Aunt Piedad was wearing city shoes. She had invisible stockings on, with straight lines down the back such as his sisters dreamed of. Her hair was in tight curls all round her head and she smelled of something strong and sweet that wasn't like any soap he'd ever smelled. She was speaking to Mama because she didn't know Mama didn't talk any more.

Aunt Piedad turned on Papa and her eyes were stony. 'Do you know where my José is, Ramón? Well I'll tell you. He's outside the church in the car. And shall I tell you who he's got in the car with him? My parents, that's who. They've been living like paupers in Las Hoyas these last six months. Maybe longer.'

What? Albi was all ears suddenly. His *abuelos*? Not bones. No vultures, then. He had to undo the thoughts in his head so fast, putting away the bones, forgetting about the skulls, it made him feel quite dizzy and he put out a hand to hold onto the back of the nearest chair.

'The priest in Las Hoyas managed to get a message to me, all the way to Teruel. Now why do you think he did that when I have a sister and a brother-in-law right here in El Rincón, less than twenty kilometres from Las Hoyas?'

It didn't really sound like a question. He watched his papa's face anxiously. Aunt Piedad was bigger than Papa and by the sound of it she might hit him any minute.

'I came to find out what's going on, and it's just as well I did.'

Papa didn't look cross. He looked embarrassed.

Without asking permission Aunt Piedad started bundling Mama's few things together. Papa didn't say a word. He fidgeted about and humphed up his shoulders and went to sit in the kitchen and pour himself another cup of wine.

'Find me a cardboard box or something if you haven't got such a thing as a suitcase, Alberto.' She paused and looked Albi up and down as if she hadn't really seen him until that moment. '*Madre mia*, I can't take you as well. There's no room in the car. Or in the flat. We'll be cramped as it is.'

Albi drew himself up as tall as he could and stalked off down to the stable to look for the cardboard box they'd used for potatoes in the autumn. She made it sound as if he was the last lamb to go on the butcher's lorry, the runt that got turfed off again because it wasn't worth taking. He didn't want to go anyway. You could tell by the smell of her that she didn't like boys.

He went to sit with his papa in the kitchen, shoulder to shoulder.

'Always was bossy, that one,' Papa murmured, lifting his cup of wine to his lips.

That didn't seem like enough to say, not for Mama going away. Wasn't Papa sad? Didn't he want to know how she would come back, and when?

Aunt Piedad marched into the kitchen with Mama following behind. Mama looked different out of bed, as if her clothes had got bigger or she had shrunk, but perhaps it was only because she was standing next to her big sister. Her hair was brushed and plaited and pinned on the back of her head the way she used to do it – that made her seem different too. She didn't look up once, just stood quietly with her eyes on the floor.

'When the Germans win this new war things will get better,' Aunt Piedad said. 'I might be able to send for you then, Alberto.'

'Your José always knew which side to cling to,' Papa said.

Albi stared in horror at his aunt, who was busy writing something on a piece of paper out of her handbag. He didn't want to go to Teruel.

'This is our address,' she said, thrusting the paper at him. 'Be sure to keep that safe – give it to your sisters. The telephone number is the tobacconist on the corner. You can always leave a message.' Aunt Piedad glared at Papa. '*Madre mia*, Ramón. You should be ashamed of yourself. Carry the box, Alberto.'

She turned back at the door and said loudly in Papas's direction, 'And this boy needs his hair cut. He looks like a girl.'

Papa stared into his cup.

Albi followed his mama and his aunt down the stairs, carrying the box with Mama's few clothes in it, but not the clogs, because Aunt Piedad said Mama wouldn't need them in Teruel. He thought his mama would mind leaving them behind when she remembered Papa had made them for her, but his mama didn't seem to be minding anything at all. She walked with her head bowed, her arm looped through Aunt Piedad's as though through a stranger's, her eyes on her feet.

All the way up the street to the church Aunt Piedad kept stopping to greet people who she remembered but who didn't recognise her, voices starting loud and going quiet. Eyes looked over Aunt Piedad's shoulder at Albi and glanced away again. 'Can't take the boy,' she said. Albi the runt, following behind.

The runt who people might take for a girl. But at least he could boast to the other boys that his aunt and uncle owned a car.

Outside the church a shabby little vehicle, all dusty from the road, was parked by the steps. Was that it? A man in a dark suit stood in the road, sweating in the spring sunshine and smoking a cigar. The man gave Albi a worried look but Aunt Piedad wagged her finger and said loudly, 'No, José. No, no, no.'

Not the runt.

But he'd stopped listening. There were two tiny old people in the back of the car.

Abuelo stared at him for a moment as if he didn't know him, then he gave a small, worried wave and said something to *Abuela,* she turned her face in the wrong direction with an anxious smile. How could they both still be alive, the skin and the flesh still on their frail bones, the eyes in their sockets, the soft white hair on their heads?

His aunt pushed Mama into the back seat. Uncle José started cranking the engine, the car coughed into life.

Aunt Piedad kissed Albi brusquely on both cheeks. 'Tell Pilar I'm sorry I didn't have time to see her. Make sure you give her that address and telephone number.'

Somebody in my family owns a car, he thought, over and over so he wouldn't cry. He didn't need to tell Carlos and Pepito how small and old it was. He stood watching the car squeeze carefully down the narrow street towards the Plaza and the piece of paper fluttered out of his hand. He bent and picked it up, mouthing the words, reading the numbers, hearing Aunt Piedad's voice in his head, *tell Pilar*.

Pilar. Aunt Piedad, so like her.

Alberto lifts down the photograph and takes it to the table, puts on his glasses. Santi wants to get a copy made. He knows why: it's Carlos's granddaughter stirring up the past. But he can hardly refuse.

It's not going to be a simple job. The frame is sealed on the back with the original brown paper and tape, after all these years it's a shame to cut it open. Leave it for Santi to sort out... He turns the frame over and Mama gazes out at him. She looks young to him now and it takes him by surprise. The last time he saw her, the day Aunt Piedad took her away, she seemed like an old woman.

The picture trembles in his hands. Poor Mama.

He shifts his gaze away, traces Ramona's pretty face with his forefinger. *She* might still be alive. Argentina is a long way away and they were never ones for writing, though they must have once: there are some old snapshots somewhere – a fuzzy interior with a Christmas tree, a child on a swing, a Ford Prefect standing on a drive. Ramona did all right for herself, just as she intended. It was Inma who was the surprise. Inma the quiet one, without ambition, marrying her doctor and living a life of comfort in Pamplona, while Pilar, whose domestic ambitions so tortured Papa – Pilar never went further than Valbono.

52

The Enamel Chest

On Good Friday the priest led the Easter procession round the village, Albi and Papa planted potatoes on the *huerto*.

Papa balanced on his wooden leg and made a trench with his mattock, Albi went along the trench dropping in seed-potatoes one by one. He listened anxiously for the sound of the church procession going past and when it did he sneaked a look, and relaxed. Pilar wasn't there.

'That'll do,' snarled Papa.

Albi jumped guiltily, but Papa meant, that'll do for potatoes.

'Only us two to eat them,' Papa said.

Albi straightened up and stared at him. Surely they should be planting the same amount they always did? Inma would be back by the winter and Ramona might come home any time. Mama too.

Papa turned away, swinging himself clumsily on his crutches over the loose, crumbly earth.

'Papa, we should plant more. We won't have enough.'

'Don't you argue with me, boy. Who do you think you are? Bring my mattock.'

Next day, when Albi went out from the Molino with the sheep, he took them to the *huerto* and let them ramble about eating the weeds while he planted two more rows of potatoes. He would have planted a third but he'd taken nearly all the potatoes that were left in the house. The *Guardia* had been helping themselves all through the winter, like they had in other houses. Other houses? Did Martín and the others like him have potatoes left?

He straightened up, surveying his handiwork. Papa could make a trench more neatly, but perhaps he wouldn't notice the extra rows, even if they were a bit crooked. Even Papa wouldn't be crazy enough to dig up potatoes already planted. Would he?

Next day, Papa sold the mule.

'Who to?' Albi asked, trying not to cry, hoping *something* good might come of it. The memory of mule-meat came into his mouth as strongly as if he had smelled it cooking.

'The glue man,' Papa said.

So there wasn't even anything to eat, and Papa was back in Julio's bar drinking again, now he had money in his pocket.

But afterwards Albi thought, it wouldn't really have been the glue man. Papa only said that to stop him feeling hungry as well as sad.

414

Soon after Easter, when it was warm enough to go barefoot again and Albi was released from his boots like a horse let out of the stable on the first day of spring, the bell in the church started ringing. Not for somebody dying, for Pilar getting married.

Not that he knew that at the time. He heard the bell ringing as he ran barefoot in the fresh spring grass, turning his face to the new sun as if he could drink it, but he only knew the reason afterwards.

Margarita from next door was the one who told him. She stood very close, out in the street by their front door, and whispered the news, her eyes anxious and excited both at once. 'Married before me.' Her voice was sad. Maybe her *novio* would never come back from the Republican army, now he'd been away so long. 'She wants her enamel chest. Can you take it to El Caballero's house?'

He said it was too heavy, he'd never be able to take it down the stairs. But he was thinking, Pilar never finished her sewing! All those years making her trousseau and then she didn't finish it.

'You owe it to Pili,' Margarita said. 'Why else do you think José Cedrillas doesn't come for the tax and yet your papa isn't in the lock up?' She tipped her head slyly in the direction of Julio's bar and raised her eyebrows. 'We could do it now, Albi. You and me.'

He couldn't say no after that.

Had Pilar married without Papa saying she could? There was nobody left to ask so he had to ask Margarita.

'He did give his permission. The priest told him he must. After Pilar said in Confession.'

Albi, halfway across the kitchen, stopped so suddenly that Margarita bumped into him. So Pilar had told the priest about Sergio in the wall. How was it the *Guardia* had not shot Papa already, then, and him too? He stared up at Margarita's face. Why did she not look more worried? She walked past him and into the back bedroom. The enamel chest was there where it had always been, against the wall by the bed where Pilar used to sleep. Margarita bent and lifted up one end and waited for him to pick up the other. He hung back, confused. The *Guardia* would surely come tonight. Now they knew.

Margarita said, 'It's just the chest. Pili already took the small things.'

Pilar, the teller of tales. Sneaking back into the house like a thief, crossing the doorstep even though Papa said she mustn't. And here he was, picking up his end of the enamel chest and helping Margarita carry it out into the street as if they were a pair of thieves themselves. And then they went carrying it right through the streets all the way to El Caballero's house, everybody seeing them, so that he wanted to sink into the ground. At El Caballero's house, he dropped his end of the chest on the doorstep and bolted.

He went to bed as soon as he'd done his jobs so he didn't have to say anything to Papa, but the *Guardia* didn't come that night. They didn't come the next night. They didn't come at all.

All the world was different but still it was the same. Pilar didn't belong to them any more and it was only him and Papa in a dirty house, but outside the leaves were bursting out all new and bright and clean, and the grass was shooting fast.

Every day he took the sheep and the goats out as usual and in the afternoons, when he took them back to the Molino, the blind man fed him a proper dinner. He was eating better than he did before everybody went away. Why did the *Guardia* not take El Ciego's ham and eggs and his good bread, and his old potatoes sprouting in their box? He was too tired to care.

Late April, the sun bright and the wind blowing warm, and Albi was in the Molino kitchen, eating his breakfast and thinking the *maquis* must surely be back on the *Meseta* now, turning their white winter-faces to the sun, stretching their cramped limbs. So why was he not taking them food, even if there were no messages?

He watched El Ciego feeling with a poker at the texture of the fire to see if it needed another log and the question came welling up his throat so fast it spilled out of his mouth before he could stop it.

'Don't they need things, the *maquis*?'

'What *maquis*?'

So the blind man did know about Pilar marrying Jesús. Albi watched over the top of his hunk of bread as the blind man picked up the long slender knife and sliced some more ham off the bone hanging from the hook in the ceiling. El Ciego reached out with the knife and laid one of the slices on Albi's plate. There was blood on the blind man's other hand. He must have caught it on the blade. He stared at the bright blood leaking gently into the bread the blind man was holding. This is the way it will end, he was thinking. No more messages, and not a word said about it, and then the *Guardia* knocking at the door.

El Ciego cleared his throat. 'You will go up to Estrellas today,' he said. 'Listen carefully. *Two days hence four four five one.* Repeat that.'

53

Papa the Hero

Like water breaking down a dam, there were messages for Estrellas every few days now, even if there were none for the *maquis*. The messages were all numbers. Numbers, and a day: two days hence, or three. Sometimes tomorrow. Andrés and

Mena were secretly staying at the farm again, even after all that trouble in the winter. How could they be anywhere else, with the busiest time of the year upon them? Though they were probably being watched. The *Guardia* would know as well as Albi that Andrés was hardly ever at Teresa's house in the daytime, now that his uncle's barn on the edge of the village was empty of livestock again.

Albi walked up and down the road in the spring sunshine, wondering who was watching, and what they could see. The days he stayed in the valley he walked the familiar paths round the village and wondered the same. Who was up on the cliffs, looking down? Who was down in the valley, looking up?

Not Carlos. He was working on the building site at the factory every day now. Bringing home money.

Albi stopped by the big rock next to the path, the one he'd been lying on that day when El Ciego came by, right at the beginning. He looked at the face of the rock and saw it had little holes all over it and small stones ledged in the holes, as if somebody had placed them there. Who might have done that? A thousand different plants were growing in the cracks and the crevices. A thousand? That was a very big number, but it would do. He stared at the face of the rock with its stones and its plants and secret places. Holes where snakes might be, so he didn't put his eye too close. Places for putting things in, a rock for hidden things. He saw a snail in its shell, upside down in one of the crevices pretending it wasn't a warm day. Pretending it wasn't even there. He could do that: be a snail. Go small, and hidden, nobody seeing him and nothing hurting. The shell was bright and clean and perfect. He got a stick and knocked it out of its crevice to see what it would do.

The snail did nothing. Just sat on the path, tucked into its shiny shell, and went on pretending it didn't exist. So he trod on it. That's the trouble with snails. They think they're safe.

He knew he wasn't. Probably Andrés and Mena weren't either.

Whenever he was sent to the Torre, Mena was there. Working in the kitchen or feeding the poultry. If Andrés was away in the fields, out of calling distance, Albi had to keep the message inside him and go back again the next day. Even though he could give Mena the messages now, he didn't want to tell her more than she needed to know. *Least said safest*, like Papa said.

It made him very quiet, those days. Even if Mena had offered to get the bird book he would have been afraid to say yes in case the message came out when he wasn't thinking. But she didn't mention the book. Mena was quiet too. It wasn't like last year.

How thin she was now. Then one morning she said she was sorry but she couldn't give him any cheese today, the *Guardia* had taken it all yesterday.

'What? All of it?' Last time he'd been here she'd had new cheeses sitting on the shelf of her cheese store.

Her voice went very tired. 'Yes, all of it. The *Guardia* are trying to persuade us to give up Estrellas all together.'

That was a funny thing to say. Did the *Guardia* go and talk to Andrés and Mena and say, *Please will you consider giving up your farm?*

If Mena and Andrés gave up Las Estrellas, what would the people do who needed Andrés to have the messages? None of the messages ever made any sense. Perhaps Mena and Andrés would be better off if they stopped trying to farm up here and came down to live in El Rincón like everybody else. He watched her kneading the bread. He couldn't imagine the Torre without her in it. She lifted the dough off the table with her floury hands and dropped it into a glazed bowl and put it to rise by the fire. Outside, Andrés was calling the dogs, bringing sheep into the yard.

'Better be going,' Albi said. He slipped out quickly so he could give Andrés the message in the privacy of the farmyard where the hens ran cackling from under his feet and the sheep clamoured in the corral.

The Guardia have been, Mena had said. It made him feel unsafe. What if they came again while he was in her kitchen?

'Don't worry about the *Guardia*,' El Ciego told him next morning, though he hadn't said a word. 'You have your permit in your pocket. The *Guardia* know those are Molino lands next door.'

How did they know? And anyway, the blind man might not mean it was safe *in the Estrellas kitchen*.

Was Mena safe? He was the one carrying messages in his head, so she must be safer than he was. Why was El Ciego so sure he didn't need to worry? Why wasn't he scared too?

Pilar stopped him in the street. 'Help me with this, Albi.'

He could see a man's shirts in the basket of wet laundry, and a man's white underclothes, looking like new. Nothing like they had at home.

Pilar was even stouter. No wonder the heavy basket made her out of breath. He took it from her unwillingly and turned to walk with her to El Caballero's house, hoping nobody would tell Papa or he'd be beaten for it later. He wouldn't take the basket up the stairs for her, whatever she said. Especially not now El Caballero was telling everyone what they could and couldn't do because the *Guardia* had decided he should be mayor again.

'You need a hair-cut,' she said. 'Running wild like a little savage. You should come to my house and I'll cut it for you.'

He scowled. What was this *my house?* El Caballero's house, more like.

She started asking about things at home. He grunted one-word answers, not paying attention. He would *never* go inside that house. Never.

Pilar grabbed him suddenly by the arm, right there in the middle of the street where anybody might be watching. 'Mena? You mean, Carmen? The *Valenciana*? *She's* been doing your washing?'

'She did a few times. Yes.'

He stood there awkwardly, the basket clutched in his arms and dripping on his bare feet. What was wrong with Mena helping if nobody else did? He didn't say it, though.

'You should have asked *me*, Albi,' Pilar said angrily, as if he'd done something wrong. Well that was nothing new. He shrugged and set off up the street again but she grabbed him by the arm again. '*We* are family, Albi. *She* is not.'

'Papa says you're not in our family any more.'

'Papa is a stupid fool.'

'No he isn't!' He turned on her in fury, not caring any more who might hear. 'He's brave. He's a war hero. And you're a bad woman for going against him and joining the other side.'

She gripped his shoulder so fiercely that the basket tipped in his arms and all the clothes tumbled out onto the cobbles. 'I *told* you, Albi. I told you! It's lies. All lies. Why will you not see it?' She shook him, staring wildly. A fat mad woman. 'That's not how Papa lost his leg. Not the way he told you.'

He stared back defiantly. He didn't want to hear what was coming but he could see by her face she was going to tell him anyway so he closed down his ears. Five and nine take away six is eight. Thirteen times three is thirty-nine. But he couldn't stop the words coming in. 'They were drunk, Albi. Papa and Manuel Gomez, that day in the forest. They were so drunk they felled a big pine tree badly. It hit Manuel Gomez and probably killed him, since he's never come back, and it fell on Papa's foot and pinned him to the ground. It wasn't an armoured vehicle, it was just an old pine tree. That's why the *Guardia* let him out of the lock up that time. Jesús told them Papa was never in the war. Never even anywhere near it. He got lucky – a truck picked him up on the road afterwards and took him to the hospital. And that's the whole truth.'

She let go of his arm and took the basket off him. He watched her pile the clothes back into it and walk away, back to the wash house to wash them all over again. He felt numb inside. It couldn't be true. It was a story she'd made up to be mean.

Carlos came sauntering up the street, whistling. He glanced at Pilar as she hurried past him. 'Something cooking in the oven, then?' he said to Albi, giving him a nudge. But Albi wasn't in the mood for Carlos's riddles. He felt like a dog that needs to go to a private place to lick its wounds. He muttered an excuse and ran back home, and sat on the manger in the empty stable where the mule used to live. He sat there for a very long time.

So? He lay in his bed, not sleeping. So? A tree or an armoured vehicle – Papa cut his own leg off the same, didn't he? Pilar hadn't said he didn't do that.

But there was no Inma to tell him which bits were really true, and there were the other things Aunt Piedad had said, and it didn't feel enough any more, however hard he tried to make himself think Papa really *was* brave.

Next morning when he looked at Papa, dirty and unshaven in the kitchen, he looked smaller. Cruder, shabbier than he'd looked, somehow, only the day before.

54

The Message

The blind man's hands sifted over Albi's face, the rough balls of his thumbs stroking his eyelids and then his cheeks. He stood very still and let the blind man do it. Why was El Ciego reading the fear on him when it was only morning, and the May sunshine was bright in the trees outside like little children playing?

'Today you go to Estrellas. You tell them, *tomorrow at sunset, six three one four. Six three one four* – repeat it back to me.' The hawk-face stared impassively at some nowhere over Albi's right shoulder as he repeated the message. El Ciego, he noticed, had said *tell them*. That was different.

'If I don't see Señor Andrés,' he said timidly, 'do I have to tell the señora?'

'Yes.'

The knot in his gut tightened.

El Ciego moved to the cupboard in the wall and started putting the leftover food away. In the Molino, at least, there was still plenty to eat, most of the time. Whatever that might mean.

As Albi went to the door the blind man said, 'The message is not for today, it is for tomorrow.' Well he knew that, the blind man had said it already. 'But they must get it by the end of today, no later. Understood?'

What was all this *them* and *they*? It used to be Andrés or nothing. And why was El Ciego being so urgent about getting the message to them? Something was different about the blind man this morning. Something that hadn't been there even yesterday. He thought of the hands on his face, soft as butterflies and strong as steel. And no Joaquín anywhere this morning, he realised with a jolt. Not even Joaquín's jacket hanging on its peg.

All round him the shadows were sharp but the sun came gentling through the cool morning air. The best time of the year, now, everything new. A nightingale was singing deep in a bush. Nothing looked any different to yesterday.

He was nearly at the summit of the escarpment when the roar of an engine broke. A truck tipped over the skyline and came fast down the switchback road towards him. Hastily, he whistled his sheep and goats off the road and the truck hurtled past. He saw the pale moons of the faces as the driver and the two passengers in the cab stared at him as they went by. The back of the truck was closed up, the canvas tightly laced. Not a cargo of *Guardia*, then.

He watched the truck as it descended, bend by tortuous bend. Far below, a truck was coming into the village on the Valbono road. Almost immediately there was another, and on the far side of the valley, a third truck was making its way along the white thread of the track towards the garrison. He watched it creep along, passing the garrison, then the pump house, until he couldn't see it any more. He turned to climb the last of the slope, up onto the *Meseta*.

They were up to something. And what was it that was happening at Estrellas at sunset tomorrow that was so very important? He suddenly wanted very much to know.

At La Torre de Las Estrellas there was no Andrés. Mena was there, but no bird book, and only a little to eat. All the day long he sat in the meadow and watched the birds, hoping for Mena to come so he could tell her the names. But nobody came.

When he left the meadow to walk home, there was still no Andrés in the Estrellas yard or in any of the corrals. Albi knocked on the closed front door. He wished he'd given Mena the message this morning, but the old dog woofed on the other side of the door and then she came.

In the kitchen she gave him some bread. A cup of goat's milk to wash it down. He wished Andrés would come in so he could keep Mena safe from this message, but he didn't. It felt dangerous to ask openly where he was. *Least known safest*, that's what Papa always said, but he meant, *least told less betrayed*. If Andrés didn't come he would have to tell Mena and she looked sad already without that. Was it because she knew now he was the bringer of messages that she looked at him differently? Or because Sergio had been his friend and used to talk to him, up in the hidden places? Perhaps that was what made it feel so different now between him and her. He wished he hadn't told her the message that day in the fog. If he'd kept it inside his chest and carried it away again he wouldn't have talked to her about Sergio those other times too, and she would look at him the same way she did before.

And here was another message, weighing him down, and this time the blind man had told him to give it to her. Should he pretend he hadn't understood and take it away with him again?

'You should go now, Albi. To be back by curfew.'

The house was as empty as a cave, only their two voices in it and the dog snoring gently on the hearth with his nose almost in the embers.

He stood up. 'There's a message.' He let the words hang in the air, giving her the chance to decline, but she said nothing, only watched him out of her secret eyes, waiting. '*Tomorrow, sunset. Six three one four.*'

She nodded. Seemed to think for a moment, nodded again.

At the door she put her hand briefly on his shoulder. 'Albi, be very careful.'

He looked back. The light casting up from the cobbled yard illuminated her face.

'And you,' he said. He wanted to reach out and touch her but she seemed too far away to be touched. 'You be careful too.'

She wrapped her arms protectively over her chest the same way she did that day in the fog and gave a tight little laugh. 'Oh, I will. I will.' It made her sound as if she was somebody he didn't know.

All the way down the road he could see movement in and around the village: trucks moving, a motorcycle roaring into the Plaza, dark figures by the pump house under the dam. As if something had happened. The thought rushed his legs so that his knees went tight on the steep slopes, but by the time he got down near the village all seemed quiet again except in the garrison, where the sharp sound of men being drilled drifted out across the river.

El Ciego put food on the table for him to take home, his face as impassive as ever, but when Albi said the message was safely delivered a flicker passed across the stern features that almost looked like relief, that was nearly a smile.

Of Joaquín, there was no sign anywhere.

Albi climbed the road to the village, his ears noting the sound of the river off the walls, his bare skin noting the warmth of the sun off the buildings, and his eyes and ears telling him – in spite of the *Guardia* being so busy in their trucks – there was no special news, because the villagers in the streets were going about their business as if everything was ordinary. Nobody's voice was excited, except for the little girls skipping with their long rope stretched right across the street so that they had to stop to let him pass. And when he got to his house he could hear his father drunkenly singing in Julio's bar further up the street.

55

The Plan

All night long, Mena in her distances hounded his dreams, Andrés a half-sinister shadow, never quite where he should be, nobody telling him the things he needed to know. He woke in the dark and lay in the silence. When this village sleeps, how it sleeps!

The long, long dark. A plan forming.

By the time daylight sidled in he had two halves of a plan but nothing to go in-between.

He had to know. All these things he was doing, and he didn't understand them. He didn't know where the *maquis* had gone, or what it was that happened at Estrellas at sunset and was only numbers. But he couldn't be there to find out because of curfew. After curfew, nobody else should be there either.

There was no-one in their house to mind now if he was out all night. Papa in his drunken stupor, pushed into the house by the *Guardia* as they marched past for curfew, would sleep where he fell on the earth floor of the passage if last week was anything to go by. If he did notice Albi was out of the house after curfew, he wouldn't remember when he woke up, and he wouldn't remember there was no errand to Aunt Ana in Las Rocas either. So now Albi had his plan. A beginning, a middle, and an end.

He went to the Molino in the morning as usual and ate the Molino food. Didn't say a word about his plan to El Ciego, who – to his relief – had no message for him today. El Ciego didn't even tell him where to graze the flock, which was just as well since Albi had something of his own to say.

'I can't take them out for long. I have to do an errand for my papa later.'

The lie squashed his voice up thin but El Ciego was distracted this morning and didn't appear to notice. Albi didn't mention an errand to his aunt, either. *Least said safest.*

Joaquín's jacket was back on its hook. The rush of water falling down the shaft of the mill-tower was nearly drowned out by the rumble of the great mill-stones in the belly of the Molino. Grain to grind, bread to bake, a mill to run – El Ciego was busy.

By dinner-time (except that he didn't have any dinner) Albi was out on the path to Las Rocas, all alone. He felt a bit lost, walking by himself without his animals, but it was quicker and quieter. A woman was walking in the same direction but too far away for him to see who it was. The path led up towards the towering face of La Peña at the back of El Rincón, and then it began to climb up between the blocky crags. Luis Irún passed him, coming down the other way with his mule. A little later, José Cedrillas with his donkey. A well-trodden path, this, carefully paved with white stones.

Up onto the top, and the long views. The valley far below with the rosy roofs of the village nestling in its green corner, the brilliant dam-water glinting beyond. The dam wall looked small from up here and La Guadaña was different again, a flat green board tilted on its long white edge. Everything looked quiet.

He turned his back on it all and walked across the ridge. To his left, rising ground blocked his view across the *Meseta*. Ahead of him, the woman was visible again, walking quickly towards Las Rocas until she disappeared into the trees. He followed, through the woods, down the steep gully of Los Cereseros, picking up sticks as he went so that when he came into Rocas he'd have a bundle of firewood on his back, enough to look like an errand to his widowed aunt. If he was lucky the *Guardia* wouldn't take any notice of him. And if they did, who would know his papa hadn't sent him, if he said it boldly enough? He could say it was an emergency, they'd heard his aunt was sick. The *Guardia* might not mind so much then, about him not having a permit to be in Las Rocas. If they noticed him at all.

The path joined the road. He crossed the bridge over the green river. Not their quick blue river – this one was green and deep. Gardens lush on every side now, and orchards stretching along the river bank, but above him the rocky houses were like man-made outcrops of the brown cliffs which gave the village its name.

'What the hell are you doing here?'

Jesús sat astride his motorcycle in the Plaza of Las Rocas, his goggles pushed up on his forehead.

Albi swallowed hard. Lucky his plan had two halves to it. He stepped closer so he didn't have to shout, hoping Jesús would believe him. 'One of the sheep wandered off the Molino land at Estrellas yesterday. I think she went down into the Barranco de las Carrascas. I can look for her from this end and Aunt Ana…'

'Have you got a permit to be in Las Rocas? Well you shouldn't be here then.'

'I have to find the ewe. She's our very best one.'

Jesús stared at him, suspicious and strangely nervous. He tapped his fingers impatiently on the handlebars. 'Get up to the Barranco as soon as you can and have a look. Quickly, mind. If you find the sheep put it in the corral at your aunt's but be sure you're back here by curfew whether you find it or not. I'll take you home on the bike. You won't get back this afternoon any other way. We'll sort the sheep out tomorrow if we have to.'

Go back to El Rincón on the motorcycle?

'Scarper,' Jesús growled. 'And be quick. It's late enough already. I don't know what you were thinking of, coming over here at this time of day.'

Albi delivered the firewood to his surprised aunt and obligingly ate the bread she thrust on him while he told her his story about a missing sheep and asked if he could leave it in her corral, if he found it, and she told him not to gobble like a turkey.

He was halfway up the path to the cliff before he remembered his plan meant staying out until after sunset. He had to be up on the cliff as the sun went down so he could find out what it was that happened at Estrellas, the thing he was part of but nobody would tell him. The rest of his plan was what he'd say to the *Guardia* when he came back to Las Rocas after curfew. Or, if he wasn't brave enough to do that, he'd stay out all night and hide among the rocks. So what now? Jesús would wait for him and mess it all up.

He'd have to say he'd made a mistake about the time, he'd spent too long looking, could hear the ewe but couldn't find her, something like that. What else could he do? But Jesús would definitely be angry.

He paused and looked back down the rocky slope. The sun was low enough already for Las Rocas to be in shadow.

Ahead of him, the path turned abruptly to run along the base of the cliff. The rockface breathed out the day's heat on his left cheek as he edged his way along the narrow channel cut in the stone. The ground fell away abruptly to his right. Above him, vultures flapped noisily as they came in to roost on the cliff. He didn't look up, concentrating on his hands and feet as he clambered over boulders. It would be very hard to get a ewe over this bit all by himself, if he'd really had a sheep to bring back.

He climbed into the late sunlight until he was standing on the very top. His guts heaved and he put out a hand to steady himself – the top of the cliff was barely a metre wide, like the fin of a great white fish sticking out above the green river, far below. He made himself look, and then he turned his eyes away to the Barranco de las Carrascas in front of him, steep and narrow, walled in by vertical cliffs where vultures stood with drooping wings like black priests watching. Behind him, the path dropped sickeningly out of sight.

He sat down, to anchor himself more firmly to the narrow ground, closed his eyes and waited for the sick feeling to stop. What was he doing here?

He opened his eyes. On the horizon at the top end of the Barranco, was the familiar broken bedstead against the sky. The Ermita de La Virjen de las Estrellas, and below it the Torre. He had to know. All this risk and secrecy, he had to know what it was for, that it wasn't for nothing and him like a dog on a rope running from person to person. He fixed his eyes on the distant Ermita, and the cluster of buildings at its feet. It was nothing, Estrellas. Just a god-forsaken ruin and an old farm with a tower, dark against the vast sky that was all rosy-gold now with the setting sun.

The sun dropped lower. He waited. It must be curfew time by now. His heart was pounding because very soon he would be in bad trouble. He glanced down at Las Rocas behind him. The earth-brown houses looked deserted. He couldn't hear any voices, but he hadn't heard the church bell either.

430

As he turned back to face Estrellas something flashed, but not from the top of the tower as he'd expected. There it was again. From the dark mass of the broken-backed Ermita, right on the very top of the hill, came another flash: glass or a mirror, catching the sun. And again. A pattern. Slightly uneven but quite clear. He waited for the sequence to come again. Six flashes, then three. A pause, one flash. Followed – as he knew it would be – by four flashes, and then nothing more.

Had he known all the time, really? The sequence began again but he didn't need to see any more. Behind him, the church bell in Las Rocas started tolling for curfew.

He turned to go back, and stopped. There was another sound, not just the bell. Distant, indistinct, insistent, a dark throb he'd heard once before, the day the aeroplane came and everyone in the Plaza ran to get under the bridge for fear of bombs. He stared wildly round the sky but there was nothing. Only vultures circling high up in the sun, and the pulse of a big engine coming closer.

And then he saw it. Below the rim of the horizon, a dark bird rising and falling as it came towards him, following the shape of the earth. Closer it came, relentless, the clamouring snarl of its engines rising until the rock vibrated under his feet. At his back, a sudden clatter of wings as vultures dropped off the cliffs and flew away. But he couldn't fly away, and there was nowhere to run to. He threw himself down on the ground.

Afterwards the details were jumbled together, impossible to tell which were real and what order they came in: the warm rush of air as the plane passed close by, the sudden shriek of metal against rock, sparks flying. The plane cartwheeling down the slope into the Barranco. The heart-beat of silence before it exploded. But what etched itself most deeply, what he was most sure of, was the strange long moment when the pilot in his glass bubble turned his insect head and stared down at him.

56

The Motorcycle

The room was small and hot, blue with tobacco smoke. Four men stood round the table, a fifth sat in the corner by the door with earphones on his head, fiddling with a machine which was making crackling noises. The standing men were so tall they kept knocking into the bare light bulb as they bent over the map.

Perhaps you have to be tall to be allowed to be a *Guardia*.

Albi sat very still on the hard wooden chair, hoping they'd forgotten he was there. The hammering in his chest had quietened down at last. They hadn't shot him but they'd been fierce in their questions: what was he doing there, what had he seen? He hadn't seen anything, only the plane. That was what he kept saying, over and over, trying not to think about mirrors, or the pilot staring down at him. *I was looking for a lost sheep. A plane came.*

They'd sent his weeping Aunt Ana back to her house and now they seemed to have forgotten him. The room was full of excited talk, all letters and numbers, but not his numbers.

'Zaragoza say it's not one of theirs.' That was the *Guardia* in the corner with the things over his ears like the man in the plane was wearing. The man with the insect head who had looked straight at him as the plane hit the rock. Was that what had happened?

I've killed someone.

He shrank smaller in his chair.

More *Guardia* crowded into the room, all of them shouting to be heard. 'I said he was flying too low! Didn't I say so?' And the other *Guardia*, the one who seemed to be in charge, snapped back, 'Whether he was or not, we're the ones who'll have to prove he wasn't shot down.'

Albi shut his ears. He didn't want to hear any more. He didn't want it to be anything to do with him. He could go to sleep here on this chair and they wouldn't notice. He could sleep until tomorrow. He could sleep until another time all together and wake up in a different life. Which one would he have? With Mama, in the old days. Before the soldiers came, certainly before the *Guardia*. Just him and his sisters and his mama and his papa, and the *abuela,* the way they used to be. And Manolo. He would have Manolo back and have it be before the war, because that would make it safer. And La Perrita, and La Gatica his little cat, and La Gorda his sheep, and his special rabbit and his speckledy hen.

'*Hostia*! You're still here, are you?'

The room was empty. When did that happen?

The big *Guardia* stood looking down at him. He seemed annoyed. 'I'd forgotten we still had to deal with you.' He stuck his head round the door and yelled, 'Ortega? Bring pen and paper and come in here.' And then in a bored voice he said to Albi, 'Sit in that chair. Facing the table.'

It was the same questions all over again. This time the Ortega man wrote them down on a notepad and underlined each one before he wrote Albi's answers underneath. The big *Guardia* made his voice stern but his eyes were distracted as if he wanted to be somewhere else. Albi gave his name, his address. His parents' names. His aunt's name, and her address. His excuse: he was looking for his lost ewe. The man studied his permit that said he could graze the Molino lands and where those were, then he handed it back. He was looking as if that was going to be the end of it, as if he was going to let Albi go, when the telephone rang on his desk. The man picked it up.

When he looked at Albi again his eyes had woken up.

'I said, what is your connection with La Torre de las Estrellas?'
I wish I'd never been inside Mena's kitchen

'None.'

'None, señor,' rapped the big *Guardia*.

'None, señor,'

'I don't believe you. How many times have you been to the Torre de las Estrellas?'

I wish I'd never seen the books in the room Mena called the library.

'I've been there once or twice. Señor. When I was passing.'

The *Guardia* looked at him disbelievingly. 'Once or twice? When you have a permit to graze the land right next door?'

I wish I'd never slept in Mena's feather bed.

'They're usually busy when I go past, señor.'

'Don't mumble. So – you'd have me believe you go all the way up there from El Rincón and when you get there you do no more than… wave?' The *Guardia* gave a little mincing wave, like a girl to her *novio*. Albi shrugged. 'You just – give a little wave – and then carry straight on? And that's it?'

I wish Mena had never come to me in the meadow…

'*Si*, señor.'

'Really?'

… with her red and white cloth and her peaches and strawberries…

'*Si*, señor.'

… and her book of birds.

The *Guardia* stared hard. 'My officer saw you on the road near Estrellas yesterday.' He paused. 'Funny that. Considering.'

Considering what? Albi's thoughts bucked like bad horses. He hadn't seen the flashing mirror. He didn't know anything. He didn't know… 'C- c- considering what, señor?'

'Considering where you were two hours ago.'

Suddenly the *Guardia* was on his feet and coming round the table. He grabbed Albi by the shoulder and pulled him roughly round to face him.

Garlic and fried liver gusted in his face. He saw a fleck of spittle on the man's lower lip as he ducked. The writing man had put his pen down neatly beside the pad of paper on the table-top and folded his arms.

He knew what he had to say. *No sé nada, I know nothing*

He fixed his eyes on a drift of white fluff on the floor and waited for the blows to come down.

The *Guardia* was back in his chair on the other side of the table, staring with narrowed eyes at Jesús, who was standing to attention beside Albi, but hadn't looked at him once.

The *Guardia* took the piece of paper off the Ortega man and laid it down on the table. He said, 'Your statement reads *I, Jesús García Baroja, inhabitant of El Rincón, came to the village of Las Rocas on this day, the 22nd May 1940, to collect rents for my employer, Don Juan Pablo Castelar Villaverde, Mayor of El Rincón, bringing with me my wife's brother, Alberto Álvarez Zapatero, aged ten years, in order for him to visit his widowed aunt, Ana Álvarez Blanco, and to look for the ewe he lost yesterday which the boy believed had wandered into the Barranco de las Carrascas. His presence so close to the scene of the crash of the National Air Force plane was therefore a coincidence. I vouch for the boy's good character.* Is that correct?'

'He was lucky he wasn't killed, señor,' Jesús said. 'And it's obvious he knows nothing.'

'Quite. Sign here at the bottom.'

Albi jerked upright. His good character? What did Jesús know of him? Now he'd be one of them. It was all going wrong but he kept his mouth carefully shut.

Jesús said, 'And he works for José-Luis Sanchez. You know – the blind miller in El Rincón? That should be guarantee enough.'

The Guardia looked unconvinced, but he let them go.

Albi let Jesús lead him outside and down to the Plaza where the motorcycle gleamed on its stand, a metal horse by moonlight. All the way back to El Rincón, riding behind Jesús under the big moon with the night wind scraping back his hair and hurting his ears, he saw nothing. He was on the wrong side now was the only thought in his head. But which side was that?

On the edge of El Rincón they stopped for the sentries. Jesús lifted the goggles onto his forehead so they could see his face and shouted something over the noise of the engine. The sentries waved them through and they drove under the gatehouse. This was what the village looked like at night, empty. Jesús coasted down through the silent streets to the Plaza and opened the throttle to ride up the further side. The sound echoed harshly off the walls. Albi looked at the shuttered houses. What was going on in all those dead-eyed rooms? Were people listening to the sound of them passing and thinking frightened thoughts?

The sentries in front of the church were standing in the road with their guns held ready. Jesús stopped to speak to them and the sentries let them pass. He coasted down the Calle San Juan and braked outside the door of number fourteen. Albi could hardly climb off the seat he was so cold. He looked at Jesús who still had the goggles on his forehead, standing up like frog's eyes in a pond, and he didn't know what to say. Jesús stared back for a moment. Then he said gruffly, 'We're family now,' and coasted away down the street, his big feet sticking out on either side, like a black frog.

Albi stood outside the door, listening to the roar of the bike receding as Jesús went back across the village to El Caballero's house where Pilar would be waiting, because now she was his wife. Then the sentries by the church shouted at him to get inside the house. He tried the door, not knowing what he would do if it was bolted, but it wasn't.

In the passage his papa was lying in the dark, asleep on the earth floor. Whether he'd fallen down coming in or was waiting for him to come home, he didn't stir when Albi stepped across him to go up the stairs.

57

The Tower

All the long day he stayed in his attic room, hiding from the world, while the gossip rattled up and down the street beneath his window. He could hear the excitement in the voices. *A plane! Who shot it down?*

Was that what had happened? But he'd been there, the pilot had looked at him. It was his fault. He'd killed a man.

But he hadn't told the *Guardia*, he hadn't said anything he shouldn't.

Outside, the sound of the whispering changed. Something else had happened. He sat up, listening: the voices were anxious now, nervous. Two names in their mouths over and over. Andrés. Carmen.

He ran down to the street, skirting round behind people, hovering on street corners, trying to hear what was being whispered. Something bad had happened, he could see by the faces, by the way words rushed from mouth to mouth. Something more terrible even than the aeroplane. This was something that belonged to El Rincón.

Cristina told him. Andrés and his wife had been seized in Old Teresa's house and dragged through the streets to the Plaza, Old Teresa hobbling after them and pleading but the *Guardia* ignored her. They tied Andrés and Carmen's hands behind their backs and threw them in the back of a truck. 'Their own truck, too,' Cristina whispered. 'The one the *Guardia* took off them last year.' Six men travelled in the back to guard them.

Where had they taken them?

'Las Hoyas,' Miguel said firmly, as if he had reason to know. 'They'll have taken them to the *Guardia* headquarters in Las Hoyas. I saw the truck going up the hill.'

Albi's eyes were stretched so wide they hurt. He turned away, his stomach churning. Miguel was probably right, but the road to Las Hoyas went past Estrellas.

He ran like a shadow through the sunset woods, passing from tree to tree out of sight of the paths. Not a shepherd boy any more, just a boy running. Slipping up the hill the long way round to Estrellas, up the mule path above the waterfall. He should have told the *Guardia* he was the one who made the aeroplane crash, then they wouldn't have been interested in Estrellas. He must talk to Andrés. Andrés would tell him what to do.

At the top of the path he turned his back on the Secret Valley and Las Cabreras and headed across-country, north-west and always uphill. Not running now but hurrying, clutching the stitch in his side. Keeping to the thin tree cover where he could, to the rocky places where he couldn't, so he might at least hide behind a boulder should a vehicle come along the track – he'd be in such bad trouble if they caught him again. But no trucks came.

It was well after curfew now, the afternoon fading. Above him, the Ermita stood against the westerly sky where the sun still cast its rays over the edge of the world. Below the Ermita, the cluster of farm buildings glowed in the orange light, the craggy tower jutting up dark against the setting sun. Not a sound, everything still, no dust hanging in the air from a truck passing, no hint anywhere of a mirror flashing. Not tonight. He clung to the hope they'd be sitting there in the gentle dusk beneath the grape vine as usual. They shouldn't be at Estrellas at all. They should be down in the village, and so should he. The *Guardia* would have his guts if they caught him, after yesterday.

But I have to know, I have to know.

In a moment he would find them sitting in the shadows, Andrés's arm about Mena's waist. He crept round the corner of the house. The door was hanging drunkenly on broken hinges.

The yard was deserted. There were no chickens, and the corrals were empty. None of it was right – not the broken door, not the shattered pots scattered on the ground, nor the tablecloth dragged outside in the dust – but nothing prepared him for the sight of the kitchen as he stepped through the doorway. The table had been tipped over, the chairs smashed, the great water jars were broken in pieces. He stood and stared. How would they ever make the kitchen nice again?

Well that decided it. They couldn't come back here, not now. Perhaps that was a good thing, if it made them stay in the village. He listened, so much wanting them to be in the house somewhere, not in Las Hoyas. Perhaps they were too shocked and upset to come down to the ruined kitchen. He called, timidly at first, then louder. Nobody answered. On the floor, by the upturned table, lay the disemboweled pages of a book. Even as he picked it up he knew it was Mena's book, not clean or heavy any longer, the birds torn across, the words broken. He hugged the pieces against his hurting heart, the rustle of the pages loud in the silence.

He went to the hallway and up the stairs, creeping like a burglar with the pieces of the book clutched to his chest. Everywhere, the same destruction, clothes turned out of chests, feather mattresses slashed, exploding like warm snow over everything. Chairs were broken in pieces, and the old bedsteads too. But there was no Mena weeping quietly in a far room. No Andrés sitting staring with wounded eyes. No dog, no cat. Nothing but smashed possessions, and in the library, a chaos of books, as if whoever did all this began to destroy the books and then gave up because there were too many, so they pulled them down and stamped on them instead. The marks of their boots were on the white pages.

Without Mena the books meant nothing. He laid the bird book down carefully on the floor with the others.

He went back down the stairs and stood in the dark hallway,

439

the shadows congealing as the light faded. A slight wind touched his face: the door to the tower was ajar and the wind was blowing out of it.

As he went towards the broken door a noise caught his ear, a faint groaning sound from up in the tower. He stood still, listening, struggling to hear over the pumping of blood in his ears, but he didn't hear it again.

It was no good, he had to go and see. Somebody must, and he was the only one here. He pulled the narrow door fully open on its damaged hinges and began to climb the steep stairs.

There was a bang as if somebody had switched on an electric light. He flattened against the wall, shielding his eyes against the sudden glare, but it was only the wind, blowing the shutter open at the corner of the stairs above him and letting in the last rays of the sun. He stood with his hand on his chest to stop his shocked heart jumping straight out from between his ribs. Then the empty summer wind blew on his face and the shutter banged again, just as suddenly, and the light went off. He felt his way up to the corner of the stair and pulled the shutter open, turning the catch to hold it flat against the wall.

That noise again, like a groan. Another floor up.

He climbed the winding stair. Above him, along the edge of the rounded beam, a string of tiny rubies glowed in the light like summer fruit hung out to dry. There was a strange smell, like the smell of iron on your hands on a cold day. He didn't stop to think about any of these things. He ran up the steep steps.

It was her sandals he saw first, through the door which was groaning on its hinges as the wind blew it backwards and forwards, backwards and forwards. Her sandals in the hay, and her feet in the sandals, twisted awkwardly. Andrés lying beside her. Such a stillness about them, he knew at once.

So much blood. Red blood spattered across the white wall, dark blood drenching the sodden hay. Black blood oozing from her distorted mouth.

58

Joaquín

He made his way back to the Molino in the dark. Where else could he go? Black blood, anthrack. The fear went with him, like the iron smell of blood in his nostrils, in his lungs, in his clothes. It stayed with him as he hid in the bushes at the back of the mill. But the *Guardia* were out and about, their torchlight erratic among the trees, their voices echoing on the paths. They would surely smell him if they didn't see him. So he crawled into the cold black terror of that place under the mill where the night was dank and the rats were running.

In the morning, when El Ciego came walking from the village, head held high and dead eyes listening, Albi was sitting on the bench by the front door.

Upstairs, in the silence of the kitchen, he talked. His voice sounded too loud as if it was no longer his. He told what he had seen and then he closed his mouth. A terrible distance had reared up between him and the blind man. The smell of blood, *This is what the blind man sees.* But the ripping of flesh, the blood-spattered wall, the drenched hay – El Ciego would never have that inside his head the way it was inside Albi's now, gnawing at his brain.

El Ciego made him lie down on the single bed in the corner and then he went out. Afterwards, Joaquín was there.

The blind man came back in, and went out again, and Joaquín was still there. Albi turned his face to the wall and closed his eyes. Joaquín will talk now, he thought. Everything is reversed and nothing is what it seemed. But Joaquín didn't say anything. Every now and then his breathing came near and his heavy hand patted gently down on Albi's rigid shoulder. He kept his face to the wall. When at last he heard El Ciego come back into the room the light had faded, as if it was growing late. He heard El Ciego telling Joaquín they must take the boy back to the village, he couldn't stay here in the Molino, not even as a secret. 'The *Guardia* are very touchy tonight,' El Ciego said. 'The boy will be safer in his own house.' The breathing came close again, the shadow of the big man taking the light away, then Joaquín scooped Albi off the bed like a baby and carried him out of the Molino, into the sweet empty air of late afternoon.

He stared at the passing world and nothing in it had anything to say to him. As they climbed the steep road into the village there were people muttering on every corner. The talking stopped when they saw Joaquín and El Ciego approaching, and the boy in Joaquín's arms. They were talking about the disaster but they looked at Albi as if he was a separate disaster, and then looked away again. In their wake there was a pause, and then one voice, then two, then a third began again, whispering where they'd left off. They don't know, he thought, in some distant part of his brain. They don't know it was me who found them.

He felt a pressure on his arm and looked down. The blind man's hand was resting on his elbow, just resting there, as they went up the street. Albi stared at the hand, strong and calloused. A seeing hand, not a blind one. He was still staring when Joaquín stopped outside the front door of the house. Carefully, Joaquín set him on his feet. The door was locked. Albi looked at it.

'The key, Albi?' El Ciego said gently, staring straight ahead.

All Albi's joints groaned as he bent to pick up the key from behind the pot of last year's geraniums beside the front door. He felt as if he'd climbed a thousand mountains, not as if he had just come home. He handed the key to Joaquín and let him open the door. What home, anyway? There was nobody in it. Joaquín lifted him over his shoulder like a sack of wheat and carried him up the narrow twisting staircase. In the kitchen the fire was dead,

442

the hearth unswept. Joaquín put him on his feet and briefly rested a great paw of a hand on his head.

'Come, Joaquín, we must go,' the blind man said from somewhere behind them. 'Your papa will be home any time now, Albi.'

Albi stood in the middle of the kitchen among the empty chairs and listened to their feet going down the stairs, then walking away up the street. The church bell began to ring for curfew. Wearily, he opened the door to the attic and climbed the precipitous stairs. He didn't open the shutters. He rolled under the blanket of his narrow bed in the dark room. He wanted so much to be asleep and never to wake up, but sleep didn't come.

Far below, the front door opened. The distant sound of his papa climbing the stairs, *lippety lippety*, his clumsy clatter in the kitchen. The steady tramp outside in the street of curfew beginning. The door to the attic stairs opened and his papa came up. Albi covered his head with the blanket and pretended to be asleep. He heard his papa swing into the room on his crutches, and the silence of him standing looking down at his son in the shadowed room. What father, what son? It was all meaningless. There was no family, there was no tomorrow, and yesterday must be forgotten. All his yesterdays must be forgotten.

Far away, as if it was the bad dream come again (because who but the *Guardia* came knocking after curfew?) there was a hammering on their front door. He lay low under his blanket but his eyes were awake now, and his ears. Wide awake, and cold fear pricking like fierce water all over his body as he pushed back the blanket the better to hear. They'd come. They'd come for him.

'I'm coming, I'm coming,' Papa shouted as he started down the stairs, *lippety lippety*, but his voice was more scared than impatient, and he was going so fast he would surely fall. Inside his head Albi shouted, *Don't let them in! Don't let them in!* but Papa carried on as if he'd heard nothing, *lippety lippety* to let the *Guardia* in.

443

Albi stared at the wall. He heard bolts being shot back, but there was no shouting from the street below. No thunder of boots on the stairs. Only a murmurous silence, and the soft click of the front door closing.

In the silence between the front door closing and the creak of the door of his room opening he dreamed many dreams, one after the other. It was Mena at the door, and Andrés behind her. It was Mama at the door, and his *abuelos*, all well and laughing again. It was the *abuela* at the door, and Old Jaime with her, not as they were at the end but as they used to be when they sat in the street and talked about what the village was like when they were young. It was Inma at the door, and she had pink cheeks and wasn't sick any more.

But it wasn't any of those people. He tried to dream it again. To have it be Mena. Especially Mena. He clung to the rag of dream and started to cry. He couldn't stop, not even when Pilar put her arms around him and pulled him against the hard mound of her swollen belly and hugged him tight. He wanted it to be Mena but it was Pilar who'd come, curfew or not. Jesús had told her what had happened, she said. (But what did Jesús know? And if he'd told her everything, why wasn't she angry?) He heard Papa's voice, uncertain, not like Papa at all. From deep under Albi's ear, resonating in her belly like a drum, Pilar's voice said, 'Papa! He's only a kid!'

He floated away, like a bird. He looked down on the valley. On El Rincón in the corner of it. At the floating summer pastures of the *Meseta*. At the map of Spain that used to hang in the classroom with *La Meseta* not even a name on it. Then Pilar said in her ordinary voice, 'And this house is worse than a pig pen, Papa. I'm going to have to take it in hand.'

59

Guilt

In the kitchen Pilar was sweeping, her broom attacking the corners and driving rubbish and fluff into great piles in the middle of the floor. But when she saw his eyes on her she stopped tutting, and looked at him as if she didn't know what to say. Which was more disconcerting than all her cleaning, so he went out of the house.

There was an old man sitting on the church steps. The man didn't look like his papa until Albi came closer, he looked like a dried insect – the shell still there but nothing left inside it. Papa nodded when he saw it was him. Albi nodded back and walked on past, down to the *fuente* where the crowds were forming.

Nobody took any notice of him. What would he know, he was just a child. And besides they were too busy, frantically whispering, grabbing at straws: who knew what, who had told that person it was true. Spreading rumour about like muck on a field.

The Guardia *killed them.*

No, it would have been the maquis. They were in it together but they fell out and the maquis *killed them to stop them talking.*

It couldn't have been the *maquis*. Albi leaned against the wall. He watched the heads bobbing and listened to the voices rising, rising, falling again. Bullets were scarce, rope was plentiful. If it was the *maquis* it would have been hanging. But then he remembered the bullets in the bacon fat and the voices buzzed in his ears like flies on a corpse.

'Of course it wasn't the *maquis* killed them.' Miguel's voice. 'It was the *Guardia*. Look at them now, crowing like cockerels on a dung-heap. It was revenge for the *maquis* shooting down the plane.'

Albi turned his head, like everyone else, to stare at the sentries standing at the road-block on the far side of the gatehouse.

'What rubbish,' Martín said. 'I had it from one of the *Guardia* in Mario's bar last night: they arrested them over something else entirely and let them go again. They didn't even know about the deaths until yesterday afternoon. They've taken the bodies to Las Hoyas for post mortem.'

Albi turned his back on them all and studied the stones in the wall, one by one. If the *Guardia* found the bullets would they know who it was had taken them to the *maquis*?

The whispering stopped suddenly as El Caballero came limping across the Plaza.

'Right that's enough speculation. For your information it was suicide. They knew we'd worked out what they were up to, and it's just as well for all of you we had because they were planning to blow up the dam. Think about that, and be grateful.' He looked round at their faces as if willing them to defy him. 'And you, Miguel – before you start spreading rumours to the contrary you should know we found the dynamite this morning, hidden in one of the outbuildings. Now get back to your work, all of you.'

He turned on his heel and walked away, a small man with sturdy shoulders.

Albi went down to the Molino and took the sheep out. He grazed them by the river, he picked up firewood for the blind man. That day and the next day and the day after. He didn't talk to El Ciego. He didn't say anything at all. A boy who didn't speak couldn't carry messages. It made things stop.

'Hey!' Carlos barely spoke to Albi anymore, now he was working in the new factory, but here he was. 'Did you hear about the plane? It was a Heinkel.' Carlos's head was newly shorn, shaved close all round the back but left longer on the top. It made him look like a man.

Albi said nothing. Carlos leaned in close. 'I saw them, you know. I saw the bodies hanging in the Torre.'

He smelled the communion wine on Carlos's breath. He closed his eyes and shut him out. It was lies, a trick. He willed himself to say nothing.

The hot breath came closer. 'I told you! I told you they'd be planning to blow up the dam. Hanging was too good for them. That's what my papa says.'

Albi clamped his hands over his ears and fled.

*

In the night, Mena comes for him. There is a light in the room as if he has a candle burning, it shines up into her face. The whites of her eyes look blind, there are no pupils in them, and round her neck a scarlet rope hangs, bright as a Republican kerchief. I told you to come, she says. Why didn't you come? He wants to say, you were going to kill me. Why did you want to kill me? But he can't. He opens his mouth but only a grating sound comes out, and she looks at him as if she never liked him, as if he wasn't her friend. I didn't kill you, she says. You killed me.

Alberto wakes, sweating. The grating sound is real. He was shouting.

He lies in the still dark and waits for the panic to subside. He can see it so clearly, as if it is still in the room with him, that dead-eyed face, no longer beautiful. The dream Mena, who has been hounding him for the last seventy-eight years.

60

Alberto, 2017

As he walks up the street arm in arm with Mari-Jé he hears voices. There are two figures on the church steps – one of them looks like Carla but the other is a stranger, a young man who is making shapes with his hands as if he's framing the view.

The city voice carries clearly, 'We'll start with the church… pan round like so, taking in the village…home in on the Plaza, your grandfather's old house…'

Carla sees them and comes down the steps. 'How are you?' Kiss kiss. Hug hug. 'Let me introduce you – Esteban – Señor Alberto Álvarez and his wife, Mari-Jé. Esteban is our cameraman. We're just doing a recce today, we'll be back next week to do the actual filming.' She turns to the young man as if revealing a secret. 'Señor Álvarez knew my grandfather.'

The young man has a sharp haircut and even sharper little black beard. He stares into Alberto's face with interest. Mari-Jé's hand tightens on his arm.

As they walk on the young man says, 'We could use him! What a wonderful face!' and Carla murmurs some reply.

Mari-Jé leans in close and squeezes his arm again. 'Don't if you don't want to, Alberto.'

Behind them, Carla says '…we'll go to Las Rocas to film where the plane…'

He doesn't wait to hear her say her grandfather saw it happen.

It's early but someone is hammering on the door downstairs. Alberto opens the kitchen window and leans out. The pale moon of Santi's face tips up towards him and for a moment – just a moment – it's the *Guardia* come knocking and he is Albi again, up in his attic room, looking down at the very moment one of the hats tilts backwards and becomes a face. But there is no hat, and the face grins. Santi's voice calls up, 'Hey *Tío*! Finished your breakfast yet?'

Alberto goes down to let him in.

Back in the kitchen, he pours Santi a coffee. They sit together at the table, Santi stirring the usual three sugars into his cup, while Mari-Jé chatters to Ana on her mobile about arrangements for the weekend. Shouting because the line is bad, or maybe because she's too deaf to hear how loud she's being. Alberto raises an eyebrow at Santi. Santi grins.

'And, Ana, bring the ham!' Mari-Jé peers at the phone and presses buttons to switch it off. 'Morning, Santi. What are you up to today?'

'Cleaning out the rabbits, if *Tío's* ready and willing. He said he'd give me a hand.'

Alberto gets to his feet. It's a pleasure to be wanted.

'Good,' says Mari-Jé briskly. 'While he's out of the house I can get this floor washed.'

Alberto wheels the barrow, Santi scrapes the muck from the boards under the wire cages.

'Carla's in town,' Santi observes, not looking at him. 'She'll be back with the film crew on Tuesday.'

Alberto pretends not to hear. The muscles of Santi's bare arms are smooth and tight under the velvet of his skin, such young muscles, primed and ready for life to begin. He looks at Santi's skin and the words spill out, taking him by surprise, 'The *Guardia* took all our rabbits. Breeding females too. And the buck.'

Santi's eyes turn to him, suddenly attentive. 'Took? You mean, without paying?'

Alberto shrugs. 'It was an insult, what they called payment. Besides, what use was money when there was no food to buy?'

It's common knowledge, a small safe thing to mention. Behind it comes another.

'We were like prisoners, once the soldiers came. They had all the guns, they had all the power. We were trapped in the village like these rabbits in their cages.' He nearly laughs. All this long winter the weight of his memories has been pressing down on him and now he talks about rabbits!

Santi bends to his shovel. 'Were you scared, *Tío*?'

'Yes.'

Small chinks in a wall, but it's easier when they are working side by side and the past comes slipping and sliding like a dam breaking, all stones and rocks and fierce muddy water, but the words coming quietly because that is who he is. A sentence here, two sentences there. The terror of being imprisoned in their own houses. The tyranny of curfew. The tyranny of hunger. Santi listens as they work, occasionally asking a question, long pauses in between that Alberto can feel safe in. And then it is dinnertime. He stops up the wall in his mind and tucks the past behind it.

'Let's go and find out what your *tía* has cooked for us today,' he says, as if that is the end of story-telling.

At the door of the shed, before they step out into the pale March sunshine, he stops and rests his hand on the boy's arm.

'Not a word to your *tía*, Santi.' He waits for Santi to nod.

The fragrance of rabbit stew wafts down the stairs. Alberto holds open the door of the bathroom, where the old stable used to be and the mule in it. 'We'll wash our hands down here, Santi. You know how your *tía* hates us washing in the kitchen.'

Upstairs, Mari-Jé has the salad ready on the table and crusty bread freshly collected from the bakery van. All through the meal Alberto feels Santi's eyes on him but nothing is said and Mari-Jé doesn't notice, she's too busy repeating the gossip she heard in the bread queue. If Santi asks, will he tell him more? He can't decide. If he does, there are some things he'll maybe steer clear of. El Ciego, perhaps?

Santi asks Mari-Jé some question, she replies. Their voices wash over Alberto's head.

If he does talk about El Ciego he won't mention Jesús saying about the blind man playing a double game. There are two ways a double game might play and who's to say Jesús knew enough to judge which way this one went. Besides, he's the same Albi he was then, he doesn't tell the things he did not see.

Santi gets up from the table. 'Well, *Tía,* I'd better get back to work. Though you've stuffed me so full I can hardly bend.'

'Aren't you going to have a lie-down?' she says sharply when Alberto stands up too. 'You'll get over-tired.'

He lifts one shoulder against her and goes out.

Her voice follows them down the stairs. 'Don't let him overdo it Santi! He's nearly ninety, remember.'

'Eighty-eight,' Alberto mutters, and Santi grins.

Out in the street the March air is warm in the sunshine, but the shadows are cold. In the shed, the rabbits lie in their cages, ears flat and indifferent along their backs. Santi feeds, Alberto fills the drinkers. For a long while neither of them speaks. Then Santi says, 'This curfew, *Tío.* Did you ever get caught out?'

They are sitting in the doorway in the fading sunlight, Alberto on an old chair, Santi at his feet. Santi's silent attention has drawn him into saying more than he intended, a detail here, an explanation there, laid out like pebbles on the floor between them. But some things run too deep for telling and now, watching Santi's bright inquisitive eyes, he's afraid of what he's unleashed.

'So, what happened to your brother?'

He breathes again: the answer to that is simple, there's nothing to tell. Like Jaime and Tomas, Manolo was one of the disappeared. There were so many in that time, dying in ditches, or in labour camps, or fleeing over the border into France and perishing in someone else's war. The families left behind never knowing what happened to them.

Santi nods. He looks strangely moved.

Alberto shuts his mouth, then, and turns his head away, leaving the silence to settle. In the depths of memory Carlos's laughter echoes faintly across the terraces, Pepito's too, and somewhere among them is his own. In the before. But in the now...

'And the couple in the Torre. Who killed them?'

He flinches, he can't help it. I killed them.

'They were planning to blow up the dam but the *Guardia* found out. He killed her, then turned the gun on himself.'

Santi looks disappointed, then incredulous. 'But surely you never believed that, *Tío*?'

'She was going to kill me, Santi. Me and everyone else. I loved her, but she would have killed me.'

It would be so much easier if he could believe it.

Walking slowly up the track in the gathering shadows, needing to be alone, Santi's question chews at his soul. He wishes he could believe it, because then she would be guilty instead of him. Would that hurt him less?

He stops. Gazes up at the darkening sky. So enviably simple, Santi's view of the world.

The truth is, however guilty he feels for what happened to Andrés and Mena, the measure of his guilt lies elsewhere. There were two bodies in the Torre but no gun. He saw them, he knows. He knew it then – it was the *Guardia*. The plot to blow up the dam, the suicide pact – all lies. He should have shouted it in the streets. He should have shouted it from the rooftops, back then while the world still remembered them. But he didn't. He didn't say a word.